SIREN

ALSO BY SAM MICHAELS

Trickster
Rivals
Vixen

SIREN

Book 4 in the Georgina Garrett Series

Sam Michaels

An Aria Book

This edition first published in the United Kingdom in 2021 by Aria,
an imprint of Head of Zeus Ltd

A CIP catalogue record for this book is available
from the British Library.

ISBN eBook: 9781789542202
ISBN Paperback: 9781800246089

Cover design © Debbie Clement

Typeset by Siliconchips Services Ltd UK

Aria
c/o Head of Zeus
First Floor East
5–8 Hardwick Street
London EC1R 4RG

www.ariafiction.com

To my beautiful granddaughter, Annabella Blofeld.

When you're a big girl and all grown up, if you ever
need reminding of how amazing you are, open this
book and read this message from your
Nanny Sam – You're THE BEST!

I hope your life is filled with beautiful stories.
Lots of love to you my darling xxx

November 1943.

Three years since Georgina
Garrett's arrest.

I

London. Holloway Prison.

'Garrett, a word.'

Georgina recognised the formidable voice of Miss Winter and looked over her shoulder to see the prison warden marching towards her. The woman's greying hair was pulled tightly back into a neat bun and her lips set in a grim line, giving her a stern look. But Georgina knew Miss Winter's harsh tone and tough appearance masked a softer side that could be bought for cash. It was a side that few of the other women prisoners ever saw and they'd given her the name 'Old Frosty Drawers'.

They stood outside of Georgina's cell amongst the cacophony of women's voices echoing throughout the prison. After almost three years of internment, the noise of cell doors slamming, keys jangling, pipes rattling and harrowing cries had become a constant hum that Georgina was now accustomed to, though she'd never get used to the sound of a woman howling for her child. And from what she could hear, poor Linda on the floor below must have been brought back from the prison hospital. She'd secretly birthed her baby alone in her cell the night before and no one had discovered it until the morning.

'Is that Linda I can hear bawling her eyes out?' Georgina asked, the upsetting noise stabbing at her heart and making her think of her own children.

'Yes. I reckon her baby only took a few breaths before he died. But Linda held him all night and was still trying to nurse him in the morning. He was blue. Horrible. I think the sight even shocked Miss Kenny and you know what a hard cow she is. We had a right fight trying to get the baby out of Linda's arms and she ain't stopped screaming since they took him away. The doctor gave her a sedative but it's worn off now.'

'For fuck's sake. The little mite didn't stand a chance of surviving. Linda ain't been well for ages. She should have been in the hospital months ago.'

'I know, Georgina, but she hid her pregnancy from us all. She's a silly girl. If we'd known, she would have received a special diet from six months onwards. Instead, she looks half-starved and was still scrubbing floors on her hands and knees just hours before she dropped. And the baby, well, let's just say that after seeing him, I reckon he's best off dead.'

'Maybe, but I'm sure Linda doesn't share your sentiments.'

'Probably not, but she's barmy and that baby weren't right. Anyway, I've got some good news for you. As from next week, you'll be assigned to domestic duties in the married quarters.'

Georgina looked down into the pint of tepid cocoa

she was holding and drew in a long, deep breath. 'No, I won't,' she ground out, seething at the thought of her potential new role.

'I thought you'd be pleased. I had to pull a lot of strings for this. It's a cushy number and gets you out of this shithole.'

'Thank you, Miss Winter, but I refuse to wait on those fascist bastards,' she whispered.

It was no secret that Winston Churchill had seen to it that Oswald Mosley had been given special privileges and was now serving his time within the walls of the prison with his wife, Diana Mitford. The woman had gained favour with many of the prisoners and was well thought of, a brilliant blonde, her beauty undeniable, and she had shown herself to have a kind heart. But she was a fascist, an enemy of the state, and Georgina remembered her run-in with the Fylfots – they were a dangerous group of men, Nazi sympathisers who'd infiltrated every major institution, and no doubt they had been in bed with Mosley too.

'You're not telling me that you'd rather be on the mangle?' Miss Winter asked.

'It's not so bad. At least it's warm. But can't you get me on domestic duties at Pentonville?'

'Oh, I don't know, Georgina. They normally only let the most trusted women work in the warden's quarters.'

'I've been a model prisoner and I've never stepped out of line. Jinny is getting released next week. She'll need replacing and you know I won't let you down.'

Miss Winter glanced nervously from one side to the other. It wouldn't do to be seen having a friendly conversation with a prisoner. 'All right. I'll see what I can do,' she said quietly, 'but don't hold your breath.'

Georgina smiled warmly at her ally and stepped inside her cell. The door closed and she heard Miss Winter turn the lock. She had another long and lonely night ahead with only her thoughts and the pathetic pint of nightly cocoa that each prisoner was given. Though as Georgina stood on tiptoes to peek through the small, studded iron-barred window, the early evening sun was just setting and she thought to herself that it could hardly be classed as night time. But this was the prison routine. Lockdown at four-thirty and her door wouldn't be unlocked again until six-thirty the following morning.

As the time dragged by and the evening slipped into the dark hours of the night, the prison didn't become any quieter. These arduous, drawn-out times of confinement were the most unbearable and worst moments for the women. Locked away alone, their minds torturing them with memories of their loved ones on the outside. Their hearts would break for their children. Many would be reliving abuse they'd suffered. Some would cry for their mothers. It was enough to drive the strongest of characters to insanity. Georgina tried to ignore the screams and sobs, the nervous titters and even the singing. She pushed away all thoughts of Alfie and Selina, her precious children being raised by their gypsy grandparents, their father, Lash, long dead. Instead, she focused on her plan.

It had come to her when she'd heard a couple of the borstal girls had tried to escape by scaling the high walls that surrounded the prison. One had fallen and broken her leg but the other had made a clean getaway. Word had spread that every police officer in London was on the lookout for the fleeing girl but they hadn't found her yet. Georgina smiled to herself, thinking good on the girl, and wished her luck. After all, no one could blame her for wanting out but few had the guts to try. Georgina did. She had the guts. She'd considered escaping on many occasions. She knew she couldn't do the five years she had left to serve. And now with the possibility of a three-penny a week cleaning job at Pentonville prison, the thought of freedom danced around merrily in her head. She could almost taste it, smell it, touch it. Her liberty was nearly within reach but it relied on Miss Winter and she hoped the guard wouldn't let her down.

In Battersea, Charlotte Mipple checked the time. It was after eleven, an agreeable time to call on Lord Quentin Hamilton for his rent money. Charlotte didn't like to chase up the posh nob fella but with the Naylor brothers breathing down her neck, she didn't have much choice.

The Naylors had become a thorn in her side and, from what she'd heard, quite a few folk were being badgered for money by them. The audacity of the pair! The Naylors were nothing more than a pair of louts who'd taken advantage of Georgina being locked away. Now that Battersea wasn't under Georgina's rule, the place had become a free-for-all. Johnny and the gang had fallen apart and thugs like the Naylors thought that they could muscle their way into the protection business. In truth, Charlotte wasn't scared of the Naylors. They didn't have the organisational skills that Georgina possessed and could never run a small empire.

No one could. But the Naylors were good at intimidating. They were just a pair of bullies really. Gawd, she wished Georgina was around to put them in their place and get the old gang back together.

Charlotte gently tapped on Lord Quentin Hamilton's door. The middle-aged, white-haired gentleman with a waxed moustache rented an apartment in the house that had once been Georgina's office and a successful brothel. Now, converted into apartments on Georgina's orders, Charlotte had a one-bedroomed flat on the ground floor. The two-bedroomed apartment opposite was kept for Georgina. It remained empty. Dina, a Russian ex-prostitute, lived in the studio apartment above, next door to Lord Hamilton and Miss Gray opposite him. Miss Gray, an old spinster, kept herself to herself and was no bother. She always put her rent in a scented envelope and would pop it under Charlotte's door as regular as clockwork. Lord Hamilton, on the other hand, was becoming difficult. Every fortnight, Charlotte would have to chase him for his rent and he'd come up with the most elaborate excuses for paying late. But, Charlotte had to admit, the sophisticated older man did have a charm that always left her smiling.

'Ah, my dear girl,' Lord Hamilton announced when he opened his door. 'Is it that time already?'

'Yes, but I've no doubt you're going to tell me the most fascinating tale and I shall leave here entertained but empty-handed.'

'Well, not being one who wishes to disappoint, please, do come in and I shall tell you what happened to me this morning.'

Charlotte rolled her eyes and shook her head in mock

disbelief. The man was brazen, though very amusing, and she followed him through to the lounge.

'Allow me to pour you some tea,' he said, picking up a fine bone china teapot and filling a matching teacup and saucer.

Charlotte sat in one of the three plush armchairs and gazed around the room. She'd sat in the same chair on many occasions but the fine artwork that adorned the walls never ceased to amaze her. Not that she knew anything about art, but she could tell they were expensive pieces. It was clear he had a few bob, yet she always had this fortnightly struggle to get him to part with his money. And though he called himself *Lord* Quentin Hamilton, she doubted his title was a real one.

'Here,' he said, handing her the cup of tea, 'Darjeeling with one cube.'

'Thanks,' Charlotte replied, wrinkling her nose. She'd have preferred a normal cup of tea instead of the posh muck he always gave her.

Sitting in an armchair adjacent, Lord Hamilton waved his arms in the air with a theatrical grace. 'Honestly, Charlotte, this war is costing me a fortune. I'm afraid I'm shy of the rent thanks to my good deed of the day. Let me explain.'

'Please do,' she said, intrigued to hear more.

'The paperboy hasn't been delivering my copy of the *Times*, as I believe he has the measles or something equally dreadful. And you know how I like to do the crossword over breakfast, it's good to tax the brain first thing in the morning. So, I went to the newsagent to collect the paper, and while there a young woman came in with three children. Now, you know I'm not a snob but it was clear that the family were in dire poverty. I try not to allow things like that to bother me but this dear child, a girl, told me it was her birthday and that she was five years old. I wished her best wishes and rather naively asked her what presents she'd received. Of course, the poor thing had nothing. Her mother informed me they'd lost their house thanks to a bomb and her husband was missing in action. I had the rent money on my person and felt compelled to help the family so I handed the mother one pound and each of the children a shilling.'

'That was very kind of you but you've had all day to go to the bank and get some more money,' Charlotte said sceptically.

'Yes, and I was on my way but became distracted when I bumped into a dear friend of mine, Lady Winslow-Jones. I haven't seen her in years. Her husband and I attended Cambridge together but he passed away some time ago. She informed me that since his death, she's been struggling with the maintenance of their rather grand house and asked me to return home with her to evaluate several paintings. I couldn't refuse, after all, Lady Winslow-Jones is the cousin of Queen Mary's lady-in-waiting.'

At this point, Charlotte found herself smiling and not believing a single word. Lord Hamilton's tales mostly involved members of the royal family, or reminiscences of his great expeditions across India or his time in the Middle East with the Sheikh of Dubai. But then he rose to his feet and walked across the room to where something under a dustsheet leaned against the wall.

'I took this from Lady Winslow-Jones,' he said and whipped the dustsheet off to reveal an oil painting in a gilt frame of someone regal looking. 'It's an original of Prince

Jacques Francois Leonor de Goyon de Matignon, Prince of Monaco by Robert Gabriel Gence.'

'He looks like a right Nancy boy if you ask me,' Charlotte said as she studied the painting, unimpressed.

'My dear girl, this exquisite piece of art is worth more than you could ever imagine and Lady Winslow-Jones has commissioned *me* to sell it on her behalf.'

'Good for you, but what about the rent?'

'I don't think you're quite grasping the enormity of this. Once I've sold the painting, which I'm reluctant to do as I believe it should remain within the royal circles, but none the less, my commission will be extravagant! Enough to pay you a lifetime of rent in advance.'

'Blimey, who'd have thought a picture of a bloke in frills would be worth a fortune,' Charlotte guffawed, still not being taken in by his story.

'It is, and I'd appreciate your patience as I am going to be incredibly busy finding a suitable buyer. But then, my dear, you will have my full attention and a full year's rent.'

Charlotte looked into his blue eyes, which were bright with excitement. Unfortunately, his enthusiasm for the painting didn't rub off on her. She had no time for fancy art and just wanted the rent that was due. Especially as the Naylor brothers were going to be badgering her for the protection money. 'One week,' she said firmly.

'Two. Two weeks and I hope to have secured a deal.'

'Fine, two weeks,' she answered with a sigh. 'But if you don't cough up, you're out.'

'Please, Charlotte, there's no need for vulgarity. And I wish you'd accept my offer of elocution lessons.'

'No, you're all right, thanks. I like how I talk and don't

want to sound like a stuck-up cow,' she said dolefully, thinking of Nancy Austin, the posh tart who'd snitched on Georgina. Granted, the woman was dead. Georgina had made sure of that when she'd rigged the safe and it had exploded in Nancy's face, but that hadn't saved Georgina from getting sentenced to eight years in prison for fraud. 'I'd better get going. Thanks for the tea,' she said, rising to her feet.

Lord Hamilton showed her out and after collecting her coat and bag from her apartment, she climbed into the car parked outside. It had been Georgina's car but now Charlotte drove it, though she didn't have a driving licence. Johnny Dymond had taught her how to drive. The pair had become good friends and, since Georgina's prison sentence, he was the only one of the old gang who she still had contact with. The rest of the men had disbanded. With their boss banged up in Holloway, the criminal business had fallen into chaos and their operations had become susceptible to scrutiny from the long arm of the law. Georgina had immediately given instructions for the brothels, The Penthouse Club and the protection rackets to be closed down. No one had been happy about it at first, but they soon realised that they couldn't operate without their leader.

Charlotte started the car and headed towards The Prince's Head. Johnny lived in a flat nearby, above a haberdashery. He hadn't been keen on taking the place at first as he thought it wasn't becoming of his flashy image, but Charlotte had persuaded him. The rent was cheap and it had two entrances, one at the front and another at the back. Good for a quick getaway if needed. Johnny was no longer working for Georgina and made his living from stealing and dealing. He hadn't long been out of prison, doing a year stretch for a bit of petty thieving. But it hadn't taught him a lesson. Charlotte didn't think that he'd ever go straight, but he needed to watch that he didn't get caught again. *Bless him*, she thought. Johnny was a smashing bloke but without Georgina behind him, she'd seen his flaws and she didn't think that he was the sharpest knife in the block.

As Charlotte pulled up at the back, she spotted Johnny coming out. He was fastening his long wool coat, the wide fur collar now his trademark. She tooted the horn and when he looked up and saw her, he smiled widely.

'What 'ave I told you about driving? I bet you still ain't got your licence, have you?' he said, talking to her through the open window.

'No, not yet. Where are you off to?'

'I've got to see a man about a dog.'

'Your car still not fixed then?'

'Nope. But it should be by the end of the week.'

'Jump in, I'll give you a lift,' she offered.

'No chance. I ain't getting in that car 'til you get your licence, young lady. Have you heard anything from Miss Garrett?'

'No, Johnny. She won't let me send any letters in and she won't send any out because she knows they'll get inspected by the Old Bill. Molly receives the odd letter from her now and then but she never mentions any of us in them.'

'She did a good job of protecting us all from going down with her. I hope she's all right in there.'

'Me too. I miss her and so does Dog. Battersea ain't the same without her.'

'You can say that again.'

'Battersea ain't the same without her,' Charlotte repeated with a grin.

'You soppy mare. Anyway, what brings you over here?'

'Nothing, really. I was at a bit of a loose end,' she lied, hoping to have had the opportunity to discuss the problem she was having with the Naylor brothers.

'It's getting dark. You should go home. I'll pop round tomorrow.'

'All right, Johnny. See ya. Are you sure you don't want a lift?'

'I'm sure, now bugger orf.'

Charlotte skilfully turned the car around and headed back to Alexandra Avenue where Dog would be waiting for her to take him for a walk. Her mind turned with thoughts of Georgina and how horrid it must be to be incarcerated. She'd once spent the night in a police cell so she understood what it felt like, but one night was nothing compared to the years Georgina had endured. Still, at least Georgina didn't have to worry about finding the money to pay off Bert Naylor and his brother Len. Since they'd found out that Charlotte was collecting rents, they'd been on her back for a pound a week. She dared not pay up. She understood how these things worked. If the Naylors weren't satisfied, Charlotte would end up with smashed windows and worse. She had planned on talking to Johnny about it but knew there was little he could do to help. The Naylors had a hold on Battersea and though they were just a couple of thugs, they commanded respect through fear, though not *her* fear. She thought they were pathetic, just big blokes with less than half a brain between them. But she had no doubt that they could throw a good punch and Charlotte didn't relish the idea of a black eye. God, she wished Georgina was out of prison. The woman would put a stop to the Naylors and have them begging for mercy. But, just as Charlotte had said… Battersea wasn't the same without her.

2

The next day, Johnny Dymond hopped off the trolleybus that took him to south-east London. He hated using public transport but had little choice until his car was back from the garage, but at least it was mild weather for the time of year. As he made his way through David Maynard's old patch, three women in London Fire Brigade uniforms drove towards him on motorbikes. One of them caught his eye and he thought she was quite a looker. As they passed, he gave her a cheeky wink and she smiled back. An old boy on the street had paused, his back bent and leaning on a walking stick. He must have seen the flirtatious exchange and chuckled.

'You're in there, son,' he said to Johnny.

'Cor, fancy that, eh? Women on motorbikes and in the fire brigade. If they all look like her, I'll consider setting me flat alight!'

The old codger laughed and Johnny doffed his fedora hat and bid him good day. He carried on his way, thinking to himself how much the war had changed things. He'd never have believed he'd see women doing the jobs that men once did, but he knew they were more than capable. He'd learned how strong and accomplished women could be from working for Georgina Garrett. She'd been a force to be reckoned with, and Charlotte had hit the nail on the head when she'd said Battersea wasn't the same without her.

Reaching his destination, Johnny rapped heavily on the large, double wooden doors. The house, tucked away up a side street that led to a small park, was owned by the new governor of south-east London's powerful criminal gang. David Maynard had once been the boss but since he'd been injured in a bomb blast, no one had seen or heard from him until a bloated and burned body had washed up on the bank of the River Thames near London Bridge. The ink on his ID papers had been mostly indistinguishable but the police had managed to work out that the body was that of David Maynard. Cor, rumours were rife after that! Who had the nerve to take down David Maynard? Turned out, it was this new bloke, The Top. He was a bit of a mystery. Johnny had never met him as all business transactions were done through one of his minions. But before Mr Maynard's blokes had gone into hiding, they'd warned everyone not to cross The Top. Apparently he was Irish and had links with the IRA and, by all accounts, he enjoyed working with explosives. His reputation commanded even more respect than David Maynard and Johnny could feel nervous butterflies flitting in his stomach.

A hatch in the door opened and a set of dark eyes peered through.

'Ralph, it's me, Johnny Dymond,' he said, leaning in closer and shifting uncomfortably from one foot to the other.

Ralph pulled open one of the heavy doors and stepped

aside for Johnny to walk in. The large reception area with a staircase sweeping up around the edge always impressed him. But the area was bare. No pictures, fancy statues or opulent rugs dressed the grand entrance, which made Johnny think the place lacked a woman's touch.

'Is The Top expecting you?' Ralph asked.

'No, mate, but I need some lead.'

'Right, follow me.'

Johnny climbed the sweeping staircase behind Ralph until they reached the landing. Here, there were several closed doors, one of them guarded by two thick-set men.

'Wait,' Ralph said, indicating to a maroon leather chesterfield near the top of the stairs.

Johnny unbuttoned his coat and sat down, resting his elbows on his legs and interlocking his fingers. It stopped him from anxiously fidgeting and, with the two bouncers snarling at him, he could feel his heart pumping.

Ralph went into the room. He came out moments later and motioned his head for Johnny to enter. The bouncers frisked him first, something Johnny expected. He hadn't been foolish enough to bring his gun with him. Once in the room, he could see the silhouette of another man stood in front of tall windows covered in heavy drapes that were almost pulled shut. A small opening allowed in a slither of natural light, the rest of the room dimly lit by a desk lamp and one wall light.

'Hello, Johnny, we haven't seen you in a while,' the man said and walked from the shadows towards him with his hand extended.

Johnny's tension instantly eased when he recognised Gary Lockwood, also known as Slugs on account of his preferred weapon of choice, a shotgun. He gripped the man's hand and shook it eagerly.

'Good to see you, Slugs. You've lost weight, you're half the bloke you used to be.'

'Didn't you hear? I got popped in the guts, fucking nearly killed me. Some geezer trying his luck here, thought he could take down The Top.'

'Bloody hell, no, mate, I never heard a thing. You all right?'

'Yeah, I am now, but me days of scoffing a good fry-up are long gone. I hear you're after some bullets?'

'That's right. Just a box or two.'

'Sorry, Johnny, I'd like to oblige but you know the rules.'

'Oh, come on, Slugs. I'm skint and I need to do a proper job, which means I'll need bullets. I've got a lifestyle to maintain and I can't do that flogging a bit of bent gear.'

'You look like you're doing all right, you flash bastard. Smoke?' Slugs asked and held out a packet of Woodbines.

'No, thanks, mate. About them bullets…'

'The Top doesn't want those idiots, the Naylors, getting their hands on any ammo so he won't sell to Battersea.'

'You know me, Slugs. I don't have fuck all to do with those two wankers. The bullets are for my own personal use, I swear. Look, let me have a word with him. I'll explain me situation.'

'No chance. The Top doesn't see anyone.'

'You have a word for me then. Come on, do us a favour, mate, we go back years.'

Slugs stubbed out his cigarette. 'All right. Wait here.'

As he went to another room through an adjoining door, Johnny craned his neck to try and get a glimpse of the elusive Top, but the door quickly closed and he was left in the room with a different set of two bouncers. The Top was well protected and Johnny was surprised to have discovered that someone had tried to take him down, though it was Slugs who'd taken the bullet.

The door opened again and Slugs reappeared looking pleased with himself. 'You're a lucky fucker.'

'Has he agreed?'

'Yeah, two boxes and at a good price. But if he gets so much of a sniff that the Naylors or anyone else has got hold of the bullets—'

'—It's all right,' Johnny interrupted. 'You don't need to drop any threats. I know the score. Nice one, cheers, mate. I owe you.'

The exchange was carried out in another of the rooms and Johnny left a happy man. It had been a couple of years since he'd last shot his gun, and maybe he wouldn't need to use it for the big job he had planned, but it was better to be safe than sorry. And when it came to the Naylors, Johnny had no intention of allowing the brothers to get their hands on his bullets. In fact, he thought, the only way the Naylors were going to get any of the bullets was if Johnny fired them into their ugly heads.

Georgina's cell door was unlocked and she walked out into the grim corridor. She could still hear Linda's howls from the floor below and then heard another woman's voice shouting at Linda to shut the fuck up. She wanted to jump to Linda's defence but Miss Kenny was ushering them along the corridor.

'Come on, get a move on,' the unsympathetic guard ordered.

She looked behind her and glared daggers at the woman. At twenty-nine years old, Georgina reckoned she was probably about the same age as Miss Kenny, but narrow lips and sharp, pointed features made the guard appear older. Georgina thought the power of her position as a prison warden had gone to her head. She was a bully and didn't care about the women she watched over.

As they slowly ambled down the stairs, she managed to glimpse into Linda's cell. The girl was hunched on the floor in the corner, her knees huddled to her chest as she rocked back and forth, crying and hollering. Georgina stood against the green iron railings and waited for several women to pass until she came face to face with Miss Kenny.

'You can't leave Linda in there in that state,' she whispered.

'Can't I? Do you think you're running the place now? This isn't Battersea, Garrett, this is *my* wing and I'll do as I see fit. Get on with it or you'll be back in your cell for the day.'

Georgina looked past Miss Kenny at the queue of prisoners waiting on the stairs. Desperate women, beaten down by the endless regime and monotony of prison life. She knew they'd love to see her challenge Miss Kenny. A fight would entertain them for a few minutes and give them something to talk about. And when Miss Kenny pushed Georgina, she was tempted to push her back. But common sense prevailed and she moved on, but not without a final empathetic glance in Linda's direction.

A short while later, she sat at one of the long tables in

the dining hall with three slices of bread and a meagre amount of margarine. It wasn't the tastiest nor healthiest of breakfasts but it would do to keep her going for six hours of work.

Jinny joined her at the table. She'd been in the prison for seven years, though she'd never told anyone what her crime had been. She was tall, like Georgina, and had the same dark hair. But where Georgina's violet eyes shone, Jinny's brown eyes were overhung by drooping eyelids, prematurely ageing her. 'Did you see Linda?' Jinny asked worriedly.

'Yes, I did. It ain't right. She needs help.'

'I saw you talking to Miss Kenny. That bitch couldn't care less if Linda hangs herself. You're wasting your breath on her.'

'I know but I had to try. I'm worried about Linda's state of mind.'

'Can't you have a word with Old Frosty Drawers? I've seen you and her in cahoots.'

'What's that supposed to mean?' Georgina asked defensively.

'Nothing. It ain't none of my business if you're bribing her or got something on her. All I'm saying is, you seem to get on all right with her. Maybe she can get Linda moved to the hospital.'

'I think she would, if she could, but welfare ain't down to her. It's down to Kenny and she ain't interested.'

Their conversation came to an abrupt end when Miss Kenny screeched, 'SILENCE!' across the hall.

'Bitch,' Jinny spat under her breath, looking at Miss Kenny with contempt.

Georgina finished her meal but couldn't stop thinking about Linda and her unbalanced state of mind. Finally, she picked up her pint of weak tea before striding towards Miss Kenny, determined to make the mean woman listen to reason. As she strode across the hall, she was aware of the women nudging each other and whispers being exchanged. All eyes were now on her as she approached the formidable warden. Miss Kenny stood with her hands on her hips, staring hatefully at her.

'Get back to your seat, Garrett,' she ordered harshly.

'I'm concerned about Linda. She shouldn't be in that cell,' Georgina replied defiantly.

Miss Kenny smirked. 'Isn't that sweet. One filthy slut concerned for another.'

'The doctor should see her.'

'I've already told you, Garrett, you don't run this place. I'm in charge and what I say goes. However, I'm a fair person. I'll get her moved, and you can move with her.' With that, Miss Kenny called to three other wardens who were quick to surround Georgina. 'Take her downstairs and then take Linda Green down too.'

'No,' Georgina protested, 'you can't do this.'

She dropped her tea as the wardens took each of her arms. Miss Kenny's smirk was now a smug look and Georgina wanted to spit in the woman's face. But she reminded herself of her plan. She had to behave. She couldn't give them any reason to turn her down for domestic duties at Pentonville. 'I'm sorry, Miss Kenny,' she said begrudgingly as she was led away.

Georgina didn't struggle with the wardens even though she knew where they were taking her – the lower corridor.

A stinking, damp row of windowless cells, each cell with nothing but a mattress on the floor. She'd spent the first few weeks of her confinement there when she'd arrived at the prison. Her heart sunk at the thought of being back there but she knew she'd have to accept her fate for now.

After being dragged down a few flights of stairs and through several doors, a putrid smell hit her. Bile rose in her throat and she tried not to breathe too deeply.

'Looks like you'll be living down here with the other lowlife rats and conchies,' one warden said as the other unlocked a cell and they pushed her in. 'You've got Jewish scum next door to you. I hope her and her dirty brat contaminate you and bring you down a peg or two.'

The door slammed shut and Georgina slumped onto the rotten mattress. She was grateful that the overhead light was low. At least she couldn't clearly see the black mould on the walls and the bugs scurrying around her feet. Her jaw clenched and her hands made fists. She'd get Miss Kenny. One day, when she was free, she'd make the evil cow pay for this.

The minutes ticked by slowly. She listened for the sound of Linda being brought down but heard nothing. Perhaps Miss Kenny had had a change of heart and had sent for the doctor after all. She doubted it, but she was relieved that Linda didn't have to endure these awful conditions.

Pushing herself up from the mattress, she went to the door and called to the prisoner in the next cell. 'Hello... can you hear me?'

A woman replied with a simple, 'Yes.'

'I'm Georgina Garrett. I've been here three years. What about you?'

'I am Ester Gutfreund, with my eight-year-old daughter, Paula.'

Ester spoke slowly and she had a distinctive accent that Georgina couldn't make out. As she digested the words, she baulked at the realisation of a child being in the prison.

'We are Jewish refugees from Düsseldorf, in Germany. We have done nothing wrong. We have no trial. They promise me, my daughter will stay with me. I do not know where my husband is. They say we will remain here until they take us to a holding camp on the Isle of Man. Please, what should I do?'

Georgina swallowed hard. She hadn't been expecting this response. She'd heard rumours that women who'd escaped the Nazis were being held in the prison but she hadn't believed the gossip. But now she realised it was true and she supposed that anyone from Germany was considered to be foe and were feared. But a child... how could anyone fear a child?

'Please, what should I do?' Ester asked again, the desperation in her voice clear to hear.

'Sit tight. There's nothing much you can do. Just... sit tight. No one will hurt you or your daughter. They won't keep you locked up forever. They just need time to work out that you're not the enemy.' Her words would be of little comfort but what else could she say?

'I sit here now for two weeks. Paula is not eating. Please, you speak for me. Make them understand before my child starves.'

Georgina's head dropped at the hopelessness of the situation. There was nothing she could say to anyone that would help Ester but she had to offer the woman some hope. 'Yes. Of course I will,' she said, trying to sound reassuring.

'Thank you, Miss Garrett. Thank you.'

Georgina rubbed the finger where she'd once worn her mother's wedding ring. It had been removed from her on arrival and if she got her way and escaped, she knew she'd never see it again. But the loss would be worth her freedom. She couldn't abide to think of that starving child in the cell next door, petrified and cold. Or Linda, mourning the loss of her baby. Her heart silently cried for these women. She desperately wanted to help them and to fight the unjustness of it all, but was powerless to do anything. Again, she slumped onto the mattress and tears streamed down her face, a part of her wishing that she didn't know of the existence of Ester and Paula.

Hours passed and Georgina finally heard the familiar jangle of a warden's keys. She jumped to her feet, hoping it wasn't Miss Kenny. When her cell door opened, she was relieved to see Miss Winter looking at her disapprovingly.

'You're supposed to be keeping your nose clean, Garrett,' the woman said and tutted.

'I have been. All I did was ask Miss Kenny to get the doctor for Linda.'

'I know, I heard what happened, but it isn't your place to concern yourself about the welfare of the women. Miss Kenny doesn't take kindly to being told what to do, and there's no point in worrying about Linda anymore.'

'Why? What's happened?' Georgina asked suspiciously.

'The silly girl killed herself.'

The shocking but not surprising news left Georgina feeling like she'd been punched in the stomach and winded. 'What happened?' she mumbled.

'She was found a while ago. She somehow managed to

shove a load of the mattress stuffing down her throat and choked. Such a waste. She was due for release in a few months.'

'Can you get me out of here and back on the block?' Georgina asked, fighting the urge to scream or cry.

'Yes, but keep your bloody head down in future.'

She nodded, but couldn't help speaking up for Ester next door. 'Just one thing, Miss Winter. The girl, in there with her mother. She's not eating.'

'All right, I'll see to it that the doctor is sent for. Now, back to your cell, quietly.'

Georgina followed the warden through the prison. It felt quieter than usual. She guessed it was subdued because of Linda's tragic death. At least the girl was at peace now and hopefully reunited with her baby boy.

'You've missed a day's work so your wages will be docked,' Miss Winter said as she escorted Georgina to her cell.

'Have you got anywhere with getting me Jinny's job?'

'I hardly think now is the right time to put your name forward.'

'Please, Miss Winter, before someone else jumps in.'

'All right, I'll mention it tomorrow. But like I said, don't hold your breath. Miss Kenny is none too keen on you and she holds more rank than me.'

'I know you'll do your best for me,' she said and smiled knowingly.

'Shush, that's enough. Get in your cell and forget about any supper tonight. You'll have to wait 'til morning for something to eat.'

Georgina nodded and resigned herself to a night of

stomach-grumbling hunger. But at least she was away from the lower corridor, though she couldn't shake off thoughts of Ester and her child. She hoped Miss Winter would be good to her word and ensure the doctor attended. Then her mind turned with thoughts of Linda.

Eventually, as night descended, she fell into a restless sleep, haunted by images of Linda's dead baby and the child in the cell downstairs, starving to death. But at least these images kept her from thinking and dreaming about her own loved ones… Alfie, Selina and the men she had loved and lost.

3

In Battersea, Charlotte had waited in all day for Johnny but he hadn't called in to see her. It had given her time to think and now she'd come to the conclusion that she wouldn't tell him that the Naylors were extorting money from her. After all, what could he do about it other than fight it out with them? She knew he would, for her, but she didn't want to see him getting hurt. No, she'd have to deal with it herself – just like Georgina would.

The terrifying sound of an air raid siren sprung into life and wailed out, snapping her from her thoughts. It had been a while since she'd heard Moaning Minnie, and immediately her stomach churned while her pulse quickened.

'Quickly, Dog, come,' she called and grabbed the animal by the scruff of the neck, pulling him to the kitchen.

She huddled under the heavy wooden table with Dog beside her, squeezing her eyes shut as she drew in several long, deep breaths to try and calm her rattled nerves. She found herself trembling as her mind wandered back to her memories of the time when she'd been homeless and living on the streets. She'd seen hideous sights during the Blitz. Bodies mutilated and mangled by explosions, melted skin and headless corpses. The images filled her head, bringing tears to her eyes. She wanted to scream. Covering her ears did nothing to blot out the relentless whining of the sirens.

'Please, go away,' she mumbled, shaking with fear, her ears pricked for the sound of planes above.

Dog licked her cheek and she opened her eyes to look at him. 'It'll be all right,' she said soothingly, trying to convince herself more than him. The black, scruffy mutt brought her some comfort but she wished Georgina was with her.

At last, the sirens quietened, and after a while they signalled all clear. Thankfully, she hadn't heard any bombs drop nearby. But then a loud knock on the door startled her. She guessed it would be Lord Hamilton coming to check on her. She knew it wouldn't be Dina. The tall Russian blonde hated her but Charlotte thought it was to be expected. She doubted the woman would ever forgive her. Poor Dina had never fully recovered from being accidently poisoned, which left Charlotte feeling awful about what had happened.

She scrambled out from under the table and went to the door to find Lord Hamilton stood with a glass in each hand.

'Brandy, my dear, to calm one's nerves.'

'Thank you, come in,' she said, pulling Dog back from jumping up and licking the man.

'It appears we're safe tonight but I fear Wimbledon or Putney may have been struck.'

'Poor souls,' Charlotte said, knees still shaking as she sat down. She sipped her drink and tried to rid her head of the disturbing memories that the sirens had triggered.

'Quite. I heard Miss Gray singing as I came downstairs. The dear lady seems to think she is Margery Booth but her notes are terribly off-key. I suppose singing aloud must bring her some comfort during these wretched times.'

'Have you checked that she's all right?' Charlotte asked, not knowing who Margery Booth was and not caring.

'Absolutely no point. The last time I called on her she dismissed me, rather abruptly too. She prefers her own company and doesn't like to be bothered.'

'Yeah, I got that impression an' all.'

Lord Hamilton swilled his brandy around the glass and asked, 'What about Dina?'

'What about her?' Charlotte replied, cringing at the memory of how the woman had come to drink brandy laced with arsenic from apple seeds.

'Well, she's a bit of an odd fish and she doesn't speak kindly of you.'

'It's a long story, you don't want to know.'

'Oh, my dear, I do,' he said with a wicked grin.

Charlotte looked over the top of her glass, studying his face. She could tell from his bemused expression that he was already fully aware of the awful facts. 'She's told you, hasn't she?'

'She may have mentioned something in passing when she was sweeping my floors earlier.'

'So why are you asking me, if you already know?'

Lord Hamilton threw his head back, laughing. 'You're a dark horse. I would never have had you marked as a potential murderer!'

'I ain't... not really. I was young and stupid and made a big mistake.'

'Dina told me that you instructed your boyfriend to crush apple seeds and disguise the poison in a bottle of brandy which she then came to drink. However, your real target was Miss Garrett.'

'See, you know it all so just drop it, please.'

'Oooh, touchy. Sorry, I'm just teasing and I shouldn't. But I gather you and Miss Garrett are the best of friends now?'

Charlotte stretched her neck. The tension she'd felt from the air raid had lifted and the brandy had given her a warm glow inside. She sighed heavily. 'Yeah, Georgina has been good to me. She's like family. Me mum don't want me living with them on the farm but even after everything I did, Georgina took me under her wing.'

'Such a pity I can't meet her. Miss Garrett sounds intriguingly delightful, albeit a tad frightening.'

'Oh, you'd love her. She's... she's... incredible.'

'Well, my dear girl, so are you. You're little more than a child and here you are, acting landlady of this building and dealing with those awful men.'

'What awful men?' Charlotte asked, sitting forward.

'Sorry, it's none of my business but I've seen those two hoodlums demanding money from you.'

'Huh, the Naylor brothers. Honestly, if Georgina was around, those two would be quaking in their boots.'

'Do they frighten you?'

Again, Charlotte sighed. 'No, not really. But I worry what damage they would cause if I didn't pay them.'

'Couldn't you discuss the situation with your friend, Mr Dymond?'

'I thought about it. I was gonna talk to him today but he didn't show up and maybe it's just as well. There's nothing much Johnny can do other than get into a fight with them, and I don't want him hurt. I'm afraid I'm stuck with having to cough up what they ask for or deal with it meself.'

'That sounds terribly unfair.'

'It is, but that's how things are,' she said, adding thought-fully, '… but then again, they don't have to be.'

'You sound like you intend to redress the balance of unfairness?'

'Yeah, I suppose I do,' she answered, wistfully. Granted, she wasn't Georgina Garrett and her name, Charlotte Mipple, didn't install fear. She couldn't fight with her fists like Georgina could, but Georgina had taught her to be clever. She'd need to outsmart her opponents. Brains and beauty, that was Georgina. Charlotte didn't have the beauty but she had the brains and it was time she stood up to the Naylors and reminded them what the Garrett name represented.

Another monotonous day had passed and now, in the pitch blackness of lockdown, Georgina tried to blot out the echoes of hysterical women, the clangs of iron bars being rattled, the cries… all sounds of another restless night on F Block. There'd been tension building all day since rumour had it that Diana Mitford was due to be released with her husband, Oswald Mosley, on the grounds of his ill health. The British Union women were delighted, but the rest of the prisoners resented her special treatment. Miss Winter had told Georgina that Diana had been granted the luxury of a daily bath, though apparently the woman had declined the offer. The prison only had enough water for four women a day to bathe so Georgina was pleased she'd had hers that morning, though she knew it would be at least a week or two until her next one.

She'd just drifted off to sleep when the familiar sound of the air raid siren wailed across London, waking her with a start. Thankfully, there'd been a lull in the Luftwaffe's aerial attacks since the devastating Blitz, but every so often the German planes would fly over, still determined to destroy London.

Instantly, the prison broke into pandemonium. Women began screaming for their doors to be unlocked, terrified of being caged and trapped while bombs dropped around them. They'd been told that the safest place to be was in their cells, unless the block took a direct hit. None the less, the wardens dashed from cell to cell releasing the frightened prisoners.

Georgina heard her door unlock and was pleased to see Miss Winter.

'Any news on Jinny's job?' she asked hopefully.

'Yes... yes, it's yours, but I'll talk to you tomorrow,' Miss Winter answered quickly and hurried to the next cell.

Georgina felt elated and wanted to shout with joy, but knew she had to keep her feelings hidden. It wouldn't be long now and she'd be free.

The women began to huddle in the corridors. A few remained in their cells to gaze out of the windows. The East End had taken a battering during the Blitz and many of the prisoners were from that area, with family and friends living there. These women would stare anxiously across the skyline, some praying out loud for God to spare their loved ones.

Jinny came to stand beside Georgina, her face ashen.

'Are you all right?'

'No, not really,' Jinny answered. 'These bombs shit me right up.'

'Well, let's be pleased for small mercies. At least they're not a nightly occurrence anymore.'

'Yeah, I suppose so, but my mother was killed in a raid. My girl was wiv her but she got out unscathed. She's wiv me sister now. I hope they're all right.'

'I hope so too; try not to worry. And sorry about your mum.'

'Thanks. It broke my heart. It was Miss Kenny who told me and I'm sure the bitch enjoyed it.'

'Probably. The woman seems to like seeing us lot in misery,' Georgina said, then her brow knitted when she noticed a familiar face walking towards them.

'Fleur, is that you?' she asked. The girl looked different without make-up and her crude bleached blonde hair was tied on top of her head exposing her dark brown roots.

'Hello, Miss Garrett. I hoped I'd find you in here.'

'Who's this?' Jinny asked, eyeing the young woman up and down.

'This is Fleur, she used to work for me.'

'What you in for?' Jinny asked.

'Turning tricks. It's me second time banged up in *Camden Castle*. Six weeks this time, but at least I ain't downstairs again.'

'Not long then, love,' Jinny said. 'I'm out in a few days, thank gawd. I won't have to wear these awful voluminous drawers and black knitted stockings no more. It wouldn't be so bad if I had garters. Without them the bloody things spend more time round me ankles.'

'Yeah, I know what you mean and this calico dress don't 'alf scratch,' Fleur moaned.

'You'll get used to it. Anyway, I'll leave you two to catch up. See you around, Fleur.'

'Come in here,' Georgina said and pulled Fleur into her cell. 'What's going on in Battersea?' she asked, excited for news from outside.

'I wish you was back. Bert and Len Naylor are throwing their weight around. I've heard they're making a good living out of taxing a lot of your old customers. Making them pay well over the top too.'

'Cheeky bastards. What else? Any news on Johnny and Victor?'

'I see Johnny about now and then. He did a bit of time a while back but he's out now and seems all right, still as cocky as ever. I've not heard anything about Victor. I think he went to work for The Top over in south-east London.'

'I've heard about him. What do you know about him?'

'Not much. He's some Irish geezer. Maynard's blokes did a runner after his body was found but before they scarpered, they made sure that everyone knew that it was The Top who killed Maynard. People are shit scared of him. I reckon he killed Victor an' all. He's probably still at the bottom of the Thames. I mean, Victor was a big bloke. I don't suppose his body floated up like David Maynard's did.'

Georgina's breath caught in her throat at the mention of David's horrific death. It had broken her heart that she hadn't even been permitted to attend his funeral. When his body had been washed up, the police had reported that David had been shot in the head before being dumped in the river. The thought of it churned Georgina's stomach.

The two men in her life that she had loved, Lash and David, had both been mercilessly gunned down.

'I know it ain't none of my business, Miss Garrett, but why won't you let anyone visit you? I saw the Barker twins a couple of months ago and they said they'd have liked to come and see you.'

'No, Fleur. I don't want visitors. No letters in and none out. I want everyone to stay away from me for their own sake.'

'That's what I thought. The Old Bill have a sniff round now and then but there's nothing for them to find. Did you hear about Livingstone Road?'

'Yes, the roof got badly damaged,' Georgina answered, unbothered. The house had been a brothel, a small part of the business she'd run that had once belonged to Billy Wilcox.

'Yeah, blown orf! Bloody bombs! It's derelict now. Least none of the girls were in there. They all cleared orf the day after you was arrested. Good job an' all. The filth were all over the place like lice.'

'I knew they would be. That's why I had everything closed down. How's Charlotte? Do you see her?'

'No, hardly ever. Never hear anything about her neither. I bumped into Dirty Gerty a while ago. She's working for the Zammits now. She's got a nice little patch up town and gets well looked after. She's living in the same house as Max the Axe.'

'None of the old gang are working together anymore then?'

'No, Miss Garrett. I dunno what happened but they all

went their own ways. Did you hear about your dad's mate, Ray? He was killed when a bomb landed on his house.'

'Yes, I heard. Very sad. Listen to me, Fleur. This is very important. When you get out of here, I want you to look Charlotte up. Make sure you do.'

Georgina's lifelong best friend, and Charlotte's older sister, Molly, had sent a letter last week that had briefly mentioned Charlotte. Molly lived on a farm in Kent with her husband, Oppo, and her son, Edward. They weren't the only ones. Fanny Mipple, Molly and Charlotte's mother, also lived with them. Her thoughts went back to the letter. Molly had said the farm was doing well and Oppo had taken on a couple of land girls to help in the fields. She'd said the weather was mild and they were getting ready for Christmas and that Charlotte was doing well in London. She said Aunty Esme had taken a trip to Swansea which she very much enjoyed. Aunty Esme was coded information for the whereabouts of Lash's gypsy family. They travelled the country and sometimes went to Ireland but Georgina was pleased to know they were in Wales. She hadn't relished the thought of having to cross the sea to get to her children. And though it was wonderful to receive news from Molly, she now wished that she hadn't allowed her friend to write. She feared that when she made her escape, the police would be sure to look for her on the farm and she didn't want Molly upset.

Bringing her mind back to the present, Georgina said to Fleur, 'Right, keep your head down, stay out of Miss Kenny's way and come to me if you get any bother.'

'Thanks, Miss Garrett. I will.'

Fleur slipped out of the cell and Georgina closed the

door. From the sound of the laughter drifting in from the corridors, it appeared the mood on the block had lifted. She lay on her bed and closed her eyes, a small smile on her face. Now she knew she had Jinny's job, by this time next week, she'd be out of Camden Castle for good.

4

Charlotte opened the door to the large bedroom and, with a sweeping motion of her arm, stated, 'The flat comes fully furnished and the bed is brand new.'

She watched PC Timothy Batten's face to gauge his reaction. His hazel eyes were wide and Charlotte was pleased to see he looked suitably impressed. She couldn't help noticing his fine features and how attractive he was but men were, and always would be, off the agenda.

'The other bedroom isn't furnished but that wouldn't be a problem, would it?' she asked, knowing the young police constable was a single man.

'No, not at all. I don't really need two bedrooms. In fact, I don't really need a whole apartment. Just a room would do. This place is smashing but I'm not sure I can afford it.'

'Of course you can. I'm letting the place go at fifty per cent discount but if you want it, you'd best be quick. First come, first served.'

PC Batten glanced around the room and sucked in a sharp breath. 'This house was Georgina Garrett's knocking shop. I don't think my station sergeant would be too happy about me renting here.'

'I'll have you know that this place is very respectable now.

There's a lord lives upstairs. Look, it's up to you. There's a housing shortage so there'll be plenty of folk ready to bite me hand off for a nice place like this. I thought I was doing you a favour but forget it. Now, if you don't mind,' Charlotte said, gesturing to the front door.

'No, wait, sorry. Perhaps I was being a bit hasty. You're right, it's not easy to find a decent place to live… I'll take it.'

Charlotte hid a smile of triumph and shook his hand. His touch left her feeling slightly flushed but she quickly dismissed her feelings. 'I'll get the paperwork drawn up. You can move in straight away if you like?'

'Yes, I will, thanks. I've cricked my neck sleeping on my sister's sofa and her kids don't give me much peace. I'll collect my things and be back later. Here's four weeks' rent.'

Charlotte exchanged the money for the keys, pleased with her transaction. She'd always vowed that she'd never rent out the apartment intended for Georgina on her release but reckoned her mentor would be proud of what she'd done. She'd used her brain and now she had a copper in the building to keep the Naylor brothers at bay. Genius!

As Charlotte showed him to the front door, Lord Hamilton was coming in and stopped to look suspiciously at the policeman.

'This is PC Timothy Batten. He'll be living in here,' she said, pointing to the ground floor apartment. 'Lord Hamilton lives upstairs,' she added.

'I see. Pleased to meet you,' Lord Hamilton answered haughtily, then brushed past saying, 'Excuse me. Charlotte, a word when you have a moment.'

She nodded, but wondered what could be bothering him.

Lord Hamilton wasn't his usual friendly and flamboyant self; if anything, she thought he'd been quite rude.

PC Batten left and Charlotte headed straight upstairs. She tapped on Lord Hamilton's door.

'Has he gone?' he asked, poking his head through and looking left to right.

'Yes, to fetch his stuff. He'll be back soon.'

'Come in, come in,' he said urgently in a hushed voice.

In the lounge, she questioned, 'Is something wrong?'

'Oh, my dear girl, how could you rent the apartment to a police constable?' he asked, sounding flummoxed.

'I don't see what the problem is. I noticed him looking at the cards on the noticeboard in the newsagent and asked him if he was after somewhere to live. What's wrong with having a copper here? It'll keep them Naylor brothers off me back.'

Lord Hamilton sighed and swept his arm across the room, indicating to the oil paintings on the wall. 'These, my dear, these are the problem.'

'What, are they pinched?'

'No, they're reproductions.'

'There's nothing illegal about reproductions, is there?'

'No, but there is if one is selling them as originals. You see my point?'

'So, that's your game, you sly old bugger,' Charlotte said with a chortle. 'I shouldn't worry. Just don't invite PC Batten in. Anyway, he'll be at work all day. He won't see what you're up to.'

'I hope you're right, Charlotte. The last thing I need is the Metropolitan Police taking an interest in my activities.'

Charlotte wasn't surprised at Lord Quentin's revelation.

She'd always suspected there was something dodgy about him and still wasn't convinced that he really was a lord. 'Do you paint them yourself?' she asked.

'No,' he laughed, 'I can't even paint a matchstick man. Paintings of this quality require tremendous skill and talent. It's quite rare, you know.'

'Do you have someone who paints them for you?'

'I did, but not these ones. They were painted many, many years ago, long before you were born. Unfortunately, I can't sell them as originals as the originals are hung in galleries, at least they were before the war. Now I suspect they've been shipped off to somewhere safe.'

'So you're stuck with them?'

'For the time being. They're worthless as repros but would be worth an absolute small fortune on the black market as originals.'

'If you say so. It's all a bit above my head. Anyway, just keep PC Batten at arm's length and I'm sure it'll be fine. I've gotta dash. I need to go and see Mr Harel about getting the tenancy papers drawn up. See ya.'

Charlotte drove to Clapham Junction where Benjamin Harel's father, Ezzy, owned a jewellery shop. Benjamin had been Georgina's trusted accountant and the manager of The Penthouse Club, but now worked freelance from a small office in the back of his father's shop. He'd been a great help to Charlotte since Georgina's arrest but she hadn't seen much of him lately. She felt sure that he'd think her decision to rent to a policeman was a wise one. It would stop the Naylors from demanding money from her, though sadly, it wouldn't keep them from extorting cash from Ezzy Harel.

*

Johnny sat at a table in the corner of the Halfway House and sucked on his cigar as he kept his eyes on the pub door. He hadn't seen much of the old gang lately and was looking forward to working again with the Barker twins, Ned, and Max the Axe. Though to get them on board, he knew he'd have to use his charm and wit to persuade them that his idea was a viable and profitable one. After all, since Miss Garrett had been banged up, none of them had been particularly successful. He himself had had the pleasure of His Majesty's hospitality for a year in Wandsworth prison. And from what Max had told him, the others were only scraping by. There was no doubt in Johnny's mind that his old gang mates worked better together rather than alone. So if Miss Garrett wasn't around to organise them, Johnny had decided that he would take up the reins.

Ned was first to come in, his flat cap pulled low and his neck hunkered down into the collar of his donkey jacket. Short and with a slim build, he carried himself like an old man though he was only forty-something. He spotted Johnny and came over, extending his hand to greet him.

'Hello, mate, good to see ya,' Ned said, smiling to reveal his yellowed teeth.

'And you, Ned, thanks for coming.'

'I got word from Max that you wanted a meet. Cor, talk about putting a smile on me boat race. How ya doing, me old mucker?'

'Yeah, good, Ned. Sit down, I'll get you a drink.'

'Bottle of stout, none of that shit out the pipes.'

Johnny stood at the brown painted bar and looked to the door again when the Barker twins came in.

'Johnny Dymond, fancy seeing you here,' one said.

'Two halves,' the other added, grinning.

'You timed that well,' Johnny laughed and shook their hands. There was a time when he could have told the brothers apart. Both in their early thirties, Nobby had a rounder face than Eric and his brown hair was slightly more receded, but now he wasn't sure who was who.

Once they sat at the table, Ned was the first to speak. 'So, what's this all about, Johnny? You didn't call us together 'cos you've missed us.'

'But I have, Ned. I've missed you all. You're right though, I do have a proposal – but let's wait 'til Max gets here before we discuss it.'

'I knew it,' one of the twins said. 'I knew there was something. Is it Miss Garrett? Are we gonna bust her out of gaol?'

'No, but I wish it was. If I thought we could get her out of that place, I'd be bang on it.'

'Yeah, me an' all. I can't fucking stand thinking of her rotting in there. She don't deserve it. At least that Nancy fucking Austin got her face blown orf. Serves her right. It was one thing to try and take over the business but a fucking disgrace to have fitted up Miss Garrett like that,' Ned said with disgust, then sniffed some snuff off the back of his hand.

For a moment, the way Ned's nose was wrinkling, Johnny thought the man was going to sneeze so he leaned to one side out of the way.

'Bleedin' stuff makes me hooter feel funny every time,' Ned moaned, his eyes watering.

''Ere, Ned, have a smoke instead,' one of the twins offered. 'Don't put no more of that shit up your nose.'

'Yeah, I fink I will, cheers, mate.'

'First things first, gentlemen,' Johnny said and held his glass of double whisky in the air. 'Cheers, to old friends and absent ones.'

'Yeah, to old friends,' the men said in unison.

'I gotta ask,' he continued, looking at the twins, 'who the fuck is who?'

Nobby and Eric chuckled.

Then Ned chipped in, 'He's Nobby, you can tell.'

'Yeah, I'm the best looking one,' Nobby said, grinning.

Johnny looked from one twin to the other. There were subtle differences in their features but nothing obvious.

'I'll make it easy for you,' Nobby said and pointed to a small mole on his cheek, close to his ear. 'Eric ain't got one.'

With that cleared up, Johnny checked his watch, wondering what was keeping Max. It wasn't like the man to be late for a meeting and when Johnny had suggested it, Max had seemed keen. Johnny had expected to walk in the pub and find Max ready, eager and waiting. He was surprised that the man wasn't already here.

'You look like life has been treating you well, Johnny. What you been up to? I heard you got yourself banged up, you silly git,' Nobby said, always more talkative than his brother.

'Yeah, I ain't as young as I used to be and not as fast. I got caught legging it from a poxy little job. But, you know me.

I'm back on me feet again and I've been doing a bit of this, that and the other. What about you?'

'We've been doing all right. We've got a cousin who works in the kitchens at Chelsea Barracks. He's been getting us butter, eggs, bacon and all sorts that we can sell on. And our nephew has got a job on a farm in Surrey. He's managed to get his hands on the odd pig or two. Mum's been claiming rations for our gran who pegged it last year and our old man claimed on the government compensation scheme for the house getting blown up. He got fifty quid. It's been tiding us over.'

'Sorry about your house,' Johnny said.

'No need, mate. It's still standing. The bombs missed it but our dad's a crafty bugger.'

'Cor, blimey, sounds like you've got a right bleedin' dodgy family,' Ned said with a chortle.

Johnny got another round of drinks and checked his watch again. Nearly half an hour had passed and there was still no sign of Max.

'It seems Max has stood us up,' he said, but then the pub door opened again and Johnny was pleased to see his friend from boyhood breeze in.

'Better late than never,' Johnny said, rising to his feet to greet him.

'Sorry about that. I got caught up in a row with some Yank and Gerty. Fucking liberty-taking wankers. Do you want a drink?'

'No, mate, we're all right. What happened?'

'Let me get meself a pint,' Max said, 'Give me a minute to calm down. I'm fucking seething.'

Johnny saw Ned's eyebrows raise and noticed Max's

knuckles were bleeding. He'd clearly been involved in a fight and knew whoever had been at the receiving end of Max's fists would be in a mess now. From the age of ten, Max had gained a reputation for fighting. He had a short fuse and explosive temper. He'd once told Johnny that he never felt pain. He'd keep going until his opponent was on the floor. And if his fists weren't enough, he'd brandish his tomahawk axe – a gift from his grandfather, apparently stolen from a real Native American Indian – hence his nickname, Max the Axe. It had been his fearless character that had first caught the attention of Norman Wilcox, who'd quickly recruited him to his gang. Max had then brought Johnny in, but unfortunately they'd soon found themselves working for Norman's mad son, Billy. Max had been one of the few blokes who hadn't been scared of Billy Wilcox. Johnny had feared Billy and felt no shame in admitting it. He'd been secretly pleased when Billy had been murdered and Miss Garrett had eventually taken over, though at first he'd been disgruntled about working for a woman.

Max returned to the table and sat next to Johnny. He drank a few glugs of beer and then sighed. 'That's better,' he said.

'So, what happened to you?' Ned asked.

'Fucking Yanks, taking the piss. I heard Gerty upstairs screaming so went up and found this American GI trying to get hold of her.'

'Ha, I bet you sorted him out, eh, Max?' Ned said.

'Fucking right, I did. Cheeky bastard. Turns out she's been working up town for the Zammits, and this American GI took a shine to her. Followed her home.'

'What, Gerty's one of the Piccadilly Commandos?' Johnny asked.

'Yeah, she's raking it in.'

'If she's on the game for the Zammits, shouldn't they be looking after her?'

'I suppose so but there ain't much they can do once she's off work and at home,' Max answered.

'I've heard about the Zammits,' Nobby said, shaking his head. 'They've got a hold on all the girls uptown. It ain't right, is it? I mean, they ain't even English and they're profiting off the back of our women. What with the fucking Ities first and now the Maltese. Anyhow, is Gerty all right?'

'Yeah, yeah, she's fine. I told her to give me a shout if she gets any more trouble from her punters.'

'You fancy her, don't ya?' Ned asked.

'No, but she's a nice girl.'

'Dirty Gerty,' Ned laughed, 'That's what all the other brasses used to call her when they worked for Miss Garrett. But you're right, Max, she is a nice girl. A tart wiv a heart.'

'Yeah, and probably with a dose of something an' all,' Max laughed. 'Trust me to get lumbered with her living upstairs from me.'

'It could have been worse. You could've had Johnny up there,' Ned added.

'Yeah, thanks, mate,' Johnny smiled. 'Right, let's get down to business, shall we?'

'I've been dying to hear this,' Max said and the others nodded in agreement.

Johnny glanced from one face to the other and lowered his voice. It felt nice to have the familiar faces around him. Men he trusted with his life. He missed the days when they'd worked for Miss Garrett and, thanks to her ingenuity, had made a good living. But without her, they'd all drifted back to doing small, petty jobs for themselves. Now Johnny had decided it was time to think in the way Miss Garrett had and turn over something worth turning over. 'I've got a job in mind, a good earner for us all. But I ain't gonna lie, there's risks involved.'

'Ain't there always?' Ned said, shrugging his shoulders. 'But it's never worried us before.'

'Yeah, but we had Miss Garrett watching our backs then,' Eric pointed out.

'If you don't want in, just say. It would be a shame 'cos there's no one else I'd rather work with than you, Eric... all of you. I trust you lot and I wouldn't suggest this if I didn't believe we could pull it off. Do you want in or out?' Johnny asked, hoping the twins would come on board.

'In, of course. Go on then, let's hear it,' Nobby replied, speaking for himself and his brother.

Johnny smiled. They hadn't even heard his plans but had agreed to be a part of them. And he hoped that once he explained everything, they'd be impressed. After all, one of the things he'd learned from Miss Garrett was the importance of planning. She'd planned everything meticulously, never leaving room for error. And with this job that they were about to embark on, error would mean one or all of them could die.

5

Georgina carried her pail to the slopping-out area, holding her breath until her lungs ached. She hoped to avoid getting a whiff of the stomach-turning stench but it was inevitable, especially if there was a queue. Luckily, this morning, the disgusting job was finished quickly, though as she made her way back to her cell she saw Fleur gagging and trying her hardest not to vomit. Placing a reassuring hand on her shoulder, she told the girl, 'You'll be fine.'

Fleur looked at her with red-rimmed eyes. 'I ain't weak, Miss Garrett, but I can't abide the slopping out.'

'It's all right,' Georgina whispered and pulled a small tin pill box from the pocket of her grey prison-wear dress. 'Take this,' she whispered, 'and rub a bit round your nostrils. It helps.'

Fleur discreetly accepted the tiny package and shoved it in her pocket. 'Thank you, Miss Garrett, thanks so much,' she gushed.

'Go on, get on your way before Miss Kenny has you up for loitering,' Georgina said and watched as Fleur hurried back to her cell.

The pill box had contained an ointment made from peppermint. Jinny had slipped it to her before she'd been released. Georgina had been grateful but she had no need for it now. Today was the last day she'd be slopping out. If all went according to plan, she'd be a free woman by this evening.

After breakfast, as the women went to work at their assigned jobs, Georgina and two others were escorted from the block. Door after door clanged behind them as they made their way through the oppressive building. The low ceilings and lack of natural daylight made the place feel claustrophobic. When they reached the outside, she breathed in deeply, enjoying the cold, fresh air. She peered up at the tall turrets of the impressive prison. Holloway had been aptly nicknamed Camden Castle, and from the outside she could see why. It looked like a medieval fortress but she inwardly smiled – it wasn't going to keep her locked up for much longer.

They passed a huge pile of coal in the yard which was mostly used for the laundry. Ha, the mangle. She'd never miss that mangle. In fact, Georgina vowed right there and then that she'd never use one again, even if it meant her clothes were left dripping. She'd never eat margarine again either. Or use a pail for her ablutions.

As they left the soot-blackened walls of the yard, Georgina glanced to her right at another wing of the prison. She knew the wing contained the condemned cell – a holding area for women sentenced to death. It was positioned next to the double gallows where they were hanged. The thought of a rope around her neck, and dropping into the pit, had woken her with a start on many lonely nights. After all, if the authorities had been aware of half the things she'd done, she had no doubt that they would have convicted her to that terrifying fate. Luckily, she'd been spared the rope and was grateful for small mercies.

They were driven half a mile up the road and through the staff entrance into Pentonville prison for men. The place had an even worse reputation than Holloway, though Georgina couldn't imagine how conditions could be any worse than those of the women's gaol. But she'd never know. Her cleaning duties in the warden's quarters was in the grounds of the prison, well away from the men.

She set to work, pretty much unsupervised. This role was a position of trust, and for the past four days she'd proved herself to be a good housekeeper, leaving each accommodation spick and span. There'd been no room for complaint from any of the female wardens. In fact, on the quiet, Miss Winter had told her that she'd been doing a good job and it had been noted. But unknown to anyone, alongside the cleaning, Georgina had also been checking how to put her plan into action.

Three hours later, Georgina heard the bells chime from a nearby church. It was one o'clock. Time to act. Her heart hammered and she felt quite giddy, yet it didn't once cross her mind to back out. The thought of holding her children in her arms was worth the risk. She was more determined than ever to escape the rigid confinement of the prison.

Being as stealthy as possible, she left water running in a bathroom with the door ajar. If anyone passed, they'd assume she was in there cleaning, just as she should be. She then snuck into the warden's bedroom and quickly undressed before throwing on a spare uniform. The skirt was a tad too short, the starched white shirt and jacket only just reached across her chest, but she managed to do the buttons up. Next, she squeezed her feet into a pair of black, low shoes. They too were on the small side, making her feet feel crushed, but with adrenaline pumping, she hardly noticed. She shoved her prison issue dress, long-legged knickers and stockings under the bed before grabbing a warden's hat and tucking her hair under.

Georgina glanced quickly in the mirror. A coat would have been ideal but there wasn't one. The warden probably had it with her at Holloway. She was lucky there'd been a spare pair of shoes. Several of the other accommodations in the block hadn't had any. Satisfied that this was the best she could hope to achieve and with no time to spare, Georgina drew in a deep breath to steady herself and then strode confidently out of the door.

The accommodation was in the fourth block in a row of seven. As she marched past the other flats, she hoped she wouldn't bump into anyone, especially a warden who might recognise her. She wanted to run but that would draw suspicion. Instead, she walked hurriedly, her head low but swinging her arms. She could feel her pulse racing and her mouth felt so dry that she could hardly swallow.

The gates were in sight now. Her legs were like jelly but she managed to keep going. She was almost there and prayed the guards wouldn't stop her or ask for identification. Luckily, from what she'd seen from Miss Winter's small bathroom window, the two male guards covering the lunchtime period were pretty lax in their duties. She'd spotted them wave several people through without checking for identification.

The skies had darkened and small spots of rain began to fall. This could work in her favour. She'd have good reason to be hurrying to avoid a downpour. But it could also work against her if the guards suspected something unusual in the fact she wasn't wearing a long, dark coat that all the female wardens wore.

Georgina picked up her pace, scurrying now, with her hand holding on to her hat so it obscured her face. Without glancing at the guards, she dashed past them as if it was the most natural thing to do in the world. As she approached the staff gate, she braced herself, expecting them to call her back. She could barely believe she'd walked straight past them. And now the gatekeeper was doffing his hat and opening the exit for her.

'Best get a move on, miss,' he said, 'or you'll get wet through.'

'Yes, thank you,' she answered, trotting past him and out into freedom.

She daren't look back and headed in the direction of Holloway Prison. Her heart pumped so hard that she could hear the blood rushing in her ears. The moment she was out of sight, Georgina dived down one of the alleyways and into the labyrinth of narrow streets around the outside of the prison.

Quickly chancing a glance over her shoulder, she was relieved to find she wasn't being chased or followed and paused for a brief moment to catch her breath. She reckoned it would be about an hour before they'd discover her missing. It wasn't long to get very far away and they'd soon work out she was in a prison warden's uniform. She had to get rid of it and fast, or risk standing out.

After overcoming the challenge of absconding, now she faced her next test – the getaway. And with no money and little knowledge of the streets around Pentonville, it wasn't going to be an easy task. But Georgina had always been resourceful and hoped she had luck on her side. 'If you're up there looking over me, Lash, help me out. I need to get back to our children,' she whispered, her eyes skyward. 'Or you, Gran, give me a hand here, or Dad, I could do with a bit of help. Any of you, just give me a sign... something... anything.'

Georgina wasn't sure what she was expecting. Maybe a flash of lightening or a clap of thunder to prove her long-gone loved ones were listening. Or maybe some miracle... a feather falling from the sky and blowing down the street to show her the way. But nothing happened and she suddenly felt very foolish and alone.

'Come on, girl, get a grip. You can do this,' she told herself as she moved on. She'd done the hardest part and walked through the gates of the prison to her liberty and now all she had to do was evade capture.

She couldn't go back to Holloway, not ever, and if they caught her, her sentence would likely be doubled. Georgina knew she'd do whatever it took to stay out of prison and if they found her, she wouldn't go quietly. She'd go down fighting, even if that meant fighting to the death.

Charlotte smugly swaggered to the front door, looking forward to seeing the look on the Naylor brothers' faces when they discovered who was living just feet from where they stood on the doorstep. She confidently pulled the door open and though the two men towered over her, she refused to be intimidated by them.

'Yes, can I help you?' she asked.

54

'You know why we're here,' Len, the younger brother sneered.

'Remind me,' she said boldly.

'We ain't got time for games, Charlotte. Just pay up or face the consequences.'

'I ain't paying you a penny so do your worse. But a word of warning… watch out for PC Batten. That's his room, just there,' she said and barged past them to point at a ground floor window. 'You know PC Batten, don't you? Local bobby, rides his bike, that one there,' she said, pointing to the constable's bicycle leaning against the wall by the front door.

She saw the brothers exchange a confused look. 'He'll be a kip now. I heard him come home this morning off his night shift. He might or might not be a heavy sleeper, so you'd best lower your voice when you threaten me.'

'We ain't threatened you,' Len quickly said.

'But you're gonna.'

'No, we wouldn't threaten you. Wherever did you get that silly idea from? You take care of yourself, Charlotte. We'll see you around.'

Before she could say anything, the brothers spun on their heels and hurried off. Good, she thought. That had showed them that she wasn't a pushover. Moving in PC Batten had had the desired effect and now she was free of the Naylor brothers. They wouldn't dare visit her again, not now they knew that a police officer lived on the premises.

Charlotte brushed her hands together as she walked back in, satisfied that she'd outsmarted them. She was just about to close the door when she recognised the familiar sound of Johnny's car hooter.

He pulled up against the kerb and climbed from his 1930s red Riley car, a cigar in his hand as he strutted towards her.

'You got your car back then,' she said, looking past him to the overly showy vehicle that was most impractical.

'Yeah, and funnily enough, that's what I wanted to talk to you about.'

'Come in, I'll put the kettle on,' she offered, pulling the door open wider.

'Was that the Naylor brothers I saw walking off from here?' he asked as he removed his fedora and sat on the sofa.

'Yeah, probably.'

'What were they doing here?'

'Nothing.'

'Bollocks. What were they doing here, Charlotte?'

'I told you, nothing. Do you want a cuppa?'

'No, I don't want a bleedin' cuppa. I want to know what business those wankers had coming here.'

Charlotte rolled her eyes. 'Don't worry about it, Johnny. I've sorted it.'

'Sit down,' he ordered.

'I'm going to put the kettle on.'

'I said, sit down,' he barked and as she took a seat he asked again, 'What did the Naylors want? And no bullshit, girl, I want the truth. 'Cos believe me, if that pair of slimy bastards are giving you any jip, I'll rip their fucking heads off then shove them up their miserable backsides.'

Charlotte smiled warmly at Johnny. 'Thanks, but that won't be necessary. Like I said, I've sorted it.'

Johnny's head tilted to one side, his eyes narrowing, and

from that look Charlotte knew he was waiting for more information. She tapped the ends of her fingers together before continuing. 'They've been getting money out of me but before you kick off, let me finish... Every week, they come round here and demand a quid from the rents. I've been paying up 'cos I didn't want them damaging the property or upsetting the tenants. But I've put a stop to it and they won't be back again.'

Charlotte could see the corner of Johnny's top lip twitching up and down. She knew it did this when he was angry.

'Why didn't you come to me?' he asked through gritted teeth.

''Cos I knew you'd go charging in with your fists flying and I didn't want to see you get hurt. Anyway, like I said, they won't be back so that's an end to it.'

'How have you stopped them?'

'I used me brain, just like Georgina would have, that's how.'

'For fuck's sake, Charlotte. Just tell me what you did,' he demanded impatiently.

'I let them know that a police officer is renting a flat here. They soon scarpered.'

Johnny leapt to his feet. 'What? A copper is living here?'

'Yeah, in Georgina's flat. Clever, ain't it? That'll keep the Naylors from bothering me.'

'Clever! Are you fucking kidding me? It's about the stupidest thing I've heard in ages!'

Charlotte, feeling hurt, looked up at Johnny. She'd been hoping for a pat on the back for using her initiative but instead he was insulting her.

'Don't look at me like that, Charlotte. You should have known better. He'll have to go.'

'But why?'

'Why? Do I really need to explain it to you... there's bodies in the cellar. Bodies that me and Miss Garrett put there.'

'Yeah, but the Old Bill never found them when they searched the place before.'

'Only 'cos we was lucky. If they do a bit of digging, that'll be it. I'll be swinging.'

'PC Batten ain't gonna go down in the cellar and he certainly won't be going down there with a shovel.'

'You can be sure of that, can you? A young copper, keen to get on with his career and impress his bosses. Work it out, Charlotte... He couldn't be better placed. I'm surprised at you. I would have thought you'd have seen straight through him. Didn't it seem a bit odd that a copper would come knocking on your door and want to live here?'

Charlotte lowered her head and gulped. 'He didn't come knocking. I saw PC Batten in the newsagent looking at the board for somewhere to rent.'

Johnny flopped back onto the chair and ran his hands through his thick, brown hair. 'You invited him here?' he asked, sounding exasperated.

Without meeting his eyes, Charlotte nodded.

'Then you'd best un-in-fucking-vite him!'

'But Georgina used to work with the police,' she protested.

'No, Charlotte. The police worked *for* Miss Garrett. She never worked *with* them. She hates the Old Bill.'

'But what about the Naylor brothers? I don't want you

fighting with them. There's two of them and only one of you.'

'Oh, sweetheart. Just 'cos they ain't likely to smash the windows in now, having the Old Bill under your roof won't protect you. The Naylors will be out of sight, waiting for you to go out and then they'll get you. They'll hurt you, then frighten the living daylights out of you so you'll be too scared to grass 'em up. Trust me, I've been in this game a long time and I know every trick in the book. In fact, I wrote the fucking book.'

Charlotte felt stupid and could feel her bottom lip beginning to quiver but fought back tears.

'Don't upset yourself. We all make mistakes but it's how we rectify them that makes the difference. You get rid of Batten and I'll sort the Naylors. Deal?'

'Deal,' she agreed, nodding her head.

'And don't worry yourself about two of them and one of me. I've got my best mate in my pocket. They won't be arguing with this,' Johnny said, patting his chest over his fur-lined lapel coat where his gun was tucked away. 'You can put the kettle on now,' he added.

While the water warmed, Charlotte went back into the lounge and asked, 'What was it you wanted to talk to me about? Something about the car?'

'Yeah, that's right. I need to use your car for a while. Mine stands out a bit too much.'

'Are you doing a job?'

'I might have something in the pipeline,' he answered, smiling wickedly. 'And you'll get a handsome cut. But don't ask me any questions about it 'cos I'm telling you nothing.'

'Fine,' Charlotte replied and swanned back out of the room, returning shortly with two cups of tea. 'But just one question... Are you doing it alone?'

'I told you, no questions. But I'll pass your regards to Max, Ned and the Barker twins,' he said and winked.

It warmed Charlotte to think of some of the old gang back together and it gave her a feeling of safety. Now she felt even more foolish for not having turned to Johnny about the Naylor brothers. She realised Johnny was right. She hadn't really thought it through properly and hadn't considered that the brothers would get to her when she was away from the house and the protection of PC Batten.

'I want that copper gone by the morning,' he said gravely.

'He will be,' she answered, though she had no idea how she was going to evict him. After all, he had a legally binding contract that Benjamin Harel had drawn up.

'I'll be back in a couple of days when he's cleared orf. We can swap cars when there's no Old Bill watching what we're up to,' Johnny said, and placed his cup and saucer on a side table before standing up and putting on his hat. 'In future, if you get any more problems with anyone, you come to me. All right?'

'Yeah. Thanks, Johnny. See ya.'

Charlotte gazed through the net curtains as Johnny sped off and she saw Lord Hamilton returning home with a newspaper tucked under his arm. He'd be another person who'd be happy to see the back of PC Batten. But rather than go banging on the copper's door now, she'd let the man sleep for a while. It would give her time to think about what she was going to say. But he had to go, she'd promised Johnny, and she hoped he'd go amenably. If he didn't, she chuckled to herself as the thought flashed through her mind of burying him in the cellar with the other corpses.

Georgina had discarded the prison warden's hat and now her shoulder-length black hair hung loose. But she couldn't get rid of the jacket. It was far too cold to be wandering around in just a shirt and would probably draw attention. She stood at a small crossroad of narrow streets, unsure of which direction to take. Left, she decided, hoping it was the direction that led away from the prison. The street was just about wide enough for a small cart to pass. Tall, neglected narrow houses flanked each side, blocking out most of the sunlight and leaving the street looking and smelling damp. A young woman in tatty clothes dragged a screaming small child indoors. She threw Georgina a filthy look before slamming her front door. A few houses further along, two women stood on their doorsteps chatting and as Georgina approached, she heard them talking unfavourably about her. One of them spat on the ground in front of her.

'Slag,' she said, scowling at Georgina.

'You've got some front walking down here. My girl's banged up in Camden Castle. Half the women on this street have been in there at one time or another. You wanna watch yourself.'

Georgina hurried on. She didn't blame the women for holding her in such contempt. They had no idea that she wasn't a prison warden. She reckoned if they knew the truth, they'd probably help her abscond, but she didn't want to drag in an innocent stranger and had no idea if she could trust them.

She turned a corner into an even narrower street and more decrepit housing. It was deserted but she heard a baby crying, probably from hunger. The sound drifted out from an upstairs window. Then a woman yelled and a bloke shouted back a profanity. From another house, someone was coughing heavily. The street reeked of poverty yet Georgina felt comfortable here. It reminded her of home with her deceased grandmother, Dulcie, and her best friend, Molly.

Muddy alleyways ran between every fourth house, which she guessed led to a shared privy. She doubted they'd look for her here and she could hide out for a while, but then what? She still had to get across London in a warden's uniform.

A door opened and an overweight man in a pair of grubby dungarees stepped out onto the street. He took a roll-up from his mouth and flicked it onto the ground as he leered at Georgina. She recognised that look in his eyes. She'd seen it when Kevin Kelly had raped her at her husband's funeral. The memory turned her stomach.

'You must be lost,' the man said, eyeing her up and down.

'Actually, I am,' she answered.

'Ha ha, fucking ironic, that is. Good luck. You're gonna need it.'

'You couldn't help me out, could you?' she asked, fluttering her dark lashes.

'Depends. What's in it for me?'

Georgina stepped towards the pot-bellied man. 'Whatever you like, but I ain't got any money,' she purred.

He glanced up and down the street and nodded for her to come inside. Georgina followed him into the dark passageway, her nose wrinkling at his putrid body odour that wafted as she walked behind him. He stopped at the bottom of the stairs and told her to go up first. The wooden staircase looked rickety and unsafe but she willingly followed his instruction. Wallpaper hung from the walls and in some areas, she could see the wooden lath where plaster had fallen away.

From the landing, he led her through to his room. Empty beer bottles littered the floor and Georgina was sure she saw rat droppings. She looked at the filthy mattress on the bare floorboards and tried not to appear disgusted.

'You're a fine looking woman,' he said, pulling his boots off, 'but what ya doing just standing there? Take your clothes off. Don't be shy. You're all sluts from that prison. The whores and the guards are as bad as each other.'

Georgina swallowed hard as she slowly unbuttoned her jacket.

'Hurry up, I ain't got all day,' he said, now naked from the waist down and semi-erect.

'Why don't you give me a hand,' she teased.

The man licked his lips as he walked towards her, his eyes fixed on the curve of her breasts. He reached out and yanked the jacket over her shoulders. She turned her face from his foul breath and at the same time, swiftly brought her knee up sharply into his groin.

He immediately doubled over, then fell to the floor, holding onto his now flaccid penis and testicles as he groaned and writhed in pain.

'Bitch,' he spat in between moans.

'Yep, I am, but I ain't a slut,' she spat, kicking him hard in the back.

The man rolled over to his front and sat on his knees. She saw hatred in his eyes and knew he wanted to kill her.

'I suggest you stay exactly where you are,' she warned.

Still holding onto his testicles, he went to stand up but Georgina was quick and swung her arm round. Her fist connected hard with his chin, which sent him reeling backwards. She shook her hand and blew on her painful knuckles. It had been a while since she'd used her boxing skills but her father had taught her well in the use of a good right hook, and it appeared she could still throw a fierce punch.

As the man lay dazed and bruised, Georgina scrambled to undress, then threw on his dungarees. It was a relief to take off the pinching shoes but she didn't relish the thought of slipping her feet into his stinking boots. Still, needs must, she thought as her eyes searched the room and she spotted a dark donkey-type jacket and flat cap. Now, fully dressed in the man's attire, she gathered up the warden's clothes before hovering over him.

'Sorry about this,' she said. 'Keep your mouth shut, don't tell anyone about it and I'll see to it that you're compensated for your silence. And if you do talk, I'll arrange for your tongue to be cut out.'

He looked back at her, grimacing, but nodded his head. She knew his type. He wouldn't go running to the Old Bill. Satisfied that he'd keep quiet, she dashed down the stairs and into the scullery, searching for something to cut her hair. The first knife she found was too blunt. Then she found a rusty pair of scissors and hacked at her mane.

She looked down into the sink at her dark locks and pulled the flat cap low over her face. As she turned, she caught her reflection in the scullery window. Having been brought up as a boy, she felt quite comfortable in the dungarees and boots.

'Hello,' she said, and smiled to herself. 'It's nice to meet you again, *George*.'

6

The next day, after a fraught night sleeping rough, Georgina had made her way through London and been shocked and saddened at the devastation she'd witnessed. Whole streets had been flattened by Hitler's bombs. Ruins now stood where grand buildings had proudly lined affluent roads. Kids played on bomb sites and many women appeared worn-out looking and drab. The war was clearly taking its toll on the people of London.

Georgina ambled through Clapham Junction feeling inconspicuous dressed as a working-class man. She passed two soldiers who didn't give her so much as a second glance. Had she been in her normal attire, they would have at least surreptitiously eyed her with admiration. But in the dungarees and heavy black jacket, her tall stature and broad shoulders helped to carry off the look of an unassuming bloke. She made sure she walked with splayed feet, her shoulders hunched and her hands tucked deeply into her pockets.

Georgina found it comforting to be back on familiar territory, though she hoped she wouldn't be recognised. As she passed a newspaper stand outside the railway station, she scanned the front covers on display. There was no mention of an escaped convict from Holloway, just headlines about troop movements. But that wasn't to say there wouldn't be coverage about her inside the papers. With empty pockets, she'd never know.

At last, and weary now from travelling, she reached Ezzy Harel's jewellery shop. The old Jewish man, the best fence in Battersea, had been friends with her father long before she'd been born. His son, Benjamin, her accountant, still cared for her financial affairs. She rang the doorbell entry system but when Ezzy looked through the plate-glass door, he shooed her away dismissively with his hand. Her masculine disguise was more convincing than she'd given it credit for. She tapped on the door and when Ezzy looked up again, she smiled.

'It's me,' she mouthed, 'Georgina.'

Ezzy's eyes widened in surprise and he hurried from behind his counter and across the shop.

'Georgina… My goodness, come in… come in,' he said.

Once inside, he quickly pulled down the shop shutters.

'You are looking like George again. Very clever.'

'Are they searching for me, Ezzy?'

'I don't know. I didn't know you'd escaped until I just saw you. Come, through to the back. Benjamin will be very pleased to see you.'

Georgina removed her flat cap and ruffled her short hair before popping her head around the door to Benjamin's small office.

'Psst,' she whispered. 'Special delivery for Benjamin Harel.'

Benjamin looked up from the books on his oak desk and pushed his round-rimmed glasses up his nose as he scrutinised her face.

She watched with amusement as it began to dawn on him that it was her.

'I don't believe it!' he exclaimed, placing his hands on his desk as if to steady himself.

'Yep, it's me,' she said, walking towards him.

'What... what... what are you doing here? You're supposed to be in erm, prison.'

'Not anymore.'

'Did they release you early?'

'Something like that.'

'You've absconded?'

'Yep.'

'You do realise they will, erm, extend your sentence if you're caught?'

'Yes, of course I do. But I have no intention of being caught.'

At last, Benjamin smiled. 'It's good to see you. Really good. Though I'm not sure about the, erm, err, boots.'

'You never met George but this was how I grew up. Ask your dad, he'll remember.'

Ezzy came into the office carrying a tray of tea. 'Oh yes, I remember George well. The young rascal who was the greatest pick-pocket in the borough. And the toughest girl I ever knew. Your father taught you well.'

'Yes, he did,' she replied fondly. 'And thanks for the tea, I'm parched.'

'What are you going to do?' Benjamin asked.

'I don't know yet but I have to see my children. I need money though.'

Benjamin picked up a letter-opener, pushed his seat back and walked to the corner of the room. He moved a coat stand to one side and lifted the edge of a rug from the floor before jemmying up a floorboard. Georgina watched with fascination as he pulled out a file of papers and what she recognised to be one of his accounting books.

'It's all here but it's not, erm, good news,' he said in his usual nervous, stuttering manner.

'I didn't expect it would be. Nice hiding place, by the way.'

After sitting back at his desk, he opened the book and gave her the grave news. 'You have very little money remaining.'

'I know. But give me a breakdown. The short version.'

'The house in Clapham didn't achieve its erm, full value. No surprises there as people aren't buying property during a war. Molly Mipple refused to accept fifty per cent of the profit. But the cost of the renovations to convert the house on Alexandra Avenue were substantial. Livingstone Road is bomb damaged. I was unable to claim any compensation from the government scheme due to your incarceration. The bicycle shop just about breaks even. Segal's restaurant on Lavender Hill was also damaged, though the property is still viable – albeit requiring repairs. The insurance company refuse to pay out as they don't cover acts of war. So the restaurant is now closed, as is The Penthouse Club, on your instruction.'

'You're not still smarting about me closing The Penthouse, are you?'

'I was disappointed but I understand your reasons... you couldn't, erm, protect me,' Benjamin answered, glancing uncomfortably sideways towards his father.

Georgina didn't say any more about it. Ezzy clearly had no idea that his only son was a queer and that The Penthouse

Club which Benjamin managed was strictly men only. It had been profitable when Georgina had been running the small empire she'd created with the local coppers in her pocket. The police had known about the illegal meeting place for homosexuals but had willingly turned a blind eye – well, they had for a price.

'So in a nutshell, you're telling me that apart from two empty business premises, a poxy bicycle shop and the house on Alexandra Avenue, I've no money?'

'You have a small amount,' Benjamin answered and scribbled a figure on a piece of paper which he pushed across the desk to her. 'Now you are no longer in prison, perhaps we could, erm, stop the payments to Miss Winter?'

Georgina looked at the measly amount. It wouldn't last long. 'No, carry on paying the old bint. *If* they capture me and send me back, I shall want her on my side. In the meantime, get word to her to keep an eye out for Fleur.'

'Consider it done. Payment of rent has been maintained on your previous residence. The house is boarded up and the name on the rent book is Colleen O'Hara, the daughter of—'

'—Yes, I know,' Georgina interrupted, 'Mary next door's daughter. Does Mary have the key?'

'Yes. Is that where you'll be staying?'

'For now. Are you able to contact Brian?'

'Brian Harris? The man who worked in your printers before the police raided the premises and closed it down?'

'Yes. If he can forge ration coupons then he can forge identity papers too. I need some, and sooner rather than later.'

'I can see to that.'

'It has to be done immediately. Arrange for the papers to be dropped with Charlotte. I'll collect them from there.'

'I don't think that's wise. Charlotte has an officer of the law residing at the premises and surely that is one of the first places they will look for you.'

'She's got a copper living at Alexandra Avenue?'

'Yes, in erm, your apartment actually.'

'Well, that's a turn up for the books. They'll never find me right under their nose and it will be the last place they'll expect me to be. Anyway, even your dad didn't recognise me so I'm sure I can fool the Old Bill.' At least, she hoped she could. Now she was back in *her* world, Georgina knew she could never return to Holloway. 'Benjamin, this is what I want you to do... sell the bicycle shop. I don't care what you get for it, just as long as it's enough to cover the costs of repairs to Segal's. Once the restaurant is fixed, I want it opened as a less formal place, you know, sandwiches, cakes and cups of tea. Perhaps Ivy could manage it?'

Georgina saw Benjamin and his father look worriedly at each other.

'Ivy, erm, err, Ivy didn't make it.'

'What, she's dead?'

'Yes, I'm afraid so. She was killed in a bombing raid. The shelter she was in took a direct hit.'

Georgina's shoulders slumped and a sob caught in her throat. Poor Ivy, she'd been such a sweet and cheeky young lady who hadn't had much of a life. First abused by her father and then raped and tortured by the Dentist who had removed her front teeth. The same man who had murdered Ethel, Molly's and Charlotte's backward sister.

'She didn't suffer. She wouldn't have known what hit her, literally.'

'Another casualty of this bastard war,' she whispered under her breath. Then, pulling herself together, she continued, 'Right. If not Ivy, maybe Dina? No, not Dina. She's not exactly the friendly sort. What about one of the girls? Do you see or hear anything of Gerty, Babs or Tilly? I'm sure they'd rather run a café than be prostituting themselves.'

'No, Miss Garrett. I've no idea what became of any of the ladies. Charlotte may be better informed.'

'All right, for now, just get the bike shop sold and the repairs to Segal's done. I'll think about who can work in there later.'

'Or the restaurant could be sold too? Just another, erm, suggestion.'

'No,' Georgina snapped. She wouldn't consider selling the restaurant, not ever. It had been a gift from David and held sentimental value. After all, it was the only thing she had left of him.

'Georgina, I think you should stay with us. We will hide you well,' Ezzy offered, his dark, watery eyes full of kindness.

'Thank you, but I won't put you in a position where you could end up in trouble with the law. The last thing you need is the police going over your business with a fine toothcomb. I'll be fine in my old house and to be honest, I'm that exhausted, I just want to sleep.'

'You must come to me if you need anything. Anything at all.'

'I will, thank you,' she said, smiling at the dear man. 'I'd best get going.'

Benjamin pulled a small metal box from his desk drawer and a key from his pocket. After opening the box, he handed her the contents. A few five pound notes and two guineas.

'I can have more cash available for you tomorrow.'

'This will do for now,' she answered, acutely aware of her precarious financial situation and outgoings, now including paying Brian Harris to forge her identity documents.

She pulled her flat cap back on and smiled, asking, 'How do I look?'

'Like a scruffy young workman,' Ezzy answered. 'But wait. Take this,' he said and dashed from the room, returning moments later with a wooden toolbox that contained several tools. 'It finishes off your look perfectly,' he said, offering it over.

Georgina smiled warmly at the man and thanked him before leaving. Her heart hammered as she stepped out of the shop and back onto the main road. It wasn't far to go to get to Mary's house but with the police probably searching for her and no identity papers, she knew she was taking a massive risk in coming back to Battersea. But it was home. The only home she'd ever known. And regardless of the danger of being recaptured, it was where she belonged.

Twenty minutes later, though a chilly day, Georgina felt warm inside as she turned onto the street she knew so well. Just round the corner from home, Mrs Peterson's shop remained unchanged. As Georgina walked in, the sound of the bell above the door delighted her, and she beamed at Mrs Peterson sitting in her usual place behind the counter.

'Hello, George,' the old woman said.

'Hello, Mrs Peterson. You're looking well,' she lied. The years had taken their toll on the elderly lady and now her lined skin appeared translucent and her white hair left her colourless, giving her a ghostly appearance.

'You've shot up. What's your gran been doing? Putting you in a bag of manure?'

'I'm sorry, Mrs Peterson, what do you mean?'

'I mean your gran must have been feeding you well. You've had a growing spurt.'

Georgina's brow furrowed as she looked at Mrs Peterson, who was obviously confused.

'What can I get you? Has your gran sent you in for her ciggies?'

'Erm, no, Mrs Peterson. I'd like a bar of chocolate, please,' she answered, not wanting to upset her.

'Course you do. Your dad treating you again? I don't know, he spoils you something rotten.'

Before Georgina could answer, a woman of about fortyish appeared from out of the back, tutting and shaking her head. 'There you are, Aunty. Come on through to the back room. I've put two bars on the fire and made you a cup of warm milk. You'll be nice and comfy.' She placed her arms over Mrs Peterson's shoulders and gently urged her towards the door to the back of the shop.

'Sorry about this,' the woman whispered to Georgina.

Mrs Peterson pointed in Georgina's direction. 'That's George. George Garrett. He's a smashing young lad,' she said.

The woman ushered Mrs Peterson through a curtain and told her to sit down and she'd be in shortly, then she turned and addressed Georgina. 'Sorry, my aunty gets a bit muddled. Can I help you, sir?'

'Er, no, thanks,' Georgina answered and hastily left the shop. It upset her to think of dear old Mrs Peterson losing her marbles but it was also reassuring to know that her masculine disguise was readily fooling people.

As she turned onto her street, all thoughts of Mrs Peterson were replaced with a rush of memories that flooded her mind. She remembered being a child and playing on the street with Molly, who at the time wore little more than rags. And how they used to have to take Ethel everywhere with them. Then her dad, the pair of them coming home together with sacks of stolen goods that they'd nicked, and him telling her off for skipping like a girl. Dulcie, her gran, standing on the doorstep and wagging her finger, warning her to be careful. There had always been the threat of Billy Wilcox hanging over her, but he was nothing more than a distant bad recollection now.

It was sad to see the windows of the house boarded over and the neglected doorstep, which her gran had always kept neatly chalked. The house, once filled with love, now looked abandoned. Weeds had grown through cracks on the short garden path and the front door needed a lick of paint. Yet even so, it warmed her heart to be home.

Before she could knock on Mary's front door, the rotund, red-haired woman opened it and pulled Georgina inside before quickly closing it again.

Crossing herself, Mary sighed. 'Jesus, Mary mother of Jesus. Thank the good Lord you're here,' she said in her broad Irish accent.

'Hello, Mary.'

'I knew you'd come, so I did.'

'Have the police been?'

'Yes, this morning. But I told them this would be the last place you'd show your face. I gave them a long line of reasons for why myself and many others can't stand the sight of you. I think they believed me. Bejesus, gal, I've been waiting for hours at that window.'

'Thank you. Sorry if I've had you worried.'

'I'm not worried for me but I am for you. They'll have every policeman in London looking high and low for you, so they will.'

'Probably, but they're looking for Georgina, not George.'

'I suppose so. Anyway, you're here now. Are you hungry? I've a pot of broth on.'

'That would be very welcome, thank you.'

'Go and sit yourself down but keep an eye out that window.'

Georgina made herself comfortable in Mary's small front room and was grateful for the large bowl of broth and chunk of bread that Mary served.

'Do you have plans?' she asked as she watched Georgina eat.

'Sort of. I need to get to Wales to see Alfie and Selina.'

'Wales. Is that where Lash's family are now?'

'Yes, just outside of Swansea. Molly's letters have kept me up to date. But for now, I just want to get my head down and get some sleep.'

'Well, you'll find everything shipshape next door. And there's fresh sheets on the bed. I can't promise everything is where it should be. The police left the house in a mess after they arrested you. But I've kept it clean.'

'Thanks, Mary, thanks so much.'

'Shush now, gal. An empty, boarded house doesn't need much looking after. You've done plenty for me and my family over the years. It was the least I could do. Here are the keys, but go in the back door and you won't be seen. First though, I've a little surprise for you, come with me, you'll like this.'

Georgina followed Mary up the stairs, where she pointed to the loft hatch on the landing ceiling. 'Get the ladder from behind my door,' Mary instructed.

Georgina did as she was asked and Mary positioned it against the wall.

'Now, there's not much room up there and mind you stay on the rafters and don't fall through.'

'What, you want me to get up in the loft?'

'Yes, go on, up you go.'

'Why?'

'You'll see.'

Georgina couldn't imagine why on earth Mary would want her to get in the loft but she humoured the woman. She carefully slid the hatch over and poked her head into the darkness. She was familiar with the loft next door and, as a child, had often climbed into it to retrieve something her dad had stolen and stashed. The lofts in the street were little more than crawl spaces and Mary's was no exception.

'Look towards your house. Can you see anything untoward?'

Georgina peered at the wall separating Mary's house from hers. Nothing appeared unusual. 'No, I can't see anything.'

'Good. But the part of the wall directly between your

hatch and mine has loose bricks. My old man knocked them through and rebuilt them using flour and water instead of mortar. Come back down now.'

Georgina slid the hatch back in place and carefully made her way down the rickety wooden ladder.

'If the police come to your house looking for you, get in the loft, kick the wall through into mine. There's a board on your side made from a packing case. It's painted to look like bricks. Once you're in my loft, slide the board over the hole. In the dark it should be sufficient to hide the hole as long as the police don't look too closely.'

'Blimey, Mary, that's genius!'

'Yes, it is that, but I can't take the credit. It was Mr Harel who suggested the idea and well, let's be honest, we've had a few years to master it.'

'Thank you. It's reassuring and I shall sleep better tonight.'

Twenty minutes later, after Mary had given her two sandwiches wrapped in brown paper along with a large bottle of ginger beer, Georgina sneaked into the back yard next door. She was about to relock the gate when Mary appeared.

'I forgot to give them to you. The electricity has been disconnected so you'll need these. And take care of yourself, pet,' she said and passed Georgina three candles and a box of matches.

'Thank you,' Georgina answered gratefully, smiling warmly at Mary before locking the gate. She then turned and looked at the yard. It had become overgrown but still nothing grew on the spot next to the coal bunker where her gran had buried her second husband. Georgina smiled wryly. This house had been filled with love but also held many secrets.

The back door boarding had been lightly tacked in place and was simple to remove. She leaned it against the wall and, with trepidation, slowly opened the door. Her heart pounded as she stepped over the threshold. Georgina wasn't sure what to expect or how she'd feel. She closed the door and found herself in darkness. After fumbling with the candles and matches, she finally had some light and looked around the kitchen with fond recollections. The table, where she'd shared so many meals with her gran, dad and husband. Her and Lash had even made love on it once. The patch of worn linoleum on the floor that her gran had obsessively scrubbed. The scuffed doorframe where Alfie had rammed his toy truck into it. The butler sink where she'd bathed Selina. It had been a busy family kitchen but now it harboured an escaped convict and Georgina wished she could turn back time to those happier days.

In the front room, the clock on the mantel had stopped ticking. The room was unusually quiet and felt cold without a fire burning in the hearth. She ran her fingers over her gran's chair and then held the candle close to a framed photograph of Alfie and Selina. Tears filled her eyes as she stared at the grainy black and white image. 'Pack it in, you daft moo,' she whispered and reminded herself that she'd be seeing them soon. But she wouldn't if she didn't keep one step ahead of the law, and she knew she'd need to keep a clear head. There wasn't time for sentiments. She couldn't afford to wallow in memories and self-pity. Drawing in a deep breath, she marched back through to the kitchen and took a chair from under the table. She'd need this to get in the loft if a quick getaway was required. And keeping focused, she took the chair upstairs and placed it in the corner of her bedroom. She grabbed a folded blanket from the end of the bed while trying not to think about how she'd once shared it with Lash. She knew it would be too painful and didn't want to be overwhelmed by her emotions. And, as she walked back across the landing, she closed the door to Alfie's room, barring the sight of his bed and any memories from there too.

'Out of sight and out of mind,' she said as she trudged back down the stairs, resigned to sleeping on the sofa to preserve her sanity. That, at least, would be bearable and though it was lumpy, she knew it would be far more comfortable than the thin mattress she'd had in prison. In fact, anything would be better than prison, and once again, Georgina thought about how she'd avoid going back, no matter what it took.

7

The next morning, Johnny tapped on Charlotte's front door and eyed PC Batten's bike with displeasure.

'He's still here then,' he said to Charlotte when she opened the door.

'Yeah, come in,' she answered.

Once in the privacy of her flat, she went on to enlighten him. 'I asked Batten to leave. I explained that it wasn't really fair that I'd rented the flat out to him when it's got two bedrooms and he doesn't need them. There's families with far greater needs. He was as good as gold and understood.'

'So why is he still here?'

'I gave him a week's notice. He'll be gone in a few days.'

'I can't wait that long. The blokes are ready and the job is all lined up. You'll have to do without a motor for a bit. I'll park mine up out the way and if he asks where yours is, just tell him it's in the garage or something.'

'All right. I'm sure I'll manage. It's not like I can drive it when he's around anyway. The keys are on the sideboard. Are you gonna give me a clue about the job?'

'No, course I ain't. Just sit tight. I'll be back with your car when he's cleared orf. By the way, have you had any more problems from the Naylors?'

'I've seen 'em hanging about and they followed me up the High Street yesterday. I suppose they're trying to intimidate me but I ain't scared of them.'

Johnny could feel his temper flaring. He could do without this right now but couldn't leave Charlotte to fend for herself against those two idiots. 'I ain't having this, the cheeky bastards,' he growled, and grabbed the keys to Charlotte's car before heading towards the door.

'Wait, Johnny, what are you gonna do?' Charlotte asked, sounding frantic.

'What I should have done a long time ago,' he answered and slammed the door behind him. He stomped down the path but then spun on his heel and walked back. He was about to kick PC Batten's bike, but instead he picked it up and carried it off before throwing it in the back of his car. He drove the short distance to Battersea Park, screeched to a stop, jumped out the car, grabbed the bike and slung it over the fence. A woman pushing a pram saw him but Johnny didn't care. After doffing his hat at her, he jumped back in his car and parked a few streets away from Charlotte's house.

A group of young boys were playing with an improvised cart and when they saw Johnny's flash car, they ran towards him. 'How fast does your motor go?' one of the lads in short trousers and with dirty scuffed knees asked.

'Fast enough. Tell you what, keep an eye on it for me and when I get back, I'll take you for a ride in it.'

The boys looked at each other with excited faces and another asked, 'Can I have a go too?'

'You all can, but only if my car is still in the same nick when I get back. I'll be gone for a few days. Do you reckon you can look after it for me?'

The boys emphatically nodded their heads.

'Good, 'ere ya go,' Johnny said and handed each of them a coin. Their little faces lit up. 'Don't let me down,' he said as he walked off and heard one of them shout, 'We won't, thanks, Mister.'

Minutes later, he was driving Charlotte's car. It felt odd to be behind the wheel of the familiar vehicle, it used to be Victor who mostly drove it. He wondered how the man was faring and what he was up to now. Last he'd heard, Victor had gone back to south-east London but Johnny hadn't seen him working for The Top. He had no doubt that the rumours were true. The Top had killed David Maynard and Victor had been caught up in it. After all, Johnny knew that if Victor had been working for David Maynard, he'd have given his life to protect the man.

Johnny pulled up outside the Halfway House and went inside to find Ned and the Barker twins waiting. He still couldn't tell them apart and looked for the mole on Nobby's face.

Ned jumped up from his seat, knocking the table which caused beer to spill over the tops of their glasses. He was clearly a bit jumpy about the forthcoming job. 'We thought you'd changed your mind. You're late, Johnny. Do you want a drink?' he asked.

'No, mate. I wanna get orf. And calm down, will ya! You're like a bleedin' coiled spring. We can't afford mistakes so just relax, eh.'

'Yeah, sorry, you're right. I'm proper wound up but I'll be all right.'

'Anyway, we've got something else that needs our attention first.'

'What's that?' Nobby asked.

'The Naylors. They've been bothering Charlotte.'

'Fucking pair of wankers,' Ned seethed.

'They've been taking liberties since Miss Garrett got banged up,' Nobby added and swigged back the rest of his half pint. 'Come on then. I'd be happy to pay them a visit,' he said, rising to his feet.

Eric stood too and they looked at Ned.

'I can't drink that,' he said, looking at his beer. 'My stomach's churning something rotten.'

They followed Johnny out to the car and climbed in.

'Shame Max ain't here. We could have set him on them,' Ned said.

'Yeah, they wouldn't have known what hit 'em,' Nobby laughed.

'Well, hopefully Max is ready and waiting for us. But let's sort the Naylors out and then we'll come back for the guns. Did you get everything I told you to?' Johnny asked the twins.

'Yeah, no problem. We got two Sten guns and a shitload of rounds from the Home Guard store at Norwood. And a Tommy gun from the Brixton store. That'll do, won't it?'

'Yeah, plenty. You can take the guns back after we've done the job,' Johnny instructed.

'Are you having a laugh? Why risk getting nicked to return the guns?'

'It's what Miss Garrett would have made you do. You know she wouldn't have stood for any of us pinching the army's gear.'

Johnny couldn't see them, but he knew Nobby and Eric,

sat in the back seats, would be rolling their eyes. When Ned chuckled, he asked, 'What's so funny?'

'I dunno, mate. Listen to us. I reckon we're all soft in the head. *She* did that to us. The fucking hardest bitch I've ever known but hey, what a woman.'

It was Nobby who commented. 'Yeah, you ain't wrong, Ned. Miss Garrett was the best guvnor we ever had. And Johnny's right. She wouldn't like us 'alf-inching the Home Guard's guns. We'll put 'em back when we're done. But shouldn't we go and get 'em first to make our point with the Naylors?'

'No need. And we don't want it being put about in Battersea that we've got an arsenal of weapons nicked from the Home Guard. The fewer people who know about the job we're gonna do, the better. If we're seen waving submachine guns around in the pub, it won't take a fucking genius to work out it was us who turned over the brewing company.'

The rest of the short journey was done in silence and it didn't take long to get to the pub that the Naylors were known to frequent. Johnny pulled into the kerb. 'Right, you ready for this?' he asked, turning in his seat to look over his shoulder at the twins.

'Fucking right we are,' Nobby answered, his mouth set in a grim line.

Johnny led the way and they marched into the smoky pub. They must have looked a sight – Johnny with his swagger, Ned snarling with his fists clenched and the twins, both big blokes, following behind. The landlord looked worried and backed away from behind the bar. Several men left their drinks on tables and hurried out of the door. The Naylors, though, smirked as Johnny approached.

''Ere, look, Bert, it's Georgina Garrett's Nancy boys,' Len Naylor said loudly to his brother.

Four other men sat in close proximity to the brothers rose to their feet when they saw Johnny and stared at him menacingly. But the Naylors' heavies didn't intimidate him. He had something in his pocket that would shit the life out of the lot of them.

Bert Naylor, a tall and broad man with mousy brown greased-back hair, took a swig of his drink, placed the glass on the table and scowled at Johnny as he spoke. 'What the fuck do you want? It had better be good, coming in here and disturbing my pint.'

'Yeah,' Len added, rubbing his square chin. 'A bunch of fucking poofters who worked for a woman.'

Johnny didn't answer. He couldn't be bothered to waste his breath. Instead, he looked sideways at Ned and smiled. Ned's eyes widened; he knew Johnny well enough to anticipate what was coming next. Johnny slowly nodded his head at Ned, at the same time reaching inside his coat pocket. He felt the comforting touch of his gun and yanked it out to point it directly at Bert's head.

A shocked gasp went round the pub and three of the Naylors' blokes dived for cover under tables. Len Naylor reached across to touch his brother's arm while saying shakily, 'Hold up, Johnny, there's no need for this.'

'There's every fucking need,' Johnny answered and squeezed his finger on the trigger. 'And it's Mr Dymond to you, you fucking arse wipe.'

'Come on, Joh… I mean, Mr Dymond. Let's talk about it, eh?' he said, all signs of bravado gone.

'There's nothing to talk about. Just get this through

your thick fucking skulls or I'll blow your tiny brains up the fucking wall... Stay away from Charlotte Mipple. If I hear you've even so much as looked at her, I'll hunt the pair of you down and you'll be eating the barrel of me gun. Understand?'

'Yes, Mr Dymond. Loud and clear,' Len answered, the fear in his voice evident.

But Bert just glared defiantly at Johnny and didn't seem as frightened as his brother. So Johnny thought he'd show them he meant business and pulled the trigger but deliberately aimed the gun just past Bert's head.

The blast from the gunshot resounded in Johnny's ears. A puff of smoke wafted from the end of the barrel, and for a moment it felt as if the world stood still. Then, as the ringing in his ears subsided, he saw the bullet had wedged in the wall between the brothers, and Bert, now sheet-white, turned to look at it.

'Do you get my message now?' Johnny asked.

Bert was visibly shaken and gulped. 'Yeah,' he said with urgency, 'I get it.'

'I ain't messing about. And if I find out that you've been near any of Miss Garrett's friends and family, I'll be back for you.'

'Sorry, Mr Dymond. You won't get no trouble from us,' Len gushed.

Johnny turned on his heel and swaggered out with Ned and the Barker twins behind him. It felt good to be back in power, like the old days when he'd commanded respect. A time when Georgina Garrett's name had carried a lot of clout and he'd been proud to be a part of her gang.

'Ha, did you see the look on Bert's face,' Nobby laughed.

'I think he might have shit himself,' Ned said. 'They soon backed down, cowards, the pair of them, only fit to pick on women.'

'All right, back in the car,' Johnny told them. 'Let's keep this professional, eh.'

''Ark at him,' Ned said. 'That lead out of his gun has gawn to his head. Professional, my arse!'

Johnny turned the engine and set off to the Anderson shelter where they'd stashed the *borrowed* Home Guard arms. It was in the back yard of a cousin of the Barker twins. 'Ned, mate. We *are* professional and don't you forget it,' he said. 'We worked for Miss Garrett, the best in the game. And we're together again. It's about time Battersea took note and wankers like the Naylors were put back in their place.'

Charlotte paced the room and chewed on her thumbnail, worried about what Johnny was going to do to the Naylor brothers. She knew he had a gun and hoped he wasn't about to land himself in trouble with the law. It had been awful when he'd been away serving time, she'd missed him terribly. She didn't want to go through that again.

A tap on her door caused Dog to bark and snapped her out of her thoughts. She held Dog by the collar as she opened the door, expecting to find Lord Hamilton on her doorstep. She was surprised to see PC Batten stood there in his full uniform and with a sheepish look on his face. The grand sight of him momentarily took her breath away.

'Sorry to disturb you, but you haven't moved my bicycle, have you?'

'No,' she answered. 'Isn't it outside the front door?'

'No, it's gone. I was hoping that maybe you'd brought it inside.'

'I haven't touched it. Do you think it's been stolen?' she asked, trying to keep a straight face. Oh, the irony of it!

'Looks like it. Oh well, I suppose it'll be Shanks' pony for me.'

'Aren't you on night duty anymore?'

'No, back on days but my shift doesn't start until two.'

'Blimey, you're keen. It's only twelve.'

'Yes, but I was hoping to get a cup of tea in the canteen before I start. I'm all out of tea leaves. I gave my ration coupons to my sister.'

'You silly bugger, you should have said. Come in, I'll make you a cuppa.'

'No, really, thank you. It's very kind of you but I wouldn't want to impose.'

'Oh, shut up. You ain't imposing. Come in, I'll make you a spam sandwich an' all.'

Charlotte pulled the door open wider and when PC Batten walked in thought she could see he looked uncomfortable.

'Sit yourself down, there's tea in the pot. Don't worry about Dog. He's a friendly boy but watch you don't get your smart uniform smothered in fur.'

Charlotte went through to the kitchen and poured the tea and hastily made a sandwich. Her mind raced. Was there anything in the front room that she wouldn't want PC Batten to see? She was sure that there wasn't but why on earth had she invited the Old Bill into her home? She'd felt sorry for him and it had been impulsive, but now she could have kicked herself. Christ, if Johnny turned up, he'd have a fit!

The sandwich prepared, Charlotte peeked over her shoulder before lifting a slice of the bread and spitting on it. She thought it was the right thing to do, though she felt a twinge of guilt, after all, PC Batten seemed like a nice bloke. But she reminded herself that thanks to his colleagues, Georgina was banged up in Holloway Prison for years to come.

'There you go,' she said, handing him a plate and placing the cup and saucer on a side table next to the sofa.

'Thanks for this,' he said, 'I must admit, I'm hungry. With this shift work, I haven't had a chance to get to the grocer's shop.'

As he tucked into the sandwich, she offered him a half-hearted smile, and inwardly cringed when he bit into the part she'd spat in. God, she wished he'd soon eat up and get going. Though strangely, there was a part of her that liked being with him. Dog sat in front of him at his legs, pleading with his eyes. Charlotte thought if the mutt could talk, he'd be asking to share the food.

'Is it all right if I give him a little nibble?'

'Yeah, I suppose so. He's an expert beggar. He'll never starve to death, that's for sure.'

PC Batten pulled off a small piece of the sandwich, which Dog gently accepted.

'He's a good boy. I like dogs,' he said, patting the pooch on the head which made Dog's tail wag.

'Seems he likes you an' all.' She'd always thought Dog a good judge of character. He'd proved that with Nancy Austin. Dog had never taken to the woman and had once growled at her. But again, Charlotte had to remind herself that PC Batten was the enemy and she wasn't to be sucked in by his seemingly kind nature and good looks, no matter how much Dog liked him.

'That's set me up for the day,' he said as he placed his helmet back on his head and went to leave. Looking awkwardly down at his feet, he added, 'Thanks for your hospitality, Charlotte. Perhaps you'll allow me to repay you by, erm, taking you out to dinner one evening?'

'Oh,' she answered, stunned. She hadn't been expecting him to ask her out and though she found herself unwantedly attracted to him, she wasn't interested in men, especially not a policeman. 'There's no need to repay me but thank you very much,' she answered politely.

PC Batten's cheeks burned red and he bumbled out of the door, clearly embarrassed at her rebuff.

'Good grief,' she sighed after closing it behind him. His proposal of dinner had come out of nowhere and had caught her off-guard. She thought about his smile, kind and genuine. There was no doubt about it, copper or not, he was a nice man but very naïve. If he had any idea of the things she'd been involved in, she knew he'd be horrified. Still, it was flattering to receive some attention for a change but the thought of a man touching her body made her skin crawl. The abuse she'd endured when she'd lived on the streets had been enough to put her off men for life.

Someone knocked on the front door, which made Dog bark. Charlotte peeped through the net curtains to see who was there. She wasn't expecting anyone and Dina, Lord Hamilton and Miss Gray never received visitors. She saw a man standing on the doorstep but couldn't see his face and guessed it was someone looking for work. It wasn't unusual to have callers asking for any odd jobs.

When she went to see what the man wanted, Dog charged out and ran to the front door, incessantly barking.

'All right, calm down, there's a good boy,' she said, reaching for his collar and pulling him back as she opened the door.

'Can I help you?' she asked.

Dog wriggled and managed to slip free from her grip. He leapt at the man, his tail furiously wagging as he jumped up and down, trying desperately to lick his face.

Charlotte had never seen Dog behave like this and tried to grab his collar again.

'Sorry about him,' she said. 'He won't bite.'

'I know,' the man replied.

Charlotte stared at him, confused. Something about his voice didn't sound right. The man looked back at her and when Charlotte saw those violet eyes, she knew. 'Georgina!' she gasped, unable to make sense of what was happening.

'Shush. Let me in.'

She was quick to usher Georgina inside, still trying to pull Dog from her. Once in the flat, Georgina crouched down and made a fuss of Dog as he lavished her with affection. He hadn't forgotten his owner and was excited to see her.

'What? How? When? Christ!' Charlotte's words tumbled out.

'I had to get away.'

'Bloody hell, Georgina, have you escaped?'

'Well, they didn't give me permission to leave.'

'Jesus Christ, they'll have every copper in Battersea looking for you!' she said, thinking of PC Batten who had only just left. In fact, they must have passed each other on the street.

'Yeah, but they'll be looking for a woman, not a bloke in dungarees. I thought you'd be pleased to see me.'

'I am... I'm just shocked. What are you gonna do?'

Now Dog had calmed down, Georgina rose back to her feet. 'First things first, put the kettle on. I didn't have any tea at home.'

They smiled at each other and Charlotte rushed forward to wrap her arms around Georgina. 'I'm so glad you're here,' she said, fighting to hold back her emotions.

Georgina, never one for being overtly demonstrative, peeled Charlotte's arms from around her. 'It's good to see you,' she said, 'but I must stink. I've had these clothes on for a couple of days.'

Charlotte stepped back, impressed at Georgina's tall stature. She'd forgotten how imposing the woman was and though her baggy dungarees hid her frame, she could tell Georgina had lost weight. 'It's really good to see you too. I've missed you. Everyone's missed you. Don't worry, we'll keep you well hidden from the Old Bill. You ain't never going back to that shithole again. Blinkin' 'eck, I still can't believe you're here! Wait 'til Johnny sees you. He's gonna be over the bloody moon!' Her words fell out as the shock wore off to be replaced with an overwhelming joy.

'I can't stay here, Charlotte. I need to get my children.'

'Yeah, of course, but you'll come back, won't you?'

'Slow down. One step at a time. I haven't worked it all out yet.'

'Yeah, yeah, sorry. I'll put the kettle on and make you something to eat. But what do I do if the police knock on the door?'

'Nothing. Just act like nothing is out of the ordinary.

If they want to come in, then let them, and they'll see me looking at a pipe under the sink. My name's George Robinson. I'm a plumber. Benjamin is arranging identity papers for me which will be dropped off to you later. In the meantime, I'll just have to blag it.'

'What does blag mean?'

'Pull the wool over their eyes. Hope to get away with it by lying. That sort of thing.'

'Blimey, you've picked up some new words in prison. And how long have you been out?'

'I got to Battersea yesterday and saw Benjamin. I stayed at my old house last night. Mary next door said the police had been there to look for me. I'm surprised they've not visited you yet. Perhaps they're watching the place and using that copper across the landing as a mole.'

'You know about him?' Charlotte asked, shocked and suddenly feeling clammy. She would have expected Georgina to be angry about a copper living in the house.

'Yes, Benjamin told me. You clever girl! It's perfect. The Old Bill ain't going to worry about searching the house for me if there's already a copper living here. Well done, but why on earth have you rented it out to a policeman?'

'It's a long story. But I'm glad you're not upset with me. Johnny told me to get rid of him so he's moving out in a few days.'

'Oh no he isn't. Can you persuade him to change his mind?'

'I don't know. I could try.'

'How well do you know him?'

'Not very. He ain't been here long. But he erm, he, he asked me out to dinner.'

'Great. Get as close to him as you can. It'll be good to have a local bobby on our side.'

'But I've already turned him down.'

'I'm sure you can easily tell him you've changed your mind. You're not a daft girl, Charlotte. You must be able to see how this can work to our advantage?'

'Yeah, of course I can. That's why I got him here in the first place. See, I was getting a bit of jip from the Naylor brothers and I thought they'd leave me alone once they knew the Old Bill was living here.'

'What do you mean?' Georgina asked, her eyes narrowing.

'Let me put the kettle on and I'll tell you all about it.'

Georgina followed Charlotte through to the kitchen and fiddled about under the sink. 'Fill the kettle up. The sink is going to be out of action for a while.'

Charlotte topped it up, her mind turning with the idea of going out with Timothy. The thought of it thrilled her, though she wished it didn't!

Georgina stood up, saying, 'There, that should do it.'

When Charlotte turned to look, she saw a pool of water beginning to form on the floor from a drip in the pipework. She was about to grab a cloth to wipe it up but heard someone rapping urgently on her door.

'Are you expecting someone?' Georgina asked.

'No, and that's not the way Lord Hamilton from upstairs knocks on me door. Christ, Georgina, I think it might be the police!'

'All right, take a deep breath. There's nothing here to worry about. I'm just the plumber, remember, here to fix your leaking pipe. Go and answer the door.'

Charlotte's lips pursed. 'Cor, you don't 'alf take risks. I'd forgotten how bloody mad it is when you're around.' She nervously tucked her long brown hair behind her ears and sucked in a long breath before blowing it out slowly. 'I can do this,' she said tensely and watched as Georgina unlocked the kitchen window before scrambling back under the sink.

'Good girl. Of course you can. Now go,' Georgina urged.

Charlotte hurried to the door and fixed a smile on her face as she pulled it open to find PC Batten standing there looking ashen.

'Where's the fire?' she asked breezily.

'I'm glad you're still at home. You'll never guess what's happened.'

'Probably not… Have the Germans surrendered?'

'No, nothing like that. But I was on my way to the station and saw a commotion on Battersea Park Road. A motorbike spooked a horse, which reared up causing the cart to lose a wheel, which then shed its load of potatoes all over the road. It was mayhem but luckily there's a police box nearby so I phoned it in.'

'Well, it sounds like you've had an exciting morning before you've even got to work,' Charlotte said, wondering why he'd come back to tell her about it.

'Yes, but when I phoned the station, you won't believe what they told me.'

'You're a policeman so I probably would,' Charlotte lied, knowing that there were some who were bent.

'Ha, yes. Well, they said Georgina Garrett is on the run from Holloway Prison. She's escaped!'

Charlotte gasped and threw a hand to her mouth. 'Are you sure?'

'Yes, that's what my sergeant said!'

'Blimey, you're right, I can't believe it! Have they sent you back here to look for her?'

'No, well, yes and no. The house has been under surveillance but they called it off last night when my sarge told his boss that I live here. I've been told to keep an eye out.'

'I don't think she'll show up here. I mean, why would she? There's nothing here for her anymore. Do you want to come in? Have another cuppa?'

'No, I really should get to work. I just thought you should know about Miss Garrett.'

'Thank you, PC Batten.'

'Please, call me Tim.'

'All right, I will, Tim,' Charlotte said, and lightly fluttered her eyelashes. 'And I've been thinking about what you said earlier, you know, about going out one evening. You caught me unawares but if you'd still like to take me to dinner, I think that would be smashing.'

'Oh,' Tim said and grinned widely. 'Yes, I'd love to. How about Saturday?'

'Great.'

'Yes, erm… great. I'll see you later. Cheerio.'

'See ya,' Charlotte said and was relieved to close the door. She hurried back to the kitchen to find Georgina just rising to her feet. 'That was embarrassing. Did you hear all that?'

'Yes, every word. You did really well, Charlotte. He never suspected a thing.'

'I know, but now I've got to go to dinner with him.'

Georgina laughed. 'And you'll have him eating out of the palm of your hand. But at least we know they're not looking for me here.'

'Does that mean you'll stay here?' she asked hopefully.

'I've got no lighting at home, and it's a bit bleak there, but with that copper in my flat I'd have to sleep on the sofa.'

'Let me get rid of him, Georgina.'

'No, with him living here, they'll leave this place alone. It'd be safer here than in my old home.'

'Yeah, I suppose you're right,' Charlotte said and impulsively gave Georgina another hug. 'With you here it'll be just like the old days, you, me and Dog,' Charlotte said. Though in reality, she knew it wouldn't be anything like it used to be. Georgina had been powerful, feared and revered. Now she was an escaped convict and would have to hide away, but for now Georgina was back and Charlotte could once again feel safe.

Johnny turned the car into a leafy lane in Surrey, surprised at how remarkably calm he felt considering what they were about to do.

'Blimey, it looks right la-de-da round 'ere,' Ned said, his eyes wide as he peered out of the window at the large detached houses behind gated gardens.

'It is, mate. We're in the land of the hoity-toity toffs now,' Johnny answered with a twinge of jealousy. He'd have liked to own a big house and an even flashier car than he already had. But he wasn't born with a silver spoon in his mouth as he imagined many of the people in this exclusive neighbourhood had been.

In fact, Johnny hadn't had the best of starts in life. His father had done a runner to avoid prison and left his mother to bring up Johnny and his four siblings alone. Johnny was the youngest of his brothers and had only ever received the scraps and hand-me-downs. His dear old mum, in an effort to support her family, had worked herself into an early grave. Maybe that's why Johnny appreciated the finer things in life now and was prepared to take risks for a good return.

'What the fuck is an illegal brewing outfit doing round here?' Ned asked, shaking his head.

'It's landowners, Ned. Most of the grain is going over to feed the nation, hence the shortage and taxes on beer. But the farm we're about to visit ain't declared their crops, and have turned the fruits of their harvest into beer which half of London has been buying up on the black market. Now all we've got to do is walk in and take their profits.'

'You make it sound easy, Johnny, but it ain't gonna be that straightforward, is it?' Nobby asked. 'I mean, if it was, we wouldn't need the shooters that are in the boot.'

Johnny shrugged. 'If they've got any sense, then it'll be straightforward. The guns are just for insurance purposes. Let's try not to use them unless we have to.'

'Yeah, right, if you say so, Johnny. But they ain't likely to just say, "Oh, here you are. Help yourself. Do you want a barrel of beer to take with you an' all."'

Johnny chuckled. 'That would be nice, but, no, probably not. Just stick to the plan and it should go smoothly enough.'

They came to a T-junction at the end of the lane with a telephone box on the corner. Johnny was pleased to see Max inside the booth, exactly where he should be. He pulled the car over and wound down the window as Max sauntered towards them, a roll-up on his lips.

'You took your time. I thought you weren't coming.'

'Yeah, sorry, we had to see to something first,' Johnny answered. 'The Naylors needed a visit.'

'I've missed the fun then?'

'Not yet. The real fun is about to begin. Jump in.'

The Barkers scooted over for Max to climb in the back of the car. 'This is cosy,' he said as Nobby tried to avoid elbowing him in the ribs.

Johnny turned in his seat. 'Give us an update,' he said to Max.

'Two cars have gone up with two blokes in each motor. None have come out. Three trucks went out first thing this morning. I couldn't see what was in the back but they was riding low so I'm guessing they had full loads.'

'Good. They've been busy delivering their beer and the cars you saw going in will be the runners from London who've collected the payments. This should be a tidy little earner. Where's the car you nicked to get down here this morning?'

'In a ditch. Shame that, it drove well. I wouldn't have minded keeping it.'

'Now we're working together again, you'll soon have enough to buy your own car.'

'I hope so but I won't be buying a bleedin' stupid thing like what you've got, Johnny.'

'Oi, leave my Betsy alone. She's a beauty and deserves a bit of respect.'

'Betsy... you've named your car. For fuck's sake, Johnny, have you gone queer?'

'Course I fuckin' ain't but if I was, we all know you'd fancy me, Max.'

'In your dreams.'

Johnny chortled as he put the car in gear and turned left onto a dirt track. They crept towards the farm, hoping to arrive with the advantage of surprise.

'Fuck me, it's a bit bumpy,' Ned moaned.

'I reckon the suspension is playing up,' Johnny answered, but any problems with Charlotte's car were far from his mind.

As they neared the farm and it came into sight, he could feel his pulse quicken. His leather-gloved hands gripped the steering wheel and he was pleased the others couldn't see his white knuckles. 'This is it, boys,' he said, looking at the rustic, stone farmhouse.

They stopped out of sight behind a hedgerow, just short of the yard, and the Barkers jumped out of the car to retrieve the stolen guns from the boot. Johnny pulled a balaclava over his head and Ned and Max did the same. The relaxed atmosphere had changed and now Johnny could feel their tension.

The Barker twins appeared with the large guns and handed them out, they too wearing balaclavas. 'All ready?' Nobby asked.

'Yep, go,' Johnny answered tersely.

The Barker twins stood behind the hedgerow, peeping round towards the farm. Johnny anxiously waited for the thumbs up.

'Come on… come on…' Ned said under his breath as he tapped his hand rapidly on his thigh. 'What's taking so fucking long?'

'Just be patient, Ned. One of them will show their face soon,' Max answered.

Ten minutes later, Johnny's heart raced when he saw

Nobby give him a thumbs up sign and the twins ran towards the farm. He counted down to twenty in his head then put his foot down hard on the accelerator and sped into the yard, the tyres throwing up a plume of dust as they screeched to a halt outside the house.

Leaping from the car, Johnny pulled his handgun from his coat pocket. They left the doors open and went to stand alongside the twins, who had their guns pointed at a young farmhand's head.

'Just let us in and you'll be all right,' Nobby threatened the young man.

The blond-haired lad was noticeably shaking and looked like he was about to burst into tears but he did as he was told and unlocked the front door to the farmhouse. Johnny, Max and Ned charged in with the Barker twins dragging the farmhand with them.

A quick glance into the first room showed it was empty. The next room's door was closed so Max kicked it heavily, causing it to swing open. Johnny looked in and saw three suited men staring at him in shock. One went to reach for a pistol on a table beside him, but Nobby pushed the farmhand through the door then quickly followed, firing bullets in the air. Eric was close behind and did the same, shouting, 'Get down… Get down. Get on the fucking floor.'

The man quickly retracted his hand from the pistol and plunged to the floor with the others. Once the twins had stopped firing and shouting, Johnny walked into the room.

Bits of plaster from the ceiling had showered the men on the floor. He could see there were six of them in total, all laid on their fronts with their hands on the back of their heads. Max frisked them and found two handguns.

'Stay on the floor and no one needs to get hurt,' Johnny said, sounding calmer than he felt. It was a cold day but he could feel himself sweating under the balaclava and his heart thumped hard and fast.

One of the burly men lifted his head and asked, 'Who the fuck sent you?'

'None of your fucking business. Where's the money?'

'You ain't getting fuck all so you might as well piss off.'

'Yeah, is that right? Perhaps if I blow your mate's brains out, then you'll tell me where the money is?'

Another spoke, quietly saying, 'Will, just tell him. Give 'em the money.'

Will shook his head. 'Nah, I ain't 'aving this. I told ya, you can piss right off.'

Johnny moved towards the bloke on the floor who'd spoken quietly. He hoped he wouldn't have to shoot anyone but he pointed his gun at the man's head and said to Will, 'I'll count to three, give you a chance to reconsider.'

Will looked furious and glared at Johnny but remained tight-lipped.

'One... Two...'

'Fucking tell him. Please, tell him where the money is!'

Still, Will didn't answer.

'Three,' Johnny said and pulled the trigger back.

'It's behind the picture,' Will said urgently. 'The money is in the safe behind the picture of the dogs.'

Max walked across the room, stepping over two men, and took the dark, wooden framed painting of three gun-dogs from the wall to reveal a grey metal safe behind.

'Well done,' Johnny said, and the man with the gun to his head sighed with obvious relief.

Max tried the safe but it was locked.

'The key?' Johnny asked.

Will indicated with his head that it was in his trouser pocket. Max stepped back over two men and rummaged in Will's pocket, quickly retrieving the small key.

'You're gonna regret this,' Will hissed. 'You've got no fucking idea who you're dealing with.'

As Max unlocked the safe, Nobby shouted in alarm, 'Johnny, quick, he's doing a runner!'

Johnny spun round to see the farmhand slipping out the door. The lad had somehow managed to sneak around the outside of the room and was making a run for it. Johnny, his gun already poised, fired. He aimed low and the bullet struck the lad in the back of his thigh. Screams of pain filled the air as the lad writhed on the floor in agony, blood oozing through his fingers as he tried to stem the flow from the bleeding wound.

'Shut the fuck up or I'll put a bullet in your mouth,' Johnny warned. He hadn't wanted to shoot the young man but he couldn't take a chance on him running to get help. The lad had brought it on himself. 'You idiot,' Johnny sneered at him and was pleased he'd stopped screaming.

Max had filled a cloth bag with wads of notes and was smiling as he stepped over the two men again and walked towards Johnny. 'Done,' he said as he passed and headed for the car.

'Thanks, gentlemen, it's been short and sweet. Good day to you,' Johnny said, smirking, and followed Max to the car with Ned behind him. As he climbed behind the steering wheel, he heard the Barker twins unloading some of their ammunition and hoped they were firing high. There was no need for any more blood to be spilled. They came out from the house, both grinning.

'Tyres,' Johnny called to them, pointing to the cars and vehicles in the yard.

Nobby and Eric opened fire again, this time shooting out all the tyres, Nobby firing from the hip. They got in the car and Johnny raced off before they'd even closed the car doors.

'We did it,' Nobby declared, sounding pleased with himself. 'We went and fucking did it!'

'You idiot,' Ned snapped.

'What? What's the matter with you?' Nobby asked.

'How many times have we gone over the rules and procedures, eh? Go on, tell me... how many fucking times?' Ned barked and Johnny wondered what had pissed him off.

'I dunno, loads. What's your problem?'

'You... you're the fucking problem, Nobby. You said Johnny's name!'

Johnny's head snapped round to look at Ned and he could see the man was furious. 'He didn't, did he?' he asked, his heart dropping into his shiny black shoes.

'Yeah, when that youngster tried to run off. He called you Johnny.'

'Shitting hell, Nobby! What are you playing at? Are you trying to get me killed?'

'Sorry, Johnny, it must have just slipped out. Fuck, I'm really sorry,' Nobby said, his voice full of remorse.

Ned looked over to the back seat. 'Yeah, that's right, you hang your head in shame. I hope it doesn't, but if this comes back on us, we'll know who to fucking blame.'

'There's hundreds in here,' Max said, looking in the bag

of money and skilfully changing the subject. 'And we've got a few extra guns. We've done all right.'

Johnny nodded; that was some compensation for having his name bandied around in front of their victims. But Ned was right, he hoped this didn't come back on them. After all, hadn't the boss said something about not knowing who they were dealing with? It was obviously someone big and probably someone to be feared. His stomach knotted. He hadn't considered that there was anyone else involved. He could have kicked himself. If Miss Garrett had organised this, she'd have checked every last detail. It wouldn't have slipped past her that someone bigger than them was running this operation. Someone like The Top, Johnny thought with a shudder of regret.

8

Two days later, Georgina yawned as she opened her eyes and stretched her arms above her head. She'd become accustomed to Charlotte's sofa, though her sleep remained restless. After all, the police could come crashing through the door at any time and knowing that a copper lived just across the landing didn't help either. She'd feel more relaxed once she knew for sure that Charlotte had him onside. Even when she had managed to doze off, her sleep had been punctured by horrific sounds and images from Holloway. She knew that place would forever haunt her dreams.

'Good morning. Did you sleep all right?' Charlotte asked, fetching her a cup of coffee and turning on the wireless. They had the wireless on all day to drown out any sound of their voices.

'Yes, fine,' Georgina lied.

She pushed herself up on her haunches as Dog jumped on her lap and tried to lick her face.

'Get down, Dog,' Charlotte chastised the mutt, then looked at Georgina. 'Sorry, it's habit. He's your dog, I shouldn't be telling him off.'

'Don't be daft, it's you who's looked after him. And you're right, he shouldn't be on the sofa,' she said, easing the dog down. 'Are you looking forward to your date tonight with Tim?'

'No,' Charlotte answered but Georgina didn't believe her. The girl's cheeks had flushed red and she'd averted her gaze from Georgina's eyes.

'Yes, you are, you fibber,' she teased.

'No, I'm not. The last thing I need in my life is a man, and even worse that he's a copper. I'm only going out with him to use him, like you told me to.'

'If you say so,' Georgina answered and threw the blankets off before pushing herself off the sofa. She glanced in the mirror over the mantel and could see the sleepless nights were beginning to show on her face. Dark circles ringed her eyes and her complexion looked dull. She couldn't even brighten herself up with a bit of red lippy, she thought, as her eyes fell on her dungarees draped over the back of an armchair. Not that it mattered. She wasn't out to impress anyone. Her only focus was to see her children. 'I hope Johnny comes round today. If not, you'll have to go and fetch him,' she told Charlotte. Now that she had her fake identity papers, she was keen to get Johnny to drive her to Wales.

'I'm pretty sure he will, and hopefully with some money for me too.'

'Are you struggling?'

'No, not at all. The rent from Miss Gray and Lord Hamilton is more than I need to live on.'

'Good. And how is Dina coping?'

'No idea. You know her, she won't talk to me, not that I blame her. She's quite chummy with Lord Hamilton and cleans his flat for a couple of bob.'

'I suppose I should let her know I'm here. As weird as the woman is, she's always been loyal and trustworthy.'

'If you say so, but the fewer people who know you are here, the better.'

Georgina knew that Charlotte was right, but being confined was getting hard and she hoped Johnny would turn up today.

A couple of hours later, Georgina heard a car pull up outside and looked through the net curtains, hoping it wasn't the police, and was pleased to see it was Johnny. She smiled as she watched him swagger to the door, cigar in hand and in his usual fur trimmed coat. She found it comforting to see that some things hadn't changed and couldn't wait to watch the expression on his face when he set eyes on her.

Johnny knocked on the door as Charlotte came through from the kitchen, her face ashen.

'Don't look so worried, it's only Johnny.'

'Thank gawd for that,' Charlotte muttered and went to let him in.

'Don't let on that I'm here. I want to surprise him,' Georgina called. She sat casually on the sofa but her excitement was mounting. Johnny had been her right-hand man and she'd openly admit how fond she was of him.

He strolled into the room, the smell of his cigar wafting in with him. As he removed his hat, his eyes set on Georgina and he gasped, stepping backwards in surprise.

'Hello, Johnny,' she said, her face beaming with delight.

'Pinch me, Charlotte… am I dreaming?'

'No, Johnny, you ain't dreaming,' Charlotte replied, chuckling.

'Miss Garrett, I never thought I'd see the day!' he said, walking towards her now with his arms outstretched.

Georgina rose to her feet and returned his embrace, albeit briefly. 'You're looking pretty dapper, unlike me, dressed like a workhand.'

'It don't matter what you're wearing, you're still a sight for sore eyes. Why didn't you tell us they were letting you out early? We would have picked you up and arranged a party. Cor blimey, wait 'til the rest of 'em hear you're back. They're gonna be chuffed to bits.'

'Slow down, Johnny, I didn't get let out early.'

'What are you on about? You're here, ain't ya?'

'Yes, but not with permission.'

'Bleedin' 'ell, have you escaped?'

Georgina nodded her head and Johnny looked impressed. 'I don't know why I'm surprised. In fact, I'm surprised you didn't break out sooner,' he said and guffawed.

'I had to wait for my chance.'

'What's the plan now? Are we setting up business again? You know I'll be more than happy to work for you and so will some of the blokes.'

'Not just yet. I need to see my children first. They're in Wales and I want you to drive me there. We'll set off first thing in the morning.'

'Anything you say, Miss Garrett.'

'In the meantime, Charlotte can make us a cuppa and you can tell me all about what's been going on and everything you know about The Top.'

Georgina listened intently but Johnny didn't impart

much more information than she already knew. 'And you're sure that it was him who killed David and Victor?' she asked.

'Yeah, I'm sorry but I'm convinced The Top is behind it. I don't see how else he could have just walked in and taken over. I reckon it was all planned when Mr Maynard was laid up in hospital. The Top attacked when he saw his opportunity.'

'Don't you think it's strange that no one knows anything about the man apart from the fact that he's Irish and has connections with the IRA?'

'Fuck knows, Miss Garrett. I did some digging and from what I can make out, the geezer used to sell to David and wanted a cut of the London action. Only he wanted a bigger cut than Mr Maynard was prepared to offer. So he took the fucking lot. Now he's got a few familiar faces round him. Slugs knows him but he ain't saying nothing.'

'Blimey, there's a name I haven't heard of in years. Do you think Slugs would talk for money?'

'No, I doubt it. He took a bullet for the man so I doubt he'd be persuaded to talk, even for a good handshake.'

'What about his protection? Surely one of them could be bought?'

'I don't think so, Miss Garrett. They don't seem like the talking sort, if you know what I mean.'

Georgina was left to ponder The Top while Johnny told her about turning over the illegal brewing company.

'This is for you, Charlotte, and your cut, Miss Garrett,' he said, offering her a wad of notes.

Georgina looked at the cash. She needed it. She needed every penny she could get her hands on, but she hadn't earned this money. 'Thanks, Johnny, but that's yours,' she said.

'No,' he protested, 'Rules are rules. You always get a cut of any jobs.'

'I *used to* get a cut.'

'I'll leave it on the side for you,' Johnny insisted. 'I've gotta get going now but I'll be back first thing. Cor, I can't wait to tell the others you're back.'

Georgina didn't need to remind Johnny to be careful about who he spoke to of her return to Battersea. Her most trusted man wasn't stupid and she knew he wouldn't put her at risk of being captured by the authorities. And she had to admit, though she'd thought she wouldn't get involved again with heading up the criminal gang, the idea of it thrilled her. If she was honest with herself, she was in dire need of the money too. Being on the run wasn't going to be cheap. She'd need cash to buy favours and silence. But, for now, she just wanted to hold Selina and Alfie close to her.

The wireless on the sideboard blared out. Charlotte wished she could switch it off and tried to ignore it, but it was impossible not to hear the news bulletins of soldiers, invasions, cities and countries under attack. The assault on her ears would trigger the horrendous memories she'd sooner forget. She thought of the kind fire warden she'd encountered, his head blown off, and how she'd had a one-sided conversation with him. God, it was awful. She shook her head, trying to shake the image away, and pulled a brush through her hair before pinching her cheeks to give them a bit of colour.

'You look lovely,' Georgina said, sitting on the sofa behind her.

Charlotte stared at her reflection in the mirror. 'No, I don't. I look plain and boring. I dunno what Tim sees in me,' she said, thinking out loud.

'Well, for someone who isn't interested in going out with him, you seem to be worrying quite a bit about what you look like.'

Charlotte turned away from the mirror and threw herself onto the armchair. Georgina had a point. If she wasn't bothered about Tim, why did she have butterflies in her stomach? 'I'm just nervous 'cos I don't want to mess it up. If I get this wrong, you could end up back behind bars.'

'That's not going to happen and you're not going to mess it up.'

'Thanks,' she answered, grateful for Georgina's confidence in her.

Her stomach flipped at a sudden knock on the door. It wasn't time for her date, so she guessed it was probably her upstairs neighbour. 'That'll be Lord Hamilton. Brace yourself, he's quite a character.'

'Are you sure we can trust him?'

'Yep, he's always wanted to meet you, and when it comes to the law, he's as dodgy as the day is long.'

When Charlotte ushered him into the front room, she could see Georgina was trying to keep a straight face. In his burgundy, silk house coat, cream cravat and curled moustache, he looked like he should be walking the corridors of a stately home.

'Miss Garrett, what an absolute delight to finally meet

you,' he said, sweeping across the room to take her hand and hold it to his lips. 'I've heard much about you.'

'Likewise,' Georgina answered, 'Charlotte talks very highly of you.'

'I'm flattered but I can assure you that her gracious compliments of me are unfounded. You, on the other hand, are far more beautiful than I had imagined. And I must say, I'm terribly excited to be in the presence of such an accomplished woman and one who has defied the authorities. That, my dear, deserves a toast and I've brought you a bottle of the finest champagne.'

Charlotte held the bottle aloft for Georgina to see before going to the kitchen to fetch glasses. She didn't have any champagne flutes, tumblers would have to do. And she only had two glass tumblers but didn't mind drinking her champagne from a cup.

Back in the front room, Lord Hamilton and Georgina appeared to be getting on well. He was telling her his usual tales of rubbing shoulders with royalty and Georgina was pretending to be impressed.

Charlotte popped the cork and poured the champagne, hoping that a glass of bubbly would calm her nerves about her impending date with Tim. She glanced at the clock again. Only fifteen minutes to go.

'You look as if you're going somewhere?' Lord Hamilton questioned with a raised eyebrow as she handed him a glass.

'I am,' she answered.

'She's going on a date with PC Timothy Batten,' Georgina told him.

'Goodness gracious me! Well, this is a day full of surprises!'

'I'm only going out with him 'cos Georgina thinks it would be a good idea.'

'Oh, I see,' Lord Hamilton said thoughtfully, 'Keep your friends close and your enemies closer.'

'Indeed,' Georgina agreed and held her glass in the air, asking, 'What are we toasting?'

'To new friends and freedom,' Lord Hamilton said and they all clinked glasses.

The knock on the door came sooner than Charlotte had expected and Dog bounded towards it, barking. Charlotte gulped down the champagne in her cup. The bubbles caused her to loudly belch as she gathered her coat and bag. Glancing over her shoulder as she went towards the door, she saw Georgina with her finger over her lips, reminding Lord Hamilton to be silent.

After dragging Dog back into the front room and closing the door, Charlotte drew in a long breath ready to greet Tim. 'Hello,' she said, shyly. 'I'm ready to go.'

'You've left the wireless on.'

'Yeah, it's company for Dog,' she answered quickly, pulling her coat on and shutting the front door behind them with urgency. She walked past Tim and out onto the street where he caught her up and marched alongside her.

'You must be hungry, you seem in a hurry.'

'Sorry,' she said and slowed her pace. 'It's cold, a brisk walk warms you up.'

'Yes, it does, but I'm used to being out on the streets in the cold.'

'Where are we going?' she asked, realising she could be walking in the wrong direction.

'I wasn't sure what you like, but as it's one of the meals that Churchill hasn't rationed, I thought fish and chips.'

'Smashing, my favourite, especially from Shooters. They cook their chips in beef dripping and you can buy a bag of crackly bits.'

'Oh, I was going to take you to a little restaurant on York Road but if you prefer to go to Shooters?'

'No, the restaurant will be fine, I'm sure,' Charlotte answered, a little anxious but looking forward to the experience. She'd never been in a restaurant before. She'd had hot chocolate once in a café with Daphne, a posh woman who'd later turned her nose up at her. Another memory she tried to push aside.

The temperature outside was rapidly cooling and Charlotte picked up her pace again, Tim keeping up beside her. 'It's chilly this evening,' she said, pulling a pair of knitted gloves from her coat pockets and shoving her hands inside them.

'We might have a white Christmas.'

Charlotte looked up at the sky and though the sun had set, there wasn't a star in sight, masked by the clouds. Not even the moon offered any illumination on the blacked-out streets of London. 'Maybe,' she mused.

'Are you going anywhere for Christmas?'

'No, probably not,' she answered. She knew she wouldn't be welcomed by her mother at Molly's farm. But now Georgina was home, she had no desire to go to Kent anyway.

'I'll probably go to my sister's. She does a good spread, even with the rations. You could come too, if you like?'

'Oh... thanks, but I'll be fine at home. Lord Hamilton

will insist on keeping me company. He did last year. In fact, we had quite a hoot.'

'I've only met him briefly in passing and haven't seen Miss Gray yet. The other lady, the blonde one, I saw her out of my window but we haven't spoken.'

'You'll be lucky to get more than a few words out of Dina. We're a funny bunch in that big house, a right mixture.'

'I know you said you'd changed your mind about me moving out but I still don't know if I feel right about staying, not when I know there are families desperate for housing.'

'I hope you will,' Charlotte said and, strangely, she felt sincere in saying it.

'If you *really* want me to stay, then I will,' he said and looked down at her.

Their eyes met and she felt those butterflies again. *You're only using him* she reminded herself. *Don't fall for a copper.*

'Have you always wanted to be a policeman?' she probed.

'No, not at all. My dad pushed me into it. He was a copper but got injured and had to leave the force.'

'Oh, blimey. How did he get injured?'

'You probably won't remember it but it was when the police station got blown up.'

'I remember hearing about it,' she answered, cringing inside. Georgina had never admitted it but it was rumoured that she'd been behind the explosion. This wasn't going well. Tim was unlikely to want to help protect Georgina if he had an inkling that it was her fault his dad had been hurt.

'It killed a few policemen but they never caught the bloke who did it. I suppose my dad was lucky to have only been injured… unfortunately.'

'What do you mean, *unfortunately*?' she asked, thinking this was sounding more promising!

'Oh, nothing, I shouldn't have mentioned it.'

'But you did. Don't you get on with your dad then?'

'No, far from it. He's not a nice man, Charlotte. Suffice to say, since joining the force I've heard things about him that I couldn't repeat in front of a lady.'

'You can tell me. I ain't no lady.'

'No, I couldn't and I wouldn't want to. I'm ashamed of him and the heinous things he's done. I'm just glad my mum isn't around anymore, God rest her soul. I dread to think what she must have put up with from him and whatever she knew about him went with her to her grave. Now, let's change the subject, I'd rather not talk about him. What about you… how did you come to look after that big house?'

Charlotte's mind raced for an answer. She couldn't tell him that Georgina owned it but Mr Harel had arranged for the name on the deeds to be changed to her son's, Alfred Hearn. But she was saved from finding an answer when they heard bells from vehicles racing towards them from behind.

Tim stopped to look. 'I wonder what's going on?' he said as several fire brigade engines passed and two police cars. 'It must be a major incident.'

'I dunno, Tim, but I don't like the look of this,' she said, her pulse quickening.

The vehicles sped in the direction they were walking and Charlotte had the urge to turn around and run home. 'We should head back,' she said, 'Something's not right.'

'I might be needed. Come on, let's hurry,' he replied, grabbing her hand and dragging her along.

Charlotte snatched her hand away from his. 'No,' she shouted. 'There's something bad going on up there. I want to go home.'

'Please, Charlotte, I can't turn my back on people who may need my help. Let's just go and see what the problem is. I'll look after you, I promise.'

Against all her instincts, she reluctantly rushed towards where the vehicles were going, all the while questioning her sanity. The engines and cars had stopped on the corner of a side road and even in the darkness, Charlotte could see a large crowd had gathered.

'What's happened?' Tim asked a bystander.

The man animatedly explained, 'They've found an unexploded bomb behind the wall of the factory there. Gotta be at least a five hundred pounder. It ain't a Satan but it's a big 'un.'

Charlotte, terrified at the news, tugged on Tim's arm. 'Please, take me home,' she said, panicking.

'It's all right, Charlotte, the bomb disposal unit will be here soon to deal with it. But let me help clear all these people away, just in case the thing goes off.'

The thought of standing so close to a bomb and being caught up in the blast was too much for her to bear. 'Please, Tim,' she begged, tears streaking down her face now.

He grabbed her shoulders firmly. 'Just do as I say and everything will be fine,' he told her and led her along the road and into a shop doorway. 'You'll be safe here. Just wait ten minutes for me. I'm going to move those people on and then I'll be back. Understand?'

She nodded, her imagination running havoc – she was now too petrified to move or speak. She squeezed her eyes shut, trying to block the awful memories from flooding in, and when she opened them again, Tim was gone. Closing her eyes again, she counted out loud. 'One... two... three... four...'

The sound of more vehicles with their bells ringing loudly passed her. 'Five... six...' Men yelling *'Stand back, stand back.'* 'Seven... eight...' She never reached nine. A terrific booming noise filled the air and she felt a gush of air lift her skirt. Her cheeks stung as fragments of flying debris hit her face. Charlotte's legs gave way and she dropped to the ground, fear rendering her unable to open her eyes. She was on her knees, trying to scramble back to her feet but her legs had no strength to support her and she staggered sideways, dropping back to her knees. Still with her eyes closed, her nostrils twitched at the smell of explosives, fire and burning bodies. And then the waft of brick dust and plaster began clogging her nose.

'No, no, no,' she screamed, well aware of the devastation she would see if she dared to open her eyes. She recognised the stench of death in the air. And the screams of pain from women and men with mutilated bodies. The harrowing shout of a mother looking for her child. The muted cry for help from under rubble. Her body violently trembled uncontrollably from head to toe. She heard a long, tormenting, low howl and realised it was coming from her own lips.

'Are you all right, miss?' A man's voice in the madness asked and she felt hands around her waist, pulling her to her feet. Still, she refused to open her eyes.

'Miss... miss... are you hurt?'

She managed to quieten herself and shook her head.

'Come, sit here,' the voice said.

She was led a few steps and could hear the sound of shattered glass underfoot. The man lowered her down, onto a doorstep, she assumed. 'You'll be all right here,' the kind voice said.

Charlotte dropped her head into her hands, and after a while she noticed a damp feeling on her fingers. Pulling her hand back, she slowly opened her eyes to look at it and saw blood on her blue woollen glove. She pulled off the glove and touched her head again, this time wincing at the sharp pain. And then she remembered… Tim. He'd gone back to help clear the crowds. A new wave of panic washed over her and she jumped to her feet, scanning the horrendous scene down the street. Plumes of smoke and dust were glowing red and orange, lit by the flames of the fires. People were running in all directions, some limping slowly, others gazing at the destruction in shock.

With trepidation, she staggered forward, desperately seeking sight of Tim. *Please, let him be alive*, she prayed, edging closer to the horror.

'Tim… Timothy…' she shouted but her voice was hoarse and lost in the sound of the roaring fires. 'Tim… Tim…'

She saw a familiar looking figure silhouetted against the glow of the fires. He'd scooped up a child and was heading towards an ambulance. Relieved he was alive, she intuitively knew it was Tim and rushed over.

Buildings had crumbled. Men and women were standing on the wreckage of piles that were once houses, moving bricks one by one and passing them down a line. The despair of what they might discover under the fallen debris was etched on their blackened faces. Charlotte tried not to look and focused on Tim. She called his name again but he couldn't hear her. As she neared the ambulance, she saw him rush back to another burning building and watched in awe of his bravery.

Someone placed a blanket over her shoulders.

'Let me take a look at that, miss,' he said, pointing to the wound on her head.

She'd forgotten about her injury. 'No, I'm fine, thanks,' she said, her eyes fixed on Tim.

He came towards the ambulance again, this time with his arms supporting an elderly woman. As he drew closer, he looked up and when he saw that she appeared unhurt, he smiled. The ambulance driver took the elderly lady and Tim pulled Charlotte into his arms.

'Thank goodness you're ok,' he said, holding her close.

Charlotte was glad to be in his arms and felt herself crying.

'It's all right,' he soothed, stroking her hair. 'Christ, you're shaking. I'll take you home now.'

They walked back slowly, hand in hand, neither of them speaking, both dazed from the bomb blast.

As they turned onto Alexandra Avenue, it was Tim who broke the silence. 'I'm sorry I dragged you into this tonight.'

'You don't have to apologise. It's your job. You wouldn't be much of a copper if you didn't want to go and help people.'

'Thank you for being understanding. I don't suppose you'll want to go out with me again?'

'Why would you think that?'

'Because I didn't listen to you when you asked me to take you home.'

'I saw what you did, Tim. I saw you rush into that burning

building with no regard for your own safety. You saved that old girl. Of course I want to go out with you again, you silly sod, but perhaps next time we can just get a bag of chips from Shooters?'

'Good idea.'

Charlotte felt him squeeze her hand a little tighter. Before now, the thought of a man touching any part of her body had left her feeling sick to her stomach, but there was something about PC Batten that felt natural and she enjoyed the feeling of her hand in his.

They were just outside the house when the front door flew open and Lord Hamilton came rushing out. 'Charlotte, oh, Charlotte, we've been so worried about you,' he said, frowning at the blood that had trickled down the side of her face. 'You've been hurt!'

'It's fine, just a graze,' she said, smiling wanly.

'We heard the blast. One of the neighbours said a bomb exploded along from York Road.'

'Yes, that's right.'

'Come inside, dear, out from the cold and let me pour you a brandy.'

Charlotte shot him a frantic look, worried he'd forgotten they were harbouring a wanted woman.

'And you PC Batten. You appear to have done a spiffing job of looking after Charlotte. I should imagine you'd be grateful of a brandy too?'

'I wouldn't say no,' he answered.

As they walked into Charlotte's flat, she held her breath and crossed her fingers, hoping Tim wouldn't spot any sign of Georgina being there. Her eyes flitted around the front room and fell on the two tumblers and bottle of champagne.

'Sit down, by the fire. I'll pop upstairs and get the brandy,' Lord Hamilton said.

Tim waited until Charlotte had taken off her coat and sat in one of the armchairs. He hovered over her and, looking at the dried blood on her face, said, 'I'll get a bowl of warm water to clean you up.'

Charlotte leapt to her feet. 'No,' she snapped, panicking. Georgina could be hiding in the kitchen!

Tim looked taken aback.

'Sorry, my nerves are a bit jangled. Just sit down, Tim. My head is fine, I'll clean it up in a minute.'

He sat in the chair opposite and leaned towards her as Dog rested his head in her lap.

'We were lucky tonight. I don't know how I came out of that unscathed. And I can't tell you how pleased I was to see you standing there. The whole time I was helping people to the ambulance, all I could think about was you.'

Charlotte felt herself blush and looked down at Dog.

'I'm sorry, I'm making a fool of myself and embarrassing you.'

'No, it's nice. I felt the same. I was so worried that something awful had happened to you. Gawd, the relief I felt when I saw you!'

Lord Hamilton swanned back into the room carrying a half-full bottle of brandy. He took the two tumblers to the kitchen and returned with a drink for them both.

'What happened out there?' he asked Tim.

It was Charlotte who answered. 'A bloody big bomb went off, that's what happened. It was horrible, really horrible, but Tim here was a right hero.'

'I've no doubt, a strapping young police officer like yourself.'

'No, I wasn't a hero. I did what anyone else would have done.'

'Take no notice of him, Lord Hamilton. He was a hero and I saw it with my own eyes. He ran into a building that was on fire and pulled out an old woman. She would have burned to death if he hadn't rescued her.'

'Well done, young man!'

Tim looked across to Charlotte and smiled awkwardly at her which made her stomach flip again, but she didn't want him to be having this effect on her.

'I say, you must both be exhausted. Now, drink up, PC Batten. I shall draw Charlotte a hot bath and then we shall leave her to rest.'

'Yes, of course,' Tim said and gulped down the brandy, pulling a face when he'd finished.

As he stood up to leave, Lord Hamilton handed him the bottle. 'You can have another before bed. It may help you to sleep.'

'No, thank you,' Tim said, passing the bottle back. 'I'm not really much of a brandy drinker and I have to get up early tomorrow.'

'Well, thank you for bringing Charlotte safely home. When we heard the explosion, you can imagine what went through our minds.'

'We... who's we?' Tim asked.

Charlotte saw Lord Hamilton was unnerved by the question and quickly interrupted, 'Him and Dog.'

'Yes, Dog and I were terrified,' Lord Hamilton said, sounding believable.

Tim said goodnight, and when he left the room, Lord Hamilton closed the door behind him. Charlotte was left wondering what on earth she'd been thinking! No matter how much she admired Tim's bravery, or the feelings he'd evoked in her and the feel of her hand in his, first and foremost, the man was a policeman and she had to keep that in mind. Or else Georgina could end up being arrested and if that happened, she knew she'd never forgive herself.

9

Georgina, dressed and ready to go, paced back and forth, stopping every few seconds to pull back the curtains a crack to glance out the window, eagerly waiting for Johnny to turn up. The sun hadn't yet risen and the street was in darkness. She didn't expect Johnny to arrive for at least a couple of hours but she'd hardly slept again and had been awake since four. Though this time, rather than lying awake listening for every sound, on edge and ready to run, her insomnia had been caused by the anticipation of seeing her children.

'Blimey, Georgina, you're up at a sparrow's fart. Johnny won't be here for a while yet.'

'I'm sorry if I woke you,' Georgina said and turned away from the window to look at Charlotte. In the low lamplight, she could see the girl's head was showing a distinct bruise from her injury of the previous night. But she was pleased to see that Charlotte didn't seem to be too adversely affected from her experience.

'Why are you looking at me like that?' Charlotte asked.

'No reason. Just making sure you're all right.'

'Yeah, I'll live, unlike some of them poor beggars last night.'

'Try not to dwell on it, eh?'

'I won't. Don't worry about me. You just make sure you have a lovely time with your kids.'

'I can't wait,' she answered, turning back to the window.

She could hear Charlotte in the kitchen and smelt the aroma of bread toasting. And though her mouth watered, she couldn't face food. Her stomach was doing somersaults.

'Some toast and jam and a strong cuppa,' Charlotte said, coming back into the front room and offering her a tray.

'I'm sorry, I can't eat. I'll take some sandwiches for me and Johnny. Maybe I'll feel a bit more settled later. But I'll have the cuppa, thanks.'

Charlotte pulled off bits of the toast and fed them to Dog. 'What a waste,' she moaned in jest. 'He's getting good rationed food, the spoilt mutt. I put loads of butter on this.'

Hours later, Georgina turned off the table lamp, turned on the wireless and pulled open the curtains to see sunlight flooding in through the taped windows, drenching the room in a golden hue. She was glad of the good weather for their trip to Wales. As she gazed out onto the street, she saw PC Batten leaving the house. She thought he looked very smart in his uniform with polished silver buttons down the front of his jacket, and his helmet gave him added height. And then it struck her that she didn't feel the usual repulsion towards him that she'd normally feel about a copper. What was different about him? Was it because Charlotte had developed feelings for him? Of course, the girl hadn't admitted it – she had in fact fervently denied it – but Georgina could tell that Charlotte was falling for him. As long as Charlotte didn't get her heart broken, Georgina didn't mind her being in love with a policeman, especially as it could work to her advantage.

Now that PC Batten was out of the way, she was eager to get going and was delighted when she finally saw Johnny driving towards the house. 'At last,' she said to herself, then called to Charlotte, 'Johnny's here.'

Charlotte came through from the kitchen with sandwiches and bottles of pop. 'There you go,' she said, handing the bundle to Georgina. 'I'll see you tomorrow.'

As Georgina climbed into her old car, dressed in her workman clothes, she refrained from looking up and down the street. She didn't want to act suspiciously or appear nervous.

'Good morning, Miss Garrett. You're looking… erm…'

'Like a bloke,' she answered, smiling at Johnny.

'Yeah, like a bloke,' he laughed.

'I think it's about time you called me Georgina. No, you'd better make it George, for now.'

'Oh, I dunno, Miss Garrett, it wouldn't feel right. You're the guvnor.'

'Not anymore, Johnny.'

'Yeah you are. Anyway, what have you got there? I'm famished.'

As Johnny set off, Georgina unwrapped a corned beef sandwich for him.

'Thanks,' he said, driving with one hand on the steering wheel. 'I reckon we should arrive before teatime.'

'I hope so. Have you got the map?'

'Yep, and some petrol coupons. Don't take the piss but there's a flask of tea under your seat an' all. Oh, and a handgun for you.'

Georgina sat low in her seat with her flat cap pulled down, watching the sights of London pass. It was heart-wrenching to see so many buildings bombed and turned to rubble, queues outside shops, housewives desperate for their meagre rations, and the distinct lack of children playing in the streets or on their way to school. When she'd given Selina to Lash's parents, it had been with reluctance but she'd known it was for the best. The decision had been made when her daughter was just months old and bombs were dropping all around them. Mary had talked her into it and Lash's parents had readily agreed. But at the time, she could never have imagined that the war would still be raging years later and children would be separated from their parents, evacuated to safety. *Damn you, Hitler*, she thought, looking at a group of soldiers proudly wearing their khaki uniforms. They were getting on a tram, going to gawd knows where. She wondered if they'd been waved off from home by mothers and wives. Were they on their way back to war? Would they return to London or would their blood be spilled on foreign lands?

'When will this bloody war be over with?' she said, her mood dampened.

'Christ knows! It's been going on too long now.'

The rhythmic motion of the car relaxed her and she felt the tension lifting from her shoulders. Her eyelids began to feel heavy and as the car trundled out of London and into the winding country lanes, Georgina drifted into sleep.

She found herself with David, his arms around her as she breathed in his scent. He was whispering something in her ear but she couldn't quite hear him. Now they were in his office and drinking champagne, laughing about the enormous carrot hiding behind the curtains. She pulled her gun from her clutch bag and David applauded her as she shot the potato sitting at his desk. Lash came in and carried her away. David gave chase, waving his gun in the air. Georgina held tightly around Lash's neck and then she heard the gunshot. Lash fell to the floor. She screamed. Then David pointed his gun at her.

She woke to Johnny's voice as he gentle nudged her arm. 'Miss Garrett... Miss Garrett...'

'What... I think I've been asleep.'

'Yes, for hours but I woke you up 'cos it sounded like you were having a bad dream.'

'Thanks. Where are we?' she asked, looking out the window at the unfamiliar countryside.

'Not long now. I've seen the sea a few times. About an hour away, I reckon.'

'Blimey, thanks, Johnny. I've been asleep for most of the journey.'

'You have and it's been nice and peaceful,' he said with a laugh.

They drove up a hill, the road seemed endless, but the higher they got, the faster her heart pounded. She knew that on the other side of the hill, Lash's family would be camped and she'd finally hold her children in her longing arms. But she feared how they might react to her. Selina wouldn't know her and Alfie may have forgotten her. Would they be scared? Excited? Shy? What did they look like now? She imagined Alfie would be the image of his father with dark hair and eyes. Would Selina look like her? Her mind raced as the car went over the brow of the hill.

Georgina tried to peer through the trees to the valley below but her view was too obscured. 'Hurry up, Johnny, they should be down there. Can't you drive any faster?'

'Sorry, Miss Garrett, but I've gotta take it slow on these bends.'

Halfway down, still she couldn't see the caravans or the horses.

The road curved to the left and then she spotted three vardos, alone, next to a stream where three horses were grazing. 'There!' she exclaimed excitedly, 'Over there.'

At the bottom of the hill, Johnny brought the car to a stop and Georgina took a deep breath. 'Wait here,' she told him. 'I'll be back soon. Let me speak to Lash's parents first. They'll offer us a bed for the night but I don't want them to be on the defence because I've walked in with a man.'

As Georgina approached the three caravans, she looked up and down the valley, wondering where the others were. And where were her children? Something didn't feel right.

She stood outside the first vardo, painted green and decorated with small but elaborate red and pink flowers. The large wheels and steps up were red, and gold coloured curtains dressed the small windows. The front door was framed by intricate wood carvings, as was a wooden box attached to the undercarriage. A wooden stand with a tin wash basin stood outside and smoke belched from the small chimney. Someone must be home.

'Hello,' she shouted, and waited.

The door opened and a lady with black hair tied high

on her head came out, wiping her hands on a cloth. She wore an apron over her long, black dress and a red crotched shawl over her shoulders.

'*Sastibe* (hello), Georgina.'

'*Sastibe*,' she parroted, unsure of who the woman was.

'Come inside. The pot is hot.'

Georgina followed the woman inside and as she did, memories of being in Lash's parents' vardo came flooding back.

'*Besh* (sit). *Martya* (spirit of the night) told me you would be coming.'

'I'm sorry, I don't know who you are.'

The woman, her face etched with the tales of a thousand lives, sat opposite Georgina at a small table. 'I'm Rukeli, your husband's *Beebee* (aunt). I've seen you many times through my third *yak* (eye).'

'Thank you for inviting me in, Rukeli. Can you tell me where my children are?'

'*Zeravo* (left) to the ocean. Your *Sastro* (father-in-law) made it so. Your children are with their *niamo* (relatives) and they travel a *lundo drom* (long road).'

Georgina couldn't believe what she was hearing and hoped her confusion was because of her limited understanding of their language.

'I'm sorry, please speak to me in my tongue. Are you telling me my children aren't here?'

'Yes, Georgina. It is for the best.'

Georgina's teeth clenched and she jumped to her feet, anger cursing through her veins. 'You've no right to keep my children from me,' she screeched, her chest heaving with rapid breaths.

'The world is at war. Your children cannot come back to you yet.'

'I still have a right to see them!' she shouted, running her hand through her short hair.

'We thought it might upset them. Your children are settled, loved and cared for. Seeing you would unsettle them. You must have patience, Georgina.'

'They're *my* children,' she ground out and felt tears stinging her eyes.

'Understand, child, they are safe and this decision was taken in agreement with the elders.'

Georgina placed her hands on the table and leaned towards Rukeli, her voice quieter now. 'Where are they? And don't tell me all that rubbish about across oceans and long roads. I want to know exactly where my children are.'

Rukeli pushed herself to her feet and hobbled across the caravan to attend to the pot on the stove. 'You've had a long journey to find disappointment. I cannot tell you what you want to know. But I can offer you refreshment.'

'I don't want bloody refreshment. I want to see my babies!'

Rukeli turned quickly from the pot, her eyes blazing. 'Check yourself, Georgina. Check your tone and remember who you are addressing. *Barearav!* (respect).'

Georgina lowered her eyes. 'I'm sorry,' she muttered, acutely aware of the reverence she should be showing Lash's aunt.

'You and your friend must rest.'

'Thank you, Rukeli, but I can't stay, not without my children,' she sighed.

'Your children will be brought to you in good time. And

do not think they have forgotten you. We tell them stories of their mother and father. Alfie remembers you. He says you are the boss. And Selina is curious. She has your eyes.'

A sob caught in Georgina's throat that she tried to suppress. Her hand went over her mouth as tears fell unashamedly.

'They are happy, Georgina. Let us take care of them with your blessing.'

Georgina recalled a conversation she'd had with Lash, when he had wanted to take Alfie to be with his family and she'd disagreed. He had asked to take Alfie with her blessing but the conversation had turned into an argument. The last words they'd shared before his death had been spoken in anger, something she had always regretted and had to live with. Now, with hesitancy, she nodded, unable to speak, and Rukeli came towards her. She took Georgina's hand in her own and closed her eyes.

'I see the man on fire,' she said and shuddered.

It had been Lash's aunt who had foreseen that Lash would die and she would be with the 'man on fire'. David Maynard had been that man, horrifically burned in a bomb blast. 'What do you see, Rukeli?' she asked curiously, even though she didn't really believe in fortune telling.

'He is on your mind. You are angry with someone else.'

'He's dead. I will avenge his death.'

Rukeli pulled her hand away and bustled past Georgina.

'He lives in your heart alongside Lash.'

'He does.'

'*Buino*. The man on fire was *buino* (proud). He has passed over, Georgina. I do not feel his *mulo* (spirit of the dead). And you will not have revenge.'

Georgina swallowed hard. Lash had always sworn by Rukeli's visions. He'd said his aunt was never wrong. More tears stung her eyes. She had nothing. No children. No man to love her. And now she'd been told that she wouldn't even have her revenge. But she sat and listened to Rukeli who was happy to recount heartwarming tales of Alfie and Selina's adventures.

Finally, Georgina bid farewell to Rukeli but hated leaving without having had the opportunity to hold her children. Back in the car, Johnny looked puzzled.

'Just drive,' she told him, fighting to hold back more tears.

Her arms were still empty but as they embarked on the arduous journey back to London, Georgina's grief turned to bitter anger. Everything had been taken from her. And regardless of what Rukeli had said, now it was time to seek retribution.

Johnny had struggled to keep his eyes open for the last couple of hours of the journey home from Wales and had smoked three cigars in an attempt to keep him awake. Thankfully, Miss Garrett hadn't complained about the smell. The fresh air blasting his face from the open window had helped to keep him alert.

His heart went out to his guvnor. She'd been so solemn after discovering she couldn't see her kids. And Lash's aunt had said that Miss Garrett wouldn't get any revenge on David's killer. Not that Johnny gave it much credence. He thought all that palm reading and tea leaf rubbish was just a gimmick used on the end of Brighton Pier to fool the gullible folk to part with their money. But, if that's what it took for Miss Garrett to back down about wanting to pay back The Top, then who was he to question it? The trouble was, The Top was powerful and could easily get rid of Miss Garrett. In fact, Johnny wouldn't be surprised if there wasn't already a target on her head. After all, Miss Garrett had once been a terrific force in Battersea and Johnny was sure she'd soon regain her crown. The Top might not like that notion! And he doubted very much that Miss Garrett could take him down first.

He'd dropped her off in the early hours, arranging to pick her up again that evening. Now he was looking forward to his bed and trudged up the stairs to his flat. After driving almost non-stop for hours, every step was an effort and his body felt stiff and ached. His back was sore too. The thought of Daisy popped into his head. She was never far from his mind but it was the smallest of things that would bring her to the forefront. This time, his aching back. He remembered Daisy's back had been painful once and he'd massaged her, which of course had led to them making love. Ah, making sweet love with Daisy. She'd taken him to levels of ecstasy that he'd never known existed. He missed her and knew he always would. *Daisy, Daisy, Give me your answer do…* He'd sung that song to her on her deathbed. She'd said yes, of course she'd marry him. But poor, beautiful, delicate Daisy had died before Johnny could make her his wife.

His precious thoughts of Daisy were quickly dismissed when he neared the top step and noticed that the door was ajar. Johnny stopped dead in his tracks.

Reaching inside his coat for his gun, Johnny walked through the darkness in a calculated manner towards his flat, ready to shoot if he had to. He flung the door open wider, holding his gun in front of him, and then he slowly tiptoed inside. It was black, almost impossible to see anything. He listened, but all he could hear was the sound of his heart thumping. Edging further in, he flicked on a light switch and glanced around the lounge in disgust at the disarray. The sofa cushions lay ripped on the floor. The contents of drawers had been thrown around and the wireless was smashed. Even the wastepaper bin had been emptied.

He moved from the lounge to the kitchenette and then the bedroom to find each room in the same mess. But whoever had been in was long gone now. He felt relieved but at the same time, would have liked to catch the bastards in the act and put a couple of bullets in them.

Johnny tucked his gun away back in his pocket, closed the front door and went straight to his hiding place. It was clear that someone had been looking for something and he guessed they were probably searching for the money from his recent job.

Stepping over his clothes strewn across the bedroom floor, he pushed an old trunk to one side and then removed a piece of skirting board. He reached into the hollow he'd made in the wall, pleased when his fingertips touched a cloth bag. Pulling out the bag, he looked inside, to see his wad of notes and a gun. They hadn't found his stash but he knew they'd be back and wondered who they were. Now he realised it was a good job that he hadn't been home, and shuddered at the thought of what they might have done to him if they'd caught him off-guard.

Johnny's heart raced as he frantically tried to think of what to do next. He couldn't stay here but he didn't know who he was running from. What if it was The Top? He was taking Miss Garrett there later. He could be offering himself up, like a lamb to the slaughter of a sacrifice.

Grabbing a few necessities and with the cloth bag, Johnny fled his flat and raced round to Max's house. His good friend wouldn't mind him kipping there for what was left of the night and at least together they had strength in numbers. Two men with guns was better than one.

10

Georgina's eyes flicked open to the sound of someone tapping on the front room window. She pushed herself up wearily from the sofa and glanced at the clock to see she'd only had a couple of hours' sleep. Pulling back the curtain, in the darkness, she saw Johnny outside with his arm over the shoulder of a woman. She gave him a quick thumbs up and mouthed, 'Just a minute,' before hurrying through to Charlotte's bedroom.

'Charlotte... Charlotte... Wake up,' she said quietly as she shook the girl.

'Eh, what, what?'

'Johnny's outside with a woman. Let them in.'

'Eh? Johnny? Outside?'

'Yes, hurry up. Something must be wrong,' Georgina answered and threw Charlotte a dressing gown from the back of the door. 'Come on, quick.'

She waited anxiously in the front room as Charlotte went to let Johnny in. When they came through, she could see the woman under Johnny's arm was trembling and Johnny looked worried.

'What's going on?' she asked.

'You remember Gerty, Miss Garrett?'

When the woman looked up through her mascara-blackened tear-streaked face, Georgina recognised that Gerty had been one of her prostitutes at Livingstone Road.

'Gerty,' Charlotte exclaimed, surprised to see her.

'She's had a bit of a shock. Well, we both 'ave,' Johnny said sombrely.

'Charlotte, put the kettle on… and the wireless,' Georgina said and told Gerty and Johnny to sit down. 'What's happened?' she asked, addressing him.

He told Gerty to go and help Charlotte make the tea and to close the door behind her. Then once alone, he sat forward and lowered his voice.

'You know that brewery company we turned over?'

'Yes.'

'It looks like we've pissed off someone pretty bad. When I got home, my place had been ransacked. I went round to Max's and… he's dead.'

'Someone killed him?'

'Yeah. Fucking 'orrible it was an' all. He was a right mess, I hardly recognised him. Whoever did it gave him a right fucking beating. There was blood splattered up the walls and by the looks of it, I reckon they stamped on his head a few times.'

'Jesus! Poor Max.'

'Yeah, poor Max. I reckon they'll be coming for me next. Good job I was in Wales with you.'

'What about Ned and the Barker twins? Have you warned them?'

'Yeah, me and Gerty went round to their houses. They'll be here in a bit.'

'How did Gerty get mixed up in this?'

'She lives upstairs from Max. She heard a lot of shouting and screaming so sneaked downstairs. She couldn't see nothing but heard them kicking the shit out of Max. You know what he was like... he didn't feel pain. He would have kept coming at them until they killed him. Gerty hid under the stairs until they'd gone, then found Max with his brain oozing out his head. It's shaken her right up, I couldn't leave her.'

'No, you've done the right thing, Johnny. But I'm worried about the blokes coming here when there's a copper across the passageway.'

'It's all right, they know to be discreet. I knew having him so close would cause problems.'

'It'll be fine. Charlotte's working on him. We've got more pressing matters to be worrying about. Who the hell have you pissed off?'

'I dunno. I think it might be The Top.'

'Bloody hell, Johnny, I hope not. We ain't strong enough to go up against him. If it's The Top, we can all say our goodbyes soon.'

'I dunno, it might not be. But if it is, we're fucked.'

Charlotte came back into the room with Gerty, and Georgina instructed her to keep an eye out the window for Ned and the Barker twins. She unconsciously rubbed her finger where her mother's wedding ring had once been, deep in thought.

Twenty minutes later, Charlotte sneaked Ned and the Barkers into her flat. Despite being told to keep their voices down, they couldn't hide their delight at seeing Georgina and she thought it a shame that the happiness of the reunion was marred by the murder of Max. And now they each had a possible death sentence hanging over their heads too.

Georgina went to Charlotte's room and dressed. When she came back into the front room, she could feel the tension. All eyes set on her as if they were waiting for her to come up with an answer to the problem. But she didn't know what to do. How could she when she had no idea who they were fighting?

'Take me to him, Johnny,' she said, her face stern.

'Who?'

'The Top, of course.'

'Are you sure?'

'I said so, didn't I? There's no point in pussy-footing around. Take me to The Top and let's get this sorted.'

She watched as Johnny, Ned and the Barker twins looked at one another then back to her. Johnny went to speak but she quickly jumped in.

'Don't question me. You came here because you haven't got a fucking clue what to do. You're scared, the lot of you. And I don't blame you. You've brought this to my doorstep and now I'll deal with it. Come on, let's go.'

'Now?'

'Yes, Johnny, now,' she answered and marched towards the door. 'The rest of you, sit tight and stay out of sight. If we're not back by lunchtime, run.'

She crept past PC Batten's door and quietly closed the front door. She got into the car and Johnny sat beside her, his face pale and she could see the tautness in his jaw.

'You can't take a gun,' he warned.

'I know, more's the pity. I'll leave it in the car.'

The sun began to rise as they headed towards Lewisham. Georgina's mind turned, thinking about how she'd approach The Top and what she'd say. That's if she even got to see him. From what she'd been told, the man refused visitors.

Before she knew it, they were in Lewisham and Johnny pulled up outside a grand house. 'We're here,' he said nervously.

'You can wait in the car if you like,' Georgina offered as she reluctantly placed her gun in the glove compartment.

'No, I'll come with you. This is my mess. It's me they're after, not you.'

Georgina didn't think it was a good idea for Johnny to accompany her and wanted to protect him but if The Top and his gang were out to kill Johnny, they'd get him with or without her. He knocked on the large doors and a small hatch opened.

'Ralph, it's me, Johnny Dymond and I'm with Miss Garrett.'

Ralph didn't respond but opened the door. When Georgina walked in, she was taken aback by the size of the stark, white hallway. They followed Ralph up the sweeping staircase where two men the size of tanks greeted them with coldness. Ralph went into a room and closed the door while Johnny was frisked. Then Georgina held her arms out at her sides as the other large man frisked her. His hands lingered too long over the edge of her breasts and she stepped back, glaring at him as he sneered at her.

Ralph returned and nodded to the men who escorted

them into the room. At last, Georgina saw a friendly face she recognised and smiled at Slugs.

'It's a bit bloody early,' he said as he walked towards her with his arm outstretched. 'But good to see you none the less. We've been expecting you.'

'Hello, Slugs,' she replied as she shook his rough hand. She'd met him on a few occasions, one of David's men who had visited the hospital when David had been injured in the bomb blast.

'Take a seat, Miss Garrett. Would you like coffee?'

'That would be very welcome, thank you.'

'I'll have one an' all,' Johnny said.

'I ain't waiting on you, you ugly git,' Slugs replied with a chuckle and turned to another two men stood by the door. 'Coffee, three cups.'

One of the men went outside and Slugs turned back to Georgina. 'You did a cracking job of getting out of Holloway.'

'Thank you.'

'Look, I can guess why you're here. I realise you ain't been around for a few years and things have changed, but you made a big mistake robbing the proceeds from the beer farm. To be fair, I can understand you'd need the money but you should have looked into it first to see who you were dealing with. The Top was surprised that you fucked up.'

'It weren't Miss Garrett. She didn't know nuffink about it,' Johnny quickly said, the desperation apparent in his voice.

Slugs looked confused.

'It was me, mate. I fucked up. But if I'd known it was The Top fronting it up, I wouldn't have gone near it.'

Slugs chuckled again. 'Oh, Johnny, mate, it ain't The Top. He gets a load of barrels as a cut but it ain't his operation.'

Georgina threw a glance at Johnny, who looked as perplexed as her.

Slugs continued, 'It's the Zammits. Those Maltese bastards have got the West End sown up with their tarts and now they've diversified into this. I hate the slimy gits but I wouldn't want to upset them.'

'The Zammits… fuck me, that's all I need.'

'Yeah, you and Miss Garrett. They ain't gonna believe you did it on your own, mate.'

Georgina rose to her feet. 'Fine. At least we know who we're dealing with.'

Slugs jumped up too. 'Wait, Miss Garrett. You can't go steaming in there. You don't know what they're like and believe me, you don't want to find out.'

'Then what do you suggest? I can't sit by and watch them take down my men one by one.'

'Here,' Slugs answered and walked over to a large desk with a leather inlay. He quickly jotted down something and handed it to Georgina. 'Jacob Flowers is the man you want to see. He's the Zammits' accountant. He'll negotiate on your behalf but he comes at a cost. He's the only geezer the Zammits will entertain.'

'What about The Top?'

'What about him?' Slugs asked.

'He obviously has a rapport with the Zammits.'

'Yeah, he does, but he's already spoken to them and they won't make a deal with him. The Zammits want your blood and your only chance is Jacob Flowers.'

'Why has The Top already spoken to them on my behalf?'

'I dunno, Miss Garrett. I suppose because you're a bit of a legend and he admires that, you know, what with you being a woman an' all that.'

'Let me speak to him.'

'Who? The Top?'

'Yes.'

Slugs sucked in a long breath as he shook his head. 'I'm sorry, Miss Garrett, but that won't be possible.'

'Why not?'

'He don't see no one. Not ever. I'm sure you've heard about his connections with the IRA. He can't risk anyone being in a position where they'd be able to identify him. I hope you understand. So, anything you want to say to The Top will have to go through me.'

Georgina's feelings had been correct. She'd guessed that she wouldn't get access to The Top but she had a pressing question on her mind. She looked down at her boots and when she lifted her eyes, she blurted, 'Was it The Top who killed David?'

Slugs, his eyes wide, turned away and he walked back towards the desk. She waited for an answer but nothing came. A short man with a thick mop of red hair came into the room, carrying a tray. Slugs indicated to him to leave the tray on the side and then the man scurried away.

Once the door closed again, Georgina continued. 'Well,

did he?' she pressed, desperate to know the truth even though there was something inside her that wanted to run from it.

Slugs, now stood behind the desk, avoided her searching glare.

'You must have known I'd want to find out what happened to him and Victor. Don't bullshit me, Slugs. Did The Top kill David Maynard?'

Slugs swallowed hard and slowly nodded.

This wasn't the response she'd wanted. It was hard to take in the fact that she was in the same house as the man who had killed David. It felt like she'd been punched in the stomach and her legs felt weak. She remembered this feeling when she'd seen Lash laid dead on the ground, a bullet in his chest.

'And Victor?' she asked shakily.

Slugs nodded again but still wouldn't look her in the eye. Guilty conscience, she assumed. Slugs had worked for David but now worked for the man who had murdered him. He clearly had no integrity, which left her with no respect for him.

She licked her dry lips and tried to compose herself.

'Get me out of here,' she whispered to Johnny, hoping her legs wouldn't give way until they were in the car.

Johnny leapt up and went to support her but she pushed him briskly away. She wouldn't show weakness, not here. She marched towards the door without any further words to Slugs, Johnny trotting behind her. She just wanted to get out from being under the same roof as the man who had helped to destroy her life.

Once in the car, she handed Johnny the piece of paper that Slugs had given her. 'Drive,' she said, staring blankly ahead as she fought to hold back tears.

'I'm sorry, Miss Garrett.'

'I know. And so will The Top be when I've finished with him,' she answered solemnly.

11

Jacob Flowers sat at his desk in his basement flat, under an impressive house above. He lived in the house with his wife, Elsie, but worked from his basement and would insist his wife spent her days downstairs too. This way, he could keep an eye on her and watch that she wasn't looking at other men.

The house had three bedrooms, a sumptuous lounge, large dining room and was decorated to the highest order. It was exactly how Elsie Flowers liked it, though she rarely had the opportunity to show it off, except at Christmas and Easter when they would entertain guests from her church. Jacob detested the vicar and hated socialising but he'd be there as the loving husband and to ensure that his wife behaved appropriately. Though meek-mannered, there was nothing Elsie Flowers liked more than money and indulging her lavish tastes. She wore expensive clothes and precious jewels but Jacob was happy to oblige his wife. After all, she was his creation. He'd moulded her to what she was. He'd designed a virtuous woman, one with standards and good morals. A woman respected in the church for her charitable work. Immaculately presented and with impeccable manners, she appeared to be the perfect wife. But she'd once been nothing more than the child of a destitute woman who'd begged and whored herself to sailors.

He'd been a merchant when he'd first encountered Elsie's mother begging in the Port of London. Something about the woman had struck him, she'd reminded him of his dead sister. Somewhat out of character for him, Jacob had showed the woman kindness by giving her a few bob now and then. Several months later, Elsie's mother had turned up at his office, her face scabby and she'd struggled for breath. She'd pushed Elsie in front of her ragged skirts and pleaded with Jacob to take her, saying she was dying and there was no one to care for the girl. She'd promised that Elsie was a good girl and would clean and cook for her keep. The child was only nine years old, her blue eyes full of sadness and brimming with tears. Jacob had immediately dismissed any notion of caring for the girl, but two days later he found Elsie sitting on his doorstep and her mother's body was discovered floating alongside a ship carrying African ivory.

He could have taken Elsie to an orphanage but after giving her a hot meal, she'd been quick to clean the dishes. So he'd allowed her to stay that night. And when he'd woken in the morning, he'd been pleasantly surprised to find she'd cleaned the house. As quiet as a mouse, she was. Never uttered a word. So, one night led to another which led to a week, a month and then a year.

Then one morning, six years after Elsie had arrived in his home, he'd looked over the top of his newspaper to see her reaching up to pull open the heavy drapes. The sunlight through the window silhouetted the profile of her slim body and he noticed the curve of her breasts. Her blonde hair glistened and when she turned to look at him with wide, innocent eyes, he'd found that her purity aroused him. From that day, he'd taken her as his lover, though had never penetrated her. Always compliant, Elsie had been happy to satisfy his *unusual* sexual desires. From then, Jacob had known that he wanted her to remain a virgin and soon married her. A small ceremony with no frills. After all, they weren't celebrating their love, just a mutual need: she required caring for and he wanted to possess her.

He tapped out the tobacco from his pipe and stuffed in some fresh, thinking how, ten years later, the relationship had changed. Elsie no longer showed any enthusiasm when she saw to his sexual needs. It was mechanical on her part, merely going through the motions. It lacked excitement. Had it always been that way? He shrugged and supposed it was better than nothing and at least he was confident that she was remaining chaste and still pure. That thought stirred his passion, but the idea of another man touching his wife turned his stomach and he knew that if she ever allowed it, he'd slit her throat.

He heard the door open that connected the basement to the house, and was surprised it was already ten o'clock. Elsie appeared with a tray, carrying his usual breakfast of black tea, one slice of bread and a smoked kipper, an apple and two peppermints.

'Good morning, Jacob,' she said dolefully as she placed the tray on his desk.

He eyed her up and down, unhappy with her attire. 'Your skirt is too short and your blouse is too tight. Go and change,' he ordered.

Elsie slipped back up to the house while he ate his breakfast, annoyed at her for opting to wear a skirt that revealed so much of her calves and a blouse that accentuated her bosom. She should know better, and he was disappointed that he'd had to tell her. He'd reprimand her later and remind her of how the wife of an important accountant and businessman should dress.

Much to his irritation, his breakfast was interrupted by someone rapping on the front door to his basement flat.

'Elsie... Elsie...' he shouted.

She came hurrying into his office and he was pleased to see that she'd already changed her clothes to something that he deemed suitable. Her loose, dark blue dress was buttoned up the front to the neck and it hung just a few inches over her ankles. He thought the single row of pearls she wore gave her outfit an air of sophistication and he smiled, satisfied.

'See who is at the door,' he told her and then popped a peppermint in his mouth.

Moments later, Elsie came back looking flustered.

'Well, who was it?'

'It's a lady, but she looks like a man. She said her name is Miss Garrett, and she wants to talk to you.'

'Does she indeed. What are you standing there for? Show her in,' he snapped.

Elsie rushed out while Jacob pushed his tray to one side and interlocked his long, thin fingers. He'd heard of Georgina Garrett. Just about everyone had. But he'd never had the desire to meet her. He found the thought of a woman conducting business quite repulsive. But if she was here, she must require his services and he wouldn't turn away her money.

Elsie showed Miss Garrett into the room, followed by

an extravagantly dressed man. Elsie hadn't mentioned anyone accompanying Miss Garrett and he watched his wife, pleased when she took her position in a seat in the corner of the room and lowered her eyes to look at the floor. He turned his attention back to Miss Garrett. She looked masculine, her clothes those of a workman, and he wondered if she was one of those perverts who liked other women. Of course, if Miss Garrett was a *she-man* it would make sense and offered an explanation of her fierce reputation in Battersea.

'Thank you for seeing me, Mr Flowers,' she said, unsmiling.

'Please, take a seat,' he offered, intrigued by the beauty he saw behind her awful clothes.

'Thank you. This is my colleague, Mr Dymond. We've been sent by The Top as I understand you may be in a position to help with a small problem I have.'

'Would you care to divulge your problem?'

'It seems there has been a misunderstanding with the Zammits. A robbery was undertaken by my men who, unfortunately, hadn't carried out their due diligence thoroughly which resulted in unwittingly turning over one of their operations.'

Jacob sat back in his chair, a smirk on his thin lips, and drummed his fingertips on his desk. Oh, Miss Garrett was going to make him a lot of money and he was incredibly gratified she'd come to him. 'What do you know about me?' he asked.

'Nothing.'

'As I thought, and that's good because my work has to be conducted with the utmost discretion. I'm an accountant, a businessman and a negotiator. The very best. There are certain, shall we say, *businesses*, who will only work with me and me alone. Consequently, if I refuse to *help* you, you'll be left high and dry.'

'You'll negotiate on my behalf?'

'For a price and that price will be significant. I trust you have the funds to meet my expenses?'

'Yes.'

'You don't know my prices.'

'Whatever they are, I can afford them.'

'Then I shall agree to negotiate on your behalf. I'll expect fifty per cent payment in advance and the remaining monies due on completion of a satisfactory outcome. Cash.'

'Fine. I'll send the money to you this afternoon but in the meantime, the Zammits are a threat to the safety of my men. I want your assurance that no further attacks will occur while you are in the negotiation stages.'

'You have my word. Here are my terms,' Jacob said and scribbled down a figure that was twice as much as he'd normally demand. After all, the woman must be desperate to have come to him and he was sure he could milk her for a small fortune. When he handed her the invoice, she didn't baulk and he wondered if he could have charged her even more. 'My wife will see you out. I'll expect payment this afternoon and to see you in my office five days from now.'

As Miss Garrett and Mr Dymond scraped back their chairs, Jacob's eyes set on his wife. She momentarily glanced from under her lashes to look at Mr Dymond and then he noticed her cheeks flush. He knew it! He knew Elsie could be turned by a good-looking face! That quick glance, her reddened cheeks and flustered manner told him all he needed to know – his wife was capable of being a slut, but he wouldn't stand for it. Oh no, Elsie Flowers wasn't going to make a fool out of him, he'd make sure of it!

Johnny tightly gripped the steering wheel as a police car passed them and Miss Garrett sunk low in the passenger seat.

'It's all right, they've gone,' he said, then asked, 'How the hell are we gonna pay Jacob Flowers?'

'For now, we'll have to use the proceeds from the robbery. That'll cover the first instalment.'

'But the Zammits are gonna want that money back.'

'Yes, Johnny, I'm fully aware of that but one step at a time. This will buy us some time while I work out where I'm going to get the rest of the money from.'

'I'm sorry about all this, Miss Garrett.'

'No more apologies, let's just get it sorted,' she said shortly.

They drove on for a few more minutes in silence and Johnny found himself thinking about Mrs Flowers. She seemed a shy and pretty little thing. There was something about her that reminded him of his first and only love, Daisy. God, he'd loved that woman with every ounce of his being and had nearly lost the plot completely when she'd died with the flu. Daisy had the same eyes as Elsie. He wondered how she'd ended up married to Jacob Flowers. The man was spindly with beady eyes and a long, pointed nose. He was sinister in his looks and nature. He couldn't fathom what Mrs Flowers saw in him. 'Bit of an odd couple, weren't they?' he said.

'Yes, and I got the impression that she's very much under his thumb. I've seen it before, men like him.'

'What, you reckon he knocks her about?'

'Without a doubt, the poor woman.'

Johnny sighed deeply. He hated the thought of any woman getting beaten by their husband. He'd seen his mother used as a punch-bag often enough by his stepfather. She'd hidden her bruises well but Johnny had known what was going on. He'd been too young to protect her, but it had all changed one day when, in a drunken rage, his stepdad had kicked off in front of Johnny's older brothers. After a terrible fight, the three young men had sent their stepdad packing. His mother had been grateful but she'd had to work twice as hard to support them and had died before Johnny had turned fifteen. He missed his dear old mum and hated his stepfather for marring his memories of her. For every loving memory, there was a dark one too. A recollection of seeing his mum crying, cowering in a corner with his stepfather towering over her with clenched fists. If he ever set eyes on that man again, he'd happily put a bullet in his chest.

His mind drifted back to Mrs Flowers. 'I don't like the thought of him giving her a good hiding.'

Georgina's head snapped round. 'Whatever you're thinking, forget it, Johnny. She's a married woman, stay clear.'

'No, I wasn't thinking that,' he protested, though he had to admit to himself that he did fancy her. She was the spit of his Daisy.

'Good. We've got enough to be worrying about without you landing yourself in it by upsetting Jacob Flowers.'

'Yeah, yeah, I know. And talking of things to be worrying

about, how are we gonna get the police off your back? You can't keep hiding and hoping they won't find you.'

'I've got something in mind but let's square things with the Zammits first.'

Johnny smiled to himself. He should have guessed that Miss Garrett would have something up her sleeve to keep her out of prison, though he couldn't imagine what. He assumed it had something to do with PC Batten. If it had been down to him, that copper would have been out on his ear. But Miss Garrett was clever and he didn't doubt that she knew what she was doing. Christ, he thought, there was so much going on. The Zammits were vying for his blood. Miss Garrett wanted vengeance against The Top. The police wanted her back behind bars. Life was never boring around her. And though the fear of being killed like Max should have been playing on his mind, he found he couldn't stop thinking about Mrs Flowers.

Charlotte had been looking out the window and was relieved when she saw Johnny pull up with Georgina. She rushed to the door to let them in and Johnny pulled her to one side.

'I'll get rid of the blokes,' he whispered, 'she ain't in a good mood. Slugs confirmed that it was The Top who killed Mr Maynard and Victor.'

Charlotte gasped and her heart sank. First Georgina had been denied seeing her children and now this. Georgina would put on a brave face, she always did, but Charlotte felt sorry for her.

Johnny quickly rounded up the men, reassuring them

that Jacob Flowers would be negotiating with the Zammits on their behalf. They said farewell, leaving Gerty to rest in Charlotte's bed. They couldn't send the girl back to her house, not with Max's corpse rotting there.

'I'll get off now as well and make the first payment to Flowers.'

'Yeah, you do that and keep your eyes off his wife,' Georgina replied.

Dog seemed to sense that Georgina was upset and sat beside her legs with his head resting on her lap. Charlotte didn't know what to say. No words would calm Georgina's simmering fury. All she could do was bring her sweet tea.

They sat quietly, each deep in their own thoughts. Charlotte's mind had drifted and her stomach was fluttering at the thought of sharing a bag of chips with Tim later that evening. Georgina broke the silence.

'I'll get Dina to put Gerty up in her flat for now.'

With her feet tucked under her legs and a cup of hot tea in hand, Charlotte was brought back to reality and asked, 'Sorry, what did you say?'

'I said, I'll get Dina to put Gerty up for a while.'

'Yeah, good idea.'

Nearly an hour passed and Charlotte brought Georgina more tea. She saw her look at the clock on the hearth, her face pensive.

'Johnny should be at Jacob Flowers' house now. I've got a day or two to work out how I'm going to get the money together to pay the Zammits back, along with the final payment to Jacob.'

'Blimey, Georgina, this is all you need on top of everything else. What can I do to help?'

'Nothing. Just work on Tim.'

'I am. He's taking me out tonight.'

'Good.'

A tap on the door startled Charlotte but she recognised the knock. 'That'll be Lord Hamilton,' she said, rising to her feet with a smile.

After she answered the door, she quietly warned him of Georgina's bad mood.

'Don't worry, my dear girl, you can count on me to brighten her up,' he said and swanned into the room, greeting Georgina with a kiss on the back of her hand.

'So nice to see you again, my dear.'

'And you. You're looking very smart,' she replied, eyeing his beige checked tweed jacket, beige trousers, rust coloured jumper with a crisp white shirt and tie. The sort of day clothes that only people from *old* money would wear.

'One likes to make the effort. One never knows who one might meet. Tell me, am I interrupting anything?'

'No,' Charlotte answered. 'We were just talking about how we can earn a good few bob, and quickly. Do you want a cuppa?'

'No, thank you. But if it's cash you want, I may be able to offer a suggestion,' he said, turning to look at Georgina with a wicked grin as he twisted the end of his moustache in his fingers.

'Do tell,' Georgina said and Charlotte sat back down, pleased to see that the presence of Lord Hamilton had seemed to lift her spirits a little.

'Art, my dear. Art.'

Charlotte rolled her eyes, saying cynically, 'Oh yeah, art

you reckon? Well how come you ain't rich? If you were, you wouldn't be living here and paying me rent money.'

'Quite. But I had the unfortunate luck of collaborating with an unsavoury character who left me penniless.'

'I'm sorry to hear that, but I don't know anything about art,' Georgina said.

'You don't have to know anything because I do! I'm the expert, and you, well, you're the muscle.'

This seemed to amuse Georgina. 'Tell me more,' she urged.

'I happen to know of an elderly gentleman, and when I say *gentleman*, I use the term loosely. Augustus Rice is quite the scoundrel. He lives in a grand home alone, in Hampshire, and has in his possession a collection of the most exquisite Old Masters, albeit not originals but—'

'—Stop,' Georgina interrupted. 'You've lost me. What are Old Masters?'

'An Old Master is an extremely skilled European painter pre-dating the eighteen hundreds.'

'I'm sorry I asked. Look, Lord Hamilton, I don't mean to be rude but this really isn't my bag.'

'Please, Georgina, hear me out. I'm going to make us both very wealthy.'

'Go on then,' she said, sighing.

'A few years ago, before the war, I worked with Augustus. He's fanatical about art, to the point of obsessional, especially anything by the Old Masters. After selling him a few paintings, he suggested that we should go into business together. The idea being, I would finance the reproductions of paintings and he would sell them abroad, in America. The

Americans adore European art and anything with history. We knew we could make a fortune. But it didn't work out how I'd hoped.'

'What happened?' Georgina asked.

'I commissioned an expert forger who didn't come cheaply. Augustus lined up keen buyers in America. It was all going swimmingly... only, Augustus never went to America. He kept fobbing me off and fabricating excuse after excuse. And then war broke out and it wasn't viable to ship crates of fine art to the States. But now I'm afraid he is threatening me. He's warned me that if I attempt to contact him again, he will inform my clients and the auction houses that I've sold them reproductions. I have a reputation to maintain. He could ruin me!'

'I see. And you want me to get the paintings from him?'

'Yes, exactly. When I sell them we can have a seventy-five, twenty-five cut.'

'Seventy-five in my favour.'

'You can't be serious, Georgina. I paid for the paintings. Twenty-five per cent profit will merely cover my original costs.'

'Fine. Thirty. You'll get nothing without me and I'm the one taking the risk in stealing them, so take it or leave it.'

Lord Hamilton twisted his moustache again, deep in thought. 'Deal,' he said, and shook Georgina's hand. 'It'll be worth it just to know that Augustus, the dreadful rascal, hasn't won.'

'But couldn't he still ruin your reputation?' Charlotte asked.

'Possibly, but not if Georgina's men terrify him into silence.

And, if Georgina is willing, I have several money-spinning ideas.'

'Oh, I'm always willing if it involves making money,' she said with a weak smile, but then her expression changed to one of seriousness and she asked, 'How soon can you sell the paintings?'

'I'd be able to sell a few of them immediately. The others may take a some weeks.'

'And what are they worth?'

'More than you'd imagine. Put it this way, my dear, the sale of one painting alone to the right person would cover my expenses for a year.'

'Good. Wait until Johnny returns and we'll make plans to collect the paintings tonight.'

'This is so exciting,' Charlotte said, clasping her hands together. 'I'm glad you're home, Georgina. Can I go on the job tonight?'

'No, you've got a date with Tim.'

Charlotte smiled. Yes, she did, and she was looking forward to it more than she cared to admit. But she knew Tim would have a fit if he had any idea what was being discussed just across the hall from where he lived, or that she was harbouring an escaped convict. They were from different worlds, him maintaining law and order and her breaking it. She wished she didn't like him as much as she did. This wasn't just a ploy to get him onside. She wasn't just fooling him and building his trust so that he'd work for Georgina. Her racing heart at the thought of him told her it was more than that. She was falling for him but knew their relationship was doomed before it had even started.

★

Johnny tapped tentatively on Jacob Flowers' basement flat door. He pushed his shoulders back and chest out, holding his head high. There was something about Mr Flowers that unnerved him but he wouldn't show it.

When Elsie Flowers answered the door, the undeniable excitement he felt at the prospect of seeing her again was soon replaced with a sinking feeling. Just as he and Miss Garrett had suspected, Mrs Flowers was sporting the evidence of a back-hander from her husband.

'Please, come in,' she said coyly, pulling her blonde hair over the obvious bruise and cut on her eyebrow.

'You don't have to put up with that from him,' Johnny whispered as he pointed to her injury.

A look of panic flashed in her eyes and she glanced fearfully over her shoulder. 'Please, don't say anything and don't talk to me again.'

He could feel his top lip twitch with anger. The woman was clearly petrified of her husband, which narked Johnny. He felt an overwhelming urge to pick her up, carry her away and look after her. But not before he'd given Mr Flowers a good kick-in.

Common sense prevailed and he sucked in a deep breath before reluctantly nodding at Mrs Flowers to indicate he'd hold his tongue. She showed him through to her husband's office and sat in the same corner she had before, her eyes lowered, staring at the darkly varnished floorboards. Christ, she looked uncannily like his beloved Daisy to the point where it almost rattled him.

Johnny refused to take a seat and slapped an envelope

of cash on the desk. Jacob Flowers sneered wryly and meticulously counted the money. 'Fine, you can go now,' he said to Johnny dismissively with a belittling shoo of his gangly hand. 'And pass a message to your *boss* that she or he, or whatever Miss Garrett likes to class herself as, can expect good results.'

Johnny seethed inside. He'd have liked to reach across the desk and grab Jacob Flowers by the scruff of his neck and haul him to the floor where he'd kick the shit out of him. Instead, he threw Mrs Flowers a sympathetic look, spun on his heel and marched out.

At the front door, Mrs Flowers unlocked it, avoiding any eye contact. Johnny reached into his coat pocket and as he left, he slipped a tiny piece of paper into her hand.

'This is where you can find me,' he said quietly.

She went to thrust it back, but Johnny squeezed her hand shut. 'I'll be there if you need me,' he said.

She looked up at his face, her eyes a mixture of fear and gratefulness. He thought she might start crying but she gently pushed him away.

Johnny didn't hang around. He didn't want to get her into trouble with her husband. He headed back to the car but looked behind one final time. She was gone and the door was closed. He hated the thought of that beautiful and fragile woman being left alone with Jacob Flowers. And he hoped he hadn't made matters worse for her by slipping her his address.

Later that night, it had gone midnight. The waning moon offered little illumination in the dark countryside of

Hampshire. Johnny, Nobby and Ned, dressed in black and fully armed, crept alongside a high brick wall surrounding Augustus Rice's house. Eric waited in the lane in the car.

'I'm bleedin' freezing,' Ned moaned.

'Yeah, me an' all but we'll be inside soon. Remember, straight in and out, no mucking about,' Johnny said, his heart hammering.

They passed the black wrought iron double gates and glanced through to look at the house.

'Cor, he must be worth a few bob,' Nobby said.

'Shush,' Johnny reminded him. Georgina had warned them that there were two large kennelled dogs. Though it was inevitable, they didn't want to set the dogs off before they'd gained entry into the house.

They made their way round to the back of the house where Nobby gave them each a leg up and over the wall. Johnny landed with a heavy thud in the dirt and Ned fell forwards into a bush.

'I'm too old for this malarkey,' he grumbled as he climbed back on his feet.

'Shut up, Ned,' Nobby snapped after he'd somehow managed to scramble over the top of the wall. 'It ain't right that Max ain't here. You're fucking lucky the Zammits didn't come for you first but you ain't stopped fucking moaning. I'm sick of hearing it.'

'Who the fuck do you think you're talking to?'

'You, you whinging bastard.'

'I'll fucking have you,' Ned said through gritted teeth and stepped towards Nobby.

'All right, all right, ladies, let's calm it, eh,' Johnny said and stood in between them. 'You can sort out your differences later. Let's concentrate on the job in hand.'

'Yeah, but I'm warning you, Nobby, I'll fucking have you.'

Even in the darkness, Johnny could see Nobby smile. The thought of Ned picking a fight with Nobby was ridiculous. Ned was half Nobby's size and had a good few years on him to boot. Though Ned could be vicious and wouldn't back down from anyone.

'Come on, hurry up. If you two don't shut up, you'll have his dogs barking,' Johnny whispered.

Ducking as they ran, they scooted to the back door. Nobby wrapped a towel around his hand and punched through a glass panel. The sound of shattering glass set Augustus's dogs off and the air was suddenly filled with the ferocious sound of them barking.

'Quick, get us in before the racket wakes him up,' Ned said urgently as Nobby carefully reached through to quickly turn the key that was left in the lock.

They scrambled inside, closing the door behind them. Johnny held his breath and listened but could only hear the dogs' incessant barking from their kennels on the front lawn.

'This way,' he said, leading Ned and Nobby through the boot room and into a large hallway.

As they made their way to the foot of the stairs, a croaky voice spoke. 'Who goes there?'

Johnny waved his hand to the others and they pressed their bodies against the wall, the staircase above them. They stood motionless and listened to each step creak as Augustus slowly came down the stairs, stopping about halfway.

'I know there's someone there, but be warned, the police are on their way.'

Nobby shot Johnny a worried look but Johnny shook his head. The police weren't on their way. Georgina had got the layout of the house from Lord Hamilton, and told him there was only one telephone in the house. It was in the drawing room so Augustus couldn't have called them, despite his threat.

'Show yourself!'

Johnny casually stepped away from the wall and out of the shadows, his handgun pointing at Augustus. The man's eyes squinted in the dark and when he realised Johnny was standing at the foot of the stairs aiming his gun, Augustus turned and fled. As he scrambled back up the stairs, he lost his footing and cried out in pain and panic.

'Stay right where you are,' Johnny called, 'or I'll shoot.'

Augustus, now laying inelegantly across five steps, turned jerkily towards Johnny, his hands in the air. 'Don't shoot... don't shoot,' he pleaded.

'Do as I say and I won't. Now, slowly, get up and come towards me.'

Augustus nodded and pulled off his bed-hat, which was almost covering his eyes. He slowly stood up, using the bannister to steady himself, and cautiously padded down the stairs.

'Right, sit there,' Johnny ordered, pointing to a large dark wooden seat that put him in mind of the electric chair he'd seen in films from America.

Augustus shuffled over and flopped himself down, pulling his dressing gown over his night-shirt. 'What do you want? Money? Well, you're out of luck, I don't have any,' he snapped, suddenly brazen.

Miss Garrett had told Johnny that Augustus Rice was a mean man who'd swindled Lord Hamilton out of a small fortune. Johnny had no sympathy for the man. His thin, white hair stood on end, making him look crazy. And though he must be scared, his eyes showed nothing but disdain.

Johnny held his gun towards Augustus's face. 'I want the key to your gate.'

'You won't find it.'

'I will when you tell me where it is.'

'I'm not telling you anything! Do you really think I'm going to help you steal from me?'

'Yes, if you value your life.'

'Poppycock! I've nothing here that common thugs like you would want. Bugger orf, be gone with you!'

'Well, well, well. You're a brave old goat, I'll give you that. But I ain't messing around, Mr Rice. I'll ask you one last time… where is the key to the front gate?'

'Up my arse!' Augustus answered and roared with laughter.

Johnny turned to Nobby. 'You heard him. Get it out.'

Nobby sauntered towards Augustus with a wicked grin, giving the impression that he was going to enjoy rough handling him and violating his dignity.

'Wait… what on earth do you think you're going to do?' Augustus screeched, looking horrified.

'He's gonna get the key, of course, and he won't be gentle,' Johnny answered.

'No… no… don't touch me. It's in the drawer,' Augustus

said defeatedly, pointing towards a long receiver table against the wall.

Nobby rummaged in the drawer and retrieved the key. Ned appeared from the kitchen with a raw chicken and three lamb chops.

''Ere, give these to the dogs. It might shut 'em up,' he said, handing Nobby the fresh meat.

Johnny was impressed by Ned thinking on his feet, not that it mattered that the dogs were barking. Augustus lived on the outskirts of the New Forest and there wasn't another house around for a mile or two.

Nobby left the front door open and, minutes later, the only noise Johnny could hear was the sound of the car engine and wheels on crunching gravel as Eric drove the car up the drive.

'Some guard dogs they are,' Nobby said when he came back into the house after unlocking the gate. 'The grub soon shut them up.'

'Just take what you want and go,' Augustus said, looking at Johnny with contempt.

'Don't worry, we will,' he said and patted the old man's cheek three times.

'Get your hands off me, you shirker. Men like you should be ashamed of yourselves. You should be fighting for your country, not robbing decent men who fought for your freedom in the Great War!'

Johnny ignored his scathing remarks and told Ned and Nobby to search the place. 'You know what we're looking for,' he added.

As the men went from room to room, Johnny whistled a tune from the *Mr Cinders* musical, *Spread a Little*

Happiness. It seemed apt, after all, everything was going as planned.

'You think this is funny, do you? Scaring an old man half to death and robbing him of his belongings?'

Johnny shrugged and continued whistling.

'Your mother should have drowned you at birth, you're a scourge on society. Though your mother was probably nothing more than a common whore.'

Johnny stopped whistling.

'Oh, hit a nerve, have I? Well, if your mother was a slut then I should imagine you're a bastard. Filth from the slums.'

Johnny leapt forward and grabbed a handful of material around the neck of the man's night-shirt. He pulled him to his feet, his face now inches from his own. 'Don't talk about my mother,' he seethed.

Augustus maintained his composure and grinned cruelly. 'Sluts from the slums. I fucked lots of them for pennies. I probably fucked your mother!'

Johnny's jaw clenched and he threw Augustus back down. The man missed the seat and fell to the floor, hitting his head on the side of the chair.

'I warned you,' Johnny said, looking down at him.

Augustus didn't move.

Johnny lightly kicked his ribs but there was no response. 'Shit, shit, shit,' he mumbled, fearing he'd inadvertently killed the man.

'What's going on?' Ned asked, looking at Augustus sprawled on the parquet flooring.

'He fell.'

'Is he dead?'

'I dunno,' Johnny answered, and crouched beside him for a closer look. 'Yeah, I think so.'

'We weren't supposed to kill him.'

'I know that,' Johnny snapped. 'I told you, he fell.'

'If you say so.'

'I do, all right.'

'Fine, keep your hair on.'

'Sorry. How we doing?'

'One more to find,' Ned answered.

'Have a look upstairs.'

'Stupid stuck-up bastard,' Ned said with disgust as he stepped over Augustus's lifeless body and a puddle of blood that had pooled beside his head.

Johnny paced back and forth. Georgina had been very specific about not killing Augustus. She wasn't going to be happy. The murder of a wealthy gent would have the police working doubly hard to solve the crime. It was something they really didn't need to contend with at the moment.

Ned came back downstairs carrying a large painting. 'Got it,' he said. 'That's all the ones on the list.'

'Good, put it in the car then come back and give me a hand with him.'

'What are we gonna do with him?'

'I dunno yet. Go on, hurry up,' Johnny answered, debating with himself on whether it would be best to bury Augustus in his garden or take his body back to Alexandra Avenue and put him under cement in the cellar with the other stiffs. He decided on the latter.

Nobby came back in with Ned, shaking his head.

'Nice one, Johnny,' he said sarcastically.

'Yeah, all right, spare me the lecture. Just give us a hand shifting him.'

'Where to?' Ned asked.

'We're taking him with us.'

'Are you joking?'

'No. Grab his feet. Nobby, you take his arms.'

'Hang on a minute, mate,' said Ned. 'You sure you've thought this through? The boot is already full and the rest of the paintings are on the roof. Where are we gonna put *him*?'

'We ain't got time to fuck about. Just grab him, will ya! He can squeeze in the back seat with you.'

'No fucking way. I ain't sitting next to a dead body all the way back to London. And there ain't room. There's stuff on the back seat and Nobby takes up most of the bleedin' space as it is.'

'Then you'll have to have him across your laps.'

'You can fuck off, Johnny. Urgh, there's no way I'm having a stiff on my lap.'

'All right, Eric can drive. You can sit in the front. Mr Rice here can sit in between me and Nobby.'

Ned shook his head disapprovingly but helped them shift the body to the car. They tried to sit him upright but he kept leaning to one side.

'Nobby, get in,' Johnny said, 'And help me to hold him up.'

'What about the dogs?' Ned asked.

'What about them?'

'We can't leave them there. They'll starve to death. Miss Garrett will do her nut if she finds out we've left the dogs to die.'

Johnny realised that Ned had a good point. 'Untie them and let them out the gate. Someone will find them.'

'What if they go for me?'

'Fucking hell, Ned. Just do it!' Johnny barked.

With a huff Ned walked up to the dogs, saying 'Good boys,' as he unleashed them. 'Off you go,' he urged.

They seemed unsure at first but when Eric tooted the car horn, they bolted, running off through the gate and along the country lane.

'Happy now?' he said to Johnny as he climbed into the car.

'Yeah,' Johnny replied shortly.

Ned locked the gate behind them and as they set off, Johnny was pleased to be away.

It didn't seem to bother Nobby that they had a dead body in the back with them, but Johnny grimaced. 'Put your foot down, Eric. I want to get back to Battersea before Mr Rice here starts stinking,' he said, winding down the window.

'At least it ain't hot,' Ned laughed. 'But I hope it don't rain. The paintings on the roof have only got a couple of blankets wrapped round them.'

They'd been travelling for about an hour when Johnny was stunned as Nobby suddenly yelled out.

'Argh... he moved. He fucking moved,' Nobby shouted.

'What?' Johnny asked, but before Nobby could answer, to Johnny's horror, Augustus made a moaning sound.

Nobby twisted in his seat, looking as if he was trying to move away from the body that appeared to be coming back to life.

'He's alive... He's a-fucking-live,' Nobby said, sounding horrified and squirming in his seat.

'Then kill him,' Ned shouted, 'Fucking kill him.'

There wasn't much room to swing their arms but Johnny and Nobby started frantically punching Augustus in the face and head, and all the while Nobby made a deep screaming noise with each punch.

Augustus's head flopped from side to side with each blow. His blood splattered over Johnny's face and across the interior of the car. After a few minutes of exertion, they stopped hitting him.

'Is he dead?' Nobby asked cautiously.

Johnny was about to say, 'I think so,' but unbelievably, they heard Augustus groan.

'Fucking die, you bastard,' Johnny said as they resumed punching him again. His knuckles were bruised and sore now but they couldn't allow Augustus to live to tell his story to the police. Kidnap would carry a heavy sentence.

'I think he's a goner now, Johnny,' Ned said from the passenger seat.

Johnny's shoulders heaved up and down as he gasped for breath and studied Augustus's battered face. Yes, the man had finally stopped breathing. But Miss Garrett wasn't going to be happy about them returning with a dead man whose blood now stained her car.

'You get off to bed, I'll wait for Johnny,' Georgina told Charlotte.

'No, it's all right, I'll keep you company. Anyway, I wouldn't be able to sleep.'

'Suit yourself. But you'll be knackered for your next date with Tim tomorrow.'

'Yeah, but I should think he'll feel a bit groggy too after that sleeping pill I slipped him.'

'You did a good job, and you're sure he doesn't suspect anything?'

'Positive. I feel awful about drugging him though, especially as we had such a lovely evening together.'

'Charlotte, the man is a copper! I know you like him and that's up to you, but never lose sight of what he is.'

'Yeah, I know. I wish he weren't in the police force.'

'At least you're making good progress with him.'

'Cor, yeah, not 'alf. He was fascinated to hear about you and then said, *there are criminals who are good people and policemen who are bad... like his dad. It's not all black and white, there's grey areas too.*'

'Do you reckon we've got any chance of getting him to work for us?'

'I dunno, Georgina. I think so but not in a corrupt way, like for money or nothing. I think he might help to protect you for my sake.'

'Good. I don't care what his reasons are, just as long as we can get him on board. I'm gonna need him to help me get the rest of the Old Bill off my back.'

'You're still not going to tell me how, are you?'

'Nope, so stop asking me.'

'It'll be good when you can relax a bit more. It can't be easy worrying all the time that the Old Bill are going to cart you back off to prison.'

Georgina bit on her bottom lip. No, it wasn't easy living in constant fear of being captured. The thought of going back to Holloway plagued her night and day, but especially when she was alone in the dark. She'd be reminded of the endless loneliness she'd felt. The helplessness at not being able to help those unfortunate women who were so callously downtrodden by the vicious wardens. Charlotte didn't know the half of it. The girl had no idea that since Georgina had escaped, she would cry herself to sleep. She'd pull a pillow over her head to try and blot out the memory of the harrowing sounds of the prison. She'd bite into that pillow to try and stop the depressing feelings from overwhelming her. But more often than not, she couldn't control the fear.

'Are you all right?' Charlotte asked.

Georgina nodded but couldn't speak, worried that if she opened her mouth, she'd scream, or worse than that, she'd sob her heart out.

'You're not, are you?'

Georgina tried to stop the tears from falling but they came anyway.

'Oh, gawd, Georgina, what is it?' Charlotte asked, looking concerned.

'Nothing, it's nothing,' she answered, wiping her wet cheeks with the back of her hand. 'It's just *that* place. It gets to you. It gets under your skin and you can't get rid of it. I know I should put it behind me but... the things I saw... the...' Georgina paused and composed herself. 'Take no notice. I'm fine.'

They heard a car pull up outside and Charlotte went to the window.

'It's Johnny,' she said.

'Tell him to bring the paintings straight in here. Tim should be deeply asleep by now. And not a word to anyone ever about what you just saw.'

Moments later, Charlotte came back into the room, her eyes wide and lips pulled back.

'What?' Georgina asked, fearing bad news from the look on Charlotte's face.

'I'll, erm, let Johnny explain.'

Johnny came into the room next, carrying some of the paintings wrapped in blankets.

'Put them in Charlotte's room,' Georgina said. 'Then you'd better tell me why Charlotte looks horrified.'

She saw Johnny swallow hard and could tell from his jumpy demeanour that he was nervous. But the fact that he had the paintings indicated the job had gone well. Ned and Nobby followed in with more artwork, tipping their hats at her as they passed her. They looked nervous too and she wondered what on earth was going on.

'Spit it out,' she told Johnny when he returned to the room.

Ned and Nobby stood behind him, Nobby looking down and scuffing the floor with his big boots, just like a naughty schoolboy would do.

Johnny lit a cigar, blowing smoke in the air before saying, 'It went well. We got every painting on Lord Hamilton's list.'

'But?'

'But we accrued a bit extra.'

'I see. Well, whatever else you took, split it between the four of you.'

'Erm, no, not that sort of extra.'

'What sort of extra then?'

'Well, it ain't just the four of us. Five came back in the car.'

'Who?' Georgina asked, her hackles rising.

'Augustus Rice.'

'Are you kidding me? There's a fucking copper living just there,' she spat, pointing towards Tim's flat. 'And you've brought home the man you robbed. For fuck's sake, Johnny, why did you do that? What if he talks?'

'He won't be doing much talking... ever.'

'He's dead?'

'Yeah.'

Georgina slumped back on the sofa as she realised they'd murdered Augustus Rice. Her mind raced. She'd only recently escaped from prison and already she had a death on her hands. Although furious, she kept her voice at an even tone and asked, 'Why did you bring a body back with you?'

'I thought it was for the best. If I'd left him there, the police would eventually discover his body. At least with him here and buried in the cellar, he'll just be missing and though they might suspect foul play, there's nothing to prove it. There's nothing to point to us.'

Georgina sighed. She supposed Johnny's reasoning did sort of make sense. 'You'd better bring him in. Then tomorrow, once Tim is at work, I want you back round here pronto to bury him in the basement and bring whatever you need to conceal him.'

'Yes, Miss Garrett. I'll take the car away now and clean it up,' Johnny said and went to hurry away.

'Wait...'

Johnny stopped in the doorway.

'I gave you specific instructions not to kill him. Why did you disobey me?'

'It weren't like that, Miss Garrett. It was an accident. He fell over and bashed his head.'

'Fine,' she said. 'So why does my car need cleaning?'

'He, erm, came back from the dead.'

Ned piped up, saying with a chortle, 'Yeah, frightened the fucking life out of Nobby.'

Nobby elbowed Ned in the ribs, telling him, 'Shut up.'

Georgina smiled. Seeing the men exchanging a bit of banter like this reminded her of the old days before she'd been incarcerated. But as heartwarming as the feeling was, it was never far from her mind that she wanted the blood of The Top to be spilled on English soil. And when it was, she'd make sure that his body would never return home to Ireland.

12

Jacob Flowers had been satisfied at the outcome of the meeting with Temi Zammit, the son of the head of the notorious West End gang. Temi was willing to negotiate but had set the proviso that he wanted to be introduced to Miss Garrett. Jacob had tried to talk the man out of it, saying that Miss Garrett wasn't the elegant beauty he'd been expecting and was more of a man than a woman. None the less, Temi had insisted and Jacob had agreed to arrange it.

Now back in his office, he perused yesterday's newspaper as he waited for Elsie to bring him his lunch. His wife had been a disappointment of late and he'd expressed his displeasure by cutting off her spending money and disciplining her with her bible. He found a good whack around the head with the heavy book saved him damaging his hands on her. And how ironic, he thought and smiled, that the book that was filled with God's love would be the same book that punished her.

He scanned the front page of the Evening Standard. Black out at five twenty-one in the evening until eight-thirty in the morning. Churchill is ill and has developed pneumonia. The Russians close on Smyela. Jacob had no idea where Smyela was or what its significance was in the war, and neither did he care. Bombers had knocked out enemy communications through the Brenner Pass. War, war, war. He was bored of it.

Elsie came into the office carrying a tray which she placed on his desk. He looked at the meal she'd prepared with the extra beef he'd acquired from Temi Zammit. His mouth salivated at the sight of the juicy looking steak. Thanks to his questionable contacts, rationing hadn't affected their larder. As he cut into his steak, looking forward to seeing the blood ooze from the meat and onto his plate, he frowned when he realised that the steak was overcooked.

'You useless woman!' he screeched. 'This steak isn't rare. It's practically incinerated.'

His eyes shot to the corner of the room where his wife sat. He glared at her accusingly as she trembled in her seat. 'This isn't fit for a dog to eat. Take it away,' he ordered.

Elsie jumped to his command and went to pick up the tray. As she did, he grabbed her wrist, gripping it hard. With his eyes now fixed on the steak, a thought crossed his mind. 'How did you manage to overcook this? Was your mind on something else? Were you thinking about another man?' he asked, his voice calm, concealing his internal rage.

'No, Jacob, not at all. I must have had the gas too high. I'm sorry, I'll cook you a fresh steak.'

Jacob squeezed her wrist harder. 'And waste good food?'

'It won't go to waste. I'll have that steak for my supper this evening.'

'Yes, you will,' he said. 'And you'll eat it from the floor like an animal would. Take it away.'

Once he'd released his grip, Elsie picked up the tray with shaking hands. Once again, she'd dissatisfied him.

She wasn't trying her best to be a good wife and he had a sneaking suspicion that he knew why.

'Stop,' he commanded before she left his office.

Elsie stood still, her back rod-straight.

'Come back here,' he said.

She turned around and walked hesitantly towards him but she wouldn't meet his scrutinising gaze. Now he was sure she was hiding something.

'Empty the tray on the side and bring it here,' he said.

Elsie complied and when she handed him the wooden tray, Jacob quickly scraped his chair back and jumped to his feet. His sudden movement caused Elsie to flinch and at the same time, Jacob swept his arm through the air, smashing the tray against her head. The force of the blow knocked her sideways and onto the floor.

'What did you and Mr Dymond discuss at the door the other day?' he asked as she lay whimpering.

'Nothing, Jacob, nothing. We didn't speak,' she answered weakly.

'LIAR!'

'I swear on the Holy Bible, no words were exchanged between us.'

'Get up.'

Elsie rose to her feet unsteadily and Jacob noticed her cheek was hugely swollen. This wouldn't do! Christmas Eve was less than one week away and she'd already invited the elders from her church to join them for carol singing around the piano. They were sure to notice her bruising.

'Come with me,' he said, leading her into the main house.

He walked her to the top of the stairs where he loosened a piece of carpet. 'Wait here.' He said, pointing to the top step before he descended the staircase. Standing at the bottom and looking up, he smiled wryly, telling Elsie, 'Jump.'

She looked confused. 'What do you mean?'

'Throw yourself down the stairs.'

'But... I can't, Jacob. Please...'

'Throw yourself down, woman, or I shall come up there and push you.'

'No, Jacob... please... please...'

'Fine, have it your way,' he mumbled as he trudged back up the stairs.

Elsie held onto the bannister. 'Please don't do this,' she begged as he unpeeled her fingers from the handrail.

'I take no pleasure from this,' he lied, 'but you need to have an unfortunate accident which will render you unable to host for our guests on Christmas Eve.'

Elsie screamed but her pleas did nothing to abate Jacob's determination. She wriggled and writhed which further frustrated him. He got behind her and with his arms around her waist, lifted her enough from the floor to launch her down the stairs.

She tumbled forward, her legs falling over her body and head as she flipped down. Then the somersault broke and she fell down the last few steps head-first on her back until landing crookedly on the floor.

Jacob had watched with pleasure, though he hadn't liked the sound of her body thudding on the hard stairs. He could see and hear she was conscious and walked down to her, wondering if she had obtained any broken bones.

'Oh my dear wife, what have you done?' he asked, crouching beside her.

Her face was contorted in pain and she looked pale.

'Don't move,' he said, 'I'll call for an ambulance.'

Minutes later, he stood over her again, disconcerted at her laboured breathing and now she appeared only semi-conscious. He'd only been gone a short time but her health appeared to have rapidly deteriorated. Yes, he'd wanted her injured but not dead! He knew he couldn't live without her. Kneeling beside her, he lightly patted her cheek.

'Speak to me, Elsie, speak to me.'

She made a garbled sound, her words impossible to understand.

'An ambulance is on the way. Goodness, Elsie, I've warned you about that loose carpet at the top of the stairs on many occasions. I feel awful for not repairing it.'

'My arm,' she groaned, her words clearer, 'hurts.'

'Yes, Elsie, just lie still. The ambulance will be here shortly. And remember… you tripped on the loose carpet, didn't you?'

'Yes,' she whispered, 'Tripped.'

He heard the sound of the ambulance bell arriving and went to open the street door before rushing back to Elsie's side.

'You tripped. Understood?'

Elsie nodded affirmation. He knew he didn't need to threaten her to make her obey. He could have said he'd cut out her tongue or something equally abhorrent but he was confident he didn't need to. After all, Elsie Flowers was fully aware of his brutality. It was all she'd ever known.

Georgina tapped her foot impatiently as she waited for Lord Hamilton to return with a sizeable amount of cash from the sale of at least one of the paintings. She felt sure she could trust the man but wished she'd been able to accompany him. But with the police probably still searching for her, she knew it would be foolhardy to make unnecessary trips outside.

Charlotte looked to be daydreaming as she dusted the furniture. Georgina could guess where the girl's thoughts were – with PC Batten. She'd come home the night before with a stupid grin on her face and everything she said had been *Tim this and Tim that*. It was nice to see her happy but she worried that Charlotte was going to end up with a broken heart. After all, Tim worked for the police and as far as Georgina was concerned, they were more bent and corrupt than most criminals she knew.

'I was thinking about Christmas,' Charlotte said, turning to look at Georgina.

'What about it?' Christmas was little over a week away but it was the last thing on her mind.

'Well, we should do something nice. Gerty's here, Johnny doesn't have any family and I'm sure Lord Hamilton would like to join us.'

'I'm sorry, Charlotte, but I'd rather Christmas passed me by. It's just another reminder that I haven't got my children with me.'

'Oh… yeah… sorry, that was thoughtless of me. Shall we keep it just us two then?'

'What's Tim doing?'

'He's going to his sister's. He, erm, invited me but—'

'—Go. Tell him you'd love to spend Christmas Day with his family.'

'But I can't leave you by yourself.'

'I'd rather you did. I'm not in the mood for Christmas or being jolly. In fact, if Father Christmas comes down that chimney saying *ho ho ho*, I think I'll shoot the fat bastard.'

Charlotte laughed, which made Georgina smile. 'You go with Tim, and don't give a second thought about me.'

Before Charlotte could protest further, they heard a tap on the window and Dog jumped up barking. Charlotte pulled the curtain back.

'It's Benjamin,' she said and rushed to let him in.

His unannounced visit didn't come as a surprise to Georgina. She'd expected he might call in today and rose to her feet to greet him.

'Good morning, or is it erm, afternoon,' he said, looking awkward as usual.

'Hello Benjamin. Please, sit down, Charlotte will make you some tea.'

Benjamin perched on the edge of one of the armchairs, placed his briefcase on the floor beside him and pushed his round-rimmed glasses up his nose. 'I have some, erm, bad news but also some good.'

'Tell me the bad news.'

'The police raided The Penthouse building last night. They smashed their way in. They had a tip-off that you was hiding there.'

'Yes, I know,' Georgina replied.

'You know?'

'Yes. It was me who tipped them off. I wanted to see their reaction.'

'I see. There were over fifteen officers. Was that the reaction you'd anticipated?'

'To be honest, I thought they might send half a dozen coppers but not more than twice that amount.'

'They obviously want you back.'

'I think I'm going to have to put my plan into action sooner rather than later.'

'Dare I ask?'

'It's best you don't, Benjamin. So, what's the good news?'

'The, erm, bicycle shop sold quickly, which was surprising, and works are underway on the renovations to the restaurant. You'll be needing someone to manage the place.'

Charlotte came back into the room with cups of tea. 'What about Gerty?' she suggested.

'That's not a bad idea. Pop upstairs and ask her to come down.'

'Gerty's here?' Benjamin asked, sounding surprised.

'Yes, it's a long story. I'll tell you about it later,' Georgina answered and rolled her eyes. It was a long story that had landed her in a load of trouble with the Zammits and was now costing her a lot of money to resolve.

A few minutes later, Gerty followed Charlotte into the room and beamed when she saw Benjamin.

'Mr Harel, how lovely to see you,' she said.

'Yes, and you Gerty.'

Georgina eyed the girl up and down. She looked smart enough and had a friendly manner. Best of all, she knew she could rely on her. 'Gerty, I have a proposition for you. My restaurant on Lavender Hill is going to operate as a café. I'd like you to work there and manage the place.'

Gerty glanced at Charlotte then back to Georgina, the colour draining from her face.

'What's wrong?' Georgina asked, thinking that the girl looked scared.

'Nothing. Nothing's wrong. It's just, well…'

'I don't bite, Gerty, just spit it out.'

'Well, I appreciate the offer and everything but I'd rather keep the job I've already got.'

'As a prostitute? Working for the Zammits at Piccadilly Circus?'

Gerty shoved her hands in her dress pockets and looked downwards. 'Yeah. I know it ain't everyone's idea of a good job but it pays well and I'm me own boss. I wouldn't earn as much if I worked in the café.'

'Suit yourself,' Georgina answered disappointedly.

'But if you don't mind, Miss Garrett, I can recommend someone else.'

'Who?'

'Babs, miss. I'm sure she'd be pleased to work there. I know where she lives and can take you to her.'

Georgina thought for a moment. Babs had been one of her women from Livingstone Road. She'd been a good worker and trustworthy too. She was quieter than Gerty but a nice girl. 'All right. But you'll have to bring Babs to me.'

'I will, Miss Garrett. I'll go straight round there now.'

Just over an hour had passed when Gerty returned alone.

'Where's Babs?' Georgina asked.

'I'm sorry, Miss Garrett, but she couldn't come. It was 'orrible, broke my heart to see the state of her.'

'What's wrong with her?'

'She's got the cancer, miss. It looks like it's eating her alive. There's nothing left of Babs, thin as a bleedin' rake, she is, and in terrible pain. I didn't know 'cos I ain't seen her for a year or more. She's got a kid now an' all.'

'I see. Is there anyone looking after her?'

'No, miss. Babs ain't got no one. She's worried sick about who's gonna look after her baby when she dies. She reckons she's only got weeks left. She's in so much pain and hoping she don't last much longer, but she's holding on to have Christmas with the baby. Her poor lad, he's gonna go in the children's home. Me heart bleeds for him, I know what them places are like.'

Georgina rubbed her finger where her mother's wedding ring had been, an idea formulating in her head. If Babs couldn't come to her, then she'd go to Babs. 'Take me to her,' she told Gerty.

What she was about to propose to Babs would be a big ask. But if she could persuade the woman to agree with her suggestion, they'd both be better off.

13

Tim had the weekend off from work and had told Charlotte he was keen to spend it with her. She'd readily agreed, encouraged by Georgina and excited at the prospect. Georgina had said she had plans in place and Tim was a part of them. So now the pressure was on Charlotte to bring Tim onside. She felt terrible for deceiving him, until Georgina had reminded her that recruiting Tim had been the original plan. She could have kicked herself for allowing her heart to rule her head.

In Woolworths at Clapham Junction, Tim picked up a poorly constructed wooden train set, moaning, 'Look at this, it's shabby, especially for the price.'

'Just like everything else, there's shortages,' Charlotte replied with a shrug of her shoulders.

'I would have liked to buy Arthur a Meccano set for Christmas but they're not making any. The factory is producing goods for the war effort instead.'

'Why haven't your sister's kids been evacuated?'

'She wouldn't have it. I tried to talk her into it but she refused.'

'Are you sure she doesn't mind me coming for Christmas?'

'Of course not. She's really looking forward to meeting

you but she hasn't stopped complaining about the lack of turkeys. We might be having lamb instead.'

'I don't mind,' Charlotte said, tentatively adding, 'but I know where to get a turkey, if you want one.'

Tim quickly glanced around before grabbing her arm and pulling her to one side away from other customers. He leaned towards her, his voice a whisper. 'Shush, Charlotte. You can't talk about things like that in public.'

'What? All I said is *I know where to get a turkey*.'

'Yes, but it'll be on the black market and you know a lot of folk don't like it.'

'What about you?' she asked teasingly. 'Wouldn't you love to see your sister's face light up when you hand her a fat, fresh turkey? I could get you some nylons for her too. And some sweets for the kids if you like?'

She wondered if he might be appalled at her suggestion but could see by his face that he was tempted by the idea.

'I realise some of your friends are a bit on the dodgy side but you're asking me if I'm willing to break the law, the very thing that my uniform stands for.'

'No, I'm not, Tim. I'm asking you if you'd like to see your sister's delighted face if you was to give her a turkey.'

'Don't split hairs. To do that would mean I'd have to break the law.'

'It's up to you but it's not like you're murdering someone.'

Tim sighed, 'Come on,' he said shortly.

Charlotte cringed. Her suggestion hadn't gone down well and now she was dreading how he'd react to her request about helping Georgina evade capture.

Once outside, as they walked towards Arding & Hobbs

department store, he took her hand in his. 'It was a lovely idea, thank you,' he said, giving it a gentle squeeze.

'The offer is still there,' she pushed cheekily.

'I must admit, I'm sorely tempted. Her husband has been missing in action for over a year now and something like a turkey on the table would cheer her up a bit.'

Charlotte stayed quiet, giving Tim time to mull over the thought.

'And nylons, you say?' he asked, giving her a mischievous grin.

'Yes, nylons, sugar, chocolate, fruit, pretty much whatever you want.'

'I know she'd appreciate some extra sugar and fruit to make a Christmas pudding. She reckons the shop only has four puddings in stock and there's a waiting list of over sixty women in front of her. She wants to make Christmas special for the kids, you know, on account of their father missing.'

'Well, if it was my sister and her husband was missing, I'd do whatever it took to put a smile on her face. She deserves it and why shouldn't she have a turkey on her table? If it ain't on hers, it'll be on someone else's.'

'Do you know what, Charlotte, you're right! I'm going to make sure my sister has a smashing Christmas. Can you introduce me to your friend?'

'Just give me a list of what you want,' Charlotte suggested, 'And I'll get it for you.'

'Thanks, but I can't ask you to break the law on my behalf. I'd rather deal with it myself.'

Charlotte swallowed hard and asked hesitantly, 'But... well... but... what if I introduce you and then you arrest him?'

Tim stopped in the street and held Charlotte squarely by the shoulders. Looking her straight in the eye, he said, 'I would never do that to you. You can trust me.'

'Really? Can I?'

'Charlotte, I'm not daft. I know all about your involvement with Georgina Garrett and her gang but that hasn't stopped me falling in love with you.'

Her eyes stretched wide and her mouth gaped.

'Yes, that's right. I'm falling in love with you, Charlotte, and there's nothing I can do to stop it.'

'But, Tim, you don't know the 'alf of it.'

'I know all I need to know and don't think I haven't wrestled with myself. My sarge had a stern word too and warned me to steer clear of you. They've got files you know, in the station, and he put yours in front of me. It made for some interesting reading.'

Charlotte gasped. 'Why didn't you tell me any of this?'

'I'm telling you now.'

'What's in that file about me?'

'Reports. Things about your background and investigations into your activities.'

'You'll know I was on the game then? I got nicked once for soliciting,' she said defensively.

'I know,' Tim answered, releasing her shoulders and bowing his head.

'See, you're ashamed.'

His head snapped back up to meet her accusing eyes. 'No, Charlotte, not ashamed. I'm not happy about it either but you did what you had to do and it couldn't have been easy. But it's in the past and that's where it's going to stay.'

Charlotte shook her head incredulously. 'How can you claim to be falling in love with me when you know what I've done? I don't believe you. Johnny was right all along... you're setting me up... using me to try and get to Georgina.'

Tim rested his hands on her shoulders again. 'No, no, Charlotte, I swear it's not like that.'

She shook him off, spitting, 'Yes it is! You don't love me. You're just looking for an arrest and snagging Georgina would be the arrest of your lifetime! Well, I hope breaking my heart was worth it.'

She whirled round and went to stomp off but Tim clutched at her arm.

'Ger orf me,' she growled, pulling from his grip.

'Charlotte, please, you're causing a scene. Let's go someplace quiet and talk about it.'

'I don't give a monkey's and there's nothing to talk about.'

'You're so infuriating but this is one of the things I love about you! Hot-headed, independent and not afraid to say it as it is. But you're wrong about me. Very wrong.'

'Yeah? Prove it!'

'How?'

Charlotte thought for a moment. She could have him right where she aimed to get him. But on the other hand, could she trust him? Risking everything, she quietly blurted, 'I know where Georgina is.'

To her surprise, Tim didn't appear shocked. 'Did you hear what I said?' she asked.

'Yes.'

'Well?'

'Well, what? Are you expecting me to arrest you and take

you in for questioning? Or am I supposed to ask where she is?'

'Don't you care?'

'Not really. I probably should, but right now you're all I care about and I don't like seeing you upset.'

The ice that had formed around her heart began to melt. 'I won't lead you to her, if that's what you're hoping?'

He pulled her into his arms and held her there, saying quietly in her ear, 'Stuff Georgina Garrett and stuff the police. This is about you and me, none of that matters.'

She stayed there, comfortable in his embrace. 'Just the one turkey?' she asked, lightening the mood.

Tim chuckled. 'Yes, just the one.'

In Soho, Georgina followed Jacob Flowers as she strode through one of Temi Zammit's clubs, Johnny close on her heels behind her. She'd expected better from the Zammits, something with more class, not a dimly lit seedy little club tucked away up a back street.

She held her head high, her chin jutting forward, and tried not to cough when she was shown into Temi's office. Five men looked up from their seats when she entered the smoke-filled room. Two were playing cards on a coffee table, one was clipping a cigar and the other two were sat each side of Temi. The man himself was stood behind his desk with his back to her, seemingly looking at a fussy painting on the wall. She could feel an aura of power surrounding him which unnerved her, causing her heart to thud unnaturally fast.

Keeping his back to her, Temi spoke, his voice gravelly. 'It's always fascinated me, this picture. The bird is consuming that man like he would a worm. But there's no emotion in his eyes. Look, come see how cold they are.'

One of the men rose from his seat and dragged the chair to one side for Georgina to pass. She stood alongside Temi and studied the strange painting.

'A copy of Bosch's Garden of Earthly Delights,' Temi told her. 'Every time I look at it, I see something different.'

The strange painting was in three parts. To the left, a depiction of a peaceful world with animals and beauty and God standing between Adam and Eve. The middle part was filled with naked bodies and debauchery in fantastic detail. The painting to the right looked like hell. Georgina wished Lord Hamilton was with her. He'd be more informed about this sort of thing.

'What do you see, Miss Garrett?'

Georgina looked closer. She was drawn to the dark world of hell, the black buildings at the top of the picture, surrounded by smoke. She pointed to it. 'It reminds me of the Blitz,' she said flatly.

'Ah, like me, hell attracts you. Do you believe in God?'

Georgina glanced sideways, surprised at how youthful Temi appeared. His greased-back black hair receded at his temples but there were no lines around his eyes. His nose hooked slightly down and, with his protruding chin, he put her in mind of Punch from the puppet shows. She turned back to the painting before answering, 'I might believe in God, though I don't answer to him.'

'I'm told you answer to no man.'

'You were told correctly,' she said.

Temi startled her when he did a sharp about-turn and

addressed his office. 'Leave,' he said loudly, pointing to the door.

His men followed the instruction without question, leaving Johnny and Jacob Flowers looking perplexed and uncomfortable.

'All of you,' Temi ordered, looking from Johnny to Jacob.

'So disrespectful. I shall be having words with your father,' Jacob warned before leaving.

Johnny's eyes met Georgina's for approval and she discreetly nodded affirmation, swallowing hard as Johnny closed the door behind them.

'Take a seat, Miss Garrett,' Temi offered, indicating to one in front of his desk.

She sat down, her face stern, concealing her nerves.

'I'm glad we've cleared up the misunderstanding between us and I'm sorry that it must have cost you dearly. Jacob Flowers overcharges and is overrated but he is my father's friend and a good accountant. You could have come to me directly. I've always got time for a pretty face that wearing men's clothes can't disguise.'

Georgina squirmed in her seat. As beguiling as she found Temi with his olive skin and dark eyes, she was in no mood for a coquettish exchange. 'What do you want, Mr Zammit?' she asked directly.

He raised his eyebrows and smiled drily. 'Please, call me Temi. If we're to work together, I think we can drop the formalities.'

'What do you mean?' she asked, her brow creasing.

'Let's have a drink and discuss it. I don't suppose you're a sherry sort of lady?'

'Champagne,' she replied, though felt quite ridiculous

requesting champagne when she was dressed in heavy boots and dungarees.

Temi poured their drinks and asked her to join him on a green sofa against the side of the office. Another elaborate piece of art hung over the sofa and Georgina wondered if Temi had heard about her heist of reproduction Old Masters.

She sat on the sofa, pushing herself up against the arm, as far away from Temi as possible.

'I trust you've made arrangements to secure your freedom on the outside?' he asked.

'Yes, things are in place.'

'Do you require any assistance from me?'

'No, thank you,' she answered emphatically, her mind racing as she wondered what Temi's intentions were.

He edged closer towards her. 'To freedom,' he said, raising his glass in the air.

'To freedom,' she parroted and clinked his glass, noticing the large gold ring he wore on his little finger. She wished he would shift back up to the other end of the sofa.

'How are you enjoying your freedom?'

'As you'd expect.'

Temi sipped his drink, looking over the top of his glass at her. She felt he was scrutinising her but she couldn't read him, though she knew he wanted something from her.

'You're a fine looking woman, Georgina. And this,' he said, waving his hand up and down in front of her, 'is your disguise to evade the police?'

'Yes.'

'It's good. You carry it off well. I'd have liked to see you dressed as a lady should. I'm sure you turn heads wherever you go.'

She didn't like where this conversation was heading and drank three large gulps of the champagne. After placing her half-empty glass on a table beside the sofa, she turned to look at Temi directly in the eyes. 'I don't want to be your friend. I don't need your help. But I'm willing to do business with you,' she told him straight.

Again, Temi's eyebrows raised and he smiled. 'I'm hurt, Georgina, genuinely hurt,' he said in jest and, smiling, placed his hands on his chest. 'You've broken my heart.'

His humour relaxed Georgina and she finally offered a small smirk.

'If I've misled you, I apologise. My intentions are strictly business. I'm a happily married man with two children and my wife is the only person I fear. She's a remarkable woman. In fact, you'd probably get on well with her!'

'Thank you,' she answered, relieved that he didn't have an ulterior motive to be alone with her. 'What business would you like to discuss. I'm assuming it's about the artwork I have at my disposal?'

'Artwork? No, it wasn't, but I'd be interested to know more. But first, something of a more serious matter... The Top.'

Her blood ran cold at the mention of his name.

'I'm a powerful man, Georgina, equally, so is The Top. You seem to appreciate straight talking so I won't beat about the bush... I want him dead.'

Georgina rubbed her finger where her mother's wedding ring had once been and checked herself that she wasn't showing a reaction to Temi's statement. She didn't know the man. It could be a trap. He could be working with The Top to try and flush out her intentions.

As if reading her mind, Temi continued, 'I know you've visited him and while there, you were told he was the man who murdered David Maynard. I also know how you felt about Mr Maynard. This leads me to believe that you'd want some sort of revenge. Am I correct?'

Georgina reached round for her glass and knocked back the remaining champagne.

'I'll get you another,' Temi offered, reaching for her glass.

'No, thank you,' she said, wanting to keep a clear head.

'I worked with Mr Maynard on several occasions. I was nothing back then, just the son of a Maltese man. My father was trying to make a name for our family. He respected Mr Maynard and was saddened to hear of his untimely death.'

'That's not enough for you to want The Top dead.'

'No, it's not. But The Top is more powerful than David Maynard was. We don't know enough about him. It concerns me that he simply walked in and destroyed Maynard. The Top could do the same to any of us. I want him toppled before he tries to crush what my father has built.'

'Why do you want me involved? Why not just do it yourself?'

'As I explained, The Top is equally as powerful as my family. And I don't want to start a war with him.'

'I see. You want me to take the risk to keep your name out of it. Any comeback will be on me.'

'When you put it like that, yes, I suppose so. But you want him dead and I can help you. With my help, you're more likely to succeed than if you attempted it alone.'

'I'll have that glass refilled now,' she said, holding it out.

Temi took it from her and went to the drinks cabinet on the other side of his office, which gave her time to think. Acutely aware that this could still be a set-up, she pushed for more information. 'How do you propose to help me?'

Temi handed her a full champagne flute. 'I've a man on the inside. He can get you in with your gun.'

Georgina thought back to the man who'd frisked her and had deliberately touched her breasts. Thinking about it now, he had the same black hair as Temi and the swarthy skin tone. It hadn't occurred to her until now that he could be Maltese.

'It was my man who informed me of your visit to see The Top. He works on the door.'

'I think I know who he is.'

'He can give you free passageway inside. Then it's up to you. But it makes it easier for you to get to The Top, doesn't it?'

She drew in a long breath. Yes, it certainly did. But could she trust Temi?

'You've nothing to lose,' he said, 'you're going to do it anyway, so you may as well do it with a helping hand from me.'

Georgina sipped the champagne, her mind turning. 'All right,' she finally said. 'Give your man the nod. I'll be going in after Christmas.'

'Good decision,' Temi said, offering his hand out to shake. 'Now, about this artwork...'

Half an hour later, Georgina left with Johnny, having arranged for Lord Hamilton to visit Temi the next day. He had been keen to discover what paintings he could purchase and Georgina was happy that the sale would be more than enough to pay the balance due to Jacob Flowers. All in all, it had been a meeting of surprises. Temi had been more approachable than she'd expected and best of all, she could look forward to putting a bullet in The Top.

14

Johnny reluctantly opened his eyes and realised that someone knocking on his front door had woken him. He grabbed his wristwatch from his nightstand and switched on the bedside lamp. Squinting at the watch face, he groaned when he saw it was three thirty-five in the morning.

The tapping on the door continued. He threw his legs over the edge of the bed and pulled a robe over his naked body, shivering as his bare feet felt the coldness of the floor. Perplexed at who would be knocking him up at this time of the night, he grabbed his gun before going to the door.

'Who is it?' he called, being sure to take precautions against gunfire, standing sideways on to the door with his back against the wall.

'It's me, Mr Dymond, Elsie Flowers.'

Elsie Flowers, Johnny thought, his face screwed up in consternation. What on earth was the woman doing at his door? He pulled it open and looked behind her before stepping outside and glancing left and right. She was alone. And when his eyes set on her, he was shocked to see her arm in plaster and bruises on her face.

She stood, her body trembling and tears on her cheeks.

'Please… can you h-help me?' she asked meekly through her chattering teeth.

He held out his arm and ushered her indoors, though it wasn't much warmer in his small lounge than outside. 'Sit down, I'll make you a hot drink,' he offered and fetched two blankets from his bed, one which he draped across her shoulders and the other over her lap.

'Thank you,' she said in little more than a whisper.

When he came back into the room with a cup of sweet tea, he was pleased to see she had stopped crying and her body was now still. He handed her the cup. When she looked up gratefully at him with her big blue eyes, he felt his heart melt for her.

'What are you doing here?' he asked gently.

'I didn't know where else to go. You gave me your address which I memorised before putting it on the coals. You don't mind, do you?'

'No, no, of course not. Did your husband do this to you?'

Elsie bowed her head, slowly nodding. 'He hit me and then to cover up what he'd done, he tried to make me throw myself down the stairs. I couldn't, so he pushed me.'

A sob caught in her throat and Johnny's chest constricted in anger. How could that vile man do this to his beautiful wife? He wanted to kill the evil bastard. 'Don't fret,' Johnny reassured her. 'You're safe here and I'll make sure he never hurts you again.'

'He'll come looking for me. He won't let me leave him. He keeps me shackled to our bed at night. I only managed to run away because I was in the hospital.'

Johnny paced the room, walking through his anger. The

thought of the poor woman shackled to her bed at night burned furiously inside him.

'Like I said, don't fret. He won't find you here and if he does, I'll see to him.'

'Thank you, Mr Dymond. I'm so sorry.'

'It's Johnny, and you've got nothing to be sorry for.'

'He'll be furious when he realises I'm not in the hospital. If he finds me, he'll slit my throat.'

'He won't find you, I promise.'

Elsie's delicate fingers cupped her tea and she gently blew on the hot liquid before sipping it. He wondered again how she'd come to be with someone like Jacob Flowers. His name might be pretty but there was nothing flowery about the man.

'You take my bed. I'll stop out here on the sofa.'

'No, I couldn't pos—'

Johnny quickly interrupted before she'd finished her sentence, 'I insist,' he said firmly. 'No arguments.'

Elsie nodded and looked at him again with those grateful eyes that resembled Daisy's. He could see the fear in them. He'd seen that look in his mother's eyes and his stomach lurched. He hadn't been able to protect his mother but he'd do whatever it took to look after Elsie.

'How bad are your injuries? I mean, do I need to get the doctor out to you?'

'No. My arm is broken but it'll mend. I was being discharged from the hospital tomorrow. That's why I had to escape tonight. See, once Jacob had me back at home, I'd be his prisoner again. He doesn't allow me to go anywhere alone, not even to the shops. I go to church on

Sunday mornings but I couldn't ask anyone there for help. It wouldn't have taken long for Jacob to find me and then he would likely kill me and whoever had helped me. When you gave me your address, you saved my life.'

'I dunno about that,' Johnny answered, feeling embarrassed.

'Oh, you have, Johnny, you really have. I could have been killed when he threw me down the stairs. Who knows what he would have done next!'

Tears began to well in her eyes again and Johnny dashed to find a handkerchief. ''Ere,' he said, handing her a white one with his initials embroidered on the corner. A gift from Miss Garrett a few Christmases ago. Christ, he thought, Miss Garrett. He doubted she'd be pleased about him keeping Elsie Flowers safe from her husband. He decided it was probably best that he didn't mention it to her for now. After all, Miss Garrett had enough on her plate at the moment.

'You're very kind,' Elsie said, dabbing the handkerchief at her wet eyes.

'Yeah, maybe, but I won't be kind to your old man if he dares to show his face here. You get yourself off to bed, sweetheart. Try and get some rest, eh. And don't you go worrying yourself about Mr Flowers. You're never gonna have to worry about him again, not with me around.'

'I don't know what to say. Thank you and good night.'

Johnny tossed and turned on the sofa but not because he couldn't get comfortable. Jacob Flowers was on his mind. He supposed he could just go round to the man's house and put a bullet in between his beady eyes. But

Jacob had connections with the Zammits and Lord knows who else. He'd already made a mistake by rushing into things and unwittingly turning over the Zammits. He couldn't afford another cock-up. No, for the time being at least, he'd sit tight and wait. After all, Jacob Flowers had no idea where his wife had run to and the man had no reason to suspect she'd be with Johnny. She was safe. For now.

Charlotte returned from an early morning walk with Dog and Tim in Battersea Park, pink cheeked and windswept. The moment she unleashed Dog, he pounded towards Georgina, jumping at her lap and panting heavily in her ear as his tail wagged with pleasure at seeing her.

'Yes, I love you too, you soppy mutt,' Georgina said, stroking his fluffy coat.

'Well, that was interesting,' Charlotte said as she pulled her knitted gloves off. 'Tim has said he's going to resign from the police and enlist with the army.'

Georgina shot Charlotte a look. 'When?'

'Tomorrow, when he goes back to work. He's gonna hand his notice in.'

'No, he can't. Not yet. You've got to talk him out of it. Just another week or two.'

'I wish I could. The last thing I want is him off fighting the Jerries. But he's adamant it's what he wants to do. He said it's for us, me and him. He can't stay in the police force and be with me at the same time.'

Georgina gently eased Dog away and rubbed her finger

as she thought hard. Maybe Tim resigning from the police wasn't such a bad thing. She needed him to be a credible witness and he still could be. And without his uniform, he wouldn't be obliged to turn her in. If he was willing to give up his career for Charlotte, he'd likely do anything for the girl, even if it was against the law.

'What are you thinking?' Charlotte asked.

'I'm thinking that it's time to act. I'm going to get the police off my back for good.'

'How?'

'You'll see. It's important that you do exactly what I tell you. Understand?'

'Yeah, of course.'

'Good. What are your plans today with Tim?'

'I'm just about to go shopping then me and Tim are popping in to see his sister.'

'Shopping? On a Sunday?'

'Yeah, the Barker twins,' Charlotte smiled. 'I promised Tim a turkey.'

'Oh, I see. Right, on your way back from Tim's sister, I need you to pop into Mary's to drop off a Christmas present. It's imperative that Tim is with you.'

'Eh?'

'Don't ask questions, just do it.'

'Fine,' Charlotte said grumpily and clicked her tongue.

'You need to be at Mary's for five o'clock. Don't be any sooner or later. Mary's package is wrapped in brown paper in the sideboard. Put it in your bag now so that you don't forget it. On your way to see the Barkers, call in to Johnny and tell him I need him here immediately.'

Charlotte nodded. 'Can I take the car? Tim knows I can drive but haven't got a licence.'

'No, shanks' pony.'

Charlotte rolled her eyes. She'd always been a moody young woman and didn't like being kept in the dark. But Georgina preferred to keep things close to her chest, at least until after her plans had been executed. Her pulse raced. This was it. As long as Charlotte managed to get Tim to be at Mary's at five on the dot, tomorrow morning she could finally discard George and be herself again, safe in the knowledge that the police would no longer be searching for her.

Jacob Flowers clutched a bunch of slightly wilted flowers as he hurried through the hospital to collect his wife. His heels clicked on the polished floor, the sound echoing in the narrow corridor. He'd insisted that Elsie be discharged today even though it was quite unusual on a Sunday. But he'd reasoned with the nurse that the beds were needed for injured soldiers and his wife was better convalescing in the comfort of her home. She'd had a word with the doctor who had agreed and now Jacob couldn't wait to get her out of here. Once he had her home, he knew he could rest easy. As it was, he'd hardly slept the past two nights. Instead, he'd been lying in his bed, tormented with images of his darling wife cavorting with the young doctors. No, it wouldn't do to have her in hospital a second longer than was required, he thought, picking up his pace to rush to her ward.

When he pushed the door open and marched towards her bed, a rather flustered looking nurse stepped in front of him.

'Oh, Mr Flowers. Thank goodness you're here,' she said, her face ashen.

'Is something wrong with my wife?'

'No, well, not in that sense. I've been calling you but obviously you didn't answer because you're here.'

Jacob glared at the woman. 'What is the problem?' he asked impatiently.

'It's your wife, sir, Mrs Flowers.'

'What about her?'

'She's, erm, gone.'

'What do you mean, *gone*?' he demanded to know. She couldn't be dead, surely? She'd only had a broken arm and a few bruises.

'I mean, erm, she's gone. Left the hospital.'

'Where? When?'

'We don't know. She must have slipped off in the night. We were hoping that she had returned home.'

'No, she hasn't. What sort of incompetence is this? I want to see your senior… NOW!'

The nurse scurried away, mumbling something about how sorry she was.

Jacob stamped his foot, furious that they had allowed this to happen. He threw the flowers angrily into a wastepaper bin and saw the nurse approaching with the ward sister.

'This situation is unacceptable,' he ground out, jabbing a thin, gnarly finger at the sister. 'I left my wife in your hands and now I'm being informed that she has gone. Gone! No one seems to know where. How can you allow your patients to simply walk out in the middle of the night?'

'I can assure you, sir, that we were as surprised as you. But this is a hospital, not a prison. Our patients are free to leave if they wish to do so.'

'Incompetence! Utter incompetence! Where is she? I demand to know where my wife is.'

'I'm sorry, sir, but your wife is only our responsibility while she is here under our care. Mrs Flowers left a note on her pillow saying she had discharged herself. She did not state to where. Now, if you'll excuse me, I have patients to attend to. Come along nurse.'

They walked off, leaving Jacob fuming. He stamped from the hospital, his mind in turmoil. Where could Elsie be? Had she tried to come home and been kidnapped or had an accident? No, that was unlikely. The truth was plain to see. She'd discharged herself to run away from him. But Elsie was penniless without him. She wouldn't get far without money. Unless, of course, someone was helping her. But who? She had no friends; Jacob had made sure of that. Maybe someone from the church? He doubted it because Elsie would know it would be the first place he'd look. But someone had to be hiding his wife. Who? Who could she have turned to? And then he was struck by a thought that stabbed at his heart... Johnny Dymond.

He'd seen the covert glance his wife had given the man. And she'd lingered too long at the street door when she'd shown him out. It had to be Dymond, he was sure of it. And he was sure that Dymond had fancied Elsie too. Not that he could blame the man, Elsie was a beautiful creature. But she was *his* beauty. His creation. She belonged to him, not some upstart in flash clothes. He'd make Dymond pay for this! And Dymond's boss, Georgina Garrett. He'd make them both pay! And once he got his hands on him, he'd make his treacherous wife watch as he skinned Johnny Dymond alive.

15

'You will look after my baby, won't you miss?' Babs croaked from the sofa in Georgina's old house.

'Yes, Babs, I promise you. Steven will have the best life.'

'I wish I could have spent his first Christmas wiv him.'

Georgina crouched beside Babs and took her limp and scrawny hand in her own. 'I know you do, but he won't remember it. He'll have a lifetime of wonderful Christmases and I'll make sure he knows all about you and how much you loved him.'

'Thank you, Miss Garrett. I can die in peace knowing my Steven will be cared for,' Babs said softly then cried out in pain. 'Oh, miss, it hurts me so much.'

'I know, love. Here, take these,' Georgina said and slipped four tablets into her hand.

Babs looked as though she was using all her strength just to put the pills on her tongue. Georgina put a glass of water to her mouth and told her to sip slowly.

'I'm scared, miss, really scared.'

'There's nothing to fear, Babs. The pills will make you fall asleep. You won't feel a thing.'

'You'll stay wiv me 'til I fall asleep, won't you?'

'Of course I will. Shush now, close your eyes.'

A tear slipped from Babs's eye. 'Tell him every day that I love him.'

'I will. Try and relax now. You'll be with your mum soon and if you see my Lash up there, let him know I miss him.'

'Oh, miss, me head feels funny,' Babs said, her words beginning to slur.

Georgina softly stroked the woman's fair hair from her brow, her heart breaking at the sight of what was left of poor Babs. The cancer had ravished her once curvaceous body and left her nothing more than a skeleton. She kissed her clammy cheek and gently squeezed her hand.

'I'm here, Babs. I'm here with you,' she said reassuringly.

Babs quietly groaned as the pills took effect and she began to fall asleep.

'That's it, Babs. You can go now. Steven will be safe.'

She sat with her for a few moments longer until she was sure that Babs was in a deep sleep. When Johnny had helped her bring Babs to the house, he'd assured her that two pills would be sufficient to make her sleep heavily. But Georgina had wanted to be doubly sure and didn't want Babs to suffer or feel any pain.

It was sad. So tragic. Such a young life about to be taken. And leaving a baby behind too. And though Georgina felt a stab of guilt, she knew this was the best for both of them. After all, Babs would have been lucky to have survived until Christmas. And at least by Babs offering herself as a sacrifice, she'd ensured her child would be taken care of and spared an upbringing in a brutal orphanage.

She turned away from Babs and glanced around at the familiar front room. The boarded windows shut out any light but even in the darkness, it felt like home. She pictured her gran, Dulcie, sitting in the chair. Her dad, Jack, whirling her round the room in high spirits. Her children, Alfie, with his stuffed horse, and Selina sleeping in a cot by the hearth. Lash, looking at her lustfully and taking her up to bed. So many memories she'd hold dear forever, close to her heart. This would be the last time she'd ever see this room again.

Georgina sighed heavily and gathered her thoughts. 'Back to work,' she said and carefully scooped Babs into her arms. The woman was as light as a feather and Georgina easily carried her up the stairs and laid her on the double bed.

She checked the time. Her heart pounded. Ten minutes. 'You'd better be on time, Charlotte,' she whispered as she went back downstairs. She reached into her pocket for a box of matches. 'Here we go,' she said, her hands shaking as she struck the match and held it to the bottom corner of the curtains in the front room. The material scorched but didn't burn and the flame from the match stung her fingertip. She struck another and held the flame in the same place. This time, the material sizzled into life as the fire ate its way upwards and across the curtain.

As the fire grew, smoke twitched her nostrils and she dashed from the front room and into the hallway. Here, she placed a newspaper on the floor under the heavy curtain that hung over the street door. She'd never understood why her gran had hung it there. Dulcie had said it was to keep out the draughts. But the curtain had never been drawn, except to clean it.

Within minutes, that curtain too was burning and the house soon began to fill with foul-smelling smoke. Covering her mouth with a damp cloth, Georgina was surprised at how quickly the flames had taken hold and as she ran back up the stairs, she saw the fire roaring across the front room ceiling.

Desperate for fresh air now and hoping that Charlotte and Tim were nearby, she opened the sash window in the bedroom and kicked down one of the boards. She stuck her head out the small gap and sucked in great lungfuls of clean air.

Stretching her neck out further, she was pleased to see Charlotte and Tim rounding the corner and approaching the house.

Black smoke billowed up the stairs and Georgina could feel the heat rising. She was no stranger to fire. Billy Wilcox had once tried to burn her to death. She'd escaped but poor Hilda had lost her life.

She looked round at Babs sleeping on the bed. The woman didn't stir. Thankfully, the pills had worked. The fire was raging now. She could hear it roaring, almost growling like a rabid beast. Turning back to the window, she took a deep breath and screamed.

'Help me... Fire...' she shouted.

Charlotte and Tim ran towards the house and she saw Tim was removing his coat. *Please don't try to be a hero and rescue me*, she thought, hoping that the fire downstairs would beat him back.

'GEORGINA!' Charlotte yelled, looking frantic.

'I'm trapped,' she called back.

Tim was now running at the front door. The heat must have been intense. He pulled back and then tried again.

Georgina glanced over her shoulder and out the bedroom door. Through the thick, black smoke, she could see the fire was coming up the stairs, licking the wooden bannisters.

She heard Charlotte call her name again over the howl of the fire.

'GEORGINA... JUMP... KICK THE BOARDS OFF AND JUMP OUT THE WINDOW.'

She took a final long gasp of air and ran through the bedroom door. The smoke was blinding and stung her eyes. The searing heat of the fire made her skin feel hot. Although she couldn't see what she was doing, she knew exactly where she'd placed the chair under the loft hatch and clambered up into the attic, quickly closing the cover behind her.

Wiping sooty sweat from her face, she inched her way over to where Mary's husband had skilfully made an escape route for her. This wasn't what the opening to Mary's house had been intended to be used for. But none the less, Mary had agreed that Georgina's plan to set the house alight had been a good one, even if it did risk damage to her own. But of course, Georgina had promised that Mary would be generously compensated.

She slid the makeshift brick-painted board to one side, kicked through the bricks and crawled through the small space into Mary's loft. As she reached through the opening to move the board back into place, she saw smoke creeping in through the loft hatch. She'd made it, and just in the nick of time.

Making her way across Mary's loft, Georgina paused for a moment and smiled to herself. She'd emerge from Mary's house as near enough a free woman. PC Timothy Batten had witnessed her last breaths at the bedroom window. The police would assume the charred and burned body of a woman on the bed was her own. The search for her would be over. She smiled with relief, though felt sad for Babs. But Babs had begged her to take care of Steven and when Georgina had explained her terms, Babs could see the sense and through her tears had readily agreed.

Georgina looked through Mary's hatch. The house was quiet but she could hear a racket from the street. Mary would be out there, with Steven in her arms. She'd be crying, saying poor Georgina and the neighbours would be shaking their heads. Mary's husband, the fire warden, would be holding everyone back. Charlotte would be beside herself and be furious with her when she'd later discover that Georgina was still alive. A wicked grin touched her lips. Gawd, she was going to get a mouthful from the girl! But she couldn't have divulged her plan to Charlotte. She needed Charlotte to be genuinely terrified. The girl had to be believable in front of Tim. There was no room for error.

Georgina crept down the stairs and into the kitchen, where she quickly changed into fresh work clothes that Mary had prepared. Her husband's trousers were a little short on Georgina but the shirt and jacket fitted a treat. She washed her blackened face and hands and slipped out the back door. As she hurried through Mary's yard, she looked back over her shoulder to see orange flames spewing from Alfie's bedroom window. Fire engine bells rang out along the street but it was too late to save the house or the life of Georgina Garrett. The world would think her dead. Some would grieve, others would cheer. But as Babs died in the flames, George died along with her and Georgina walked into the alley behind the houses and to her freedom.

16

'I say, you look quite enchanting,' Lord Hamilton said as his eyes roamed over Georgina's smart red skirt suit. Her fitted jacket was trimmed with black piping and shiny black buttons down the front. It nipped in neatly at the waist, emphasising her shapely figure. She'd finished off the outfit with a pair of black heels and a red wide-brimmed hat.

'I had Dina choose it for me. She's got a good eye for clothes.'

'I'll say! Ravishing, absolutely ravishing!'

Georgina could feel her cheeks burning to match the colour of her jacket. She'd never been very good at accepting compliments.

'I don't know why you're being nice to her after what she put me through,' Charlotte huffed as she threw herself onto the sofa with her arms folded tightly across her chest.

Georgina looked at Charlotte's sulking face and tried not to chuckle. 'Not this again,' she groaned.

'Can you believe she let me think she was burning to death in that house?' Charlotte asked Lord Hamilton.

He too, seemed amused. 'Actually, yes, I can. The more I come to know about Georgina, the more I'm in awe of her.'

Again, Georgina could feel herself blushing.

'So, tell me, why have I been summoned? I do hope it's something terribly naughty,' Lord Hamilton asked.

'If you don't mind waiting for the others to arrive, then I'll explain everything. Charlotte will make you a cup of tea.'

'Others?' he questioned.

'All will become clear,' Georgina answered as Charlotte stamped to the kitchen.

Lord Hamilton smiled in Charlotte's wake. 'You do know that she's only behaving like this because she was terribly upset at thinking she'd lost you? The girl adores you.'

'Yes, I know. She'll get over it. Charlotte's always been a moody girl, especially when she doesn't get her own way. Anyway, she's putting on an act of grief for Tim's sake.'

'I hear that they are getting on swimmingly.'

Charlotte marched back in. 'Yeah, that's right, we are. But he ain't gonna be very happy when he finds out that she's still alive and I've been lying to him.'

'If he loves you, he'll understand and he'll forgive you. Now, go and answer the door and stop banging around with a face like a smacked arse.'

Lord Hamilton laughed at Georgina's term of phrase. 'Smacked arse,' he repeated through chortles.

Charlotte showed in Benjamin Harel, soon followed by Johnny Dymond and then Ned and the Barker twins. Dina joined them too. Finally, Brian Harris arrived.

Georgina stood in front of the window and proudly surveyed the faces crammed into the room. These were her loyal and trusted people. Men and women who would lay down their lives for her. A fraction of the workforce she'd once commanded, but she had every intention of building her business again.

'Thank you for coming, and—'

Ned interrupted. 'Georgina Garrett is back, thank gawd,' he declared. 'I wasn't keen on seeing you dressed like a bloke, but now you look like the boss again, miss.'

'Well, this is why I've called you here today. A lot has changed while I've been away. Most of you are making a living and getting by without me. But, as you quite rightly said, Ned, I'm back. Things will never be as they were but if you're willing, I'd like to have you back on my payroll.'

'Count me in,' Ned chirped. 'When we was working for you, we never had it so good.'

'Yeah, us an' all,' Nobby said, speaking for his brother too.

'You don't need to ask me,' Johnny added.

'Or me, I suppose,' from Charlotte.

Georgina looked across to Lord Hamilton.

'Oh, yes, most definitely,' he enthused.

'Pew,' Dina spat. 'I vill work for you but I never sleep wis man.'

'That's fine, Dina, you don't have to,' Georgina assured her. 'Right, starting with the newly refurbished café on Lavender Hill, my office will be in the back. No one will think twice about people coming and going through a café. Charlotte, you will manage the café for now.'

'Me! Oh, come off it. Can't I do something else?'

'It's only temporary until Fleur is released from prison. And I want you close by me.'

Charlotte tutted but nodded in reluctant agreement.

'Benjamin, The Penthouse. Obviously, we can't open and operate as it once was, not without the Old Bill turning a blind eye like they used to.'

''Ere, Miss Garrett,' Ned interrupted again, 'can't Charlotte have a word with her fella? He's a copper.'

'No, Ned, he's resigned – and he doesn't have the rank. But I'm going to open it as a nice little nightspot and also an art gallery.'

'An art gallery?' Ned parroted.

'Yes, that's right. Dina can work behind the bar. You twins on the door. Lord Hamilton, do you think you can manage the place with some help from Benjamin at first?'

'Yes, my dear, standing on my head. But what art are you intending to display?'

'We'll talk about that later. I've got a meeting tomorrow with that Dutch artist bloke that Temi Zammit told you about. I want you with me.'

'What about me?' Ned asked. 'What job have you got for me? Am I gonna run the insurance?'

Georgina smiled warmly at his enthusiasm. He'd always been one of the most outspoken men in her gang, even though he was one of the shortest. 'No, Ned, no insurance. There's little point in extracting money from businesses for protection when Hitler could bomb them out. We'll look at that once this bloody war is over. In the meantime, you're going to head up our goods in and goods out.'

'What, you mean the black market? But Nobby and Eric already have their toes in that.'

'Yes, they do, but not on the scale I'm talking about. The twins will back you up for muscle.'

'What we got that we can flog then, Miss Garrett?'

'Brian will discuss that with you. He's been busy lately, haven't you, Brian?'

'That's right. I had a feeling you'd be back so I made sure we were prepared.'

'Oh, blimey, Brian, 'ave you been printing dodgy ration coupons again?' Ned asked, his eyes wide.

Brian didn't answer but smiled.

'But that's what Miss Garrett got banged up for!'

'Moving on,' Georgina said firmly. 'As we find our feet again, I'll have other jobs for you. I'm looking at a few jewellery shops but not on our patch. Easy targets, you know the sort, and we've got a ready-made outlet for the goods with Benjamin's father's shop. We'd be foolish not to take advantage of that and Ezzy Harel has always been the best fence in Battersea.'

'Yes, he's, erm, missed you,' Benjamin said quietly, looking embarrassed.

'As you know, I officially died on Sunday. The authorities are holding my funeral tomorrow, a pauper's grave. I know some of you will want to pay your respects to Babs but she was quite specific about her wishes. She didn't want anyone there. She hated funerals. So, let's take a minute to think about Babs, eh?'

In the silence, Nobby bowed his head and Georgina saw him discreetly dash away a tear. She'd heard that he and Babs had once had a thing going.

Ned broke the silence. 'How's Babs's kid?'

'He's fine. He's with Mary until Molly and Oppo come to collect him after Christmas. He'll have a smashing life on the farm with them.'

'Yeah, growing up with the spawn of Billy Wilcox,' Ned added bitterly.

'Don't ever refer to Edward like that!' Georgina barked.

Ned looked taken aback. 'Sorry, miss, it ain't the boy's fault. I'm sure young Edward won't turn out anything like his father.'

'No, he bloody well won't!' Charlotte said adamantly.

It was Nobby who spoke next, changing the subject. ''Ere, I read about you in the paper, Miss Garrett, about you getting burned to death. Cor, the things they said about you!'

'I know, it wasn't very flattering,' she laughed.

The meeting continued for another hour and then Charlotte reminded them that Tim would be home from work soon so they should leave.

'It's about bleedin' time that you got that boyfriend of yours on the payroll,' Ned grumbled to Charlotte as he left.

'He's going to fight the Jerries so shut your mouth, Ned!' she retorted, her eyes narrowing at him.

Once they'd gone, Georgina sat down on the sofa, exhausted but running on a high. She'd found it quite exhilarating to be back as the head of her gang, albeit a small gang now. She'd vowed to herself that she wasn't going to return to that way of life. After all, she had her children to think about. But without money, what sort of future could she offer them? So the decision had been made and this time round, she'd do things better. She'd learned lessons from her mistakes. In future, she'd be more careful about who she trusted.

*

Charlotte thought that Tim had been behaving strangely all afternoon. He seemed distracted and she worried that he knew something about Georgina. They'd been to see a short play at the Streatham Hill Theatre. It was one of the few playhouses showing matinee performances and, as someone commented, actors now played in the suburbs instead of the West End on account of most of the big theatres and cinemas being closed. Even Streatham ice rink had been given over to the war effort. Instead of skaters enjoying the ice, the place was used as a food storage depot.

Charlotte had been enthralled with the grand art deco style of the theatre but rather bored by the play. And all the way through, she'd noticed Tim fidgeting.

As they disembarked the tram at Clapham Junction, she said lightly, 'Oh, did I tell you? I'm starting work here tomorrow. Just up Lavender Hill, running a new café.'

Tim looked down at her and blinked several times. 'I'm not sure how I feel about that.'

'What do you mean?'

'I know women are taking on all sorts of roles because of the shortage of men around but call me old-fashioned, I say as I find. And I don't like the idea of my wife working.'

Charlotte froze in the street as crowds bustled past. 'Your w-wife?' she stuttered, eyes wide.

Tim dropped to one knee, right there, on the pavement. He fished in his pocket and pulled out a small velvet box.

Charlotte gasped. She glanced around. People had stopped going about their business and were watching her and Tim. Christ, what was he playing at! She could feel her cheeks flushing and wanted the ground to open up and swallow her. 'Get up, you idiot,' she hissed.

He continued regardless. He opened the box to reveal a sparkling diamond ring, though she doubted they were real stones.

'Charlotte Mipple... I want to know you'll be here when I get home. Will you make me the happiest man and marry me?'

Now it was Charlotte who was left blinking. Her mind raced. Everyone standing nearby seemed to be holding their breaths, waiting for her to answer. But how could she accept his proposal? Though she was sure she loved him, there was so much he didn't know. And being his wife, he'd expect his rights in the bedroom. She wasn't sure she could face *that*!

'Go on then, put the poor chap out of his misery,' a man's voice called from the small crowd surrounding them.

'I... erm...' she muttered, staring at his pleading eyes. She couldn't hurt him and turn him down in front of everyone. And though she had her doubts, she found herself saying, 'Yes.'

A cheer went up from the crowd and Tim leapt to his feet and pulled her into his arms.

'Nice one, son,' a bloke said and patted Tim on the back.

'Congratulations,' a woman cooed.

Tim slipped the ring onto Charlotte's finger. It was a perfect fit. She held her hand in front of her and looked at the ring with misgivings. She loved him, yes, she was sure of that, but could she bring herself to share his bed? After everything she'd been through, the thought of doing things like *that* repulsed her.

'Mrs Charlotte Batten. It's got a nice ring to it, don't you think?'

'Yes, I suppose it has. Anything's gotta be better than

Mipple,' she said, smiling, though the smile didn't reach her eyes. 'So this is why you've been acting odd all day?'

'Yes. I've been a bag of nerves. Sorry, I hope I didn't ruin your day.'

'No, Tim, not at all,' she replied, but putting a ring on her finger had. 'Are you sure we're not rushing things?'

'I know you're upset about Georgina dying but I'm going to basic training straight after the new year. I don't know when I'll be back, or if I'll be back, but I know the thing that will keep me going is the thought of coming home to you.'

Charlotte felt awful for doubting her decision. To think he could be killed abroad left her feeling bereft. She silently chastised herself. Of course she could have sex with him. All she had to do was lie back and close her eyes. It wasn't something women were supposed to enjoy. It was their duty and it was the least she could do considering her future husband was risking his life for their country.

She threw her arms around his neck and planted a kiss on his cheek. 'I love you,' she gushed, and couldn't wait to get home to tell Georgina the news.

17

Jacob Flowers sat in his car along from a tall house in Alexandra Avenue. His sources had told him that this was where he'd find Georgina Garrett. He didn't believe for a moment that the woman was dead, burned to a crisp in a house fire. No, she was far too astute for that. And just as he had suspected, there she was, striding from the house dressed as a woman, with a dapper looking older gentleman. She looked quite different from when he'd last seen her. Glamorous, he supposed, but in a cheap sort of way. The woman lacked the class and sophistication he'd taught his wife. In fact, he found Miss Garrett to be vulgar and most unladylike, even though she was now sporting heels and a hat.

Jacob ducked low in his car as Miss Garrett and the gentleman passed in theirs. Good, they were gone, giving him the opportunity to check if they were hiding Elsie. He strongly suspected that Johnny Dymond had aided Elsie's escape but he knew his wife – she'd *never* stay at a man's house unchaperoned. It simply wasn't the done thing, not for a woman of her standing in the community. No doubt Dymond played a part in helping her, but it was more likely that Miss Garrett was protecting her.

Keeping his eyes peeled, he strode up to the house and fiddled with the lock. He'd seen locks picked many times and it always looked easy. But this one wouldn't budge.

'Damn it,' he spat, and kicked the door in frustration.

This caused a dog to start barking from inside. And then to his surprise, an elderly woman opened the door.

'Can I help you?' she asked.

He could see by the scarf over her hair and the shopping bag in her hand that she was on her way out.

'I was calling to see the young lady in the ground floor apartment. I'm her uncle, from Northolt.'

'Charlotte. Such a lovely girl, you must be very proud. Please, do go in, though I'm not sure that she's at home,' she said, indicating a door.

'Thank you, if that's the case, I shall wait for her.'

'Rightio, cheerio,' the old lady said, and went on her way.

Jacob crept inside. The dog was barking noisily just behind the door that the old woman had indicated. It was sure to raise the alarm to any other residents. Or Elsie.

He tapped on the door but, as expected, no one answered. He hoped he'd have more success with the lock and the hairpin this time and could hardly believe it when after just a minute, the latch released.

Jacob pushed the door open just a crack. 'There's a good dog,' he said soothingly, but the animal growled and bared its teeth.

The damn dog wasn't going to back down but Jacob wanted him quietened. He calmly reached inside his coat pocket and curled his fingers tightly around the handle of a long, sharp knife. There was only one way to mute the animal. He had to do whatever was necessary to find Elsie. And if she wasn't hiding in here, then killing the dog would leave a clear message of his intentions. Johnny Dymond and Georgina Garrett were going to be made to understand that they had messed with the wrong man!

Charlotte had to admit to herself that she'd rather enjoyed her first day in the café. She hadn't opened to customers but had received many enquiries from passers-by, all of whom had said they were looking forward to her opening in the new year. Most of the day had been spent cleaning, the rest of it writing simple menus.

Georgina had been in and out a few times. Charlotte hadn't gleaned much about how her meeting with a Dutch artist had gone but she assumed it had been successful as Georgina seemed happier than she'd been in a while.

Charlotte was just about ready to lock up and head home when a loud knock on the front window startled her. When she looked up, her heart skipped a beat to see Tim standing outside.

'I've come to walk you home,' he offered cheerily.

'Great, just a tick, I'll grab my coat.'

As she walked beside him, she looked him up and down. 'You do look very smart in that policeman's uniform. But I never thought I'd be engaged to a copper!'

'I'll soon be changing this uniform for another,' he said, his mouth set in a grim line.

'Do you regret it?'

'No, Charlotte, not at all. I'd do anything for you and to be honest, the more I hear about my dad and his colleagues, the more ashamed I feel to wear this uniform.'

'You never did tell me about your dad.'

'Best left, eh, sweetheart.'

Sweetheart. He'd called her sweetheart, one of Johnny's favourite terms. Johnny called all the girls sweetheart but it sounded different when Tim said it and her stomach fluttered.

It was Christmas Eve tomorrow and the streets were busy with people milling in and out of the shops, many with wrapped packages under their arms. Charlotte felt a jolt of excitement until she thought of home. It didn't feel much like Christmas there. Georgina hadn't wanted a tree put up. They were hard to come by but Nobby had offered her one which she'd politely refused. Georgina had even turned her nose up at the pretty ivy wreath Charlotte had made, dipping the leaves in Epsom salts to give it a bit of sparkle. Oh well, she was sure that Tim's sister would appreciate it and was looking forward to spending the day with her. Especially now as they were to announce their engagement. It would be a proper celebration, unlike the dull 'congratulations' Georgina had proffered.

The sun had set as they turned onto Alexandra Avenue and the full moon was rising from behind the houses. Charlotte dreaded every full moon. It illuminated London, giving the Luftwaffe an ideal opportunity to attack, their targets easily seen. Tim was chatting away about basic training and telling her he'd write as often as he could. She happily listened but with one ear pricked for the familiar drone of any incoming aircraft.

As they approached home, Charlotte glanced behind and saw Miss Gray laden down with two shopping bags.

'Go on ahead,' she told Tim. 'I'm going to give Miss Gray a hand.'

'I'll take her bags.'

'No, it's fine, Tim. You get the kettle on, I'm parched. I'll get changed quickly and join you in your place in ten minutes.'

Tim pecked her cheek and as she turned to walk back towards Miss Gray, she smiled when she heard him whistling a happy tune.

Charlotte greeted the old lady with a smile and was just about to relieve her of her bags but stopped rooted to the spot as an ear-piercing scream came from the house. She tensed, knowing it was Georgina.

'Sorry,' she blustered to Miss Gray and ran to the house as fast as her legs would carry her. The street door was open and as she dashed up the path, she saw Tim crashing through her flat door.

The screaming had subsided now. Charlotte's heart thudded fast. She rushed into her apartment, and the awful sound of Georgina's sobs reached her ears. She ran into the front room and stopped dead in her tracks. Her mind couldn't comprehend what her eyes were seeing. Georgina was sat on the floor in a pool of blood with Dog on her lap. He looked injured. His face wasn't right. Blood. So much blood. Was Georgina hurt too?

'He's been stabbed, Charlotte,' Georgina cried, tears

unashamedly running down her cheeks as she rocked back and forth, holding Dog close to her. 'Please, do something,' she begged, looking beseechingly at Tim. 'Make Dog better... Charlotte, help him...'

Charlotte stepped forward but Tim held up his hand to stop her. 'There's nothing you can do for Dog,' he said sadly.

'No...' Georgina cried, her face crumpling. 'No... he can't be dead... Dog... come on, boy... wake up. It'll be all right... come on, Dog, there's a good boy.'

Charlotte could feel her eyes welling too. She stared at Tim, desperate for him to do something. But he looked back at her with coldness.

She hadn't heard him come in but Lord Hamilton appeared and was trying to encourage Georgina to put the dog down and to stand up. She refused, holding Dog tighter and now rocking faster.

'Get Johnny Dymond,' Lord Hamilton said to Charlotte.

Charlotte stared blankly at Lord Hamilton. He looked worried. But her mind seemed to be closing down. She couldn't think straight.

'Charlotte, did you hear me? Get Johnny here.'

She nodded but still her mind was blank.

Georgina began wailing. 'He killed Dog,' she cried and held out a piece of bloodied paper. 'Why? Why kill Dog? Dog never did anything wrong...'

Lord Hamilton went to grab the piece of paper from her but Tim intervened. 'I'll take that,' he said gravely.

'What does it say?' Lord Hamilton asked.

Tim read it aloud. '*Bring my wife back to me. A gift on Christmas Day. Jacob Flowers.*'

'His wife,' Lord Hamilton mumbled incredulously. 'What utter nonsense!'

It made no sense. None of it. But Charlotte's unshed tears began to fall as she slowly processed what was happening. Dog was dead. He'd been murdered in the most horrific way. Her loyal and loving soppy mutt had been killed. That was Dog's blood. She'd loved him so much and now the pain at the realisation of his death stabbed at her heart. Her throat felt tight as she fought to hold back from sobbing. She ran towards Tim, desperate for comfort, but instead of pulling her into his arms, he stepped back and glared at her angrily.

'You used me,' he said. 'You lied to me and you used me. Fool that I am, I should have known better. I was warned about you. They were right.'

'What?' Charlotte asked, dumbfounded.

He didn't respond and stamped out of the room.

'Wait... Tim...' she called after him but as she peered up the hallway he was out of sight.

She thought about chasing after him but the sound of Georgina's heart-wrenching crying reminded her that she was needed here. Charlotte tried to drag her eyes to the corner of the room but she couldn't stand to look at the pitiful sight again.

'W-what should I do?' she asked Lord Hamilton.

'I told you, get Johnny.'

Charlotte thought that was a good idea. Johnny would know what to do. But how could she get him? He didn't have a telephone. Oh, dear God, Dog is dead. The thought punctuated her thinking process. Johnny, she had to get Johnny. But Dog is dead.

'All right, I can see you're in no fit state to do anything. Just stay here,' Lord Hamilton said.

Charlotte sat on the sofa and closed her eyes. Georgina's cries had petered down to whimpering now. The sound was none the less painful to hear. Moments later, she heard Tim's voice again. He had come back.

'Come on, come over to my flat. You can't stay here,' he said, pulling her gently to her feet.

She searched his eyes but still only saw anger and disappointment there. 'I can't leave Georgina,' she said.

'Go to mine. I'll bring her.'

Charlotte walked across to Tim's in a state of numbness. She recognised this feeling of detachment, of feeling nothing. She'd learned this response when she'd been living on the streets and witnessed the mutilated bodies blown apart by Hitler's bombs. This was her mind's way of dealing with things.

She sat at a small drop-leaf table in Tim's flat, relieved when she saw him leading Georgina in. Lord Hamilton followed, holding her clutch bag and fresh clothes for Georgina to change into. Tim suggested she wash her hands and face.

'You can't leave Dog alone!' Charlotte said, jumping to her feet as her mind cleared.

Tim held her squarely by the shoulders. 'He won't know. He's dead, Charlotte.' His tone was very matter-of-fact and lacked any empathy.

How could he be so cold? She took a sharp intake of breath through her nose and jutted her chin forward, saying acrimoniously, 'Yes, thanks for pointing that out, Tim.'

He shrugged, dismissively turning away from her.

Hurt, but too emotionally drained to work out what was wrong with Tim, when Georgina went to wash and change, Charlotte asked Lord Hamilton if he knew what had happened.

'No, not really. We arrived home together and Georgina came upstairs with me for coffee. Moments after she left, I heard her screaming so came running back down. I was just behind you two.'

'Jacob Flowers will pay for this. She'll make sure of it.'

'I've no doubt, and the bounder deserves it! Right, Tim, if you don't mind me using your facilities, I think we could all do with a cup of tea.'

Tim shrugged and once they were alone, he whispered to Charlotte, 'I should turn *her* in. And you.'

'What are you on about?'

'Don't play the innocent with me, Charlotte. You've led me a right merry dance. Christ, I've given up my career for you.'

The penny dropped and she realised he was annoyed because she hadn't been altogether truthful with him about Georgina. 'Please don't be angry. I wanted to tell you the truth, really I did.'

'So why didn't you? Instead you've had me feeling sorry for you that your best friend is dead. And you managed to get me to vouch for her death. I bet you've been having a right laugh behind my back.'

'No, Tim, it wasn't like that, I swear.'

'How can I ever trust you? You're a liar. You could lie to me about anything.'

'I won't, I promise.'

'I don't believe you. See, that's the problem. I'm never going to believe a word that comes out of your mouth.'

'Are you saying you don't want to marry me?' she asked, her bottom lip beginning to quiver.

'How can I?'

'But... I love you.'

'You don't. You just wanted a reliable witness. Well, you made a big mistake. I'm still a policeman, Charlotte, and I've a legal obligation to report Georgina Garrett as very much alive. Who was the poor soul that burned in the fire? Christ, were you a part of a murder?'

'No, Tim, let me explain.'

'Forget it. You can explain it to the judge.'

'Please, Tim, don't do this.'

He pushed past her, heading to the door. At the same time, Georgina came through from the kitchen in clean clothes and, to Charlotte's horror, she was pointing a small gun at Tim.

'Stop right there,' Georgina ordered and cocked the barrel.

Tim whisked around, his eyes widening when he saw the gun aimed at him. He didn't hesitate in throwing his arms in the air.

'You're not going anywhere or telling anyone about me.'

'How are you going to stop me? By shooting me? Are you going to kill me in cold blood, just as you did to that poor woman in the house fire?'

'If I have to, I will. But I'd rather not.'

'Please, Georgina, don't kill him,' Charlotte pleaded and quickly ran across the room to jump in front of him, defiantly shielding his body from any bullets that might come from Georgina's gun.

'Don't be stupid, Charlotte, get out of the way,' Georgina growled.

'No, I won't. I won't let you kill him.'

'Charlotte, move out of the bloody way,' Georgina hissed.

'If you want Tim dead, you'll have to kill me an' all.'

Tim whispered from behind. 'Please, Charlotte, do as she says. There's no point in us both dying.'

'What the hell is going on in here?' Lord Hamilton asked, aghast, glancing from Georgina waving her gun to Charlotte standing protectively in front of Tim.

'Tim is going to the police. I was trying to persuade him otherwise when Charlotte decided she wanted to get involved.'

'She's threatening to shoot my fiancé!'

'For God's sake, Charlotte. I wouldn't have shot him. What kind of monster do you think I am?'

'You was pointing your gun at him!'

'I was only trying to get his attention. I find a gun is the most effective way. It's better than shouting.'

Tim moved Charlotte to one side. 'All right, you've got my attention,' he said, lowering his arms.

'Good. Lord Hamilton has made tea. Shall I be mother?' Georgina asked, indicating for them all to sit down.

Charlotte sat next to Tim on the sofa and was pleased when she felt him discreetly take her hand, hoping this meant he'd had a change of heart.

Georgina poured the tea into Tim's mismatched cups and saucers, handing Lord Hamilton one and then Tim. 'Please don't blame Charlotte,' she said. 'I'll be straight with you. She never wanted to dupe you in the first place. Charlotte has been soft on you since she first met you. It was me who put pressure on her to get you to the right place at the right time and she had no idea about the fire.'

'Look, I don't care if you're dead, alive or otherwise. But I don't like my future wife deceiving me.'

'She won't do it again. It's not in Charlotte's nature. She's always straight and bluntly honest. Please, give her another chance. And if you want to go to the police about me, that's fine, you do that. But by the time they get here I'll be gone, and they won't find me.'

Tim looked up at the ceiling, his leg jigging. As he was thinking, Charlotte noticed Georgina's eyes had fixed on a black and white framed photograph. Her jaw had dropped and she looked deathly pale.

'What's wrong?' Charlotte asked.

'Who is in that photo?'

Tim followed Georgina's stare. 'My mum and dad.'

Georgina violently shuddered and her breathing became rapid.

'What is it, Georgina? What's wrong?'

She closed her eyes and drew in a long breath. 'Nothing. Nothing at all.'

Charlotte didn't believe her and from the look on Tim's face, neither did he. 'Have you met my parents?' he asked. 'Do you know my mum and dad?'

Georgina swallowed hard and sat forward. 'I met your father once,' she answered, snarling.

'He's a piece of work,' Tim said with equal disgust.

'You can say that again.'

'Where did you meet him?'

'In Battersea Bridge police station, when he violated me with his truncheon. He tried to ram it up my arse. I was fifteen at the time and had been wrongfully arrested. Nice man, you must be proud to follow in his footsteps,' Georgina answered, tight-lipped.

Charlotte gasped and Tim hung his head in his hands. 'I'm so sorry,' he said, sounding genuinely apologetic for his father's shameful actions.

'It's not me you oughta be going to the authorities about. It's him, your father. Your own flesh and blood!'

'You already knew, didn't you?' Charlotte asked him accusingly.

Tim's head shot up. 'Yes, and no. I knew he'd attacked women in custody. But I didn't know you'd been one of them,' he answered, looking at Georgina ruefully.

'There were others?' Georgina asked, sounding shocked.

'Oh yes, there were many others. He was stopped when the police station got blown up and left him injured. But if that hadn't stopped him, I dread to think how many other women he would have attacked.'

Charlotte had an inkling that Georgina had something to do with the explosion in the police station and now looking at Georgina's face, she was sure of it.

Tim continued. 'You're right, you know. My father should be behind bars. But I can't condone you killing an innocent woman to cover your fake death.'

'It's not what you think, Tim,' Charlotte cut in. 'It was a woman called Babs who died in the fire, but she had cancer and was already at death's door. She was lucky if she had a day or two left to live and was in so much pain. Georgina promised Babs that she'd take care of her baby. It's what Babs wanted. Georgina gave Babs pills to make her sleep. She never felt a thing. No one was murdered. Georgina ain't like that.'

'Is that true?' Tim asked, looking at Georgina.

'Yes. Except the bit about me not being like that. I am... I'm very much like that and I'm going to kill Jacob Flowers.'

'Yeah, well, after what he did to that poor dog, I can't say I blame you.'

'Do you still want to turn Georgina over to the police?' Charlotte asked tentatively.

He thought for a moment before answering. 'No, after what my father did, how can I? That would make me a hypocrite. Either I stand up for law and order, or I don't.'

'Oh, Tim,' gasped Charlotte, putting her arms around him.

'And, as I'm going to marry you and you're going to want Georgina at the wedding, I suppose I'd better turn a blind eye.'

'You still want to marry me?'

'Of course I do! Charlotte, you stood in front of a loaded gun and were willing to take a bullet to save my life.'

'Actually,' Georgina quipped, 'it wasn't loaded.'

If Charlotte hadn't been so devastated about the horrific death of Dog, she might have laughed.

Tim rubbed his clean-shaven chin and sighed. 'I suppose you'd better bring me up to date,' he said.

'About what?' Georgina asked.

'Everything I need to know about you so that I don't unintentionally drop you in it. Well, at least until I leave for the army.'

A sob caught in Charlotte's throat. Such a bittersweet moment. She'd nearly lost Tim. She'd almost sacrificed her life. But now everything was all right. All right that was, except for Dog. And if Georgina didn't make Jacob Flowers pay for what he'd done, Charlotte most certainly would.

18

Jacob Flowers was infuriated at being called into Temi Zammit's office on Christmas Day! The cheek of the man, he thought. Temi was nothing like his father and needed to have more respect. Jacob intended to have strong words with the man. After all, he had more important things to be dealing with. If his wife didn't come home today, both she and that disgusting Dymond fella would be dead by tomorrow. Jacob was sure Elsie was with Dymond and now he'd learned of the man's whereabouts. They had until the clock struck midnight.

When Jacob arrived in the West End, the club was closed but Temi was at his desk with his usual minions around him. Jacob detested the thugs. He doubted they had a brain between them. *Bloody lowlife foreigners*, he said in his head as he eyed them with condescension.

'What is so important that I've been summoned here today of all days?' he asked in an irritated tone as he sat in front of the desk.

'A festive drink?' Temi offered.

'No, thank you. I'd like to conclude any business as soon as possible,' he answered, keen to return home.

One of Temi's men placed a drink on the desk, which

Temi picked up and slowly sipped, his eyes unflinching as he stared at Jacob. 'Are you sure you won't join me?' Temi asked.

'I'm sure,' he answered, beginning to feel uncomfortable.

'Have you found Mrs Flowers yet?'

Jacob was taken aback by the question and wondered how Temi knew of Elsie's disappearance. Not that it was any business of his. 'I'm not here to discuss my personal life,' he said sharply.

'No. You're here to offer me an explanation of where my money has been going.'

Jacob reached into his briefcase and extracted a file. 'All the information is here,' he said confidently, dropping it onto the desk. 'Though you may struggle to understand it. But that's why you hire me to do your accounts. It's very specialised. It will look merely like columns of numbers to you.'

'You're probably right. It's not the books I want to see. Looking at your accounts will be a waste of my time because I know that you have cooked the numbers.'

'W-what are you talking about?' Jacob asked, feeling flustered now.

Temi leaned back in his seat and placed his hands behind his head. 'Mrs Flowers has been very vocal, which leads me to believe that you've been stealing my money,' he said casually but with an air of a threat.

Jacob could feel his heart beginning to race and his head perspiring. It hadn't occurred to him that Elsie would talk about his work, especially to the Zammits. 'The woman is an imbecile and doesn't know anything about accounts, money or business,' he blustered. 'I've worked tirelessly for your family since the day your father arrived in this country. How dare you question me in this manner! I'm insulted that you'd listen to a woman and doubt me!'

Temi smirked, leaving Jacob feeling unsettled. His act of outrage hadn't fooled Temi and he feared what the man would do next. He was known for his brutality, far worse than his father. Jacob had heard of men who'd crossed Temi and been left paralysed or brain damaged, even dead. But surely the friendship he had with Temi's father counted for something? And would Temi really believe the word of a woman?

'Jacob, there's no point in denying it. I'm fully aware that you cream money off the top of the payments that are supposed to go to the police, the magistrates and the local councillors. Luckily for you, so far they've been happy with their lot and haven't disrupted my business. But you're a sly, greedy bastard and I know there's a lot more money besides that you've stolen from me and my father.'

It seemed Elsie had told them everything but Jacob was far too terrified to hold his hands up and admit his guilt. Now he could only hope for an outcome that didn't involve him getting hurt.

'Would you like that drink now?'

He nodded. And when he took the glass from Temi's man, his hand shook uncontrollably. But what he hadn't noticed was the door behind him opening. Heels clicked across the office floor. Jacob stared into his whisky, his mind filling with all the awful scenarios of what Temi might do to him.

'I'll leave you in Miss Garrett's capable hands,' Temi said.

Jacob's eyes shot up from his glass and he looked with

confusion over the desk at Temi. Then he heard Georgina Garrett's voice behind him.

'This is for Dog,' she said.

Before he could turn to look at her, he felt a sharp pain in his neck and a warm sensation trickling down towards his chest. He struggled to draw in a breath and felt as though he were drowning. He tried to clear his throat by coughing but instead seemed to suck in more liquid. Panic rushed over him followed by a feeling of doom when he realised she'd slit his throat.

As his blood spurted from his body, he reached to his neck to stem the flow. His hands touched the gaping hole that went almost ear to ear. Wet with his own blood, no amount of pressing or trying to hold his neck together would stop it from pumping out.

She'd killed him. The bitch had killed him. But he wasn't dead yet. He fell to the floor and saw her standing over him, her face expressionless. Lightheaded now, he tried to claw his way towards her. She stepped back, out of his reach. He tried again, slipping in his own blood on the polished floor as he attempted to crawl to her feet.

He saw her turn to look at Temi and heard her say, 'Sorry, he's making quite a mess.'

'Don't worry,' Temi replied, 'my men will clean it up. That's why I suggested you kill him here. It's easier for me to dispose of a body.'

Jacob, spent, instinctively tried to breathe his final breaths but heard a gurgling, bubbling noise in his throat. His own blood, what was left of it, was choking him. It should have been Elsie. It should have been Elsie with a sliced throat. Elsie was his last thought.

19

On New Year's Eve, Georgina sat at a table in The Penthouse with Lord Hamilton and Johnny, though she was in no mood to celebrate. She'd enjoyed spending the day with Molly, and Charlotte had been excited to see her sister. Of course, Charlotte had spoken of nothing else other than Tim. Molly had taken Babs's baby back to the farm in Kent. When she'd first held Steven, Molly had gazed at him in the tender way that a mother looks at her child. Georgina saw the moment and instantly knew that Steven would have a good life with Molly but it had reminded her of how much she missed her own children. She missed Molly too. And though they hadn't seen each other for years, their friendship had picked up just where they'd left it.

'I'm just going to check if Elsie is all right in the cloakroom,' Johnny said, scraping his chair back.

'No you're not,' Georgina snapped. 'You're staying right where you are. Elsie will be fine. The Barker twins are on the door.'

Johnny didn't argue with her and sucked on his stinking cigar.

'Can you put that bloody thing out? The smell gets right up my nose,' she growled.

'Can't a bloke even enjoy a smoke? Cor, you're in a right mood tonight,' he said flippantly.

'Watch your mouth, Johnny,' she said. 'I've got you out of the shit twice now. I didn't break free from Holloway just to sort out your mistakes.' Georgina glared at him. Yes, she was in a foul mood and didn't care who knew. Christmas had been miserable without her children. And the new year wasn't bringing her anything to look forward to. Granted, good things had happened. She had money coming in now. She'd avenged Dog's death. The police weren't searching for her. But what was the point of it all if she had no one to share it with? No one to love. No one to love her back. The Top would pay for what he'd done!

Johnny couldn't argue with her and stubbed out his cigar.

She glanced around her club. It was only half full but Georgina didn't think that was too bad considering it had opened just two nights earlier. The atmosphere around her contrasted her mood. It felt light and jolly, though Dina's face behind the bar soured it.

Georgina summoned her over and said quietly, 'I realise it goes against your nature, but try and smile.'

Dina flashed her a half-hearted false grin but then looked stroppy again.

'What is your problem?' Georgina asked, her patience worn.

'Nothing.'

'Then smile. All you have to do is serve drinks and be friendly. Either do it or you can find somewhere else to live and work.'

Dina strode off, flouncing her long blonde hair. But when

she stood back behind the bar, Georgina was satisfied to see her looking more approachable.

'That was a bit harsh,' Lord Hamilton said as he topped up their glasses with champagne.

'No, it wasn't. Dina acts like the world owes her a living. Well, it doesn't. She works for me and I have standards.'

'As I can see,' he replied looking around the club. 'I must say, this is all very tasteful. The piano, the ambient lighting and, of course, the outstanding paintings.'

'Thanks to Benjamin, except for the paintings of course. I trust he's shown you the ropes?'

'Yes, it's all tickety-boo. I've already had two enquiries about the artwork.'

'Good. Just be careful about who you take out the back to see the Old Masters. Only the most select customers. We don't want to land in deep water. These paintings on display are fine to be sold as replicas but the ones out back, well, you and me know they're fake but we don't want anyone else finding out.'

'My dear Georgina. I've been an art dealer for many years now. You don't have to tell me how to do my job.'

'You're right, sorry. I wouldn't know a fake from an original.'

'And neither would most people, which is how we are going to become extraordinarily rich.'

'Cheers to Geert Neerhoff,' she said, clinking glasses with Lord Hamilton.

'Yes, cheers to Geert Neerhoff. The man is a genius in his field. And I've never known of an artist who can produce such accurate work at the rate he can. I'm surprised I hadn't heard of him until Mr Zammit introduced us.'

'Well, by all accounts, Geert is a very private man. But then I suppose if he's painting reproductions and passing them off as originals, he can't exactly shout it from the rooftops. Good for us that he needs someone to sell his work. And talk of the devil...' she said, her eyes on the door.

Oleg Volkov walked in, his large frame filling the entrance. From across the club, Georgina could see the man had a meanness about him. 'Are you sure about this?' she whispered to Lord Hamilton.

'He has money. He wants original art. Yes, I'm sure, though to be perfectly honest, I would never have dealt with him without you by my side.'

Georgina drew in a deep breath to compose herself. She wouldn't allow the Russian man to intimidate her, though she did feel extremely nervous about flogging him paintings that she was going to pass off as originals.

'Good evening, Mr Volkov, pleased to meet you. I'm Georgina Garrett, you already know Lord Hamilton and this is Mr Dymond,' she said, offering her hand to shake and a pleasant smile.

He put his large hand in hers but she found his grip to be surprisingly gentle.

'Good evening to you, Miss Garrett,' he replied, his ice blue eyes looking deeply into her. 'Lord Hamilton, Mr Dymond,' he added with a slight nod of his head.

'Please, take a seat. What would you like to drink?'

'Vodka, of course.'

Georgina indicated for Dina to come to the table. She was hoping that having a Russian waitress would be of benefit.

'Yes, Miss Garrett, you would like drinks?' Dina asked, glancing sideways at the guest.

Georgina covertly watched Oleg's reaction to Dina, pleased when she saw his eyebrows rise in surprise.

'Your accent? You are Russian also?' he asked.

'Yes.'

'What is your name?'

'Dina.'

'Where are you from?'

'Battersea.'

'Where are you from in Russia?'

'I do not know.'

Oleg looked doubtful so Georgina went on to explain. 'Dina's father returned to Russia when she was a child and her mother died shortly after. She doesn't remember much about her early life.'

'I see, but you speak the tongue of our motherland?' Oleg asked.

'*Da.*'

'*Mozhet byt', vy khoteli by podelit'sya butylkoy vodka so mnoy? Ya khorosho plachu.*'

'*Net.*'

Georgina listened, intrigued at the unfamiliar language, and wondered what they were saying.

Oleg threw his head back and laughed. He turned to Georgina. 'Your woman is not for sale?'

'No, only my paintings are on offer.'

'I apologise for my rudeness. It is wrong to speak in Russian in front of my gracious host. I asked Dina if she would like to share a bottle of vodka with me. Please excuse my presumption, I hope I have not caused offence.'

Dina glared at Georgina and spat, 'He also said he would pay well for me. I am not a whore!'

Again, Oleg laughed. 'I should know better than to upset a Russian woman. They are, well, Russian,' he said, shrugging his shoulders in mock exasperation.

'You haven't offended me, but I can't speak for Dina.'

'Good. Then perhaps I can buy Dina a glass of vodka, nothing more.'

'Thank you, Mr Volkov, I'm sure she would find that very acceptable. And we can conduct our business later. But only a glass, not a bottle. Dina is working, after all.'

Oleg stood. 'One glass. It is good for me to speak with a beautiful woman in Russian. I have missed hearing the sound of my language.'

'Come,' Dina said and marched back to the bar.

Georgina saw her pour them both a neat vodka and then she sat on a stool opposite him.

'I hope Dina is an asset and can be trusted,' Lord Hamilton whispered.

'Don't worry about Dina. She can be trusted. And she *hates* men.'

'I've always found her to be affable enough, maybe a bit stand-offish. I'm a man, I've never had the impression from her that she hates me.'

'You have no desire to take her to your bed.'

'True. There's only one woman for me but unfortunately she's already married.'

'Oh, who have you got your eye on then?'

Lord Hamilton leaned in closer towards Georgina, his voice hushed. 'Elizabeth Bowes-Lyon. She's an incredible woman.'

'What? The queen consort?'

'Yes. I knew her before she married Bertie. She was being

courted by James Stuart when he was equerry to the then Prince Albert. Alas, I couldn't win her heart but Albert did, the lucky man. I'm quite sure Albert was aware of my affection for his wife, hence the cold shoulder I went on to receive.'

'You know the King? And is James Stuart the same man who is in the coalition government?'

'Yes, dear, that's him. I haven't spoken to him since 1922. We fell out over something trivial. And as for knowing King George, yes of course I knew him. But obviously we called him Albert back then.'

Georgina had never believed Lord Hamilton's fanciful stories of him mixing in royal circles, or that his title was a real one. But if this was a tale, it was a very tall one!

She looked back over to the bar, saying, 'Excuse me,' and headed towards the ladies' toilet. She managed to catch Dina's eye and covertly indicated for her to follow.

In the toilet, Georgina asked, 'What have you discovered about him?'

Dina's nose wrinkled. 'He is a horrible man.'

'I don't doubt that, but did he tell you anything about himself?'

'He was sent to gulags where…'

Georgina cut in, 'Where is gulags?' she asked.

'It is labour camps for criminals. He became very powerful and worked his way up to *vorami v zakone*. These are the "thieves-in-law", the elite criminals who control the gulags. He has the symbol tattooed on his wrist. He likes to show off but I am not impressed, even when he told me he made a lot of money. A very much lot of money. And then Joseph Stalin offered him and many others their freedom if they joined the army to fight Hitler's invasion of our country. It goes against the code of the thieves-in-law. They should not ally with the government. But Oleg did. He craved his freedom. But he did not stay and fight for Stalin. He escaped here and brought his money with him.'

'Good work, Dina. Stay here for a minute or two. It'll look suspicious if we walk out together.'

Georgina saw Oleg was back at her table and talking with Lord Hamilton. 'Sorry about that, there was a small problem on the door,' she said as she joined them. 'I'm very select about the clientele I allow in my club.'

'As I can see,' Oleg answered, clearly impressed.

'I trust you enjoyed your time with Dina?'

'Yes, very much. But I am not foolish enough to think that she enjoyed her time with me. A strange lady.'

'Indeed. Dina is quite unique. Now, about the painting you wish to purchase…'

Oleg had been suitably impressed with the reproduction artwork and appeared to believe the works were originals. He agreed to pay handsomely for two pieces, shaking Georgina's hand to seal the deal.

'There is one particular painting I would like in my possession. I don't believe it has been shipped from this country to Canada for safekeeping as many other fine paintings have been. You are obviously a very resourceful woman, Miss Garrett. Do you think you could acquire it for me?'

Georgina thought for a moment. Geert Neerhoff was capable of producing replicas of just about any painting. It meant anything was possible. 'Leave the details with Lord Hamilton. I'll see what I can do. Now, if you'll excuse me,

I have business to attend to. Please, stay as my guest and enjoy the New Year's celebrations. Good evening to you.'

Johnny drove Georgina home, the short journey spent in silence. She hated the thought of walking indoors without Dog bounding up to greet her. She had loved that dog. She pushed her pain away and instead concentrated on Oleg's request. If she could pull it off, it would be very lucrative. But it came with danger. Oleg was a man to be cautious of – after all, he'd been a renowned criminal in his country. She thought about how best to approach it. She could commission Geert to reproduce the original and pass it off to Oleg as the real thing. But it was risky. She already feared the consequences of him finding out that the paintings he'd just purchased were fake. Was it worth jeopardising her life for again? Or maybe, just maybe, she could get her hands on the original painting that he'd requested.

Geert Neerhoff sat naked in the alcove, looking from his studio window onto the dark streets below. He pulled hard on a cigarette and watched the exhaled ribbon of smoke curl up and around the small alcove, illuminated by the moonlight. The graceful swirling of the smoke looked beautiful. He wished he could capture it in his paintings. But Geert lacked imagination. Yes, he was a brilliant artist, one of the best, but only when copying great masterpieces. His own work lacked vision and depth.

'I suppose you'll be rushing home to spend New Year's with your wife?' Eva asked.

Geert turned to look at his nude lover, lying on the sofa with just a wool blanket draped over her legs. He sighed heavily and answered, 'I should, but what's the point? She rarely knows who I am.'

'Come back here then and keep me warm,' Eva purred.

'The offer is tempting, but I must finish my work.'

'Oh, come on, Geert, you can do that tomorrow. It'll be romantic to see the new year in *together*.'

He walked across the small studio and stubbed out his cigarette, immediately lighting another. 'Eva, you don't understand. Temi Zammit wants this painting in two days. It's a birthday gift for his wife. You know I'm already neck deep in debt to the man. I can't afford to be late with this.'

'But I thought you said he'd introduced you to that woman who is going to buy your paintings. Surely you'll be able to pay Mr Zammit what you owe?'

'Miss Garrett isn't paying much for my work, a pittance of what my paintings are worth. What she pays will barely cover the rent on this studio and the fees for Doris's nurse. I had to accept, what else could I do? It's better than nothing.'

Eva sat up and pulled the blanket over her shoulders. 'It's not fair. I bet Miss Garrett is making a small fortune on your work. Why can't you sell the paintings yourself?'

'I don't know who to sell them to. Temi Zammit doesn't pay me anything. The paintings I do for him go to paying off my debt. I've tried galleries, markets, even advertisements in the newspapers. I'm a poor artist, Eva. I'll never be in a position to buy you furs and diamonds. Well, not until Doris dies.'

'Your bloody wife is the bane of my life,' Eva huffed. 'Can't you just put a pillow over the old girl's face? I mean, let's face it, she wouldn't be any the wiser and you'd be putting her out of her misery.'

'Eva! Don't be so wicked,' Geert said with a mischievous smile, 'though it would solve my financial problems. But no, I couldn't murder Doris. She's old and senile but she's still my wife.'

'Some blinkin' wife. She's more like your grandmother!'

'She wasn't when I married her.'

'Yeah, well, you should have thought about the future. Fancy that, a bloke of twenty marrying a woman of forty-five. Yuck, the thought of it turns my stomach.'

'Doris was a very attractive woman and she seduced me. I was young, it was exciting. But you're right. I couldn't see past the end of my nose. It never occurred to me at the time that twenty years later, I'd end up looking after an old woman. But when she dies, the house and her savings will be mine. We just have to be patient.'

'If you say so. But do you love her?'

Geert sat on the sofa close to Eva and took her hand in his. 'I care for her. But it's you I love,' he said, and held her hand to his lips. 'I don't want to leave you but I'd better get some work done and then go home. Doris will need feeding.'

'I thought the nurse did all that stuff?'

'She does but I've had to cut her hours down. She only comes in twice a week now.'

'You're a bloody saint, you are. Caring for her like you do. Not many men would do what you do.'

'It's only fair. I've always been a struggling artist but when I came from Holland with nothing and met Doris, she gave me a home and paid for everything so that I could indulge my painting. She has looked after me for years. Now it's my turn to look after her.'

Eva stood up and allowed the blanket to fall from her shoulders. She walked across the studio and gathered her clothes from a stall in front of an easel. He watched, admiring her hourglass figure and pert bottom. Her blonde hair, the same colour as his own, tumbled down her back. He'd have liked to paint her and capture her beauty but didn't believe his efforts would do her justice.

'I'll see you tomorrow then,' she said sullenly. 'Happy New Year.'

'Wait, Eva, I'll walk you home. I don't like the idea of you being out in the dark alone.'

'But I thought you had work to do?'

'I do. I'll see you home, check on Doris and then come back to my studio.'

Eva lived with her mother and two sisters a few streets from his studio and after walking her to her front door and tenderly kissing her goodnight, with a heavy heart, he headed for his own home in a smarter part of Battersea.

When Geert walked indoors, the house was in darkness but he could hear Doris moaning from the bedroom. He threw his coat and hat over the newel post and trudged up the stairs.

'Mother... Mother... Is that you?' Doris called as he approached her bedroom.

It seemed she wasn't having one of her rare lucid moments. Doris's mother had been dead for years. He pushed open the door and turned his head in disgust at the rancid smell. Doris had obviously soiled herself again.

'You filthy bitch,' he muttered as he flicked on the light switch.

Her rheumy eyes blinked against the light. 'Mother... Mother...'

'It's me, Geert, your husband,' he said as he impatiently stamped towards her.

'Who are you? Get out... GET OUT!'

Doris was sat in an armchair that he'd covered in old sheets. Her blankets were on the floor at her feet. He rolled his eyes, thinking *here we go again*. The nightly struggle to get her into bed was wearing. She'd fight him at every opportunity, spitting and scratching him. But if he wanted her money, he had no choice but to tolerate it. Doris had made sure of that! As her illness had set in, his wife had consulted a solicitor. The house and her savings would only come to him if he cared for her and didn't put her in an institution.

Doris flailed her arms in the air. 'Don't touch me,' she screeched.

Geert managed to grab her arms and pulled her from the chair, unceremoniously throwing her onto the bed.

'I'll call the police,' she screamed. 'Don't rape me!'

Huh, he thought, there was no chance of that happening! The woman stunk of urine and faeces. He pulled the covers over her thin, pale legs but she kicked them off.

'Suit yourself, but you'll get cold,' he warned.

'Who are you?' she asked again, calmer now.

'Geert, your husband.'

'No you're not, I'm not married! Go away, leave me alone,' she said and let out a long, screeching cry.

Geert slapped her hard around her face. 'Shut up, woman. Shut up,' he hissed.

Doris screamed louder.

He put his hand over her mouth until she eventually stopped struggling and quietened down. Oh, he'd have liked to have left his hand there and silenced her for good. But he didn't and she gasped for breath. He looked down at her with contempt. He'd told Eva that he cared for Doris. That was a lie. Maybe once he had, a long time ago. As a young man, he'd been infatuated with her. But Doris was a manipulative woman and had controlled his life. He resented that he'd had to beg her for every penny he needed. She'd used her fortune to rule over him. And as her money had been in trust from her father, there had been nothing that Geert could do about it. But soon, he hoped, very soon, he'd be inheriting Doris Neerhoff's wealth.

'Die soon, bitch, die,' he hummed sweetly as he flicked off the light and left her to rot in her own mess.

20

'Christ, Elsie, is that the time?' Johnny said as he studied the face of the wristwatch in his hand. He slammed it back down on the bedside table and threw the blankets off before jumping out of the bed. 'I'm late, Miss Garrett won't be happy,' he muttered, scrambling to put on his clothes.

Elsie wiped sleep from her eyes and then stretched her arms and yawned.

'Come on, you'd better get up too. You're supposed to be working in the café with Charlotte,' Johnny told her.

'It's going to feel strange to earn my own money,' Elsie said as she threw her legs off the bed. 'I'm looking forward to it. I really need some clothes and things. I know you collected what you could from Jacob's but I'd really like to wear more fashionable clothes. Jacob would never allow it and now, well, I can wear what I like.'

'Yeah, that's great, Elsie, but get a move on. You can think about shopping for clothes and all that later,' Johnny said impatiently. He was now fully dressed and annoyed that Elsie was still naked and standing in front of the wardrobe gazing at her dresses.

'I think I'll throw these away. They were all Jacob's choice, not mine.'

'Great, you do that. But just put one of them on for now, eh, sweetheart?'

'Do you like any of them?'

'Yes... no... I don't know, I don't bloody care. You look lovely in anything. But hurry up, we're late.'

Elsie spun round from the wardrobe, her loose blonde hair falling teasingly across her face. 'I'm tired, Johnny. You kept me up for most of the night with your love-making. Let's take a day off and get back into bed,' she purred, and crawled back under the covers.

'I'd love to but we've both got jobs to go to.'

'I wouldn't have to work if I could claim Jacob's house.'

'Without declaring him dead and without a body, there's no chance of that.'

'I wish you'd collected my jewellery too.'

'I'll buy you some jewellery, just hurry up and get ready.'

'You?' Elsie asked incredulously. 'You couldn't afford to buy me the sort of jewellery that Jacob did.'

Johnny thought she had a point. He didn't have the money to buy her expensive jewels but he could *steal* them. It was becoming clear that Elsie had a taste for nice things. And if the woman wanted lavish gifts, then he'd ensure she got them. He'd have to wait until tonight. Then, once it was dark, and taking advantage of the blackout, he'd rob a shop. He'd spotted one when he'd taken Miss Garrett to see the Zammits. It didn't appear to have the usual shutters, which made it an easy target. A quick smash and grab. He would have it clean away on his toes and back into bed with Elsie before midnight. If Johnny could have, he would have given Elsie all the diamonds and gold in the world. But for now, a nice haul from a West End jewellers would have to do and he knew it would put a smile on her pretty face.

'All this talk of art and paintings. Everyone I meet lately seems to be into art. It's a new world to me. I didn't know there was so much money in it,' Georgina said as, under her desk, she crossed one leg over the other.

'My dear, the art world has always been there. You've just never noticed it before,' Lord Hamilton replied. He cocked his little finger as he sipped the cup of tea Charlotte had brought through from the café to Georgina's office.

'This painting Oleg wants, you say you know the owner?'

'Yes, quite well, in fact. I've seen the original painting many times and have always admired it. It's a small piece, he has it hung in his library.'

'Do you think you could take it and replace it with Geert's painting?'

Lord Hamilton sat bolt upright, nearly spilling his tea. His brow furrowed as he asked, 'You want me to steal it?'

Georgina smiled. 'Yes.'

'But, but what if I get caught in the act?'

'Well, make sure that you don't.'

He placed his cup and saucer on Georgina's desk and stood up, twiddling his moustache as he walked from side to side, a worried expression on his face. 'I assumed your men would creep in during the night and make the swap. I'm not sure this is something I could do.'

'Yes, you can and it'll be a breeze. It makes more sense for you to do it than it does to risk my blokes getting done for burglary. Go and see Geert and tell him what we need.

I want the painting in three days. If it's only a small picture, like you say, that should be plenty of time for him.'

'Three days! The paint won't even be dry!'

'It'll have to be. Look, I appreciate you're new to how my business operates but you'd better get used to the pace. I don't do all this for the fun of it. I'm in it to make money, not to sit on my backside waiting for paint to dry. You said you wanted in. Are you sure you still do?'

Lord Hamilton sat back in the seat opposite Georgina's desk. 'Yes, I most certainly do,' he said with a grin. 'It's terribly exciting. A tad scary but absolutely thrilling.'

'Good. Now go and see Geert. You've plenty of time before The Penthouse opens.'

Once Lord Hamilton had left Georgina's office, Charlotte stuck her head through the door.

'Can I get you anything?' she asked Georgina.

'No, thanks. Is Elsie in yet?'

'No, not yet. Late on her first day. I shall be having words with her.'

'Yeah, make sure you do. And Johnny's going to get a mouthful from me too.'

'Do you think they're all right?'

'I've no reason to think they're not. Do me a favour – shut the door. When they get here, make Johnny wait in the café. I don't want to be disturbed.'

Georgina clasped her hands together and rested her chin on them, staring at the closed door. Christmas had passed and so had the new year, yet The Top was still alive and well. He'd murdered the man she loved and though she tried to shake the feeling of needing revenge, she couldn't. It was eating at her, gnawing her flesh and chewing her bones.

Images of The Top gunning down David played out in her mind. They intruded on precious thoughts of her children. She'd tried to push the imagined pictures of David's last moments away but day and night, they crept back in. It was time to take action. She had a lot to lose, possibly her life. But while The Top lived, she knew she'd never have any peace. It had to be done. The Top's blood needed spilling and then, if she survived, she could finally get on with her life.

21

That night, after a tense day with Miss Garrett and taking an earbashing from her, Johnny was in the West End. He hadn't dressed in dark clothes or worn a balaclava. But he did have his trusted gun with him, tucked away in the inside pocket of his coat. He swaggered along the street, passing the jewellery shop that he intended to rob and inconspicuously checked the security. This was going to be a doddle, he thought. The street was quiet and he hadn't seen a copper walking about all evening.

It was bitterly cold, which he believed worked to his advantage. The freezing January weather kept folk indoors. But it also meant Johnny didn't want to hang around for longer than he had to. He reached the end of the street and turned around, heading back towards the shop. His pace quickened and so did his pulse.

Johnny glanced over his shoulder. No one was behind. He stopped outside the shop and looked left and right. It was clear so he quickly pulled a hammer from his coat pocket and a cloth bag from the other. He glanced around again. The street was still empty. This was it. He had to act now and be fast. He held his fedora in front of his face and whacked the shop window. The sound of shattering glass was immediately drowned out by the screech of an alarm.

Johnny was panting now. He nudged a couple of hanging glass shards with his elbow. The glass fell, giving him enough room to reach inside to the jewellery on display. The sound of the alarm bell rang in his ears, making him feel panicky. He grabbed handfuls of whatever he could, dropping some bits of jewellery as he shoved it into his bag. There was no time to stop and pick up the items he'd dropped and he reached inside again, this time taking pearl necklaces and several rings. That was it. He had enough. But as he went to turn to run away, he spotted a spectacular brooch of a peacock decorated with red, blue and green precious stones. Elsie would love it, he was sure of it. He put his arm back through the broken window. As he reached for the brooch, the sound of a police whistle pricked his ears.

'Shit, fuck, shit,' he muttered, quickly retracting his arm.

A sharp piece of glass caught him, ripping through his coat but not his skin. He glanced at his arm and then at the brooch that still sat on display. It was too late. He couldn't get it now. Police torches illuminated him from the shadows. Two or maybe three policemen were running towards him. One was shouting at him, telling him to stand still. The other blew hard and long on his whistle.

'Sorry, chaps, you ain't getting a feel of my collar tonight,' he whispered under his breath and ran in the opposite direction.

As he pounded along the street, the sound from the coppers seemed to be getting closer. Johnny ran as hard and as fast as he could. He dashed around a corner and nearly bumped into a young couple holding hands.

'Beg your pardon,' he said breathlessly and carried on sprinting.

'Stop that man,' he heard a policeman yell.

Around another corner. His car wasn't far away. Just a few more streets to go.

'POLICE... STOP!'

Temi Zammit's club was within sight. He thought about running in. Maybe Mr Zammit would hide him from the Old Bill. No. Get to the car. Come on, Johnny, run faster. Run.

He turned another corner and into an alleyway which led to the street where he'd parked his car. Almost there. Keep going.

Johnny was halfway along the alley when he saw a figure step in front of him, blocking his exit onto the street. The figure was tall, with a policeman's helmet on his head.

Johnny came to an abrupt halt.

'There's nowhere to run,' the copper said, staring at him.

Johnny peeked over his shoulder. The coppers chasing him weren't in sight but he could hear them coming. He looked back towards the copper in front of him. The man had taken several steps closer and had his truncheon poised.

'Don't be a fool. We've got you covered. Come quietly.'

Johnny looked over his shoulder again. He could see the lights from the policemen's torches. Without thinking, he reached inside his coat, pulled out his gun and then aimed it at the policeman.

The copper threw his hands in the air. 'Don't shoot,' he pleaded.

Johnny felt like a caged animal and reacted instinctively.

He squeezed the trigger of his gun, firing a shot directly at the policeman.

The noise from his gun echoed through the alley but the copper didn't make a sound as he fell to the ground. Johnny ran past him. It was too dark to see where his bullet had hit the man but he noticed the copper's eyes were closed. Had he killed him? Shit, he hoped not but he couldn't hang about to find out.

Johnny was pleased to see his car now in sight. He could only hear one whistle blowing now. He didn't check behind him as he jumped in his car and threw the bag of stolen jewellery onto the passenger seat before speeding off.

He took the back streets to Battersea, hoping to avoid any police blocks en route. If he'd killed that copper, word would be out and every man in uniform would be searching for him. If they caught him, he'd hang for it. He'd swing in the gallows with a rope around his neck. But as he climbed the stairs to his flat, he finally breathed a little easier. He'd done it. He hadn't been caught and now he couldn't wait to see Elsie's face light up when he presented her with the bag of jewels.

The next morning, Georgina noticed Johnny was shifting from one foot to the other as she read out loud the headline from the paper.

'It says here that the policeman was shot and killed while in pursuit of a man who'd robbed a jewellery shop. I can't believe anyone was foolish enough to turn over that shop. Temi Zammit's dad owns it. Whoever did it will have the Old Bill and the Zammits after them. Blimey, if it was me,

I think I'd prefer to have my day in court rather than face the Zammits.'

Georgina noticed Johnny swallowed hard. Surely he didn't have something to do with it?

'Please tell me this has nothing to do with you?' she asked.

'No, course not,' Johnny answered.

He hadn't looked her in the eye and Georgina wasn't convinced. She was about to question him again but was interrupted by a light tap on her office door.

Elsie came in carrying a tray of tea and a plate of biscuits. 'I made these myself,' she said, looking proudly at Johnny and smiling.

Georgina noticed Johnny was frowning at Elsie, and then she saw that Elsie was wearing a pair of earrings that looked like real diamonds. 'Leave us,' Georgina abruptly told the woman.

Johnny ran his hand through his hair. He seemed worried and now Georgina knew why. 'It was you, wasn't it?' she asked gravely.

He pulled back a seat from in front of her desk and slumped onto it, hanging his head in his hands. 'I've fucked up good and proper.'

Georgina sighed heavily. 'Yes. You have. Why, Johnny? Why the fuck did you do it?'

'I dunno. I wanted to treat Elsie. I didn't mean to kill the copper and I had no fucking idea who owned the shop. Shit, this is bad.'

'It really is. I don't know if I can protect you this time. Temi Zammit is a reasonable bloke but his father, well, you know as well as I do what the man is like. The man is merciless. Fuck, Johnny, what's happened to you while

I was in prison? Has your brain turned to mush? It's been one thing after another but this… this tops it. Whether it's the Old Bill or the Zammits who get you first, either way, you're dead.'

Johnny picked up a biscuit from the plate, took one bite and threw it back down. 'I did it for Elsie. Christ, she can't even cook,' he said, grimacing.

'Tell her to get those earrings off. And get rid of the jewellery.'

'What shall I do with it? Take it to Ezzy Harel?'

'No,' Georgina snapped. 'Don't you dare put him at risk. I don't care what you do with it. Throw it in the Thames or something. Just get it out of your flat.'

'I could hide it for a while until the fuss dies down.'

Georgina slammed the flat of her hand down on her desk. She leaned forward towards Johnny and hissed, 'I said, *get rid of it.*'

'All right, all right, I heard you. I'll dump it but it seems a shame. There's a good few bob's worth in the bag.'

'Worth dying for, is it?'

'No, course not. I was just saying.'

'Well, don't.'

'Sorry.'

'Do you think anyone saw you?'

'No, only the copper and he can't say nothing. Cor, last night, when I was running away, I thought about hiding in Temi Zammit's club. Bleedin' good job I didn't, eh?'

Georgina couldn't bring herself to answer Johnny. She'd always respected him and thought he had half a brain on him, but now she was beginning to doubt his intelligence.

'Once I've dumped the stuff, do you reckon I should lay low until it blows over?' he asked.

'I suppose so. I'm not willing to discuss it with Temi. You've already stepped on his toes and got away with it. I doubt they would be forgiving for a second time.'

'I'm sorry, Miss Garrett. If I'd've known—'

'—That's your problem, Johnny. You rush into things. From now on, don't even have a shit before checking with me first. Do you understand?'

'Yes. Yes, Miss Garrett.'

'Good. Now go and get those earrings from Elsie and as I said, get rid of them and the rest of the stuff.'

Once Johnny had left her office, Georgina pulled open the drawer in her desk. Her gun sat there with a box of bullets beside it. She picked the pistol up, loaded the bullets and placed it in her handbag. From now on she'd need to carry her weapon everywhere. If the Zammits discovered who had robbed their shop, it wouldn't just be Johnny they'd come after. It'd be Johnny's boss too. She'd also pay the price for Johnny's crime.

'I'm sorry, sweetheart, but I have to take them back,' Johnny whispered to Elsie.

She held her hands to the earrings. 'But I love them, Johnny. Please, can't I keep just these and you can get rid of the rest of the jewellery?'

'No. The lot has to go. But I'll get you some more, I promise.'

'But I like these ones.'

SAM MICHAELS

'I'll get you even bigger and better diamonds. But I need those back now.'

Elsie unclipped the earrings and slapped them into Johnny's waiting hand. She had a face on her like a petulant child, not that Johnny could blame her for sulking. After all, she'd been delighted with her gifts last night and now he was snatching it all back.

'I bet the police don't know what's missing from the shop. If they saw the earrings they wouldn't know they're stolen,' she said miserably.

'It ain't the police I'm worried about. Turns out the shop I robbed belongs to the Zammits.'

Elsie paled and looked at Johnny with wide eyes.

'Now do you understand why I need to get rid of all the jewellery?'

Elsie nodded. 'Oh, Johnny, I know everything there is to know about the Zammits. Jacob worked for them for years and he told me stories that used to give me nightmares.'

'Exactly. But don't worry about it now. If we just keep our heads down we should be all right,' Johnny urged and kissed her cheek lightly before heading back to his flat to dispose of the haul. He'd been reluctant to dump a small fortune but could see it made sense to get rid of any evidence. But he reckoned that if the Zammits ever discovered it was him who'd robbed them, it would make no difference if he had the jewels or not. They'd still kill him.

22

Two days later, Lord Hamilton breezed into Georgina's office looking very pleased with himself.

'I did it. I exchanged the original painting for Geert's reproduction and Henry Dudley never suspected a thing.'

'Well done, I knew you could do it,' Georgina answered and gestured to him to take a seat.

'I must say, it was all quite thrilling. Though it's not something I relish the idea of repeating. I'm an art dealer, not a thief.'

'Oleg is meeting us in The Penthouse tonight before the customers arrive. Make sure you and Dina are there early. He'll pay handsomely for the original and we can sleep tightly knowing that we haven't ripped him off... again.'

'You seem a little nervous of Oleg,' Lord Hamilton said.

'I am. He's a dangerous man. But a very wealthy dangerous man and I regret that I sold him a couple of fakes. From now on, if Oleg requests any art, we only sell him originals. Keep the repros for those who aren't likely to kill us if they discover we've ripped them off.'

'Kill us! Goodness,' he spluttered. 'I hope you're joking.'

'Of course I am,' Georgina quickly lied. She'd made a

mistake. She wanted Lord Hamilton on board and didn't want to scare the man off.

'I'm glad to hear it,' he said.

'Yes, well, I'm going to be busy for the rest of the day so I'll see you this evening.'

Once alone in her office, she picked up her bag and looked inside. Her gun stared back at her. Snapping it shut, her mind whirled. Would today be the day that she killed The Top? Or would she be the one to die? But if that happened she wouldn't have a legacy to pass to her children. No, today she wouldn't die and neither would The Top. But he would one day, just as soon as she'd made a nest egg for her kids.

Johnny came in without knocking, which irritated her. His slapdash attitude lately had already got them into trouble and now she had the Zammits to worry about again. 'Drive me to see Temi,' Georgina told him before he'd had a chance to sit down.

'Do you think that's wise?'

'Do you think you're in any position to question my judgement?'

Johnny lowered his eyes and Georgina threw on her coat. As she passed Elsie in the café, she was pleased to see the woman was no longer wearing the earrings.

In the car, Johnny asked, 'Why are we going to see Mr Zammit?'

'That's my business.'

Johnny must have realised she wasn't in the best of moods with him and remained silent for the rest of the journey. He didn't even light up one of his stinking cigars, though if he had she'd have told him to stub it out.

Once outside Temi's club, Georgina told Johnny to wait

in the car. What she had to discuss with Temi didn't concern Johnny and the fewer people who knew of her plans, the better.

'Georgina, such a pleasant surprise. You look wonderful,' Temi greeted her, a genuine smile on his face.

'Thank you. I hope you don't mind me calling in unannounced?'

'Of course not. You're welcome here anytime. In fact, this is perfect timing. My wife will be here shortly and I'd like you to meet her. She's heard about you and I think she wants to make sure that you're not throwing yourself at me,' Temi said, laughing heartily.

'Should I be worried?'

'Only if you choose to do just that and throw yourself at me.'

'In that case, there's nothing to worry about.'

'Oh, Georgina, you break my heart again.'

The door opened and all of Temi's six men jumped to their feet and removed their hats. Georgina turned around to see a raven-haired woman stride into the office. The woman eyed Georgina with her black eyes.

'Ah, my darling, we were just talking about you. This is Georgina Garrett. Georgina, meet my wife, Lora Zammit.'

'Pleasure to meet you, Mrs Zammit.'

Lora stepped closer to Georgina but didn't offer her hand. 'Likewise,' she said sharply.

'Please, take a seat, Georgina. Perhaps you'd like to share a cup of tea with my wife?'

Georgina sat on the sofa and, though she had no desire to share a cup of tea with a cold fish like Lora Zammit, she smiled sweetly and said, 'Thank you. That would be nice.'

Lora sat at the other end of the sofa and Georgina could feel herself being slyly scrutinised. She'd have liked to tell the woman she had no designs on her husband and never bloody would. Instead, she asked, 'I love your hat. Where did you get it?'

'In Marie Macon's, a French boutique. It's very exclusive.'

'I see both you ladies have an eye for fashion. Perhaps you'd like to take Georgina shopping with you one day?'

Lora didn't answer her husband and merely sniffed. It was clear the woman was no more enamoured with the idea of shopping together than Georgina was. The tension between them felt thick and it was obvious they'd taken an instant dislike to each other.

'What is your purpose for visiting my husband today?' Lora asked, looking down her nose as she addressed Georgina.

'To clarify something, but it's a business matter and private.'

'I know my husband's business.'

'I'm sure you do but—'

'—So you can discuss it now,' Lora interrupted.

Georgina took a deep breath and rose to her feet. She was done with being polite to the obnoxious woman. 'Look, Mrs Zammit, I've no interest in your husband other than business. I don't expect you to take my word on that, after all, you don't know me, but it's the truth. Now, if you'll excuse me, I'll come back when your husband isn't busy and I can discuss my business with him alone.'

Georgina smiled tightly at the woman and walked towards the door. She heard Lora call, 'Wait, please.'

When she turned back she saw that the woman's face

had softened. 'I get to see my husband every night and every morning. Please, stay and discuss your business, whatever it is. I'll make myself busy in the nearby shops and will spend lots and lots of his money. Ha, look how horrified he looks now,' she said and laughed as she pointed at Temi.

Georgina saw another side to Lora now and laughed too. 'Thank you. I won't take much of his time.'

'Take as long as you like. The longer you take, the more I'll spend. Right, I'll be back later. Oh, and Georgina, you must come round for afternoon tea one day.'

When Lora left, Temi ordered his men out too. As the door closed behind them his expression changed and he looked at her gravely. Her heart began to race as she feared he suspected her of being behind the theft from his father's jewellery shop.

'Sit down, Georgina,' he said, indicating a chair in front of his desk.

She managed to look composed as she took the seat, hands clutching her bag on her lap, and said, 'It... it was nice to meet your wife.'

'Yes, I think she likes you. You haven't been to visit The Top yet,' he said, changing the subject.

'No, that's what I wanted to talk to you about,' she answered, relieved he hadn't mentioned his father's jewellery shop.

'Have you changed your mind?'

'Of course not, but I'll do it in my own time, when I'm ready. I just wanted to ensure that your man will still be expecting me.'

'Yes, he will. But how long are we talking? Days, weeks, months?'

'I don't know. Weeks, maybe months.'

Temi leaned back in his chair and patted his cheek with his index finger, deep in thought. 'This isn't what I wanted to hear, Georgina. The Top is a constant threat to me and my business, and to you too. Are you sure you're up for the job?'

'I'm sure. But don't try to put pressure on me. I don't work for you.'

'Maybe not, but I'm not prepared to wait weeks or months for the man to be taken out. In fact, I was hoping he'd be dead by now.'

'He will be, though not yet. There are several things I need to secure first.'

'Anything I can help with?'

'No, not really. I'm only just out of prison and before I risk my life, I want to make sure my children will be looked after financially. Once I have a few business transactions under my belt, I'll be ready.'

'Money is the only thing holding you back?'

'Yes.'

'Ha, well, that's easily remedied. How much do you want? What will be a sufficient figure to leave for your children? Not that I'm suggesting you'll die. But I'll give you the money you want. If you kill The Top and don't get killed yourself, you will return my money. That way, we're all happy.'

Georgina was taken aback by Temi's offer and hadn't been expecting it. As she thought about it, Temi spoke again.

'Of course, if you are too proud to accept my offer, I can easily have The Top killed by my men. But then you'll miss out on the sweet revenge that I know drives you.'

Georgina rubbed her finger where her mother's wedding ring had been. Would knowing that The Top was dead be enough to satisfy her? Or did she need to put the bullet in his head herself?

'I want five thousand pounds,' she said bluntly.

'Five thousand,' Temi spluttered. 'I'll give you two. That's more than enough for each of your children to buy a house. And I know you already own a café, a club and a large house. Don't take liberties with me.'

'All right, two will suffice.'

'Good, I'm very pleased you've accepted my offer. I'm not worried about losing my money, Georgina, because I know that you *will* kill him.'

Georgina was glad that Temi had faith in her. She had her doubts but quickly dismissed them. 'Leave the money with Benjamin Harel, my accountant. The Top will be dead by the end of the week.'

Geert Neerhoff roughly spooned a mouthful of porridge into his wife's mouth. His stomach turned at the sight of most of it dribbling down her chin.

'Look at the mess you're making, you dirty cow,' he moaned spitefully.

Doris just gazed back at him blankly, unaware of who he was.

'I don't know why I bother. I should let you starve to death,' he snapped and slammed the bowl down on the bedside table. 'You needn't think I'm getting you a nurse again. I've got my own money now and I'm keeping it for me! You can rot in hell for all I care.'

'Don't like you,' Doris mumbled.

'I don't like you either but I'm stuck with you until you die.'

'Want my mother.'

'She's dead, Doris. Your mother has been dead for years. So has your father. I'm all you've got in this world so you should be nicer to me. I'm the one who feeds you, washes you and cleans up your shit! I've always been at your beck and call, always. And for once in my life, I don't have to ask you for money. I don't *need* you, Doris, not anymore. I could leave you here to fester in your own piss in that bed and no one would ever know.'

Doris showed no reaction to his words and rolled a piece of scraggly grey hair around her finger as she quietly hummed a tune.

'Did you hear me? Oh, why do I bother?' Geert spat venomously as he rose to his feet from the edge of her bed. 'I'll tell you why, Doris. I bother with you because I want your house and your money. I've waited this bloody long for it, I'm not walking away from it now. Just hurry up and die, woman. I swear you keep yourself alive just to spite me.'

Geert pulled his arm back, ready to give her a backhander. Doris cried out and cowered against her pillow. 'I could slap your ugly face so hard, you bitch,' he ground out. 'Give in, Doris. Give in. Just fucking die!'

She started humming that incessant tune again.

Geert picked up her unfinished porridge and stamped across the bedroom floor, slamming the door behind him as he left. In the kitchen, he scraped the food into the bin and threw the bowl into the sink. It cracked in two. Geert stood with his hands on his hips, looking at the broken bowl. He wasn't sure for how much longer he could tolerate his poorly wife. But if he wanted to get his hands on her fortune, then he'd have to put up with her for as long as it took. Granted, he had some disposable cash of his own now but it wasn't enough. And why should he walk away from Doris empty-handed after everything he'd done for her? He'd have to bide his time but he hoped it wouldn't be for much longer. After all, Doris was becoming frailer as each day passed. She'd once been a curvaceous woman with plenty of flesh on her bones. But now her ribs jutted through her chest and her skinny legs didn't have the strength to support her.

Geert looked up to the ceiling and shook his head. Doris's room was above. He could just about hear her grumbling, calling for her mother again. He couldn't stand to hear her whining. Grabbing his coat from the back of a kitchen chair, he checked the pocket. The ring he'd bought for Eva was tucked inside. It wasn't an expensive gift but he'd enjoyed buying it for his mistress and was sure she'd show him her appreciation. The thought of Eva's firm body wrapped around him made his groin stir. Without a second thought for Doris, he headed to his studio where he'd arranged to meet Eva. He'd find comfort in her arms. Their love-making would be passionate. And she'd be pleased with the cash windfall that Geert had acquired, though he was worried that the transaction would bring repercussions. But if there were, he felt confident that the man he'd struck a deal with would protect him. After all, it was in both their interests to keep him safe.

*

Later that evening, Charlotte cleared the dinner plates away. Georgina had noticed that she'd hardly touched her food and had instead been pushing it around her plate. Charlotte returned from the kitchen looking miserable. She'd been moping around since Tim had left yesterday for basic training.

'Why don't you come down to The Penthouse with me tonight? I've got a bit of business to conduct but once that's done, we can have a nice evening together,' Georgina suggested, hoping to cheer Charlotte up.

'No thanks. I'm shattered. It was busy in the café today.'

'You've got Elsie there to help you.'

'Huh, some bleedin' help she is!' Charlotte sniffed.

'Isn't she pulling her weight?'

'No, she bloody ain't, the lazy mare. She spends more time flicking through her fancy magazines than she does serving customers. You wanna hear her cooing at pictures of this dress or that hat. And all she talks about is what posh frocks and jewellery she had when she was with Jacob. I'm telling you, Georgina, there's something not right about her.'

Georgina hadn't noticed, but then why would she as she hadn't spent any time with Elsie. But what Charlotte said set alarm bells ringing in Georgina's head. She trusted Charlotte's judgement of people. The girl had been right about Nancy Austin and said from the off that Nancy was a wrong 'un. Unfortunately, Charlotte had been spot on and the years Georgina had spent behind bars were a testament to that.

'You're the boss in the café, Charlotte. If she ain't doing her job, you need to have a word with her?'

'I have. I've talked to her until I'm blue in the face but it just goes over the top of her head. It's like she's in a world of her own. I know she's Johnny's girlfriend but I just ain't keen on her at all.'

'All right, leave it with me. I'll speak to her. It's a shame she's not working in the cloakroom at The Penthouse anymore. But I'll have a chat with her tomorrow.'

'You'll be wasting your breath. I reckon when her old man knocked her about, he knocked all the sense out of her an' all. Don't get me wrong, I feel sorry for her after what she went through with him, but I just can't like her. I don't know what Johnny sees in her.'

'He's easily turned by a pretty face. Are you sure you don't want to come with me tonight? I'd be pleased of the company.'

'I'm sure, thanks. I'm going to write a letter to Tim.'

'He only left yesterday.'

'I know. But I miss him. And I miss Dog too.'

Georgina baulked at the mention of Dog. She missed the soppy mutt as well but did her best to keep thoughts of him from her mind. Especially the memory of how she'd found him, dead with his throat cut. At least Jacob Flowers had paid for what he'd done. She'd enjoyed inflicting the same fate on him as he had on Dog.

'Well, you have fun writing your letter. Say hello to Tim from me. I'd best get off,' Georgina said and grabbed her handbag. She took a red lipstick out of it and stood in front of the mirror over the hearth to apply the colour on her lips. She then checked her stockings. The seams up the back of her legs were straight. She was pleased with the stockings and the three crates of them that she'd acquired. The popular but hard-to-come-by nylons were selling on the black market like hot cakes. There were still women who couldn't afford them though, and would make do with drawing a black line up the backs of their legs. Georgina thought her gran would have laughed at that if she'd been alive to see it.

A car pulled up outside. Georgina looked through the nets to see it was Johnny. She was glad he'd brought her car and not his own. 'Right, I'll see you later. Don't wait up,' she said to Charlotte as she pulled her coat on.

By the time she was outside, Johnny had opened the passenger car door and was holding it, ready to close it after she had climbed in. He was trying his best to get back in favour with her but she was still angry at his lack of judgement lately.

'Straight to The Penthouse?' he asked once she'd sat inside.

'Yes.'

'Everything all right?'

'No, not really, Johnny. I'll be having words with your Elsie tomorrow. Charlotte said she's been skiving in the café. She's leaving Charlotte to do the lion's share of the work and it ain't fair.'

'Has she? I'm surprised to hear that. Elsie comes home feeling pretty worn out. She said she's been grafting too hard to make me any dinner.'

Georgina didn't say anything but raised her eyebrows at Johnny. He started the car and drove off with a frown on his face, clearly digesting what he'd just been told.

They arrived at The Penthouse and Johnny was quick to jump out of the car and run around to Georgina's side.

She'd already opened the door herself and was climbing out by the time Johnny appeared.

The Barker twins looked half frozen but greeted her with warm smiles as they opened the entrance doors. 'That Russian bloke is already here,' Nobby said as she passed him.

At the cloakroom, the young lady Dina had employed appeared nervous. Georgina never really understood why she had that effect on so many people. It wasn't as if she was an ogre! But, not wanting to keep Oleg waiting any longer, she didn't have time to offer any reassurance to the girl now.

Johnny led the way down into the club, swaggering in his usual manner.

'What's the time?' she asked him.

Johnny checked his watch. 'Six-forty.'

'We're late. I hope Dina is keeping Oleg entertained.'

'Poor Oleg,' Johnny replied and guffawed.

Yes, poor Oleg, indeed, thought Georgina. But Oleg was one of the few people who seemed to enjoy Dina's company.

When they walked into the club, Georgina's eyes squinted as her focus adjusted to the dim lights. She spotted Oleg standing by the table where Lord Hamilton was seated and walked towards them with a wide smile. No doubt her Russian customer had already heard from Lord Hamilton that they had the painting he'd requested and trusted Oleg would be willing to pay handsomely for it.

'Johnny, tell Dina to bring us a bottle of champagne,' she said quietly.

Georgina glanced towards the bar. Dina was stood behind it, her hands placed on top, but something appeared amiss.

Even in the low lights, she could see Dina looked distressed. Her eyes were wide with fear and was she crying?

'Wait,' Georgina whispered hastily to Johnny.

She walked towards the bar and as Dina became clearer, Georgina could see the woman's mouth was taped. What was going on? Had Oleg done this? And why had Lord Hamilton allowed it? Perhaps Dina had given Oleg some cheek. That wouldn't have surprised Georgina but the man had no right to treat her staff in this way.

Georgina marched angrily towards the bar, throwing Oleg a filthy sideways look. She wasn't sure, but she thought he smirked back at her. Tears were streaming down Dina's face. Georgina whipped the tape from Dina's mouth.

'My hands, my hands,' Dina shrieked, looking at them on the bar.

Georgina looked too. It took a few moments for her mind to comprehend what she was seeing. Dina's hands were bruised and swollen. Blood oozed from the backs of them. And then, horrified, she realised why. Dina's hands were nailed to the bar!

'Don't move,' Georgina told her.

'I can't.'

Johnny had already reached into his coat and had pulled his gun on Oleg, aiming it across the room. Georgina spun to look at the man. He'd thrown his head back in laughter.

'You won't shoot me because I will blow Lord Hamilton's head off before your bullet hits me,' Oleg warned, his gun now pointed at Lord Hamilton's face.

Georgina stamped towards them. As she drew closer, she could see Lord Hamilton's hands were on the table. She had no doubt that he'd also been nailed to it.

'What the fuck is going on?' she screeched at Oleg. She noticed his gun had a long muffler on the end of the barrel, something she'd only ever read about but never seen. If Oleg fired his gun, the muffler would silence the noise. The Barker twins would have no idea of the bloodshed down here.

'Tell your man to place his gun on the floor and kick it to me,' Oleg answered slowly.

Georgina nodded to Johnny, who carried out the instruction but with obvious reluctance.

Oleg used his foot to drag Johnny's gun closer and bent down to pick it up, keeping his own weapon aimed at Lord Hamilton.

'And you, Georgina, do the same with your gun,' Oleg said.

Georgina sighed, knowing she had no choice. She opened her bag, placed the gun on the floor and slid it towards Oleg.

Oleg picked it up and growled, 'Take a seat,' gesturing to the table. He then turned to Johnny, saying, 'Lock the doors. We wouldn't want to be disturbed by the pair of idiots upstairs.'

Georgina sat at the table as Johnny pulled a lock across the top of the double doors. As she'd feared, Lord Hamilton's hands were nailed down just as Dina's were. She placed a hand on his arm and could feel him trembling. 'It'll be all right,' she whispered.

The only thing that moved were Lord Hamilton's eyes as he glanced sideways at her. The rest of his body remained rigid with fear.

'Right, you've got me where you want me. Now tell me what this is about,' Georgina demanded.

'Let us have a drink first. Dina, bring me vodka and champagne for Miss Garrett.'

'I'll get the drinks,' Georgina said, scraping her seat back and knowing that Dina couldn't move.

Oleg immediately pointed his gun at her. 'No, Dina will bring them… or I will shoot her.'

'You've nailed her hands to the fucking bar! How do you expect her to bring us drinks? I'll get them.'

'No. Sit back down,' Oleg hissed. 'Let me make myself clear, Georgina. I have no affinity with you. I will happily fire my bullets into your head, and then still make Dina bring me a drink. Do not be a martyr and waste your life for nothing.'

Georgina looked over to Dina, feeling helpless, and slowly sat back down.

'Good. Dina, those drinks. Come now, I'm waiting.'

'I can't,' Dina sobbed.

'If I have to fetch the drinks myself, I will kill you. It's your choice, Dina. Bring me vodka or die.'

'But… I can't… my hands,' she cried, furiously shaking her head.

'DO IT!' Oleg barked.

Dina screwed her eyes shut and screamed in pain as she tried to lift her hands from the bar. 'I can't,' she cried again.

'Your choice,' Oleg said and turned his gun towards her.

'THAT'S ENOUGH,' Georgina shrieked. 'How dare you do this to her! Whatever your problem is, it's with me and has nothing to do with Dina.'

Oleg laughed, a long, wicked laugh that made Georgina's blood run cold. She thought the man was as mad as Billy

Wilcox had been, and that sort of unpredictability scared her.

'I want Dina to bring me a drink. It's not too much to ask. It is her job,' he said with a shrug. Without warning, he turned his gun back towards Lord Hamilton and to Georgina's disbelief and horror, Oleg fired a single shot.

Lord Hamilton slumped forward. His head hit the table hard. Georgina could barely bring herself to look but knew instantly that he was dead. His blood seeped from the bullet hole in his head and spread across the table before dripping onto the floor. She glared at Oleg in disbelief, only managing to croak, 'Why?'

'He was boring me,' the man answered nonchalantly.

Dina had fallen silent. Johnny had lowered his eyes and was staring at Lord Hamilton's blood that was inches away from his shiny shoes.

Oleg's gun had hardly made a noise and Georgina realised that no one was going to come to her aid. Once again, she was alone and inwardly prayed, *please, Lash, help me. For our children, help me get out of here alive.*

'You are so much more attractive when you're not snivelling, Dina,' Oleg said. 'I won't ask you again, bring me a vodka – or do you want to be shot dead like Lord Hamilton?'

'Wait, Oleg,' Georgina said quickly. 'Dina will bring you a drink, but first I want to know why you are doing this.'

Oleg pulled out a seat and sat a couple of feet away from the table. He stretched his long legs out in front of him and cocked his head to one side as he scrutinised her. 'You fooled me Georgina,' he said. 'And I don't like to look a fool.'

'Is this about the paintings I sold you?'

'Of course it is. I bought them from you in good faith, believing they were originals. Tell me, did you see me as stupid? Did you laugh behind my back?'

'No, Oleg. It wasn't like that. I admit I sold you fakes and I regret that. I'm sorry, it won't happen again. To make it up to you, I've managed to acquire the original painting you asked for.'

'I know about the original, I have it, here, see,' Oleg said and picked up the wrapped painting from another table. 'As I put a six-inch nail through Dina's hand, Lord Hamilton was eager to give me the painting. He said I could take it free of charge. He also offered me a refund on the first paintings I bought from you. Wasn't that nice of him?'

'Yes, it was, and as Lord Hamilton said, you'll get your money back for the other paintings. You've also had an apology from me. Isn't that enough?'

'Yes, but I still haven't had a vodka,' Oleg said with an evil leer.

'Dina will get you a drink if you promise to allow her to live.'

'Of course. She brings me vodka, she doesn't die.'

'Good,' Georgina said and looked over to Dina. 'Bring Oleg a bottle of vodka and two glasses. One for him and one for yourself.'

Dina's eyes widened in fear as she nodded. It was clear she knew what she had to do if she wanted to stay alive.

'But one more thing, Oleg. How did you find out that the first paintings were fake?'

Oleg casually leaned sideways in his seat and placed his elbow on the armrest, his gun now aimed at Georgina, and answered, 'Your artist. The Dutchman. He told me and I paid him.'

Georgina bit her lower lip as she seethed inside. Geert Neerhoff had sold her out and now Lord Hamilton was dead. She swore to herself that if she got out of The Penthouse alive, she'd kill the double-crossing Dutchman.

Georgina looked back to Dina and saw that her face was as pale as her hair. Georgina didn't want to do it but there was no other option. 'Dina, bring the vodka now,' she ordered.

Dina's jaw clenched and her eyes closed. She drew in a long breath and screamed in agony as she tried to pull her hands off the bar. Georgina couldn't watch but when she looked, Dina had only managed to free one of her hands. She was whimpering now and looked close to passing out.

'Dina, free your other hand. Do it. NOW,' Georgina shouted, cringing at the thought of the pain Dina must be in.

Georgina admired her bravery as Dina gritted her teeth and drew in a long breath. With a determined but agonising scream, her other hand was finally free. She stood in shock, gaping at her bloodied hands and the holes that went through them where the nails had been.

'Well done,' Oleg congratulated her. 'You see, Georgina, our Russian women are strong. Now, Dina, please, bring the vodka and join me.'

As Dina walked machine-like to fetch the vodka, Georgina wondered if the Barker twins had heard the screams, but as they were stood outside the club, she doubted they would have. But what about the new girl in the cloakroom? She must have heard something. Why weren't the twins kicking down the doors?

'Are you planning on staying for long? Only it will be opening time soon and I need to make arrangements to get the place cleaned up,' Georgina asked coolly as she looked at Oleg's gun, still aimed directly at her. Inside she was quaking, but she couldn't let Oleg see her fear.

'No, just for one drink. Your club is of no interest to me and we have concluded our business. I suggest you stay out of art dealing from now on, Georgina. You're not very good at it, and if he could speak, I'm sure Lord Hamilton would agree with me. By the way, you will need to find yourself a new attendant for the cloakroom. Your lady is with me now.'

So that explained why the girl was so nervous, Georgina thought, wrinkling her nose like she had a bad smell under it. Yet another person easily bought.

Dina approached the table, her sore hands shaking as she carried a tray. As she placed it on the table, Georgina heard a terrific bang and to her great relief the double doors to the club burst open. Rapid gunfire sounded overhead. Georgina threw herself under the table, grabbing Dina's arm and dragging her down too. Holding her body over Dina's, she looked across to see Johnny had ducked under the next table. She could hear bullets ricocheting off the walls, glass lampshades smashing and wood splintering.

'Keep down,' she told Dina, shielding her, then mouthed to Johnny, 'Who is it?'

He shook his head, obviously with no idea. She knew it wasn't the Barker twins. They didn't have that sort of gun power.

The firing ceased as Oleg's body fell beside her. He had at least three bullet holes in his chest. Georgina gasped at the sight of him. His eyes were open but empty. Thank goodness he was dead… but who the hell had killed him?

'Stay down,' Georgina whispered to Dina before carefully climbing back to her feet. She glanced around. Her club had been badly shot up and standing in the doorway, her eyes fell on Temi Zammit. He had two men on each side of him, all of them sporting firearms.

'Is he dead?' Temi asked, looking at Oleg's lifeless body on the floor.

'Yes, he is,' Georgina answered. She picked up Oleg's gun, thinking that the muffler would come in useful. As she unscrewed the silencer, Temi saw Lord Hamilton slumped across the table.

'Oh, shit, we didn't kill him too, did we?' he asked.

'No, Oleg did that.'

'Fuck, we were too late. But I'm glad to see you're alive.'

'How did you know?' Georgina asked.

'Our artist friend, Geert Neerhoff. He dropped off a painting today and told me he was in a position to clear his debts to me. I was curious to know how, so I made sure he told me. He said he was working with a Russian man. You know me, Georgina, I make it my business to know everything that is going on and I knew you had sold Oleg some dodgy artwork. He's not a man I'd ever work with. I know his past. I knew he'd kill you and I couldn't allow that to happen.'

Georgina's legs felt weak and her mouth dry. She lowered herself unsteadily onto a seat. 'But what if you'd come bursting in here and killed my customers? What if you'd got it wrong?'

'I never get it wrong. Your men on the door are turning

away any customers tonight. I suggest you pour yourself a stiff drink and get this place cleared up. Good night, Georgina.'

'Wait,' she called after him. 'Why? Why would you do this for me?'

Temi walked over to her and leaned down. She could feel his warm breath on her cheek as he whispered in her ear, 'Because you're going to kill The Top so I need you alive. And now, you owe me.'

23

'I'm warning you, Elsie, don't be late for work today. As it is, Miss Garrett intends to have words with you. You don't want to upset her more than she already is,' Johnny said as he pulled on his coat. 'Come on, get up.'

'But, Johnny, it's so cold. I want to stay under these warm covers,' Elsie answered and pulled the blankets up to her chin.

'Get dressed, that'll keep you warm.'

'I had a lovely, thick dressing gown when I lived with Jacob. He bought it for me from Harrods. It had matching slippers too.'

''Ere,' Johnny said impatiently. He took his dressing gown from the back of a chair and threw it on the bed. 'It ain't from Harrods but it'll have to do.'

Elsie looked at the dressing gown with disdain. 'I want a new one. My own one.'

'Then get out of bed, go to work and you can buy yourself one with your wages. Christ, Elsie, what you earn is for you to spend on yourself. It's not like I'm taking money from you towards bills and food, is it?'

'Huh, even four weeks' wages from the café wouldn't be

enough to buy anything from Harrods. Don't you want me looking nice?'

'Of course I do. You always look lovely.'

'I don't. I look like a cheap washerwoman. Jacob would never have allowed me to lower my standards and wear dresses from the Co-op, yet that's all I'll be able to afford.'

Elsie's bottom lip pouted. Johnny thought she looked like a spoiled child and that she was behaving like one too. He didn't have time for one of her tantrums this morning and kissed her forehead.

'I've got to go. I'll try and find time today to get you something nice. Now, be a good girl and get up and go to work.'

He headed out, leaving Elsie sulking in his bed. He had bigger things on his mind and Elsie with her desire for expensive dresses seemed trivial to him.

Johnny pulled up outside Miss Garrett's and tooted his horn. She soon appeared and as she climbed into the car, Johnny tried unsuccessfully to stifle a yawn.

'Keeping you up, are we?' she asked.

'No, sorry, just knackered after all that excitement last night.'

'It was a bit crazy.'

'How's Dina?' Johnny asked.

'She'll live, but her hands ain't in good shape. The poor woman, I don't know how she found the strength to free them like she did. She's pissed off with me. She reckons whenever I'm around, she nearly gets killed.'

'Dina is always pissed off with someone. But, yeah, you're right about how strong she is. I don't know if I could have done what she did and I'm a tough bloke.'

'Well, as I explained to Dina, a certain person is going to pay for it. Did you bring Max's axe?'

'Yeah, it's wrapped up in a cloth under your seat.'

'Good. Let's go. He won't be expecting us at this time of the morning.'

It was still dark when they pulled up outside Geert's house. Johnny got out of the car first and looked up and down the quiet street. This was a well-to-do area of Battersea, a far cry from the rows of two-up, two-downs that he was more familiar with. He glanced up at the large house where Geert was reported to live and saw a thin sliver of light from behind the curtain of an upstairs window.

'Someone's home,' he said.

'Good. Knock on the door.'

Johnny loudly rapped the heavy brass knocker three times and waited. No one came to the door. 'Do you want me to kick it in?' he asked.

'No, that will draw too much attention. Knock again.'

He did but still no one answered.

'What now?' he asked.

'Have you got your penknife?'

'Yes.'

'Jemmy the window. It's a sash, so you should be—'

'—Yeah, I know how to do it,' Johnny interrupted.

He squeezed past a large shrub in front of the downstairs bay window and after a few minutes of fiddling, he managed to slide his knife between the frame and the inside lock.

'I'm in,' he called quietly to Georgina.

After carefully lifting the window, Johnny clambered through. Inside, he found the room in darkness and as he stepped forward, he bumped into a table, nearly knocking off a vase. He could hardly see a thing. Geert could be hiding in a corner waiting to jump him, so Johnny reached into his pocket and pulled out his gun before treading cautiously through the room. He opened a door to the passageway and heard a muffled noise coming from upstairs. He thought it sounded like a woman calling for her mother.

Johnny ignored the sounds and dashed along the hall to open the front door for Georgina. She marched in carrying Max the Axe's tomahawk. He wondered what she intended doing with it and assumed she was going to lodge it in Geert's skull, though he thought it was a strange choice of weapon for her. But it would be quieter than firing her gun and she'd already made it clear that she didn't want the neighbours to hear what was going on.

'What's that noise?' Georgina asked.

'I don't know. It sounds like a woman crying.'

'Any sign of him?'

'I haven't checked down here, but at this time of the morning, I reckon he's probably still in bed.'

'All right, but still check these rooms. I'll wait here in case he tries to sneak downstairs and out of the front door.'

Johnny found all the other rooms in darkness and returned to say to Georgina, 'If he's here, he's upstairs.'

She led the way and he followed close behind her. The sound of the woman crying became louder. It was coming from a room at the back of the house and walking quietly towards it, Georgina opened the door. The light in the room was on but Johnny couldn't see much past Georgina, but when she stepped to one side he gasped at the sight of an old woman lying skew-whiff in a large bed. Her matted white hair and pale face gave her a ghostly appearance and the smell that emanated from her turned his stomach.

'Who the fuck is she?' Johnny asked.

The old woman didn't seem to notice them in her room and continued calling for her mother.

'I don't know, maybe she's Geert's mother, the poor cow. He's obviously not taking good care of her.'

Johnny heard a door open further along the landing and stepped out of the woman's bedroom, just as Geert ran past him. 'Stop or I'll shoot,' he yelled.

Geert was halted in his tracks, and when he turned to see a gun pointed at him, the colour drained from his face.

'Ah, there you are,' Georgina said sweetly when she too walked out of the old woman's bedroom. 'Didn't you hear us knocking?'

Geert looked down the stairs to the front door and Johnny warned, 'Don't even think about trying to make a run for it. You ain't faster than my bullets.'

'Who's the old girl?' Georgina asked.

'My... my wife,' Geert stuttered. 'She's unwell.'

'I can see that. Now then, Geert, let's have a chat. Maybe in your kitchen,' Georgina said and walked towards the stairs. 'After you,' she added, indicating with her gun.

Johnny followed, his mind racing. Geert had said the old lady was his wife. He thought she must be a good thirty years older than him and wondered why he'd married her. He didn't like the idea of it!

In the kitchen, Georgina instructed Geert to turn the light on.

Johnny blinked and when his eyes adjusted to the bright light, he saw the well-appointed kitchen was a mess.

Bowls and plates were piled in the sink. The rubbish bin overflowed and there were half-empty bottles of milk scattered along the kitchen worktops.

'Sit down,' Georgina calmly said to Geert.

The man looked visibly shaken as he sat at a large farmhouse type table.

'Close the door, Johnny,' she ordered and turned back to Geert with a sickly smile.

'I know why you're here. I'm sorry, I had no choice. Oleg made me tell him everything,' Geert blurted.

'Is that right? I understand he paid you well?'

'No, no, no, no, no, no. He never paid me a penny. He threatened to kill my wife. I *had* to tell him.'

'That's a very different story to the one I've heard. But you artistic sorts are very creative. Seems you're creative with your tales too.'

'No, Miss Garrett, I swear I'm telling the truth.'

'Of course you are, Geert, that's what they all say. But I know a liar when I see one. Tell me, did you go to Oleg purely for money?'

Geert covered his face with his hands and slowly nodded. 'I was desperate,' he said.

'You have no idea what desperate is,' Georgina snarled. 'But you will by the time I've finished with you.'

'Please, Miss Garrett, don't kill me. Who will look after my wife? I'm all she has.'

'Whatever gave you the idea that I'm going to kill you? No, that's not my plan, though maybe it should be. Your greed caused the death of Lord Hamilton.'

Geert's head snapped up and he looked surprised. 'Did Oleg kill him?'

'Yes, he did. Unfortunately for you, whatever sly little scheme you had going with Oleg has backfired on you. Oleg is dead too.'

Geert looked down at the table. 'I'll give you all the money Oleg paid me. And I'll paint whatever paintings you want, for free, of course.'

'Where's the money?' Georgina asked.

Geert pointed to a cupboard in the corner. Johnny opened it and retrieved a tin box. He looked inside to find it filled with cash. 'Yep, it's here,' he told Georgina.

She walked around the large table, her heels clicking on the flagstone floor. 'See, the thing is, Geert, it's not all about the money.'

'I can make you as many paintings as you'd like.'

'Well, I'm not in the art business anymore,' she said, and then added, 'and neither are you.'

'What do you mean?' Geert asked, looking from Georgina to Johnny.

Johnny saw Georgina nod at him. He knew what to do. As he walked to stand behind Geert, he pulled a handkerchief from his trouser pocket and took a scarf off from around his neck.

'Don't struggle,' he warned Geert and placed his hands on the man's shoulders.

Geert turned his head to look at Johnny with panic in his eyes. Johnny crudely shoved the handkerchief in Geert's mouth. Geert tried to resist and thrashed his head from side to side but Johnny soon had Geert's mouth stuffed and he secured the handkerchief by roughly tying the scarf around his head. Geert groaned, but was unable to talk or scream. His moans were muted cries, no one would hear him calling for help. Johnny stood behind Geert's chair and pressed down on the man's shoulders as he husked in Geert's ear, 'Don't try and do a runner. You'll only make things worse for yourself.'

Georgina placed her gun on the table and slowly unwrapped the small axe. When Geert saw it, he moaned harder and kicked out with his legs. Johnny pushed the end of the barrel of his gun into Geert's temple. 'Sit still, you little shit,' he growled.

The feel of the cold metal against Geert's head seemed to subdue him and he settled down. 'That's better,' Johnny said.

Georgina slowly waved the axe back and forth in front of Geert's face. 'You remember I said you're not in the business of painting anymore?' she asked.

Geert nodded while Johnny thought to himself that if Georgina was going to whack the man over the head with the axe, he hoped he could jump out of the way of the blood splatter. He'd recently had his coat cleaned and repaired and didn't want it messed up again. But she'd told Geert that she wasn't going to kill him so what was she up to? Then it dawned on him and he smiled wryly. She said he wouldn't be painting anymore and now he anticipated her next move. 'Put your hands on the table where I can see them,' he growled.

Geert did as he was told and Johnny looked over Geert's head and met Georgina's eyes. She smiled at him, affirmation that he'd done well. It had been a while since he'd pleased her and he liked being back in her good books. He spotted a mop and bucket by the back door and an idea sprung to mind. 'Keep an eye on him,' he said and then began to rummage through the kitchen drawers.

'What are you looking for?' Georgina asked, once again pointing her gun at Geert.

'You'll see.'

She didn't question him further and Johnny soon found a ball of string. He fetched the mop to the table and placed the long handle across Geert's arms at elbow height, tying it on with the string. Geert didn't dare protest as he stared down the barrel of Georgina's gun. Once the mop was secured to Geert's arms, Johnny tied string around both ends of the mop. He then wound each end to a table leg. 'Done,' he said proudly to Georgina. He was confident that no matter how much Geert might try, there was no way he'd be able to lift his arms off the table.

'Good work, Johnny,' Georgina answered and swapped her gun for the axe.

Johnny stood behind Geert again and pressed down on his shoulders.

As Georgina pulled her arm back and over her head, she said to Geert, 'You'll never paint again.' Then with a swift and hard movement, she brought the axe down across Geert's right hand.

Johnny felt Geert's body tense with pain. Geert thrashed his head from side to side, again his screams were muffled by the gag. Blood spewed from the gaping wound that had severed his hand from his wrist.

Georgina brought the axe up again and Johnny turned his face. He heard the axe thud into the wooden table and Geert's stifled cries. When he looked back again, Geert's fingers had been cut off across the knuckles but at least his hand was still intact and he had a thumb.

Geert's head lolloped sideways. He'd passed out. Johnny wondered if the man would bleed to death but couldn't care less if he did. Yet strangely, there wasn't as much blood as Johnny had expected to see.

'Are we done?' he asked Georgina.

'Yes, that'll do. Untie the mop from the table legs and push the chair across to the stove. Stick his arms in the flame to cauterise the bleeding.'

'But me coat will get messed up.'

Georgina glared at him. He knew that look and didn't argue. As he shoved Geert's bleeding stumps in the naked flame the stench of burning flesh made Johnny gag. Geert came round, tried to scream again and then slumped back into unconsciousness.

When Johnny was satisfied that the bleeding had stopped, he poured a jug of cold water over each of Geert's arms. That was it, he was done, unwilling to show Geert any further care. He heard Georgina call him from the hallway and was surprised to find her carrying the old woman.

'We'll drop her at the hospital. Hurry up, Johnny, open the door. She stinks, bless her.'

The old woman was quieter than she had been. Maybe she sensed that Georgina was helping her. Maybe she was just happy to be out of her filthy bed. Johnny didn't relish the idea of having the woman in the back of the car but he agreed with Georgina, they couldn't leave her in the house.

As they drove to the hospital, the woman's stench made Johnny want to heave. He had to wind down the window for fresh air.

'Wind it back up. She'll get cold,' Georgina instructed.

Johnny rolled his eyes but the old woman was so frail that he thought Georgina had a point. He thought his boss to be a complex woman. One minute she was severing hands, the next she was rescuing an old lady. One thing was for sure – there was nobody like Georgina Garrett.

24

Benjamin Harel sat at Georgina's desk. He pushed his round-rimmed glasses up his nose and snapped shut the accounting book. 'Apart from The Penthouse out of business while it's under repair, your figures are looking a lot healthier,' he told Georgina. 'Though I'm not counting the two thousand pounds on erm, loan, from Mr Zammit as I expect that will, erm, be paid back shortly?'

'Yes, it will. In fact, all being well, you can return his money to him on Monday.'

'I don't want to think about the alternative.'

'Don't worry, Benjamin. I shall endeavour to remain well and healthy and Temi Zammit can be paid back in full.'

'I hope so. I don't suppose you will, erm, tell me what it is you're doing?'

'You know I won't. I'll tell you after, I always do, don't I?'

'Yes, I'm always the last to know,' Benjamin answered as he packed away his books. 'I shall see you on Monday?'

'Yes, you will. If not, you know what to do with my money and assets.'

Benjamin looked sad as he nodded his head.

'I'll be fine,' she said reassuringly. 'Now go, and give my love to your dad.'

Charlotte entered Georgina's office as Benjamin left. She frowned as she stamped in.

'I've had it with her,' Charlotte grumbled, throwing her head towards the door. 'I thought you was going to have a word with her?'

'Yes, I am, but I've been a bit busy.'

'You ain't kidding. Bodies have been dropping like flies since you got out of prison. And I'll tell you what, if Miss bleedin' Fancy Pants out there don't pull her socks up, she'll be joining the body count an' all.'

'What's she done now?'

'Nothing! That's the whole point. She ain't done a bleedin' thing. I've been serving customers, wiping down tables and preparing food while Elsie has been sat on her good-for-nothing lazy arse with her stuck-up nose in a magazine. I'm gonna go for her, so help me God, I'll scratch her bleedin' eyes out. See how she gets on then with looking at her stupid magazines!'

'All right, calm down. Send her in to me, I'll talk to her.'

'I don't know why you're bothering. There's plenty who'd be grateful of the job.'

'I'm bothering because she's Johnny's girlfriend and we look after our own.'

'Yeah, well, Johnny needs his head testing. You know he's gone out nicking for her again?'

'You're kidding me? After the fiasco with the Zammits' jewellers?'

'Yep. She got that fur stole from Johnny, and that expensive hat. She told me he brings her something home every day. Bragging about it, she was. Apparently, "*my*

Johnny said I'm his queen and he'll have me dripping in jewels soon."'

'You're right, Johnny does need his head testing. The silly sod. He'd better not get himself nicked for pinching stuff for her. I won't be happy. Anyway, send her in.'

Moments later, Elsie breezed into the office and sat at Georgina's desk.

'You weren't invited to take a seat,' Georgina snapped.

Elsie raised her eyebrows, but rose to her feet.

'Do you realise what a fortunate position you're in?' Georgina asked.

Elsie shrugged her shoulders.

'Allow me to spell it out for you. You're a woman with no means of her own. But you have a roof over your head provided by a man who doesn't knock you about and asks for little in return. A man who brings you gifts, expensive ones an' all from what I've observed.'

Elsie just shrugged and, suppressing her anger, Georgina continued, 'You have no experience or qualifications in any type of work. Actually, you've never done an honest day's work in your life. Yet here you are, provided with secure full-time employment for a reasonable salary, and let's face it, it's not overly taxing working in my small café, is it?'

'No, I suppose not.'

'Good, I'm glad we agree on that. So, would you like to explain to me the reason why you are allowing Charlotte to do all the work?'

Elsie pursed her lips then shrugged again.

'I see. Do you want the job?'

'I don't know. Maybe,' Elsie answered belligerently.

Georgina's temper snapped and she said angrily, 'Fine.

You can leave anytime you like. You're not a prisoner here as you were with your husband. In fact, I'll make it easy for you. You're sacked. Get your coat and hat and leave. And you needn't think you're getting paid for the time that you've sat in *my* café, drinking *my* tea and eating *my* cakes.'

'But—'

'—No buts. I don't want to hear it. Go. Now.'

Elsie sloped off, leaving Georgina shaking her head in disbelief. Charlotte had been right – Elsie's attitude had been appalling. Georgina wished Johnny good luck with the woman, glad that Elsie was no longer her problem.

Charlotte stuck her head through the office door. 'She's walked out!'

'I know. I sacked her. Get hold of Fleur. She should be out of Holloway by now. I'll have to leave that with you because I've got enough to be getting on with,' Georgina answered as she thought about her next task.

'No problem. I like Fleur and she's a grafter,' Charlotte smiled.

'Once you've trained her up, you can jack in the café if you like?'

'No, I think I'll stay. I know I said I didn't want to do it but, actually, I quite enjoy working here. Gotta dash, there's a customer.'

The door closed and Georgina rubbed her forehead. She had a splitting headache but needed to think clearly. It was Thursday. Tomorrow would be Friday. The Top would be dead by the end of the week. She would kill him. That's what she'd told Temi Zammit and it's exactly what she intended to do.

★

Geert Neerhoff opened his eyes to excruciating pain in both his arms. The searing agony was almost unbearable but he couldn't scream. He felt like he was choking and struggled to breath. He cried out but there was no sound, just a muted groan. The pain at the end of his arms intensified. Why couldn't he call for help? Panic coursed through him. Was he dreaming? Having a nightmare? His eyes, wild with fear, looked around. He recognised he was at home. In his kitchen. He couldn't talk. Oh, God, he hurt *so* badly. Then he realised he was gagged and at that moment, the terrifying memories flooded back. He raised his arms in front of his face and stared in shocked horror at the charred and swollen stumps where his hands should be.

Vomit rose in his throat at the disgusting sight. The gag. The vomit. He couldn't expel it from his throat. He couldn't swallow it back down. He couldn't cough it back up.

Instinctively, he tried to undo the knot at the back of his head that secured the handkerchief in his mouth that was killing him. He had no fucking hands!

He couldn't breathe, slowly choking to death on his own puke.

Geert jumped from the seat and ran to the kitchen drawer. A knife, a pair of scissors. Anything to cut off the scarf so that he could breathe again. He reached for the handle of the drawer and tried to hook his blackened thumb under it. The pain. Then it dawned on him again. He had no fucking hands! He wouldn't be able to hold a knife, let alone use it to free himself. He wanted to call Doris to help. His lungs ached.

Geert staggered towards the table, desperate to breathe. A feeling of floating out of his body washed over him. He saw his severed hand and reached out for it. Using his arm, he scraped it towards him but then collapsed to the floor. His hand fell from the table and landed on his face.

Geert Neerhoff died in severe pain while staring in horror at his disconnected hand that covered his eyes.

25

On Friday morning, as Charlotte got ready to go to work in the café, Georgina tried her best to behave normally around the girl. But inside, her heart was racing with fear.

'Charlotte, sit down a moment, please.'

'Is everything all right?' Charlotte asked as she sat on the arm of the sofa.

'Yes, everything is fine. I just want you to know that if anything ever happens to me, you'll be looked after.'

'Why are you saying things like that?' Charlotte asked worriedly.

'No reason. But you know my line of work comes with danger. Anything could happen. I want you to feel assured that with or without me, you'll be taken care of.'

'Shut up, Georgina, you're scaring me. Are you doing something today?'

'No, nothing out of the ordinary,' she lied.

'Then shut up and don't talk like you're going to die!' Charlotte cried.

'I'm sorry, I didn't mean to upset you.'

'So stop being so bloody morbid!'

'All right, calm down. I wish I hadn't said anything now.'

'Yeah, me an' all, Georgina. I hate the thought of losing you. It's bad enough having to worry about Tim off fighting at war, without worrying about you too.'

'You don't have to fret about me. You know I can take care of myself.'

'Yeah, I know. And make sure you do, eh?'

'Always, Charlotte, always. Now, time's getting on and you'd best be off to the café.'

'Ain't you coming?'

'Later. I've got a few things to do first.'

'Like what?' Charlotte asked, her eyes narrowing.

'None of your business, young lady. Now, bugger off.'

Charlotte huffed but called cheerio as she closed the door behind her. Georgina looked at the clock on the mantel again. Only two minutes had passed since the last time she'd checked. Her hands felt clammy as she wrung them together.

'Come on, Johnny,' she mumbled under her breath.

At last, Georgina saw the car pull up and rushed out of the house. She checked her waistband for the umpteenth time. It was there. Her gun, fully loaded and with the silencer attached, tucked in the back of her belt. She wore a smart, dark blue jacket that matched her skirt and hid the weapon well.

'Good morning, Miss Garrett. Where to?' Johnny greeted her cheerfully.

Georgina stared straight ahead. 'To see The Top,' she answered, and swallowed hard.

'The Top. Any reason why?'

'Yes, Johnny, because I said so.'

'Fair enough.'

'Did you get me some more of those sleeping pills?'

'Yes, here,' Johnny answered and pulled them from his pocket to pass them to her.

'I suppose Elsie has had plenty to say?' Georgina asked.

'About what?'

'About me sacking her.'

Johnny's head snapped round. 'You've sacked her?' he asked, surprised.

'Yes. Keep your eyes on the road. I sacked her yesterday. Didn't she tell you?'

'No, she never mentioned it.'

They drove the rest of the way in silence. Georgina thought Johnny was probably wondering why Elsie hadn't told him that she'd lost her job. It seemed strange but maybe Elsie had been too embarrassed to say anything. Yet somehow she doubted that.

They passed a young mother pushing a navy blue and cream pram with one hand, while dragging a young lad along with the other. It made Georgina think about her children. Her stomach churned. She might never see them again. Was attempting to kill The Top really worth it? She pondered this for a while, and finally decided that yes, it was. She couldn't live with herself in the knowledge that The Top was alive and David was dead. And Temi Zammit had made a good argument. If The Top wanted to, there was nothing to stop him coming after the Zammits or her. The world would be a better and safer place without The Top in it.

Once outside the house, Georgina turned to Johnny. 'Wait for me in the next street. If I'm not with you in an hour, drive off. Go, and never look back. Do you understand?'

'Whoa, hang on a minute. What are you up to?'

'Don't question me, Johnny, just do as I say.'

'You're going in there to try and knock him off, ain't ya?'

'He killed David Maynard.'

'Yeah, I know, but, please, Miss Garrett, don't do this. You'll never get to him and... well...'

'I know what I'm up against.'

'I'm coming with you.'

'No, you're bloody well not! I told you to wait round the corner and you'll do as I say.'

'I can't let you do this alone.'

'Yes, you can, and you will. I'll have a better chance alone. If we both go in, the pair of us could end up dead.'

'Then let me do it.'

'Don't talk daft.'

'I ain't. My job is to look after you. If you want The Top taken out, then I'll do it.'

Georgina looked into Johnny's eyes and felt an overwhelming feeling of gratitude. He would sacrifice his life for her, yet she'd been nothing but annoyed and snappy with him lately. She reached out and touched his arm. 'Thank you, Johnny. Thank you for everything. But I'm doing this and that's an end to it. You know how stubborn I can be. You won't change my mind.'

'For fuck's sake!' he ground out, his jaw clenching.

'I'll see you in a while... I hope,' she added, mumbling under her breath.

As she climbed out of the car, Johnny said softly, 'I think the world of you, Miss Garrett.'

'I know. And I do you an' all. Now, clear off,' she said firmly, but with a soft smile. She could see he didn't want to leave her. 'Go,' she ordered firmly.

Georgina waited to see Johnny's car reverse up the road and around the corner. Then she walked across to the large house and rapped on the heavy wooden doors. Her heart was pounding so hard that she thought it might burst out of her chest. 'Stay calm,' she told herself.

When the hatch opened, she said clearly, 'Georgina Garrett. I'm here to buy.'

Ralph slammed the hatch shut then minutes later he opened one of the doors. She knew the routine and followed him through the grand but stark hallway and up the stairs. The familiar two bouncers were stood outside a door. She looked at the one who had frisked her before. He stepped forward but she didn't see any recognition in his eyes. Now she worried that he wasn't one of Temi's men and would find her concealed weapon. She held her arms out at her sides as the bouncer's hands roamed up her legs and over her body. Again, he was too *friendly* with her breasts but she ignored his sly grope. She held her breath as his hands felt around her waist and to her back. There it was. He must have felt the gun but he didn't acknowledge it. She finally breathed again. He was indeed one of Temi's men.

Once given the all clear, Georgina was shown into the room where Slugs met her with a wide grin.

'It's nice to see you again. Who 'ave you been shooting up?' he asked.

'No one, why?'

'I was told you're here to buy. I assume bullets?'

'Ah, yes, that's right. It's been a while since I've used a gun so I was doing a bit of target practice.'

'On anyone I know?' Slugs asked with a chortle.

'No, nothing like that. So, Slugs, aren't you going to offer me a drink?'

'Sorry, where are my manners? What would you like?'

'Champagne. Always champagne.'

'It's a bit early for that, ain't it?'

'It's never too early for champagne. Anyway, it's past ten.'

Slugs pulled on a cord, which Georgina guessed rang a bell somewhere inside the house. The short man with red hair came into the room. She'd seen him the last time she was here when he'd brought her coffee.

'Champagne for Miss Garrett,' Slugs ordered.

The man tugged his forelock and dashed away through a door where two large, unfriendly looking men sat on each side.

'No Johnny with you today?' Slugs asked.

'No, he's running a few errands for me. I thought it would be nice just the two of us,' Georgina answered and smiled teasingly at Slugs.

'Oh, erm, right,' he replied, appearing uncomfortable.

The short man came back in with champagne in a silver ice bucket and a glass.

'Aren't you joining me?' Georgina asked Slugs.

'Champagne ain't my tipple.'

'What's your tipple, then? Brandy? Whisky?'

'I'm happy with a bottle of stout.'

'Bring a bottle of stout for Slugs,' Georgina told the short man.

Again, he tugged his forelock and hurried off. She thought he seemed a funny little man, like a character from one of the silent films her dad used to enjoy.

Slugs poured a glass of champagne and handed it to Georgina. She deliberately met his eyes and lightly fluttered her dark lashes. Then, taking a seat on the sofa, she patted beside her. 'Come and sit with me,' she purred.

Slugs glanced over at the two men on the door before sitting awkwardly on the edge of the seat next to her.

The short man appeared again and handed Slugs a bottle of beer.

'Cheers,' Georgina said and held her glass aloft to clink with his bottle.

'Yeah, cheers,' Slugs parroted and took several glugs.

Georgina crossed one leg over the other, deliberately allowing her skirt hem to slip above her knee. 'You're rather a man of mystery to me,' she said.

'Am I? Nah, there ain't nothing mysterious about me.'

'Well, I don't know much about you. Are you married?'

'No one would have me,' he answered with a nervous titter.

'I would,' Georgina husked and looked over the top of her glass as she sipped the champagne.

'Get out of it, you're mucking about with me, ain't ya?'

'No, Slugs, not at all. I've always had a sweet eye for you. You know, I was in prison for a long time… and since I've been free, well, let's just say, a girl gets lonely.'

Slugs swigged down the rest of his stout while Georgina sidled closer to him and whispered in his ear, 'Get rid of those two lumps and we can have a bit of fun, eh, what do you say?'

Slugs licked his lips and she saw a spark of passion in his eyes. Good, this was going exactly how she'd planned it.

He jumped to his feet and turned towards the men on the door. 'Go and check the back door. And while you're in the kitchen, have a tea break. I'm all right up here,' he said and winked at them.

Slugs waited for the men to leave and then turned back to Georgina. 'I've always fancied you,' he said and pulled his braces from his shoulders before unbuttoning his trousers.

Georgina rose to her feet and ambled towards him. She planted soft kisses on his neck as she undid his shirt buttons.

'No,' Slugs said, grabbing both her hands. 'I'll leave me shirt on. Me belly's pretty messed up, I wouldn't want you to see it.'

'That's fine, Slugs,' she said softly and reached her hand down to his engorged manhood.

'Oh, yeah, Georgina. That's good,' he said, and closed his eyes as she pulled back and forward on his foreskin. 'Take your clothes off. I wanna fuck you.'

Georgina stepped back and slid her jacket off, letting it fall to the floor. 'Sit down,' she purred. 'And watch me undress.'

Slugs was quick to sit on the sofa with his manhood standing proud.

'Cor, Georgina, you're right bleedin' dirty, ain't ya?'

'I can be,' she answered and kicked off her shoes. Then she peeled off one stocking and placed it on the sofa next to

Slugs. Then, ever so slowly, she did the same with her other stocking.

'You're a tease,' Slugs smiled. 'But I like it.'

'Do you like this?' Georgina asked and grabbed her gun from her belt.

'What the fuck?'

'Shush, Slugs, don't make a fuss, there's a good man. It's just a bit of fun.'

'What's your fucking game?'

'Don't worry, I won't hurt you.'

'What are you, the black widow or something? I ain't into no weird stuff.'

'It's only weird the first time you try it,' she said with a wicked smile. 'Now, you're going to swallow these pills.' Georgina pulled two small tablets from the pocket in her skirt. 'Don't panic, they're only sleeping pills. You'll nod off and once you're asleep, I'm going to tie you up with my stockings and wrap my belt around your mouth. I'll drag you to behind the desk, and hopefully no one will find you for a while and you'll have a peaceful kip. That doesn't sound too bad, does it?'

'You're fucking mad if you think I'm going to take those pills.'

'Slugs, please don't make this difficult. You see this,' she said, running her finger along the silencer, 'it muffles noise. I'll shoot you if I have to and no one will hear a thing. But honestly, you seem like a nice man. I'd really rather not have to kill you.'

'If you want The Top, you'll have to kill me to get to him.'

'Really? Wouldn't you rather just have a restful sleep?'

'I ain't taking no pills,' Slugs growled.

'Is there any way I can persuade you to change your mind? You know what the alternative will be.'

Slugs leapt from the sofa towards her. Georgina had thought he might try to disarm her and reluctantly pulled the trigger, aiming directly at his head.

Slugs fell backwards, landing on the sofa. He didn't scream in pain or even whimper. His death had been instant.

'I'm sorry, Slugs, but you left me no choice,' she said and reached out to close his eyelids before slipping her shoes back on. She hadn't wanted Slugs to die. She'd given him an option and clearly explained the details. But, due to his misplaced loyalty to The Top, Slugs was dead.

Georgina marched towards the door that she'd seen Slugs go through before. She was sure she'd find The Top behind it. Her heart hammered as she pulled the handle down and pushed the door open.

She stepped inside a dim, windowless room and closed the door behind her. She was in, so close now. Her heart pounded hard, she could hear her blood rushing in her ears. She could see a man wearing a hat sitting on a sofa with his back towards her. The Top. A floor lamp stood beside the sofa and the wireless blared out news bulletins about troop movements. Apart from The Top wearing a hat indoors, it all felt so *normal*.

Quickly but cautiously, she approached the sofa with her gun pointing to the back of The Top's head. Georgina stopped in her tracks when the man held his arm up. He didn't turn round, yet he knew someone was there. Did he think it was Slugs who had entered the room? She saw a piece of paper in his hand. If he thought she was Slugs, it was meant for him.

Now she stood directly behind him. She took the piece of paper and tried to glean a look at The Top's profile but it was impossible to see anything without giving herself away. Georgina glanced at the paper in her shaking hand. Big letters were scrawled across it.

Give Georgina whatever she wants

Georgina dropped the paper to the floor and pushed the end of the gun against the back of The Top's neck. 'Huh, whatever I want, eh? I'll tell you what I want,' she ground out.

The Top didn't move.

'I want to kill you. Your life as payment for taking David Maynard's life.'

Still, The Top didn't move and said nothing.

'Put your arms up where I can see them.'

The Top did as she'd instructed and slowly lifted his arms.

'I want to see who you are,' she said and inched around the sofa with her gun held towards him. Once in front of the man she stood with her arms outstretched, holding the weapon in both hands.

The Top had lowered his head and Georgina stared hatefully at the man but she couldn't see his face. 'Look at me,' she growled.

The Top sucked in a long and slow breath before lifting his head to meet her eyes.

Georgina gasped, blinking rapidly. Was she seeing things? Was it really him? He looked different, his face badly scarred, but there was no mistake. It was him. 'David?' she muttered, unable to believe her eyes.

He nodded.

David Maynard wasn't dead. He was very much alive and was gazing lovingly at the woman who was holding a gun pointed at his chest.

26

Georgina felt as though she'd been winded by a kick in the stomach. The room began to spin and she panted for breath. She staggered backwards, her mind racing and bombarding her brain with questions. 'Why?' she asked as she fought to hold back tears. Part of her wanted to run into his arms, the other part wanted to punch him.

David offered no explanation.

Georgina put her hand out and leaned on the wall to steady herself. 'How could you do this to me?' she asked.

David now lowered his head to stare at his hands in his lap.

'You know how much I grieved for Lash yet you allowed me to grieve for you too. Why? Have you lost your mind? Did you get some sort of sick enjoyment from knowing the pain I was in?'

His silence provoked her anger. She gritted her teeth and stamped towards him. In frustration, she knocked his hat off his head, which revealed large patches of red and purple scalp where his dark hair had once been.

David looked up now and glared at her before scrambling to pick up his hat, which he quickly placed back on his head.

'I thought you loved me,' Georgina cried. 'I thought we

were going to be married. I don't understand, David. Why did you let me think you were dead?'

Finally, he spoke. 'You can see why,' he answered flatly.

'No, David, I can't.'

'Look at me,' he yelled, seeming to come to life as he rose from the sofa. He grabbed her shoulders and lightly shook her. 'Look at me! I'm not the same man I used to be.'

Georgina gazed back at David. His face was disfigured almost beyond recognition but his eyes were the same.

'You see, Georgina. This is me now. I'm grotesque. A monster.'

Georgina shook herself loose of David's grip. 'Are you *that* vain that you thought I wouldn't love you because of a few scars?'

'It's more than just a few scars. I can see the disgust in your eyes.'

'Yes, you bloody can! But not from looking at your face. I'm disgusted at you for putting me through years of pain. You're pathetic. Calling yourself The Top and hiding away in here, while I've been left to believe that you're dead! For fuck's sake, David, to get to you, I killed Slugs.'

'Shit.'

'And Victor... what about Victor? Is he alive too?'

David nodded. 'He fell in love with a nurse at the hospital and signed up with the army. Don't be angry with Victor. I swore him to secrecy.'

'The body that washed up... you arranged that. Who was he?'

'Just a bloke who'd been killed when his house was bombed. He was no one. I needed a body and he fitted the bill.'

Georgina turned away to gather her thoughts. David was alive, she should be happy, yet all she could feel was a burning anger, a sense of betrayal and of being deeply let down by the man she loved. She spun back on her heel. Tears rolled freely down her cheeks. 'I'll *never* forgive you for deceiving me like this,' she hissed.

'I don't expect your forgiveness and I certainly don't expect your love. But I want you to know that I never stopped loving you.'

'Love,' she spat. 'You don't know the meaning of the word. If you did, you would never have done this to me.'

'I thought I was protecting you.'

'From what?'

'From being lumbered with a hideous creature.'

'Oh, I see, now you're trying to get my sympathy. Well, it won't work. You got burned in a bomb explosion, David. Didn't it occur to you that if you had lived, I'd have expected you to have scars?'

'I don't think you'd have expected this extent of scarring. You're a beautiful woman, Georgina. You can have your pick of men. You can do better than this,' David said solemnly and turned away from her. 'It's best you leave now.'

'Yes, I'm going. I never want to set eyes on you again and don't you dare think it's because of your injuries. I never want to see you again because you're a coward, a liar and a selfish bastard. I hate you. I hate you for ruining *us*.'

'I understand. But a word of warning, Georgina. Don't trust the Zammits. I know you've had a few dealings with Temi. He's full of charm but he's a snake.'

'Don't tell me how to run my business. You've lost all rights to have any say over anything I do. And anyway, why should I believe a word that comes out of your mouth? You proved what a fucking liar you are!'

Before David could say another word, Georgina marched from the room and out of the house. In the next street, she saw Johnny leaning up against the car. When he spotted her, he ran towards her.

'Thank God. Thank God you're alive.'

'Get in the car.'

'Is he dead? Did you kill The Top?' Johnny asked as the car screeched off at full speed.

Georgina gulped, her mind still whirling. 'No, I didn't kill him. I could have but I didn't.'

'Why? What happened?'

She rubbed her forehead as she answered, 'Because The Top is David Maynard.'

Charlotte was fascinated to hear stories from Fleur about her time in, as Fleur called it, Camden Castle. Georgina never spoke about what it was like inside, and until now Charlotte hadn't realised how brutal it must have been for her.

She was pleased to be working with Fleur, though the woman had been aghast when Charlotte had told her she was engaged to an ex-copper.

'Mind you, he sounds like a lovely fella,' Fleur said after Charlotte had read out loud her latest letter from Tim.

'He is, I'm very lucky. I mean, fancy him giving up his job for me.'

'Not many blokes would do that,' Fleur agreed.

'Enough about him, look busy, here comes Georgina.'

As soon as Georgina came through the door, Charlotte could see that she was upset. But she wouldn't ask what was wrong in front of Fleur. Georgina stormed past them, past the counter and into the back. Charlotte heard the door to the office slam shut.

Johnny was hanging about uneasily by a corner table. Charlotte walked over to him and whispered, 'What's up with her?'

Johnny rolled his eyes and looked around to make sure that no one was in earshot. 'She's had a bit of a shock. You ain't gonna believe this, Charlotte, and make sure you keep it to yourself. David Maynard is alive. He's The Top.'

'No way! Are you sure?'

'Yeah, Miss Garrett saw him.'

'How come she's upset then? I thought she'd be over the moon to know that David's alive?'

'You know her, she's a complicated woman. I reckon she's pissed off with him for letting her think that he's been dead for all these years. I dunno, I could be wrong. She never said a word in the car all the way back here from Lewisham.'

'Bugger. Sit yourself down, Johnny. Fleur will bring you a cuppa and a sandwich. I'll see if Georgina will speak to me.'

'Good luck with that. She'll likely bite your head off.'

Charlotte gave instructions to Fleur and then she gently knocked on the office door. When there was no answer, she pushed it open and snuck her head inside. Georgina was sat behind her desk but facing the back wall.

'It's only me,' Charlotte said quietly and closed the door

behind her. 'Johnny told me about David. I just wanted to make sure that you're all right?'

Georgina's chair spun round and Charlotte was surprised to see that she was openly crying.

'Oh, Georgina, you're upset,' Charlotte said and went to her friend. She fished out a handkerchief from the cuff of her jumper and handed it to Georgina, saying, 'It's clean.'

Georgina took the hanky and dabbed at her red-rimmed eyes. 'You haven't seen me crying.'

'No, of course not. Do you want to talk about it?'

'Not really. What's there to talk about? He lied to me. He didn't love me enough to trust me. He let me think he was dead. That's cruel, really cruel.'

'Why did he do it?'

'He said it's because he's been left badly scarred after that bomb blast. To be fair, I almost didn't recognise him. But he must be bloody shallow, or he must think that I'm shallow, if he couldn't see that I'd still love *him*, not his face.'

'He's a man, Georgina, they ain't got a bleedin' clue. I'm sure he didn't mean to hurt you.'

'Don't defend what he's done!'

'Sorry, I'm not. I wouldn't. I'm just saying blokes are dumb.'

'Indeed, they are. And David is the dumbest! What he did to me was so bloody selfish. Anyway, that's it. I'll never forgive him so that's an end to it,' Georgina said and sniffed. As though determined to change the subject, she added, 'I see Fleur looks like she's doing well.'

SAM MICHAELS

'Yeah, she is. She's been smashing, and the customers love her.'

'Good. I should go and say hello to her, and I could do with a cuppa. Do I look like I've been crying?'

'No, you look fine,' Charlotte lied. 'But perhaps wipe the mascara smudges away and put a bit of powder on.'

Georgina pulled a small compact from her bag, wiped her eyes and powdered her nose. Charlotte couldn't help but notice the gun in Georgina's bag with a long contraption attached to the barrel. She recalled the conversation they'd exchanged that morning. Putting two and two together, she realised Georgina had discovered that David was The Top because she'd gone to kill him!

'Right, come on,' Georgina said, snapping her bag shut and smiling, though the smile didn't reach her eyes.

'I can't believe you,' Charlotte moaned, shaking her head.

'What?'

'You went to see The Top to murder him, didn't you?'

'It doesn't matter, Charlotte. It's all finished with now.'

'It bloody does matter! Do you realise how dangerous that was? Hang on, don't answer. I know you do and that's why you said all that stuff to me this morning about how I'll always be looked after. Gawd, Georgina, you could have been killed! Why? Why would you do something so stupid? What about your kids? Was you prepared to leave them without a mother? What about me? You care more about getting revenge than you do about any of us!'

Georgina glared at her, her violet eyes blazing. 'How dare you talk to me like that!'

'Well, someone's got to. What would your gran have said? Or Molly? I bet you never told Molly, did you? No, because you know full well that Molly would have given you a right good talking to.'

'You don't understand, Charlotte. I had to do it. I thought The Top had killed David. How would you feel if someone murdered your Tim and was walking around a free man? You'd want his murderer to pay for what he'd done.'

'Maybe, but I'd also consider the risk to myself and how my loved ones would feel if anything happened to me. Ha, and you've got the nerve to call David selfish... you're just as bloody selfish as him. The pair of you are made for each other.'

Charlotte gave Georgina a scathing look before spinning round. She went to walk out of the office but heard Georgina call, 'Wait.'

'Why? Do you want to have a go at me for telling you the truth?'

'No, I want to say you're right. I didn't think about anyone else. I'm sorry. And I needed telling, thank you.'

Charlotte softened and said jokingly, 'Yeah, all right, but don't let it happen again, young lady, or I shall send you to your room with no tea.'

'Yes, Mum,' Georgina joked back.

Back in the café, they found Fleur up to her elbows in soapy suds with her hands in the sink. There was only Johnny and one customer, an old man, reading a newspaper and eating a rock cake.

When Fleur saw Georgina, she quickly pulled her hands from the sink and dried them on her apron. 'Hello, miss, fanks for giving me this job 'ere.'

'You're welcome, Fleur. Work hard, don't give Charlotte any lip and you'll get on fine.'

Fleur smiled at Charlotte. 'It ain't the first time she's been my boss. I was a good worker before, weren't I, Charlotte?'

'Yes, and you are now.'

Fleur beamed with delight, clearly eager to please.

'How did you get on in Holloway?' Georgina asked quietly.

'All right, I suppose. All hell broke lose when you bunked it. Cor, Miss Kenny was spitting feathers. Blimey, she was a right piece of work. Mind you, she got her comeuppance. She fell down those horrible metal stairs, and rumour has it that she was pushed. Good riddance, I say.'

'Who's Miss Kenny?' Charlotte asked.

'One of the wardens,' Georgina answered. 'I was going to have her paid a visit but seems it's already been taken care of.'

'What? You were going to have her done over?' Charlotte asked.

'After what she did to me, she deserved it. I'm not sorry she's dead. As Fleur said, good riddance. Keep up the good work, Fleur,' Georgina said and returned to her office.

'Yes, miss. Of course, miss,' Fleur called after her.

Charlotte watched Georgina marching off, thinking that it didn't pay to get on the wrong side of her. Nasty things could happen if you did.

She went to speak to Johnny. 'She's all right now. What a turn up for the books.'

'I can't believe it, Charlotte. It's good news though. At least we won't have to worry about The Top. David Maynard won't ever be a threat to us and Miss Garrett.'

'Erm, I hope you're right. I hope he ain't got the 'ump 'cos of Georgina telling him where he can go.'

'I hadn't thought of that!'

Charlotte assumed Georgina hadn't thought of that either. If David Maynard wanted to, he could crush Georgina and they'd all be taken down with her.

27

On Monday morning, Georgina called into Ezzy's jewellery shop to see Benjamin and came out carrying two large brown envelopes.

She climbed into the passenger seat of the car and told Johnny, 'Right, now to Temi Zammit's office.'

'What's in the envelopes?' he asked.

'Money. It's Temi's money and I'm returning it.'

'How come you've got Temi's money?'

'It was for my kids if I died. I didn't die so now he can have it back.'

'What? He was in on you taking out The Top?'

'Yes. He wanted him dead too.'

'How's he going to react when you tell him that The Top is still alive?'

'I don't know and I don't really care.'

Johnny thought Georgina's lax attitude could get her into trouble. It seemed to him that if she'd been working with Temi Zammit to bring down The Top, the man wouldn't be happy that she hadn't kept her side of the bargain. 'Are you going to tell Mr Zammit who The Top is?'

'I don't see any reason why I should keep David's secrets.'

Johnny didn't think that was a good idea. She could

end up pissing off the Zammits *and* David Maynard! Granted, the woman was strong, but Georgina didn't hold the power she once had. Either the gang from the West End or south-east London could be a threat to her precarious position as she tried to wrestle back control in the south-west.

They soon arrived at Temi Zammit's club and as Georgina strode in, Johnny followed, half expecting to be told to wait outside. He was surprised when she allowed him to enter the office with her. Johnny had an uneasy feeling about this. If anything kicked off, he'd be no match against Mr Zammit's six men.

'I've been expecting you,' Temi said, without his usual friendly smile.

'I'm returning your money,' Georgina said, her tone equally frosty as she threw the two large envelopes on top of his desk. 'It's all there.'

'Leave us,' Temi instructed his men.

They filed from the office but Johnny waited for Georgina to tell him what to do.

'And you,' Temi said to Johnny.

Johnny pushed his shoulders back in defiance. He wouldn't be told what to do by this greasy Maltese man.

'He stays,' Georgina snapped.

'You failed to kill The Top.'

'I didn't fail. I chose not to. There's a difference.'

'Why would you allow him to live?'

'I have my reasons. You've got your money back. That's an end to it.'

'We had an agreement.'

'Let me make this quite clear, Temi. I don't work for you,

therefore I can do as I see fit. If you want to go after The Top, that's up to you but I don't want to be involved.'

'He's paid you off, hasn't he?'

'No, but even if he had, it's none of your business.'

'Aren't you forgetting something?'

'I don't think so.'

'You owe me.'

'For intervening with Oleg? I don't think so. I never asked for your help and I didn't need it. In fact, I should be billing you for the repairs to my club.'

Temi laughed loudly. 'You've got some nerve.'

'Yes, I have. Now, I think we're done here. Good day.'

Georgina had walked in boldly and she marched out with just as much gusto, her chin jutting forward and standing tall. Johnny admired her courage but worried that she was maybe being a little foolhardy in not giving the Zammits, and David, the respect they commanded.

'That told him,' she said, sitting beside him in the car.

'It's not my place to tell you how to run the business, but ain't you cutting off your nose to spite your face?'

'What do you mean?'

'Well, you've told Mr Maynard to go and take a running jump and now you've pretty much told Mr Zammit to bugger off too.'

'I know what I'm doing, Johnny. I have to show these men that they can't push me around and that they don't intimidate me.'

'I get that, but—'

'—No buts,' Georgina cut in. 'Take me home. I'm taking the rest of the day off.'

'Yes, Miss Garrett,' Johnny answered, biting his tongue.

He dropped Georgina off in Alexandra Avenue. She told him she was moving into Lord Hamilton's flat and would spend the day clearing through his things. Johnny had offered to help, but thankfully she'd politely declined his offer. This gave him more time to spend with Elsie. He was looking forward to arriving home early for a change and hoped he'd be able to persuade her to have an afternoon nap. Though a nap wasn't really his intention.

As Johnny opened his front door, he could hear Elsie singing. She still hadn't mentioned getting sacked from the café. He hadn't wanted to upset her so he hadn't broached the subject either. 'It's me, sweetheart,' he called.

'In here,' Elsie called back from the bedroom.

He walked in to find her holding a dress against herself and looking in the mirror. 'What do you think?' she asked, twirling round.

'Very nice. Is it new?'

'Yes, and this one too,' Elsie answered, holding up another dress that had been on the bed.

'Lovely. Erm, Elsie, how did you pay for them?'

'With the money from behind the clock.'

'Oh, Elsie, that was the rent money.'

'Was it? Oh dear.'

She didn't appear to be the least bit concerned that she'd blown two weeks' rent money on two dresses. But she was smiling so widely and looked so happy that he didn't have the heart to have a go at her.

'Did you bring me home a gift today?' Elsie asked.

'No, sorry, sweetheart, I haven't had a chance.'

'Aw,' she said, pouting sulkily. 'Well, you can make up for

it tomorrow and bring me two gifts. Something to go with each of my new dresses.'

'Sure, love, if that's what you want.'

'It is. After all, it's not like I've got much else to look forward to, is it?'

'What do you mean by that?' Johnny asked, feeling slightly put out.

'I'm bored, Johnny. Really bored. You're at work most of the time and the only thing that I have to entertain me is shopping.'

'I know, but if I didn't work, you wouldn't be able to afford to shop.' Johnny gave her a *knowing* look but didn't mention her losing her job.

'I suppose. But you hardly earn a fortune, do you?'

'I earn enough and you don't go short.'

'You don't understand, Johnny. I'm having to make do. These new dresses are cheap and nasty. I'm used to the expensive clothes that Jacob used to buy me.'

'Sod Jacob! He might well have dressed you in expensive clobber but you paid a high price for it. And anyway, there's a war on. Everyone is having to *make do*.'

'There's no need to snap.'

Johnny sucked in a deep breath and walked out of the room. He'd lost any enthusiasm for taking an early afternoon *nap* with her. If anything, she'd managed to put him in a foul mood. It's not that he expected her gratitude, but he found it infuriating that she kept harping on about what Jacob used to buy her. Maybe there was just no pleasing some women!

★

Georgina looked sadly at the three piles of clothes from Lord Hamilton's wardrobe. He'd always dressed smartly and they were of good quality. She decided the items could go to charity. Though the shirts and trousers weren't the normal sort of attire that men in Battersea would wear, she was sure the items would be of use to someone. It was silly really, she hadn't known him for very long but she missed him and his elaborate stories.

She shook her head, thinking *death follows me,* and an image of the Grim Reaper standing behind her flashed through her mind. Then her mind wandered to David Maynard. She still loved the man. She couldn't deny that, but she was too angry to even consider forgiving him.

'This won't do,' she said aloud, and decided she needed to get away from everything for a few days. She would visit the farm in Kent. Molly would be pleased to see her and make her welcome, as would Oppo. Fanny, Molly's mother, probably wouldn't be so happy but *fuck her*, Georgina thought, her mind made up.

She went back downstairs, and after packing a few things she found a pen and paper to scribble a note to Charlotte, explaining that she'd be back soon. Yes, this was just what she needed, she thought, and smiled. The café was ticking over nicely, The Penthouse was closed for now and the Barkers were making lots of money selling the black market goods. They had enough supplies to last them for at least a week. A short break away from Battersea and everything associated with it would do her good and give her a chance to collect her thoughts.

A few hours later, the train from Clapham Junction

pulled into the station at Kent. Georgina had telephoned ahead and as arranged, Oppo was waiting to meet her.

'Now there's a sight for sore eyes,' he said, his arms outstretched.

'Hello, Oppo,' she said, and hugged him.

He took her small case and led her to his van, limping as he had done since he'd been a child. 'Molly's thrilled to bits that you're coming to stay with us.'

'I'm guessing Fanny isn't?'

'She didn't say much, just shrugged her shoulders.'

'Blimey, Fanny didn't say much. Well, that's a first.'

Oppo just chuckled and they were soon trundling down the quiet country lanes towards the farm. The air smelt so fresh and clean, and already Georgina could feel herself relaxing.

'I hope you've brought some sensible clothes,' Oppo said, glancing sideways at her elegant coat, hat and gloves.

'No, why would I? I'm not planning on working out in the fields with you,' she said and laughed.

When they drove up the driveway, Molly was standing at the open farmhouse door, bouncing a baby on her hip.

'How's Steven?' Georgina asked Oppo.

'He's a good baby and settled in fine. Eddy loves having who he thinks is his little brother around.'

'That's good,' Georgina said, pleased that though she had thrust Steven at Molly, it was working out well.

'I'm sorry you never got to see Alfie and Selina but you will soon. I think the war is close to ending. Germany is losing ground.'

'I hope you're right,' Georgina answered and swallowed hard as a lump formed in her throat. She yearned to see and hold her children. She'd known that her feelings of desperately missing them would resurface at the sight of baby Steven and Molly's boy, Edward.

As Georgina climbed from Oppo's small truck, Molly rushed towards her.

'I've missed you,' Molly gushed.

'Yeah, I've missed you an' all. I hope the kettle's on, I'm gasping.'

'Of course, and Eddy's waiting up to say goodnight to you. Come on, let's get you inside in the warm.'

It felt so homely in the farmhouse and after popping up to say goodnight to Eddy, Georgina was fed a wholesome meal. Later that night, as she lay in bed, engulfed in the quiet of the countryside for the first time since she'd escaped from prison, Georgina slept long and peacefully.

28

Georgina had been away for four days, which had given Johnny plenty of extra time to go out nicking to get gifts for Elsie – though he kept a close eye over his shoulder for the Old Bill. If they ever caught up with him for shooting that copper in the alleyway, he knew he'd swing for it.

Johnny had brought Elsie an array of gifts – handbags, jewellery, scarves and hats. Yet she still wasn't satisfied and continued to complain. That evening, he arrived home with a porcelain cup and saucer. He could picture her delicately sipping tea from it and enjoying a fine biscuit from a box that he'd nicked from a posh shop in Chelsea.

'Hello, sweetheart, I'm home,' he called through his flat.

When Elsie didn't answer, Johnny placed the gifts on the kitchen worktop and then went from room to room in search of her. But Elsie wasn't home and he couldn't find a note from her either.

The minutes ticked by, and then hours passed. Johnny looked at his watch again. It was after nine. Where was she? As the time passed slowly by, he was becoming more and more worried. He wracked his brains trying to think of where she could be. As far as he knew, she didn't have any friends to visit and the shops would be closed now.

It made no sense. Something must have happened to her. Maybe she had been involved in an accident? It was the only explanation.

Johnny grabbed a pen and paper and left a note for Elsie to say he had gone out to look for her and if she came home, she was to sit tight and he'd be back soon. He signed it with three kisses.

Later, after hours of traipsing the streets and checking the local hospital, Johnny returned home, hoping to find Elsie there. But he found his flat empty and now he was at his wits' end.

The next morning, tired but anxious, Johnny drove round to see Charlotte. He hoped she may have news of Elsie, though he doubted it. Charlotte had disliked her and Elsie reciprocated those feelings.

'Bloody women,' he cursed under his breath as he tapped on Charlotte's window.

After a minute or two she pulled back the curtains, looking surprised to see him.

'You timed that well,' Charlotte said, when she opened the front door.

'Timed what well?'

'I was just about to leave for work. You can give me a lift.'

'Yeah, sure,' Johnny replied. As he set off for the café on Lavender Hill, he asked, 'Have you seen anything of Elsie?'

'No. Should I have?'

'I dunno. I'm worried. She didn't come home last night. It

ain't like her. I don't suppose you've got any idea of where she could be?'

'No, not a clue. But good riddance to her. If you ask me, you're better off without her.'

'I didn't ask you, so I'd appreciate you keeping your opinions about Elsie to yourself.'

As they pulled up outside the café, Johnny noticed a familiar figure standing outside, but surely his eyes were deceiving him? 'Do you know who that is?' he asked Charlotte.

Charlotte eyed the woman up and down, then turned to Johnny. 'No, I've never seen her before but she looks a bit well-to-do. Do you know her?'

'Yeah, I think I do. I'm pretty sure that's Temi Zammit's wife.'

'Blimey! What's she doing here?'

'I dunno but I'd better find out,' he answered and climbed out of the car.

As Johnny walked towards Lora Zammit, he thought she looked nervous. She was holding a handkerchief to her nose and glancing up and down the street.

'Mrs Zammit,' Johnny said and doffed his hat.

Lora removed the handkerchief for long enough to say, 'I'm looking for Georgina Garrett.'

'She's away at the moment. Can I help you? I'm Johnny Dymond, I work for Miss Garrett.'

'No, you can't help me. I need to speak with Georgina.'

'Charlotte's just opening the café. Would you like to come in and have a cuppa?'

'No.'

'I'm sure you've had a long journey here. A coffee instead?'

'No. I don't have time. I shouldn't even be here.'

'Yeah, well, the fact that you are means it's obviously important. Miss Garrett should be home any day soon. Can it wait? Or do you want me to pass her a message?'

'No, it can't wait. Do you have her telephone number?'

'I have a number for where she's staying, but she doesn't want to be disturbed.'

'Mr Dymond, please. This is serious. I need to speak to her immediately. Her life may depend on it.'

It was Johnny who looked up and down the street now. Seeing that no one was watching, he quickly bundled Lora inside the café.

'What do you think you're doing? Get your hands off me,' Lora demanded.

Once inside, Charlotte closed and locked the door. Lora didn't put up any resistance as Johnny managed to easily pin her to the wall. He faced her squarely with his hands on the wall at each side of her head. In a low, growling tone he asked, 'Why is Miss Garrett's life in danger?'

Lora glared angrily at him and he snapped threateningly, 'You'd better start talking.'

'You know who I am. Therefore you know who I'm married to. My husband would *kill* you if he knew you were threatening me.'

'Yeah, but I'm sure you won't tell him, will you, Mrs Zammit? After all, you've said you shouldn't be here.'

Lora lowered her head. 'No, I daren't,' she said shakily. She fought to compose herself and Johnny felt awful for intimidating her. But Miss Garrett's wellbeing had to come first. 'Would you like that cup of tea now?'

Lora nodded.

Charlotte dashed behind the counter and Johnny urged Lora towards a table near the counter and away from the window.

Charlotte brought them both tea and pulled out a seat too.

'Best you leave me and Mrs Zammit to have a chat,' Johnny told the girl.

Thankfully, the normally mouthy Charlotte didn't protest and slipped into the storeroom. Johnny leaned back in his seat and asked Mrs Zammit, 'Do you want to tell me what this is all about?'

'How do I know I can trust you?' she asked.

'I tell you what. There's a telephone in the office. You tell me why you want to speak to Miss Garrett and if I think she needs to hear it, we can ring her and you can talk to her. How does that sound?'

'I'd rather talk to her first.'

'That's not going to happen. Don't take this the wrong way, but if you don't tell me what the fuck is going on, I'll ring your husband and ask him. I'm sure he'd be interested to know why you're sitting in Miss Garrett's café.'

Lora's eyes widened. 'No, you mustn't say anything to my husband!'

'Fine, start talking then.'

Lora drew in a long breath and then said, 'Mrs Flowers visited my husband yesterday. After she talked to him I heard him issuing orders for Georgina's death.'

'Elsie? Elsie Flowers?'

'Yes. I think Temi paid her very generously for information about a robbery at his father's jewellery shop. He believes

Georgina was behind it and now wants her blood. She killed one of his best policemen.'

Johnny could feel his jaw clenching. This explained Elsie's disappearance but he'd never expected her to sell him out. She'd dropped Miss Garrett in it too, but another thought crossed his mind and he asked, 'Why are you going behind your husband's back to warn Miss Garrett?'

Lora lowered her eyes but Johnny had already seen they were filled with unshed tears as she spoke. 'I don't always agree with my husband's business practices and this is one of those occasions,' she answered, and dabbed at her nose with her handkerchief.

'You're risking everything just because you don't agree with him?'

'Something like that. Look, Temi puts on a good show. Everyone thinks he's the perfect husband and I'm the spoiled wife. But believe me, Mr Dymond, behind closed doors he's a very different man. He frightens me. He's had many mistresses, but he won't let me leave him. He'll *never* let me go.'

'So you're here to get your own back on him?'

'No, it's nothing like that. I like Georgina, it's as simple as that. I saw something in her that I admire and wish I had her courage. Temi made a move on her, I'm sure of it. He wouldn't have been able to resist. But Georgina turned him down. There's no woman I know who would say no to Temi. And I don't believe that Georgina had anything to do with the robbery. It doesn't seem her style.'

'You're right, she didn't. It was me. But I didn't know it was Temi's father's shop.'

'Even if Temi found out, it won't make any difference.

You work for Georgina so I'm afraid she's being held responsible. And from what I could tell, Mrs Flowers laid the blame solely at Georgina's door.'

'I don't know why she'd do that. She knows it was me.'

'You really don't understand women very well, do you? It's obvious that Elsie Flowers wants Georgina out of the way because she mistakenly feels that Georgina stands in the way of her stealing my husband. He's a powerful man and very generous with his lovers. Mrs Flowers has known of my husband's indiscretions for years. Her husband did Temi's accounts. She would have seen how much money he lavished on his tarts. That woman has always had a liking for expensive things. And now she has a liking for what Temi can give her.'

Johnny refrained from slamming his fist down on the table, but anger coursed through his veins. Elsie Flowers had taken him for a ride and made a fool of him.

A tap on the window caused Lora to flinch. Johnny saw it was Fleur and Charlotte ran out of the storeroom to let her in. Johnny rose to his feet and said quietly, 'I have to get word to Miss Garrett.'

Lora scraped her chair back and she too rose to her feet. 'Yes, you must. I have to go now, but please take care of Miss Garrett and yourself too… all of you,' she said as she looked from Charlotte to Fleur.

Once Lora had left, Johnny said urgently, 'Temi Zammit is after Georgina and may hit the café. Fleur go home, sweetheart, and lay low until I tell you it's safe to come back.'

Fleur, her eyes like saucers, nodded and hurried out, calling, 'All right. I'll see ya.'

'Charlotte, the café ain't opening so you can go home too.'

'Why is Temi Zammit after Georgina?'

'Elsie told him it was Miss Garrett who turned over his father's shop. And it won't just be Miss Garrett that they're after.'

'Shit! The bitch! I knew it. I knew she couldn't be trusted.'

'Yeah, well, we'll worry about that later,' Johnny mumbled as he fished in his pocket for the key to Georgina's office.

Johnny picked up the telephone receiver and held it to his ear. He wasn't looking forward to having this conversation with Miss Garrett but he couldn't hide it from her. At least she was safe where she was. He doubted the Zammits knew about Molly Mipple and the farm in Kent. At least, he hoped they didn't, for all their sakes.

Charlotte paced back and forth behind the counter while keeping an eye out of the window. She could ring that bleedin' Elsie Flowers' neck and would if she ever set eyes on her again.

Johnny emerged from the office. 'I can't get through to her. The line doesn't seem to be working.'

'Keep trying,' Charlotte spat.

Another ten minutes passed and Johnny came into the café again.

'Well, what did she say?'

'Nothing. I still can't get through. Fuck, I'll have to drive down there.'

'Hadn't you better tell Ned and the Barker twins what's going on? They're at risk an' all and ain't got a clue.'

'Yeah, yeah, you're right. Come on, I'll drop you at the Barkers'. They can keep an eye on you for now.'

'You can sod right off. I ain't staying with them or anyone else for that matter. Don't worry about me, Johnny. It's Georgina they're after.'

'But they'll take us all down with her. I ain't leaving you here by yourself and you can't go home in case they go there looking for Miss Garrett.'

Charlotte chewed on her thumbnail while she thought. What would Georgina do? Certainly not run off and hide with the Barker twins. And neither would she wait at home like a sitting duck. Knowing Georgina, she'd face the problem head on. But Charlotte knew this was too big for her to deal with. 'I'm coming with you to Kent,' she told Johnny.

'No, you ain't. I don't want you anywhere near me or Miss Garrett and you know full well that she'd do her nut if I didn't look after you properly. Just go home and don't answer your door to anyone.'

Charlotte huffed. They treated her like a little girl and seemed to forget she was almost a married woman. 'I have to do *something* to help.'

'Laying low is the best thing you can do to help me. You'll be one less person to worry about. And that's final.'

Charlotte reluctantly agreed. She could see that Johnny wouldn't change his mind and they were wasting valuable time by arguing about it. 'Fine, I'll stay out of the way, but not at home. I'll go to Fleur's.'

'Good girl,' Johnny said and looked at his watch. 'Christ, look at the time. I've got to find Ned and the Barkers before

I go to Kent. Shit, I'd better let Dina know an' all. At this rate, I won't get to Miss Garrett until teatime.'

'Hurry, Johnny. You go, I'll lock up and as I need to go home to pick up some stuff, I can warn Dina to lay low too.'

'All right, and thanks,' Johnny said, dashing off.

Nearly two hours later, Charlotte was sitting on an uncomfortable wooden seat in Fleur's front room. She reached out to put her cup and saucer on the table.

'Your Morrison shelter doubles up nicely as a table,' Charlotte said, shuddering at the thought of sleeping under it like a caged animal. It looked just like a large rabbit pen but with a heavy top. And there was only just about enough room for one person to lie in it.

'Yeah, awful thing. I hope I never have to get inside it. Her downstairs gave it to me when I moved in. I was grateful for it as a table if nothing else. It ain't like I've got much.'

'It's not too bad here, Fleur. Now you're earning decent wages in the café, you'll soon have this place looking nice.'

'Yeah, I will. Are you sure you'll be all right on the floor tonight?'

'No problem. It's dry, warm and safe enough.'

'Are you allowed to tell me why we have to hide out here together?'

'No, Fleur, sorry, I'm not. But you know Georgina. She'll soon get it sorted and everything will go back to normal.'

'I hope so. I like me job in the café. It's a lot better than being a prossy. I didn't think anyone would ever give me a normal job.'

As she reached out for her tea, Charlotte's eyes roamed

the sparsely furnished room. The single bed in the corner looked rickety and the mattress appeared to be as thin as cardboard. There were several nails banged in the wall, which Fleur's clothes hung on. A wash bowl and jug sat on a small wooden cupboard that had the front door missing. Charlotte could see half a loaf of bread on the shelves inside, a cup, three small plates and a tin of sardines. The Morrison shelter took up most of the space in the centre of the room, a wooden chair on each side. Thick, dark curtains hung at the window. They looked to be in good shape. There was a small rug on floorboards in front of the window. It was threadbare but at least added a bit of colour to the room.

Charlotte thought back to her days as a child. She had grown up in poverty. This room reminded her of the two rooms she'd shared with her family. Georgina was staying with them on the farm now, a far cry from their humble beginnings and probably enjoying a big pot of Molly's stew with fresh vegetables from the farm. Charlotte missed Molly and her mum. But her life was different now. Georgina felt like her family. Oh, gawd, poor Georgina, blissfully unaware that the Zammits had put a target on her head.

'Do you think it's all right to pop to the shops? Only I ain't got much in for us to eat.'

'No need,' Charlotte said with a smile. She reached down into her bag beside her and pulled out two buns, a wedge of sliced bacon, a loaf of bread and a small lump of cheese. 'I shoved this lot in me bag before I left. I didn't want it going to waste.'

'You ain't 'alf clever, Charlotte,' Fleur said, smacking her lips together.

Charlotte had thought quickly enough to have picked up a few provisions but she didn't think she was nearly as smart as Georgina. If she was, she wouldn't be sat in Fleur's room. She would be out there, predicting the Zammits' next move and beating them at their own game, just as she hoped Georgina would.

29

'He went out like a light,' Molly said to Georgina when she came into the cosy front room. 'That story you read him must have worn him out.' She'd just tucked Edward into bed though at gone eight, it was well past his bedtime.

'He really is a credit to you, Molly.'

'And me,' Oppo piped up from the armchair beside the roaring log fire.

'Yes, to you both,' Georgina added. She'd never mention his name but every time Georgina looked at Edward, she hated to admit that he reminded her of his father, Billy Wilcox. Edward had his father's eyes, but surely he wouldn't grow up to be evil like Billy? From what she'd seen of the child, Edward was very well behaved and affectionate with his mother. Though Georgina had a suspicion that Steven had screamed earlier because Edward had sneakily pinched him. Only time would tell and Georgina hoped that Molly's and Oppo's influence would sway Edward from growing into a vile monster like his father was.

'I'm going over to the barn for an hour. I've got to try and get my plough repaired before morning. Fanny's taken to her bed to read. You two can have a good girlie chat,'

Oppo said as he heaved himself out of the comfortable chair.

After Oppo had gently closed the door behind him, Molly jumped up and went to sit beside Georgina on the sofa. She grabbed Georgina's hand and held it tightly.

'I've been so worried about you behind bars,' Molly said. 'Was it awful?'

'Yeah, it wasn't exactly a picnic,' Georgina answered.

'Well, I'm glad you're out now and even more glad that you're here!'

'Me too. It's lovely here, Molly. A proper home and family. This is what I want for my children.'

'There's nothing stopping you from having it. Move down here with us. Oh, Georgina, imagine… it would be smashing. Edward and Alfie could be best friends, just like me and you have always been.'

'I dunno, Molly. It's just a dream, ain't it. Don't get me wrong, I'd love it, but I've got work to do first and I need to make a living. I know the farm turns a profit but I couldn't expect Oppo to support me and the kids.'

'You know he would and he'd never question it.'

'Yeah, I know, but I've never had a man support me. I'd need to make my own money and what the hell could I do out in the sticks?'

'I don't know, we'd work it out. We'd think of something.'

Georgina sighed. 'I don't know if I'm capable of living a normal life. I've been stealing and fighting for as far back as I can remember.'

'I remember the first time I saw you fighting. Do you remember? It was when Billy was picking on me. I thought you was a boy!'

'Yeah, I remember. You, in rags and stinking of horse muck. I remember everything, Molly. Sometimes I wish I didn't.'

'Well, there's a lot of things that would be best forgotten. Like what the police did to you in the cells. And when Billy tried to burn you alive, and when he had Malc and Sid beat you to a pulp. I wish I could forget what he did to me too. I try not to think about being locked in the attic and giving birth to Edward up there. I don't think I'd ever been so frightened. But we can't change what's happened. Though I wish we could.'

'Do you? Do you wish things had been different? I mean, look at you now... you're happy with Oppo and you've got a beautiful son.'

'Yeah, I'm happy now but I wish I'd been happy as a kid too. Don't you? Don't you wish you could change the past?'

Georgina thought for a moment. 'I don't know, Molly. I suppose I wish that me gran was still alive, and me dad, of course. But the past has made us who we are today.'

'Can you imagine what you would have been like if things had been different when we were kids?'

Georgina smiled wanly. She'd had years in prison with nothing to do other than to think. And much of what she'd spent her time mulling over had been about her past. A tear slipped from her eye. 'My gran and my dad loved me. They did their best for me. Me dad even gave his life to save mine. But Billy, the police, Kevin Kelly and Ruby's dad before them when I was just a tot... they damaged me, Molly. Proper damaged me. I know I ain't like other women. I'm different. I'm not normal.'

'Don't talk daft, of course you're normal. But yeah, you are different but in a good way. You're stronger than anyone else I know. And I've never met anyone who cares about people as much as you do. You got damaged but they never broke you and it brought the best out of you.'

Molly looked into Georgina's eyes; she too was crying now.

'Look at us, silly pair of cows,' Georgina sniffed. She let go of Molly's hand to wipe her cheeks. 'As my gran would have said, there's no point crying over spilt milk.'

'I loved Dulcie. And your dad. I always wanted them to be my family. I used to think you was so lucky.'

'Yeah, I was,' Georgina said thoughtfully. 'They were the best.'

Fanny came rushing into the room, her face pale as she gasped for breath. 'Can you hear that? Listen, it's the bloody Jerries again, I'm sure of it,' she exclaimed as she pointed upwards.

'Don't be daft, Mum. The Germans ain't dropped bombs on England for ages now.'

'Shush… listen.'

They all held their breaths and looked towards the ceiling. Georgina could hear a distinct droning noise and yes, it did sound like incoming planes. She leapt from the sofa and dashed outside into the cool, night air.

Oppo ran across the yard from the barn. The sound of the planes became louder. Georgina stared up into the sky and there, illuminated by the moonlight, she saw twenty or so Luftwaffe planes, bombers flanked by fighters.

'Oh, no, not again,' Molly said, standing beside Georgina now.

'Here come more and they look like they're heading for London. They sound like they've got full loads too.'

'Come inside, come on,' Oppo said, ushering the women back into the house.

'Shit, Molly, I need to call Charlotte and warn her. She'll be alone and terrified.' Georgina dashed to the telephone and picked it up but she couldn't hear the normal low hum from the line. She clicked the receiver down and tried again. Still nothing. 'I don't think the telephone is working.'

'Here, let me try,' Molly offered and took the phone from Georgina.

'No, there's nothing,' Molly said nervously. 'Oppo, the telephone's dead.'

Oppo came from the front room and tried the line. 'Old Jake has probably knocked down the pole again. He's as blind as a bat. He shouldn't be allowed out on his tractor.'

'Yeah, it wouldn't be the first time but that's no help to us now. Those planes are going to drop their bombs on London. We need to speak to Charlotte to warn her,' Molly cried desperately.

'I'm sorry, love, but it'll take a few days before they get the line up and running again. There's nothing we can do. But don't worry. Charlotte will have fair warning. The sirens will sound so she'll know to take cover,' Oppo reassured.

'Oh, Georgina, it's awful. I hate to think of Charlotte all alone and scared. I've been so worried about her.'

'I know, but Oppo's right. There's nothing we can do. She'll be fine,' Georgina said. 'Dina is in the house and Johnny will probably check on her.'

'I know she doesn't get on with my mum, but I wish

Charlotte would change her mind and move back here. It would put my mind at rest.'

'She won't, Molly. She likes living in town. Country life isn't for her. And anyway, she's going to be a married woman soon.'

'Yeah, I know. But every time the Germans fly over, I worry meself sick until I hear from her.'

'I'll go home tomorrow. I'll leave first thing in the morning and once I've seen Charlotte, I'll phone the post office in the village and leave a message for you.'

'Thanks, Georgina. I'm sorry if it's cutting short your visit.'

'No, it's time I got back to work anyway.'

'Cocoa?' Fanny asked as she brushed past them, heading towards the kitchen.

'Yes, please,' Molly answered, 'Though it won't help me to sleep. Nothing will.'

Georgina was about to offer her best friend some reassurance but Oppo interrupted.

'I can hear a car,' he said and walked towards the front door. 'Who would be calling here at this time of the evening?'

When he pulled the door open, Georgina was surprised to see Johnny pulling up outside. 'What on earth,' she mumbled, her pulse quickening. Johnny wouldn't have travelled from Battersea unless something was very wrong. She pushed past Oppo and went to meet Johnny as he climbed from the car. 'What's wrong? Please tell me it's nothing to do with Charlotte?'

'It's nothing to do with her,' he answered but his voice was grave.

'What is it then?'

'The Zammits. They're after you and probably the rest of us too.'

'Fuck. This is all I need. Why? Do you know why?'

'Yeah,' Johnny replied, looking uneasy. 'Elsie told them it was you who turned over the jewellery shop.'

'What? But why did she do that?'

'Apparently she's after Temi and his money and you're in her way.'

'That doesn't make sense. I've no interest in the man.'

'I know, but it seems Elsie thinks you have. Talk about stabbing me in the back.'

'Shush,' she whispered as Molly came towards them. 'Don't mention this.'

'Is everything all right?' Molly asked suspiciously.

'Yes, everything is fine but this lot can't cope without me. Johnny's driven up to take me back. That's handy, ain't it?'

'Yes, very. But are you sure everything's all right?'

'I said so, didn't I? How about you get Johnny a cup of that cocoa too. He must be knackered.'

'Yes, of course. Sorry, Johnny, come in,' Molly invited.

'Yeah, thanks. Just give me a minute to stretch me legs.'

'All right, I'll leave the door on the latch. We don't want all the heat escaping.'

Molly went back inside and Georgina turned to Johnny, her eyes blazing. 'How did you find out?'

'Lora Zammit came to the café this morning. She was looking for you to warn you about her husband's intentions.'

'This morning. And I'm only just finding out now!'

'I tried to ring you, but couldn't get through. And then the car broke down on the way here. I got here as soon as I could.'

'I see,' Georgina said grimly. 'All right, come inside, drink your cocoa and then we're going straight back to London.'

'Wouldn't you be safer here?'

'Yeah, probably, but it would only be a matter of time before they'd find me. I'm not hiding, Johnny. If Temi Zammit wants a fight, he's going to bloody well get one.'

Charlotte sat on the edge of Fleur's bed, her stomach full.

'That was the best bacon sandwich I've ever had,' Fleur said as she flopped down beside her.

Charlotte was about to agree but was stopped by a loud hammering on the door. The young women glanced at each other, fear in both their eyes.

'Shush, don't say a word,' Charlotte whispered as she looked around the room. There was nowhere to hide. If it was the Zammits on the other side of the door and it wasn't opened, they would kick it in. She swallowed as bile rose in her throat. That bacon sandwich might have been her last.

'Fleur, are you in there, pet?'

With a huge sigh of relief, Fleur said, 'It's Mrs Wise from downstairs.'

'Thank gawd for that.'

Fleur walked across the room and pulled open the door and Charlotte tried to look past Fleur to get a glimpse of the woman.

'Hello, Mrs Wise,' Fleur said. 'I'm sorry, were we being too loud? I've got my friend, Charlotte, come to stay for a few days.'

'No, no, pet, nothing like that. It's that café you work in. My old man's just come home from the pub and said the café you work in is up in flames!'

'Oh my gawd! Thanks, Mrs Wise. Thanks for letting me know,' Fleur said and closed the door, turning swiftly to look at Charlotte. 'Did you hear that?'

'Yeah, I heard,' Charlotte said, her mind reeling.

'Someone has set it alight, ain't they?'

'Yeah, I think so. You wait here. I'm going to take a look.'

'No, Charlotte, I don't think you should. I reckon you're better off staying here with me. There'll be nothing you can do.'

'Maybe, but I've got to see for myself.'

'All right, but I'm coming with you.'

They grabbed their coats and raced out the door, both running down St John's Hill and then up Lavender Hill. Charlotte could see the glow of the fire and the fire trucks outside. She had no doubt in her mind that the Zammits had done this.

As they approached, a fire warden held them back. 'Keep your distance, miss,' he warned.

Charlotte stood with the crowd and watched as the café was razed to the ground, the flames licking the flats above. She felt Fleur's hand slip into her own.

'I suppose it's lucky that we weren't inside,' Fleur said. 'Come on. You've seen it now. There's nothing left of it. Let's go home.'

'You go, I won't be long,' she said as her eyes roamed over the faces in the crowd. She didn't recognise anyone who could be a Zammit but she didn't know who she was looking for. An unknown enemy. It was a terrifying thought to think there could be someone in the crowd who wanted them dead!

After a while, the flames were dampened down and the crowd began to disperse. Charlotte turned around and headed back towards Fleur's. As she walked down the hill, the noise from the commotion outside the café became quieter. But then she heard something in the distance that made her blood run cold. Surely not? It couldn't be, could it? Charlotte looked skyward and saw the dark outline of German planes flying above.

She stood transfixed, her neck stretched back as she stared upwards. Bright searchlights from Battersea Park roamed across the night sky and the sound from the anti-aircraft guns on Clapham Common reached her ears. But why hadn't the warning sirens sounded?

'Take cover, miss,' a man warned as he darted past her.

Charlotte glanced after the man and then her eyes fell onto a young woman who, just like her, was standing frozen to the spot. She was holding an umbrella over her head and staring blankly back at Charlotte with empty eyes. Charlotte tried to pull her gaze away from the woman to peer up at the dogfight that was playing out over their heads. The Germans had taken them by surprise but the RAF were hot on the heels of the Luftwaffe. Shrapnel from their guns suddenly bounced off the woman's umbrella.

Charlotte felt someone tugging her arm. An American soldier was pulling her down the street. 'You can't stay here,' he said urgently.

As she was dragged along the road, she looked over her shoulder to see another American soldier had taken hold of the woman and was forcibly yanking her along. She dropped her umbrella but made no attempt to pick it up.

Charlotte looked up at the man holding her arm. He was tall, like Tim, and probably about the same age. He reminded her a lot of Tim. This is the sort of heroic act that he would do. But he wasn't Tim and she snatched her arm free of his grip. She didn't want to die with a stranger.

'What are you doing, miss?'

'I'm going home,' Charlotte answered firmly, and to her own flat, not to Fleur's.

She ran away from the kind American soldier and towards Alexandra Avenue. As she sprinted away from the mayhem at Clapham Junction, explosions rattled somewhere in the distance and the distinct smell of burning buildings wafted through the air. Battersea hadn't been hit so far tonight but other parts of London had been attacked. Tomorrow's newspapers would be filled with the details of the casualties and the tragic death toll.

Charlotte reached home, gasping for breath. As she put her key into the front door, she noticed her hand visibly shaking. 'You're home now,' she told herself, reassuringly.

Once inside, in the hallway, she could hear Miss Gray singing upstairs. The old lady always sang her way through a bombing raid. Charlotte didn't know what Dina did to get through it. She imagined the brave Russian woman took it in her stride. After all, Dina rarely showed any emotion apart from anger.

As she pushed open the door to her flat, Charlotte thought how eerily quiet it felt. Dog didn't bound up to greet her. Georgina was away in Kent. Tim off at basic training camp. And Lord Hamilton dead. Gawd, she missed the old toff.

He would have been down here now with his brandy and a funny story to tell. But there were only the three of them left in the building, Miss Gray, Dina and her. A strange and somewhat unfriendly bunch.

Charlotte closed the door and, feeling a bit dizzy, she slumped to the floor. She hugged her knees up to her chest and rocked back and forth, trying to push the images from her head of bomb blasted bodies. As tears poured from her eyes, she leaned to one side and lay on the floor, curled into a foetal position. The fear had subsided but was replaced with an overwhelming feeling of loneliness.

The Zammits were nothing to fear compared to the Luftwaffe, she thought as she cried herself to sleep right there on the floor just inside her door.

30

Johnny hoped the car would get them back to London without breaking down again. He'd never really understood how engines worked so if the car failed them now, they'd be stuck on the dark country lanes. It was unlikely that anyone would pass them at this time of night. He'd been lucky on his way to Kent. When the engine had spluttered and lost power, he'd been stranded at the side of the road for nearly two hours. An old boy in a tractor had stopped and towed him back to his farm. An hour later, the car was fixed. Johnny had been grateful but he knew that sort of luck didn't come around twice in one day.

As they eventually neared London, it was clear to see that the city had been badly hit by the German bombers. They could see an orange hue in the night sky. London was on fire again.

'I hope Charlotte's all right,' Georgina mumbled.

'I'm sure she will be,' Johnny answered but his mind wasn't on Charlotte. He was more worried about what the Zammits were going to do and concerned that Georgina was out of her depth. 'What are we going to do about Temi Zammit?' he asked anxiously.

'I don't know yet. I'm thinking.'

Johnny took her answer as his cue to keep quiet. They drove the rest of the way in silence but he noticed she was rubbing her finger, a sure sign that Georgina was deep in thought.

As they came into Battersea, Johnny sighed with relief. There was no sign of more bomb damage and the fires looked to be on the other side of the Thames. Westminster probably hadn't fared well, he thought, feeling sorry for the poor folk who'd been hit.

He pulled up outside Fleur's house. Georgina went in but came back minutes later without Charlotte.

'Where is she?' Johnny asked.

'Fleur said she hasn't seen her since the Jerries flew over. They were up the Junction. The café has been torched.'

'Fuck. The Zammits?'

'Yeah, probably. But at least no one was inside.'

'Where to now?'

'Home. Charlotte will be there.'

Johnny hadn't turned the engine off in case the car didn't start again. He set off for Alexandra Avenue, his mind turning. Burning down the café was a clear message that the Zammits meant business and he feared it was only a matter of time before they caught up with him and Georgina.

'Wait here,' Georgina said when they arrived at her house.

'No. I'm not leaving your side,' Johnny answered and got out of the car before she could protest.

Inside, Dina came running down the stairs. Her hands were still thickly bandaged. Johnny wondered how she managed to dress or feed herself but Dina wouldn't thank him for prying into her business so he kept his mouth shut.

'Miss Garrett, I have a message for you,' Dina said calmly

but with urgency. 'Four men come here and tell me you are to meet them at West One Club. At dawn.'

'Do you know who the men were?' Georgina asked.

'No. Gangsters. I think they want to kill you, yes?'

'Yes, probably. Did they say anything else?'

'No.'

'Have you seen Charlotte?'

'She is indoors. I hear her cry like a baby,' Dina answered with contempt.

Georgina exchanged a worried look with Johnny. She quickly fished a key from her bag and opened the door but it wouldn't open fully.

'Charlotte... Charlotte...' Georgina called through the gap and peeked inside. 'Johnny, she's on the floor!'

Johnny rushed over. He looked through the small gap to see Charlotte rising to her feet. 'Charlotte, it's me and Miss Garrett.'

'I'm sorry,' Charlotte muttered. 'I must have fallen asleep down there,' she said as she let them in.

Johnny could see her eyes were swollen from crying. 'What's happened?' he asked.

'Eh? Oh, the café got burned down.'

They went into the front room and it was Georgina who challenged Charlotte now. 'I know about the café but what happened to you? You've been upset.'

'Nothing. Nothing happened to me.'

'Are you sure?'

'Yes. I just got scared when the planes flew over.'

'You're supposed to be at Fleur's,' Johnny snapped.

'Yeah, I know but she ain't got room to swing a cat and I felt safer here.'

'Did you know the Zammits have been here and spoken to Dina?' Georgina asked.

'No,' Charlotte replied, her eyes wide.

'See, you ain't safe here,' Johnny said. 'I'm taking you back to Fleur's and this time, stay bloody put!'

'Do as he tells you,' Georgina urged. 'It's for your own good.'

Charlotte rolled her eyes but nodded in agreement. 'What did they do? Is Dina all right?'

'Yes, she's fine. I've been summoned to meet them at one of their clubs.'

'Are you going to go?'

'I don't have much choice.'

'You can't! Please, Georgina, don't go. It'll be suicide.'

'I'm damned if I go and damned if I don't. I'll work it out. But I want you at Fleur's for now. Johnny will run you there.'

'I'll be straight back,' Johnny said to Georgina before walking out the door and gently pushing Charlotte out with him.

He waited for Fleur to let Charlotte in before rushing back to Georgina. When he got there, he found she'd changed into a smart pair of trousers and a fitted jumper and was counting out her bullets.

'We haven't got nearly enough ammunition, guns or men,' she said gravely.

'I know.'

'I'll have to outsmart them but I'm at a loss, Johnny. I don't know how to get us out of this.'

Johnny sucked in a deep lungful of air and, bracing for an explosion, offered an option, 'You could ask David Maynard for help?'

'No! Absolutely not. There's nothing between me and David anymore. I won't be beholden to him for anything.'

'If we want to get out of this alive, it's our only choice. The Zammits ain't mucking about. They *will* kill both of us.'

'Maybe. But let's see what they've got to say for themselves first.'

'What, you mean meet them at the club?'

'Yes. Perhaps I can talk to Temi and strike a deal. It'll cost me but Temi loves money. I'm sure I can come to some sort of arrangement with him.'

'I'm sorry, Miss Garrett, but I think this has gone past the talking stage. Yeah, Temi loves money but he ain't averse to slaughtering those who've wronged him. And as far as he's concerned, you've done just that.'

Georgina huffed and ran a hand through her hair in agitation. 'Who am I trying to kid? You're right. He wants me there to kill me. But this ain't just about his father's shop. He's pissed off that I didn't finish off David.'

'Whatever his reasons, he won't stop at you. We'll all cop it.'

'Not if I can help it,' Georgina said, sounding more assured. 'Get the men ready. I'll meet Temi at dawn, but I'll make sure I have a little surprise for him. Something to make him sit up and listen.'

Johnny had no idea what Georgina meant but had a feeling that she had a plan. He looked at his watch. They had about five hours before sunrise. Maybe just five hours left to live.

★

'You know what to do?' Georgina asked Nobby Barker.

'Yeah. Don't worry, me and Eric have got this,' he answered in his low voice.

'Good. Time's ticking on, you'd better hurry. Take the car. Don't fuck this up. Everything is riding on it.'

'We won't,' Nobby replied.

The Barker twins left to carry out Georgina's instructions. She had every faith in them. She looked to Ned. He was stubbing out a roll-up in the ashtray, the fifth one he'd smoked in quick succession.

'Do you think you can do it, Ned?' she asked him.

'Yeah, course I can. I won't let you down, Miss Garrett.'

'All right. Off you go with the twins. I'll see you soon.'

Ned lit another roll-up as he left. Georgina thought he was more nervous than he was letting on, but Ned's part in her plan was small with little risk. She felt sure he'd pull it off.

'I need another coffee. Do you want one?' Georgina asked Johnny.

'I'd rather have a stiff drink,' he answered with a tense laugh. 'But there's no chance of getting one at The Penthouse now, more's the pity.'

'That's two of my businesses gone up in smoke, thanks to Temi Zammit. Ned said the building next door is destroyed too. It must have been one hell of a fire.'

'Good job the club was closed.'

'Yes, it was,' Georgina said as she pushed herself from the armchair and went into the kitchen to boil the kettle again. She held onto the sink and arched her aching back. Things weren't looking good for her unless she could persuade Temi to have a discussion. That was going to be a challenge in itself but she was hoping that the Barker twins would be returning soon with her bargaining tool. Something that would *make* Temi listen.

Before long, there was the sound of a light tap on the window. Georgina looked out, glad to see Nobby.

'They're back, let them in,' she told Johnny.

Nobby came into the room as Georgina picked up her bag. 'Ready?' she asked him.

'Yep, ready,' he answered.

They followed Nobby to the car. Eric climbed out from the driver's seat. Johnny handed him the keys to his own car and said, 'Look after my girl.'

'I'm a better driver than you, mate. Your car is in safe hands,' Eric replied and shook Johnny's hand. 'Me and Nobby will see you later. Good luck.'

Georgina opened the back door and eased herself in. She pulled her gun from her bag and told Ned, 'Good job. You can go with Nobby and Eric now.'

'Right you are. She's been as good as gold,' Ned said, referring to their captive passenger. Ned climbed out and dashed off with the Barkers to get Johnny's car.

'Let's go,' Georgina said to Johnny.

He turned the engine and they set off as Georgina pushed the barrel of her gun into Lora Zammit's chest. She didn't like to hear the sound of a woman crying and snapped at Lora, 'Shut up.'

'Please don't do this, Georgina. You know I tried to help you. I tried to warn you.'

'Yes, I know. Thanks for that. But, unfortunately, your husband hasn't left me with any other options.'

'But my children... please promise me that you won't hurt them.'

'That's down to your husband. You'll need to persuade him that I'm not to be harmed. If I don't return safely, then the people who are holding them will know what to do.'

Lora cried harder. 'Please, Georgina, they're just babies. You're a mother. You must understand how desperate I am.'

'I said shut up! I've already told you, your children's wellbeing will be down to the choices your husband makes,' Georgina growled. She hated using Lora's kids as a threat but in reality, she'd never harm them. They were safe with Charlotte and Fleur for now. Though she couldn't let Lora know the truth. The woman had to be convinced that her children's lives were at risk so that she in turn could convince her husband.

The sun began to rise over the buildings. They were just minutes away from the West One Club. It was one of Temi's smarter premises, often frequented by influential guests from parliament and the councils. Sometimes top ranking police officers too. The club sat a few minutes away from Piccadilly in a small tree-lined street. Georgina had never been inside but she knew that a dead-end alley ran alongside the club from which a back door could be accessed. But the alley would have two of Temi's men guarding it and there would likely be at least another two on the front door. The Zammits had ensured the club was impenetrable to uninvited customers.

Johnny pulled the car up right outside the club. Temi's men would be expecting them, but not with Temi's wife.

'Don't fight me and if you do as you're told, you and your

children will be fine. Do you understand me?' Georgina hissed.

Lora swallowed hard and nodded.

'Right, let's do this,' Georgina said to Johnny.

He got out of the car first and opened the back door for Georgina. She pushed Lora out and climbed out next, all the time holding the gun into the small of Lora's back. 'Take her,' she said to Johnny.

Johnny stood behind Lora and wrapped his arm loosely around her neck while holding his gun to her head. 'You heard Miss Garrett. Just do as you're told,' he said and eased her forward.

Georgina walked a step or two in front. 'Let us pass or Mrs Zammit dies,' she said clearly to the three men on the door.

She could see the looks of confusion on their faces as they weighed up the situation and stepped aside. Georgina walked into the club. The corridor was much brighter than she'd expected. She heard Johnny tell Lora to keep walking.

A set of double doors in front of them was guarded by another two of Temi's men. When they saw Lora Zammit with a gun to her head, they quickly lowered their weapons and one of the men pulled open the door.

'Mr Zammit will fucking kill you for this,' he snarled as Georgina walked past him.

Through the doors led to the main club area. Georgina's nose wrinkled at the musty smell of stale alcohol and tobacco. The club was mostly in darkness but she saw Temi sat at a table near the stage area. His face was illuminated by a crystal lamp on the table. He sneered at his wife. Georgina strode slowly past another four men and towards Temi. She stopped several feet away from him. Johnny stood beside her with Lora.

'I see you've brought company,' Temi said. His gun was in his hand, which hung at his side.

'I thought we could have a chat,' Georgina said casually, hiding her fear.

'You want to talk. Why is it that all women want to talk? What if I don't want to talk? What if I would rather shut you up forever?'

'No, Temi,' Lora cried, 'you have to listen to her. She has our children.'

Temi's eyes narrowed. 'An effective threat, Georgina, I applaud you.'

'You should have put protection on your family. But I'm glad you didn't. So are you ready to talk now?'

'What is there to say? You are going to plead for your life. So go on then, beg.'

'That wasn't what I had in mind.'

'If you want to live, woman, let me see you beg on your knees.'

Lora cried out again, frantically this time. 'Please, Temi, think about our children. My babies,' she sobbed.

Temi raised his arm and fired his gun. The booming sound echoed off the walls. Georgina recoiled but quickly realised that she hadn't been shot. Lora groaned.

Georgina looked to her side to see Johnny was holding Lora's head in his arms. She was laid on the floor, gripping her stomach. Blood seeped through her pretty pale blue dress and spread across the material.

'My babies... please don't kill my babies,' Lora whispered. Johnny took her blood covered hand in his own and leaned his face closer to hers. 'Your children won't be hurt,' he said quietly.

Georgina wasn't sure if Lora had heard Johnny's reassurance before she'd slipped into unconsciousness. The thought of the woman possibly dying in fear of her children's lives made Georgina feel physically sick. Bile rose in her throat.

She swallowed down the vomit and glared at Temi. 'You bastard. How could you shoot your wife down like that?'

'She got on my nerves,' he answered flippantly. 'Was there still something you wanted to discuss?'

'If I don't walk out of here alive with Johnny, your children will be joining their mother in death,' she warned and waited for his response. Georgina had known Temi was merciless with his enemies but she'd underestimated his callousness. Surely a threat to the lives of his children would resonate with him. After all, she'd assumed he was a family man.

'I've already agreed to have a discussion with you so go ahead, talk, but you and your boyfriend can put your guns down first.'

Georgina crouched down and placed hers on the floor. It left her feeling naked and vulnerable. She looked at Johnny. His beige wool coat was covered in Lora's blood. She could see he had a tight grip on his gun and made no move to give it up.

'It's all right, Johnny,' Georgina said quietly.

Johnny looked back at her. She recognised that expression in his eyes.

'No, Johnny, don't do it,' she said, but it was too late.

Johnny aimed his gun at Temi. Another almighty boom

sounded and Johnny fell to the floor alongside Lora. Georgina dropped to her knees beside him, relieved to see he was breathing and his eyes were open.

Johnny grimaced in pain. 'It's just a flesh wound,' he said, holding his hand over his wounded shoulder.

'I warned you,' Georgina screamed at Temi. 'Your children!'

'He was going to shoot me. I haven't killed him,' Temi said in his defence.

Georgina helped Johnny from the floor and onto a seat at a table. Then she turned back to Temi. 'We need to resolve this before anyone else gets hurt.'

'I'd love to hear your suggestions. I mean, you must know the reasons why I want you dead?'

'I'm guessing it has something to do with Elsie Flowers lying about me stealing from your father's shop?'

'Yes, but I know you didn't do it. It was that bastard, and he gunned down one of my most loyal coppers,' Temi said, pointing at Johnny slumped at the table. 'But you knew he'd done it. You should have come to me, Georgina, and owned up. Instead, you covered for him. Then you tortured and killed my artist who, incidentally, died owing me money. But do you know what really pissed me off?'

'I didn't kill The Top?'

'That's right, you didn't. I found out why... because The Top is David Maynard. You see, that's put me in a very difficult predicament. You know I backed you killing him because I felt he could have been a threat to me. Well, the threat has become a whole lot bigger. See, me and Mr Maynard, we're probably on par – but if you team up with him, where does that leave me?'

'God, you are just as fucking pathetic as him,' Georgina said in disgust.

Temi looked taken aback.

'It's all about the egos with you men. *My gun is bigger than your gun. I've got more power than you've got.* You should listen to yourselves. You and David sound like schoolboys arguing in the playground. I'll never work with either of you!'

Temi placed his gun on the table and began to slowly applaud her. 'Nice speech,' he grinned sardonically.

It wasn't lost on Georgina that although Temi had disarmed himself, the rest of his men were pointing their guns at her. Now would be the opportune moment for Ned and the Barker twins to act, but something must have delayed them. Ned, by now, should have innocently walked past her car and stuffed a lit rag into the petrol tank. She was expecting an explosion right outside the club. It would be a distraction to the bouncers guarding the alley. Nobby and Eric would use it to their advantage to slip in through the back door. But nothing had happened. She feared they may have been caught by Temi's men – but if that was the case, why hadn't they been dragged through here to be held at gunpoint with her? 'Come on,' she urged under her breath. But instead of an explosion, she heard the unmistakable sound of the air raid sirens.

'It seems we have some more unwanted visitors,' Temi said, pointing up towards the ceiling.

'Ironic really. There are brave men out there fighting for our freedom yet we're using that freedom to kill one another.'

'And there lies the problem, Georgina. You're quite right,

I want you dead but I have a dilemma as you have my children. How do you suggest we overcome this?'

'Call a truce?'

'We both know that will never work. The trust has been broken between us. If I let you walk out of here, you know that as soon as I have my children back, I'll come for you again. And you'll be gunning for me too... No, a truce will never work. It's your life or my children's lives. But here's the thing, I don't believe you'll harm my children. You're tough but you're not a child murderer.'

Georgina folded her arms across her chest and cocked her head to one side. 'You don't know me, Temi,' she drawled.

'I think I do,' he replied as he picked his gun up from the table.

The sirens were still wailing outside as Temi pointed his gun at her. Georgina turned her head to look at Johnny and held his gaze. She wanted a loving face to be the last thing that she saw, not Temi's smug face.

'Sorry,' Johnny mouthed helplessly.

She smiled warmly at him. 'It's all right, Johnny,' she whispered and braced herself.

Images of Alfie and Selina flashed through her mind. They'd never know their mother but she would always look over them. Was it her imagination or could she feel Lash breathing softly on her cheek?

Georgina closed her eyes and waited for the bullet to rip through her flesh. She was ready to face death but had one last thought – *please, make it quick*.

★

'Oh, no, not again,' Fleur moaned as she woke to the sound of the air raid warning sirens blaring.

Charlotte hadn't been to sleep. She'd sat up all night worrying about Georgina. The two young children in the bed with Fleur woke up and began crying.

'I want my mummy,' the little girl of four years old sobbed.

'Mummy,' the six-year-old boy cried.

'What are we going to do?' Fleur asked, her voice high pitched with panic.

Charlotte's heart pounded hard. She gulped. 'Let's get the kids in the Morrison.'

'But what about us?' Fleur screeched.

'I dunno, we can shelter under the bed.'

'Why can't they get under the bed?'

'They're just kids, Fleur. Come on, help me get them in the cage.'

Charlotte and Fleur each gathered a child in their arms and tried to encourage them into the shelter. Both children were screaming and hysterically crying.

'I don't want to go in there,' the girl shouted.

'This ain't going to work,' Charlotte said. 'Come on, I've got an idea.'

'What? Where are we going? It ain't safe out there!'

'Fleur, calm down, will you? You're not helping. We can go to the public shelter in the next street. It'll be safer. This house is so bleedin' rickety, I reckon if a bomb landed ten streets away, this place would shake and fall down. Come on, hurry.'

They'd slept in their coats, but Charlotte's had been over her lap. She plonked the sobbing girl on the floor and quickly threw it on, before grabbing the child again and rushing out the door.

'Hurry up, Fleur,' she called as she ran down the street.

'I'm trying but he's heavy.'

Charlotte stopped to wait for Fleur to catch up. 'Quick, swap kids,' she said. 'The girl is lighter.'

They exchanged children and resumed running. As they turned into the next street, Charlotte saw an old couple going into the brick built shelter which ran along the middle of the road with rows of terraced houses on each side.

The old couple saw Charlotte and Fleur running towards them.

'In you come,' the old lady said and ushered them through.

It was dark inside and didn't smell very pleasant. The screams and cries from the children filled the shelter.

'It's frightening for the little 'uns,' said a middle-aged woman. She had a scarf over her head but was still wearing her night clothes. ''Ere you go, this will quieten 'em down.' The woman pulled a couple of sweets from her dressing gown pocket and offered one to each of the children.

'I want my mummy!' the girl screeched again.

'Ain't she yours?' the woman asked.

'No. We're babysitting for a friend,' Charlotte lied.

'Blimey, I should think their mother must be worried sick about them.' The woman tried again to persuade the children to take the sweets and they did, finally quietening down.

'I know that bloke over there,' Fleur whispered in Charlotte's ear, 'he used to be a customer of mine.'

Charlotte glanced across to the man who looked uneasy stood alongside his wife. 'Just ignore him,' she told Fleur.

There must have been at least twenty or thirty people in the shelter. Charlotte's eyes roamed over their faces. Some looked pale with fright, others appeared annoyed and a couple looked as if they were still half-asleep.

'Anyone bring a flask?' a voice said from the back.

'Yeah, we did,' the old man said.

'Us an' all,' another called.

'I've brought some biscuits.'

'There's some sandwiches here if anyone is hungry?'

'Right, let's have some breakfast and a sing-song, eh? Mrs Jones, you pour the tea. Mrs Higgins, pass the biscuits. I'll start the music.' The man was stood just a few feet from Charlotte in the cramped space. He pulled a harmonica from his pocket and began playing a tune that she recognised. *Run rabbit, run rabbit, run, run, run.* But much to Charlotte's amusement, when people started singing the lyrics, they sang, *Run Adolf, run Adolf, run, run, run.*

Charlotte found herself joining in and bobbing the young boy up and down on her hip in time to the music. Mrs Jones handed her half a cup of black tea. Mrs Higgins offered her a plain broken biscuit. Even the young boy was smiling now. Charlotte placed him on the ground and watched with delight as he began to dance with his little sister. And then something occurred to her. She wasn't terrified. She wasn't plagued by the images of the mutilated bodies she'd seen during the earlier Blitz. In fact, she'd been calm and had taken control of the situation and had got Fleur and the children to safety. Tim would be proud of her, she thought with a soft smile.

Charlotte looked down at the young boy and ruffled his hair as she realised that she'd put her own fears aside to look after others. She'd protected the child as best she could, just like a mother would have done. She thought of Tim again. Maybe one day, once this blasted war was over, she would bear Tim's children. The thought had always horrified her but now it gave her a warm feeling. Charlotte knew that she had grown up and was ready to be a wife and mother.

Georgina's eyes were squeezed shut as she waited for Temi to put a bullet in her. Then over the noise of the air raid sirens, she heard a huge explosion which sent a whoosh of air blasting through the club. The chandeliers rattled and bottles chinked. The whole building had shook. Had the Jerries bombed the street or had Ned finally managed to explode her car?

She opened her eyes to the sound of gunfire. Bullets tore past her head.

'Get down,' Johnny shouted from under the table.

Georgina looked around for her men. She couldn't see Ned or the Barker twins but several other blokes were firing at Temi's gang and she was caught in the crossfire.

'Get down,' Johnny yelled again.

Georgina looked at the empty seat where Temi had been. She hadn't seen him leave. Everything had happened so fast but seemed to play out around her in slow motion.

The firing ceased. Three of Temi's men stood with their hands in the air. The rest were shot dead.

Georgina quickly took stock of the scene. She saw one of Temi's blokes spread-eagled across a table with a fatal gunshot wound to his chest. The man's gun had fallen to the floor and sat just feet away from her. Georgina ducked and scurried over to the gun. She picked it up and held it close to her face as she hid behind a seat. Who were these men?

The club doors opened and a dark figure strode in. She couldn't make out who he was but could see he was flanked by at least six other men. She was sure Ned was one of them.

The dark figure spoke. He called her name and when she heard his voice, she instantly recognised it and rose to her feet.

'David. I should have guessed. Was all this for my benefit?' she asked, gesticulating to Temi's dead men.

'Of course.'

Georgina knew she should be grateful but couldn't bring herself to thank him. Instead, she dashed to Johnny's side and knelt beside him. 'Are you all right?' she asked tenderly.

'I'll live,' he answered weakly. 'Lora, she's breathing,' he added.

Georgina glanced over her shoulder and urgently called to David, 'They need a doctor.'

A few of David's men rushed across and swooped Johnny and Lora up.

'They'll take them to the hospital,' David said as he approached her.

'Where's Temi?' she asked, remembering he'd escaped.

'With Nobby and Eric. Your men caught him trying to do a runner out of the back door. By the way, that was a nice touch with the car blowing up outside.'

'What are you doing here?'

'Saving your bacon.'

'How did you know?'

'Anyone can be bought, Georgina. After you came to see me, I questioned how you'd managed to get past my bodyguards with a gun. It didn't take much to work out that one of the blokes was working for Temi. And for the right price, he jumped ship and tipped me off.'

Georgina gazed up at David. In the dim light, his scars were hardly noticeable and his eyes still held their mischievous twinkle. *Stop it*, she told herself. 'I suppose you're expecting me to be grateful now?' she snapped.

'Well, it wouldn't hurt to say thank you. Especially as two of my men have been shot.'

'Thank you,' she said begrudgingly. 'But nothing has changed,' she added and stamped off towards the back door to deal with Temi Zammit.

'Wait,' David called.

Georgina stopped walking and stood still but kept her back to David. She could feel him coming closer. Part of her wanted to turn around and run into his arms. He'd saved her life but could she ever forgive him for making her believe that he was dead?

David was standing so closely behind her now, she could smell the scent of his cologne. He still wore the same one he always had. The smell of him rekindled exciting memories. And when he touched her arm and stroked his hand down, over her wrist and to her little finger, her body tingled. Georgina gasped, thrilled at his touch.

'Marry me?' David husked in her ear.

His proposal came as a shock and though she tried to fight her feelings, she knew she was losing. Georgina slowly turned around to face him. She searched his eyes and saw the love she'd craved from him for years. She'd lost him once and knew she didn't want to lose him again.

'Yes,' she answered. 'I'll marry you. But I'm still really bloody angry with you!'

David threw his arms around her and kissed her with fervent ardour. As she melted into his firm embrace, her anger ebbed away.

David's men began clapping and cheering.

'Congratulations, miss,' Ned shouted joyfully.

Georgina reluctantly pulled away from David's arms. 'There's still some business to sort out. I need to see to Temi,' she whispered, somewhat breathless from David's passionate kiss.

'There's no need for you to deal with men like him anymore. You can leave all that to me.'

'Oh no, David, that's not how things are going to be. If you think I'm going to be *that* sort of wife, then you can think again.'

'All right, that's fine with me, *Mrs Maynard*. Whatever you say. *You* are the boss.'

Georgina had never believed in fairy tales. She thought they were unrealistic and life wasn't like that. But once this damn war was over and her children were back at home, she hoped that maybe, just maybe, her story would end with '*and they all lived happily ever after.*'

31

16 months later.

Tuesday 8 May 1945.

Georgina could hear a terrific commotion through the open window of her grand lounge where she'd once gunned down Slugs. People were cheering and high-spirited music filled the air outside. Car horns tooted and she could hear what sounded like saucepan lids clanging excitedly. She peered out of the window, perplexed, and saw a family who lived further along the street had dragged a piano from their house and there were men, women and children dancing around it.

The lounge door burst open and David came hurtling in, his huge smile indicating to Georgina that he had good news.

'What's going on?' she asked her husband.

'It's over, Georgina. We've won the bloody war!'

Georgina staggered away from the window and dropped

onto the sumptuous sofa. 'Really? It's really over?' she asked, hardly daring to believe it.

'Yes, Germany has surrendered. Victory is ours.'

A smile began to creep across her face. 'You know what this means, don't you?'

'Yes, I do. Alfie and Selina will finally be coming home. You've waited so long for this day to happen.'

'Oh, David,' Georgina exclaimed. She leapt to her feet to throw her arms around her husband's neck. 'At last.'

'Do you have to do that in the middle of the day?' Charlotte asked.

Georgina pulled her arms from David and saw that Charlotte had come into the room.

'Dina let me in,' Charlotte said as she removed her hat and threw it onto the drinks cabinet.

'You've heard?' Georgina asked. 'The war is over!'

'Yeah, of course I've heard. You can hardly fail not to. I was on my way over when pandemonium broke loose. There's bonfires and parties everywhere,' Charlotte said solemnly. 'But it's not over for Tim, is it? He's still out in Burma fighting the Japs, so God only knows when he'll be home.'

'I'm sorry, love, but I'm sure it won't be much longer. And the moment he is demobbed, we'll get my dressmaker to make a start on your wedding dress. That's something to look forward to, eh?'

'Yes, I can't wait for him to get home and make me his wife. But I'm not jinxing anything. Your dressmaker ain't allowed to cut the material or anything until I know that Tim is home safe and sound. I'm not tempting fate and bringing bad luck.'

'It's fine, I understand.'

David cleared his throat. 'Erm, excuse me, Charlotte, would you like a drink?'

'Yes, why not. I suppose we should celebrate. Tim or no Tim, the blinkin' war in Europe is still over. Champagne?'

'Sounds like a good idea to me,' David replied.

As he popped the cork, Johnny Dymond flew into the room. 'It's over!' he declared.

'Yes, Johnny, we were just about to have a glass of champagne. Care to join us?' David asked.

'Yes, please, boss.'

'Don't call me that, not in front of the *real* boss,' David said jokingly and indicated towards Georgina.

'Actually, I think now would be a good time to announce my resignation,' Georgina said as David handed her a champagne flute. She held the glass aloft. 'A toast, to victory in Europe and to me stepping down from the business.'

'What do you mean?' David asked, frowning.

'My children are coming home. I've a lot of time to make up for. From now on, they will be my sole focus and you, my dear husband, can take over running everything without me.'

'That's definitely worth toasting,' David said and chuckled. 'I'll finally get my own way.'

'You'll still keep me on as your driver though?' Johnny asked Georgina.

'Of course.' Georgina felt that Johnny had to stay on as her driver whether she needed him or not. She'd come to realise how reckless he could be without her guidance and felt compelled to keep an eye on the silly sod. 'Do me a favour, go and give Dina a shout. She should be celebrating with us.'

Johnny slipped out of the room and returned moments later with Dina. She refused a glass of champagne and her face barely cracked into a smile.

'The children shall be returning soon, Dina. I'd like you to prepare their beds.'

'Vil you be collecting zem or are ze gypsies bringing zem here?'

'I should imagine that we will be collecting them.'

'May I come wis you?'

'If you like. Any reason why?'

'I think I leave wis zem. I travel across Europe wis zem. Zey take me to Russia, yes?'

'You want Lash's family to take you to Russia?'

'Yes.'

'I see. Well, they did say that once the war was over and my children back home, they would move east for a while. I'm sure they'd be happy to offer you safe passage with them.'

'Thank you, Miss Garrett.'

'Dina, it's Mrs Maynard now, remember?'

'Yes, Miss Garrett, I remember.'

Georgina rolled her eyes. Dina had never addressed her as Mrs Maynard even though she'd married David more than six months ago. Neither had Dina ever spoken to David.

'If you're going to be needing a new housekeeper, Gerty would be interested,' Charlotte suggested.

'Dirty Gerty?' Johnny asked.

'Yeah. She came round the other day and asked about any jobs going. She's had enough of whoring now. She said life as a prossy ain't the same without the Zammits' protection.'

'Tell her to come and see me,' Georgina said. 'I shall need someone. My kids are going to be keeping me busy. I shan't have time to look after this big house an' all. I'll miss you, Dina. What will you do in Russia?'

'Find my papa.'

'You'll need money. David will see to that. You've been very loyal to me and you'll always be welcome back.'

'I vil not be back. I go home and I stay.'

'You must write to me and let me know how you get on.'

Dina said nothing and merely stared at Georgina blankly, just as she always did. Life had not been kind to Dina. The woman appeared to be without feelings or thought, machine-like in her ways. Georgina hoped that Dina would find some happiness and comfort in Russia, though from what she had read in the newspapers, the Soviet Union occupied much of eastern Europe under a communist dictatorship. It seemed a grim prospect for Dina to be venturing in to.

'Who fancies coming up town with me for a party? Everyone's flocking up there,' Johnny said and then he knocked back the champagne in his glass. 'That's if you don't mind, Mrs Maynard?'

'No, you go, Johnny. Take Charlotte with you, and Dina if she wants. I'm going to celebrate here with my husband and maybe we can call in to The Penthouse later. My new manager will have the champagne corks popping, I'm sure,' Georgina answered and walked over to David who draped his arm over her shoulder and pulled her close.

'Ladies... do you want to party?' Johnny asked.

'Not really,' Charlotte answered sullenly, 'but I'll keep you company if only to keep you out of trouble. Are you joining us, Dina?'

Dina pushed her nose haughtily into the air and turned before walking out of the room.

'She's never going to forgive me, is she?' Charlotte mumbled.

'I doubt it but don't lose any sleep over it. She won't be here for much longer,' Georgina answered.

A loud explosion outside startled Georgina. 'Fireworks,' she said, holding her hand on her racing heart. Holloway Prison and nightly bombing raids, even the V2 bombs, they were all behind her now, yet a loud and sudden noise still made her pulse quicken. There had been many nights when she'd woken in a cold sweat after a nightmare about being back behind bars in that awful place. She thought of Ester and her daughter, Paula, the Jewish refugees who'd been in Holloway before being shipped to the Isle of Man. She wondered what had become of them and if they would now return to Germany.

'See ya,' Johnny chirped. 'I'll be back tomorrow.'

'No, I want you, Ned and the Barkers outside Holloway Prison tomorrow. Elsie Flowers is due for release. See to it that she doesn't enjoy any of her freedom,' Georgina ordered. 'And don't forget, you and me were nearly killed because of her. Don't you dare go soft on her and fall for her sweet and innocent act again.'

'I won't, I'll never forgive the bitch for setting the Zammits against us. Do you want her freedom gone for good? I'll happily put a bullet in her.'

394

'No need. Just drop her at the police station. I've lined up another charge against her. She'll be back inside Holloway for a very long time.'

'Good,' Charlotte snapped. 'She won't be getting any fancy dresses in there!'

'Indeed.'

'What's she gonna be charged with?' Johnny asked.

'Murdering her husband. I found out where Temi's men disposed of Jacob's body. The police have sufficient evidence to charge her with his death, including witness testimonials and an incriminating piece of evidence that places her there.'

'What evidence?'

'An earring that she must have accidently lost when she buried him and that several witnesses have identified as hers. And Lora Zammit has agreed to take the stand to say that her husband and Elsie were having an affair. She will state that Temi told her that Elsie killed Jacob and begged him for help to get rid of the corpse. Lora might be incriminating herself but she needs the money and I'm paying a good price for her statement. David is going to speak to his *friend* on the force to protect Lora from prosecution.'

'Elsie will hang,' Johnny said without remorse.

'Possibly. But it's no more than she deserves.'

'Once again, I take me hat off to you, boss. It's genius!'

'Thank you. Anyway, off you go and make sure that Charlotte gets back to Alexandra Avenue safely tonight.'

Once alone, David poured Georgina another glass of champagne. 'I hope I don't frighten the kids,' he said, handing her the drink.

'Frighten them... why would you frighten them?' But as Georgina asked the question, it dawned on her what he meant. She saw past his disfigurement. In fact, she hardly noticed it. But David's scars clearly played on his mind. 'I love you and so will my children,' she said firmly.

'I won't try and be their father and I won't mind if you talk to them about Lash. He should be remembered. I've gotta say, I can't wait to meet them.'

'I'm scared, David. They won't know me.'

'It won't take them long to adjust. They'll have nice big bedrooms instead of a cramped caravan and the park is right next door. I can't see any reason why they won't love living here.'

'Because they'll be living with strangers,' Georgina answered sadly.

'Strangers who will love them and spoil them rotten,' David assured. He tilted her head back and gently kissed her. Then told her, 'So stop worrying.'

'We'll see.'

They were interrupted by the trill of the telephone. 'That'll be Molly,' Georgina said.

'You speak to Molly and I'll organise getting word sent to the Hearns. The sooner we get your children home, the better.'

Georgina went to the telephone, grateful for David's love and warmed by the way he cared for her. She was so close to the perfect life that she'd always wanted. She had a kind and loving husband and she'd soon have her children home. And now she had financial security to offer them. There was only one blot on her landscape: The business. It had risks. Dangers came with it and though Georgina mostly felt confident that they ran a tight ship and had few enemies, there was always that niggling doubt in the back of her mind. One day, someone might challenge David. He could be killed. All of this could be taken away from her. Her world could come crashing down around her. It felt that now with her children returning, her priorities had changed. It was her duty to keep Alfie and Selina safe.

'Hello, Molly… I take it you've heard then?'

'Yes! Oh, Georgina, isn't it wonderful!'

'Yes, it really is. David is organising for Alfie and Selina to come home. In the meantime, Johnny has taken Charlotte up to town to celebrate. It's mayhem here, you should hear it. They're partying in the streets. There's music, singing, fireworks and everything. It's all very jolly. I ain't ever seen anything like it!'

'I can imagine. I can't stop crying, I'm so happy.'

Georgina lowered her voice, hoping that David couldn't hear. 'I want you to do me a favour. But keep it between us for now.'

'Go on.'

'Have a look around, see if there's any business opportunities for me in Kent.'

'Like what? There's nothing down here worth robbing,' Molly said with a chuckle.

'No, I mean, a business investment. Something that I could buy that would earn me and David a good living.'

There was a short pause and then Molly excitedly asked, 'Are you thinking of selling up and moving to Kent?'

'I don't know. Maybe. It's about time me and David had a change of direction with the business. You know what I mean… get into something more stable and less dangerous. But, shush, don't say anything. I haven't spoken to David about it yet.'

When Georgina replaced the telephone receiver, David asked, 'Spoken to me about what.'

'Ah, you heard.'

'Yes. What are you and Molly concocting now?'

'Nothing. I just wanted to put out some feelers before I came to you.'

David looked at her, expecting more.

Georgina sighed. 'Don't be angry with me but I was thinking that maybe you and I should think about packing this all in and doing something legit. Like farming.'

David threw his head back and roared with laughter. 'Farming... me and you as farmers? You can't be serious?'

'Yes, I am, deadly. Or if not farming, something else. I don't know, don't mock me. I just want a long life with you, David. I can't stand the thought of it being cut short. And I have to ensure the safety of Alfie and Selina.'

David pulled her into his arms. 'I understand. I know what you're saying. I'm not sure that a country life with my pipe and slippers is for me, but let me think about it for a while.'

Georgina rested her head on his shoulder. At least he hadn't instantly dismissed the idea of a new life in the country. But he was right, farming probably wasn't for them. But there had to be something that they could be successful at... something other than being the heads of one of London's most feared criminal gang.

'I love you,' she whispered.

'I love you more.'

Georgina closed her eyes and pictured Molly's big fireplace in the cosy stone farmhouse, surrounded by green fields and fresh air. It was the idyllic place to raise children.

The more she thought about it, the more she wanted it. She just had to convince David that it was the right move for them. But she was sure that David would come round to her way of thinking eventually. After all, Georgina *always* got her own way in **the end**.

Acknowledgements

Special thanks to my hubby, Simon, for getting on with the boring stuff so that I can spend time writing.

To my wonderful mum, Kitty Neale, for always encouraging me and for reading my manuscripts and telling me how brilliant they are!

To my fabby editor, Hannah Smith and my agent, Judith Murdoch.

And thank you to all my readers and friends on social media. You put up with my bad jokes and endless spamming of pictures of my pets and sunsets. Your support and comments are always very much appreciated xxx

Acknowledgement

About the Author

S AM MICHAELS writes gangland sagas set in Battersea, South London, which is where she was born and bred, the council estates being her playground.

After leaving school at sixteen with no qualifications, Sam married soon after and had a son. The marriage ended quickly, and as a single mother, she worked in various retail positions until undertaking an Open University degree. This led to Sam becoming an analytical scientist and then into technical sales where she met her husband.

A few years later, they moved from Hampshire to Spain. It was then that her mother, the *Sunday Times* best-selling author, Kitty Neale, inspired Sam to put pen to paper. She now writes her novels in sunnier climates with the company of her husband, four dogs and six cats.

Hello from Aria

We hope you enjoyed this book! If you did let us know, we'd love to hear from you.

We are Aria, a dynamic digital-first fiction imprint from award-winning independent publishers Head of Zeus. At heart, we're committed to publishing fantastic commercial fiction – from romance and sagas to crime, thrillers and historical fiction. Visit us online and discover a community of like-minded fiction fans!

We're also on the look out for tomorrow's superstar authors. So, if you're a budding writer looking for a publisher, we'd love to hear from you. You can submit your book online at ariafiction.com/we-want-read-your-book

You can find us at:
Email: aria@headofzeus.com
Website: www.ariafiction.com
Submissions: www.ariafiction.com/we-want-read-your-book

f @ariafiction
🐦 @Aria_Fiction
📷 @ariafiction